Cover by Vivien Reis

Map & Chapter Header Imagery by Lydia Blagden

EBook ISBN: 979-8-9922076-2-0

TPB ISBN: 979-8-9922076-3-7

The Gods & Goddesses of the Arkts

Amia	Goddess of the Arts
Baldrei	God of the Sun
D'Ak	God of the Harvest
Freyite	Goddess of Love, Beauty & Birth
Kel	God of Death, Darkness & Destruction
Loor	Goddess of the Moon & Wild Things
Rahn	God of the Seas
Svati	Goddess of Kindness
Tsu	God of the Skies and Keeper of Paradise
Voskulle	God of War

A Guide to Lithen Magic

Blooded Lithe	To increase ruthlessness, strength, and speed
Bronze Lithe	To increase strength
Cobalt Lithe	A sleeping aid
Crystal Lithe	To give oxygen
Cyan Lithe	Treats anxiety and calms
Emerald Lithe	To calm, induces euphoria
Fuschia Lithe	To cause euphoria and hallucinations
Plum Lithe	To slow signs of aging on the skin
Silver Lithe	To control the winds
Tawny Lithe	To give energy
Twilight Lithe	Treats pain and numbs
White Lithe	Raw power

THUNDERING HEARTS

THE SONGS OF BEASTS
BOOK TWO

SAMANTHA GONDA

CHAPTER I
ARIA

From the deepest pits of the Dahs through the winding rivers of Skierka, the beat of wraithskin drums echoed across the Arkts. Primal and unrelenting drumming. *Thu-Thump. Thu-Thump. Thu-Thump.* A sun cycle had come and gone since the drummers first took up their sacred duty. Still, they beat on.

The syren's leader, cruel and cunning as they came, had let out the cry that allowed her clan to feel the beating of her heart. An ancient magic that bound her clan. A silent, biological bell that rang internally within the ears of each the syrens in her clan, the moment their queen decided to call upon war. Fists met wraithskin. Over and over and over. The slide of blades sharpening and the thumping of the drums continued. A dark understanding and a lust for blood overtook the clan on the night their leader finally made the call.

They were called to war. Called to violence. Called to carnage. Sharp grins shone through the dark waters. The drumming, the tempo of Aria's heartbeat, awoke the ancient ones and alerted the nomadics to the news.

The Crown Prince of Skierka was dead and the syrens were at war.

The echoing of her own heartbeat had thrilled Aria, like her people, it was a day that she had longed for. The time had finally come to seek vengeance upon those that had enslaved her kind. It was the greatest of honors for a syren, to shed enemy blood, to die in battle. It was exactly what she was made to do, exactly what she was raised to do. And yet, she had concocted a plan, a bloodless coup, to ensure the safety of her people. They had seen enough violence under the heavy thumb of Skierka and Aria could not bear to see any more of her people suffer. Every syren hunted by a Skierkan, every syren whipped bloody until they mined enough white lithe to meet the Skierkan's greed, she felt all of it. Too much pain. Too much misery. She didn't want this for her people.

But nothing had happened as she had hoped. Nothing happened as she expected. And Aria the bloodthirsty, Aria the ruthless, Aria the fearless was so deeply afraid that she had hardly slept at all for the past year. Her heart rushed, racing against the echoing drums. Silently she prayed that her people would think her quickening heart was from anticipation for the glory of battle and not out of the icy fear that sat where her heart should have been.

She had lost her mother long, long ago. Her sister was far away, completing a mission in the heart of the enemy territory. And he was gone. Killed by her own sister. Not that her people knew that.

Raask. His name was her undoing.

Her people rallied at the news of his death. They drank their finest liquors and danced in the currents with a hope they hadn't known for generations. They congratulated Aria, for concocting such a brilliant plan. Their queen had returned, and with the news of their greatest enemy's death.

She should have been made happy by his death. Paired with the news of their traitorous General, the Skierkans were at their weakest since their land was established. It was the perfect time to strike, and her people did not disappoint.

A year had passed and Skierkan blood continued to stain the black shores red. The syrens were continuing to make major strides.

The Zojz trench, along Skierka's northern coast, where the waters were completely blackened and rotten with the cancerous charge of untamed white lithe the one place in the entire realm where this most powerful substance could be found, the very place where they kidnapped and enslaved the syrens to mine for the lithe, was now controlled by Aria.

Her people celebrated accordingly.

They wore intestines as scarves and belts. Eyeballs hung off of chains and piercings, and were lazily nibbled on by lovers. They had feasted on the bones of the Skierkans and drunk the bile straight from their guts.

Cries of victory and pleasure continued to echo throughout the labyrinth of underwater caverns within the Zojz trench as earlier that day, the Abisian syrens had massacred an entire warship of Skierkans. Ashes continued to rain down on the syrens like a blanket of heavy snow. They sank all the way down to the bottom of the Zojz trench where the syrens had made their makeshift keep.

Throughout it all, the drums of war continued to beat.

Many of her people were blessed with the magic of syrenic fire. The kind that burned without oxygen, in the deep pits of the Dahs. Syrenic fire, unlike the magic of the Fire Monger King's, flickered between the darkest of blacks and a silver. The Abisian syrens came from the depths of the Dahs, so they did not need the fire to see in the dark, they only enjoyed it as a weapon or as a way to celebrate.

The syrens gifted with syrenic flame lit their bodies and hair as they danced and drank, celebrating their bloody victory. The ones who were capable of casting burnless fire had enchanted fish and eel to keep the party interesting. Her people had seen devastation after devastation, but if there was one thing they knew how to do, it was to party. To lose miseries in the decadence of pleasure and violence was worship to the syrens. And Aria, who had brought them to victory, was the Queen of the revelries.

She sat upon her makeshift throne and watched as her people surrendered themselves to their primal natures. Not that she had a genuine throne anywhere, no those had been burned long, long ago. Her people had crafted this throne out of a large deposit of white lithe. Her finest craftsmen had carved the stories of their ancestors into the spikes that sat in neat rows across the entire surface of the throne. An old syrenic tradition. To bleed constantly for their kingdom. A reminder. An honor.

Her tail, long and sleek, curled beneath her on the spiked throne. Her claws tapped against the edge, in rhythm with the drums and her own heartbeat. She held her head up, resting in the palm of her hand as she considered her next course of action. Her people would need to rest, but they couldn't afford to give up this lead. There was no time for rest for the enslaved. No time for rest for the revolutionaries. This was war. But celebration? Her people needed this. They were built to gorge themselves on blood and pleasure. She would allow her people to celebrate their victory, for one moon cycle, and not a second longer.

Yes that would do. One moon cycle.

"Even after a great victory, you look displeased." The smooth voice of her General, Taura, had cut through her murky thoughts, pulling her attention back to her people. "Does bloodshed no longer excite you, my Queen?" She teased, dancing away.

Aria rolled her eyes in mock annoyance. "Do you call that bloodshed? I think a quick dinner is a more appropriate title to what that was." The Skierkans were so unbelievably unprepared for battle over the Zojz trench. The cancerous waters burned the skin off of the humans. And the ones who would not be dragged under died under the heat of the syrenic flames, effectively cauterizing the Zojz from the rotten souls of the Skierkans.

Each boat they sent, Aria had sunk.

To lose the Zojz was to lose the production of white lithe. They'd have to rely on the hordes they had already accumulated, which to Aria seemed like plenty. Evidently it was not. So they would keep sending boats, and she would keep sinking them.

She had to move past this trench and take the next step. The land. Only, her people were not prepared for such a battle. They were creatures of the sea. Capable of travel via the land, but battling on land was far different than in their natural forms. They were smaller, weaker when they masqueraded as humans.

And their allies were meek. Training them was taking too long.

They had won back their seas. Freed the enslaved. Captured the white lithe mines. But none of it would matter if they couldn't take the land from the Fire Monger King. She wanted his head on a stick. To see the life creep out of his eyes. Nothing would be enough until she had tasted his last breath on her teeth.

Aria felt Taura's stiff presence return before she saw her. "What is it now?" She asked, not bothering to hide her frustrations with the General. Taura had known her longer than most and better than almost all. They had bled together and grown together. Aria's mother had taken in Taura's pregnant mother, a Surtrian Syren, who had escaped, seeking asylum among the Abisians who had a reputation for fighting the Morloks and hiding the pregnant women among them. Taura believed it was her sacred duty to protect Aria now. And Aria, she saw her as a blood sister, another life to protect and shield from the Morloks. An asset, of course, for Taura was one of the greatest warriors of their times. But still a chink in Aria's armor, for the love she had for her.

Taura laughed at the agitation in Aria's voice. Her long braids shook gently in the current with each rasp. "Laugh now." She commanded her queen, "Your people are watching you." Aria listened, and laughed with the same feral and frightening yip of her mother. Taura's violet eyes met hers with the sharpness of a blade as she spoke under her breath, "You know as well as I that they will only respect the cruel. But they are exhausted. They need some hope, and as their leader, you need to guide them."

How could she give what she herself so desperately needed? But the truth of Taura's words weighed heavily on her shoulders, sinking into her very bones.

Aria arose from her spiked throne, each head snapped towards her in unison as she floated down from her raised dais. "Won't you be joining me, Taura the Terrible?" Aria shouted, loud for all to hear. Taura's fangs glinted as she smirked in response. "My Queen, I was afraid you'd never ask."

Taura's dark hand met hers as she led them to the center of the cavern. The syrenic fire flickered from a radiant silver to black, alighting the darkness. The drums echoed through each corner of the caves and her people sang. Their voices crisp and enchanting and haunting, filled the trench with songs of fury and pride. Their jaws snapped in time with the drums. And Aria, in the center of her people, among the bones of their enslaved families and ancestors, began to dance.

Her tail swished beneath her. Her hand arose, high over her head as she allowed herself a moment of freedom from the war. From grieving. From worry. She left it all behind on her makeshift throne as she threw her head back and sang. She allowed her magic to seep through her voice, and her people followed suit, creating a chamber of their seductive and hypnotizing magic. Their music, their voices, it felt primal and far more intoxicating than any spirit. The music, the magic, the current and the constant thrum of the syrenic fire and the drums of war, all of it, she lost herself in all of it. Her body moved of its own accord, answering only to the rhythm, as she left her mind on the dais. They had taken the Zojz trench. They had done it.

Her blue—black tail intertwined with Taura's bright green tail as they danced and laughed, the same way they would as children on the holy days of dancing and feasting. The bloodthirsty Queen of the Abisian syrens and her Surtrian General threw themselves into the revelry. Dancing with each of their warriors, giving gratitude for the blood that they had shed and a promise for a shackleless future. Aria promised them each a return to glory when she had come back home a full sun cycle prior, and tonight as they danced, she felt a glimmer of it.

Her people kissed her palms as they danced, drawing blood with their fangs or their claws as they grabbed for her. Her hands were marked with the scabs and open wounds of their praise and love and respect that they only knew how to show with blood. And Aria, she would bleed for them, each and every one of them. She would have done it even when she was hopeless and alone in the Morlok dungeons, praying to Freyite for mercy. But it felt different now that a spark of hope had lit from deep within her gut.

But hope was not something to trust. And Aria should have known better.

The first explosion was a blur. As the dancing and magic and liquor had already overtaken the dense waters of the caverns, chaos had already ensued. The flashing silver lights of the syrenic fire along the walls of the cavern along with the eels and fish darting around, created a sense of movement that made the first couple of explosions almost unnoticeable. Blood was already in the water from the prayers over Aria, as her people had grabbed and nipped and clawed at her at every chance —in show of solidarity and respect. But her people were skilled, and knew how to draw a mere drop of her blood.

Aria threw her head back once again, singing songs of glory and hope, when her eyes suddenly widened. There was blood in the water, syrenic by the smell of it, and it was not hers.

Taura's dark gaze met hers the instant she smelled it. Simultaneously they turned and watched as their people began to catch fire. Silver and black, with the quickest flash of orange at staggering intervals.

Bits of her people's organs floated around the cave. Their bile and violet blood leaked into the water as one-by-one they were shred to pieces from the inside out. Her people were dying, and she did not know how to stop it. Aria watched in horror as her army dwindled, dying in the graveyard of the ancestors they were trying to avenge. Were they watching? Just as Aria?

Taura grabbed Aria's stump of an arm, pulling her out of the cavern as their top soldiers covered her from all sides. She couldn't turn away from the horror. It took until she was nearly out of the cavern for her to realize she was being pulled away from her people as they lay dying.

With all of her strength and then some, Aria pushed and twisted, screaming and thrashing. If her people were dying, she would die with them. She needed to die with them. She couldn't do it anymore, any of it. How foolish they were, thinking they could win this war, the same war their ancestors fought and lost. She lost as well.

She would go down with her people. She begged her soldiers, she begged Taura to release her. But Aria only had one hand to pull her through the waters and Taura was her general for a reason; her strength easily towed Aria out of the cavern. Out of the carnage. Out of her duty and responsibility to her people.

The last thing she saw in that cavern were flashes of a deep orange, nearly red in the explosions. The orange of the Fire Monger King's magic. The Morloks had done this. In one fell swoop, they had nearly obliterated Aria's entire army. Violet blood dripped from Aria's hair and scales, it saturated her entire body in a thick sheen with bits and chunks of her people littered throughout. When Taura and her soldiers, the ones guarding and not taking part in the revelry, had deemed Aria far enough away from the cavern, they stopped and watched.

Aria had long stopped thrashing and screaming, instead she listened to the sounds of her people dying. The hollowed screaming and the explosions. The orange flicker of Morlok magic. The heavy stench of blood. Aria's nostrils flared and her claws dug into her palm. And for the first time in Aria's life, she did not pray to Freyite, Goddess of Love, Beauty, Birth and Mother to the Syrens. She dug her sharp claws into the fragile stump of what remained of her left arm until pain was all that she knew, all that she felt. She watched as her violet blood flowed freely into the trench, and she made a promise to the God of War, Voskulle. She would not stop until she had the Fire Monger King's heart. And until then, she would kill all that stood before her.

As Voskulle accepted this prayer as a promise, Aria's blood disappeared from the water.

CHAPTER 2
VIGGO

Dark circles marred the skin of the heir to Helk and former General of the fearsome Skierkan army. Stubble from several missed shaves stuck out from his jaw at every angle, casting a dark shadow across his face. Viggo desperately and discreetly smoothed his facial hair. Doing his best to do it without drawing more attention to his disheveled appearance, a disgrace to the formal table of the Surtr king—at which he now sat. He hoped they would just write off the smoothing of his jaw stubble between his thumb and the front of his finger as a sign of thinking and not as the desperate self-soothing tick it was.

The battle rooms of the Jungle Palace, a room for strategy and for once, long ago, impressing foreign diplomats. It was a great room, once, with long windows that overlooked the beautiful and lush jungle below. Dark green walls and thick ropy vines mirrored the infamous jungle of the islands. Only instead of wildness, the room was precisely laid out. Thick vines braided into intricate designs crossed the unwindowed parts of the wall. Tall ceilings. A grand table of dark wood. He heard that it was once polished daily; it was now littered with scratches and crumbs. The windows held smudges and layers upon layers of pollen. This once grand room was falling apart, just like the people in it.

The royals, the leaders, they had been at it for hours, endless arguing and pleading, before Viggo finally caught a glimpse of himself at the bottom of the silvered fruit platter. He had been in Boai, the main island of the Surtr Islands, for longer than he ever intended. In this time he had grown tired of the sweet fruits of their lands, at some point their sweet and vibrant taste had turned sour on his tongue as the days turned to weeks and weeks turned to months. Nothing was going as he planned.

Between his two fingers, Viggo picked up a hunk of raw white-and-purple marbled fish with a hot pepper garnish and plopped it into his mouth. It was his least favorite of the delicacies in Surtr. He was not one for very hot foods. It hurt his mouth and his throat and even his gut. But he figured he deserved whatever ache he could give himself. From across the table Skender caught his eye. His tall and lean friend, one half of the Twisted Twins of the North and heirs of the Rakkei people, gave a slight shake of his head. Skender was the only one who saw what he was doing with the overly spiced foods. The burning hot baths. The thin armor he wore on the battlefield. But now was not the time to pick apart his self-harming tendencies.

The Empress of the D'Ami Cos had finally come. She sat across from Viggo, avoiding eye contact with the former Skierkan Bruin. She wore a long and flowing white gown embroidered with gold threaded prayers to their patron Goddess Amia. Her dress was far more formal than the times she had met with Viggo in the past. But that had been another time, another life, and a different Viggo.

He used to have an excellent relationship with Alaia Vitello, the Empress of the D'Ami Cos, the nation Southeast to the vast island of Skierka. Viggo would secretly bring the refugees to their lands, and Alaia opened her borders to the displaced people without a second thought. Amia, Goddess of the Arts and Founder of the Universe, Wife to Tsu, the God of the Skies, had believed that great arts and intelligence could be found within every single soul. And there was nothing the Amicans loved more than finding true artistic geniuses and sponsoring them to represent their lands across the Arkts. They were also vehemently against war philosophically. However, from what Viggo could gather, they loved the art and literature and music that erupted from it. And their inventors, who were considered artistic geniuses in the art of war, didn't seem to mind the great sums of money that came to them and their country when other nations purchased their advanced weaponry or their consultation on battle strategy.

Hypocrites. All of them.

It never really bothered Viggo before as they were the only nation to take in the Surtrians he tried to save from enslavement to the Morlok King, his father in another life. But now he needed them. And worst of all, he needed their charity. There was no money left. And hardly any Surtrians left to fight. Last he had heard from Aria, the syrens were holding their own in the Zojz and the Dahs. But to take over Skierka, they would need to take the land. Viggo was not holding up his end of the bargain.

He thought more Skierkans would rebel against the king. He did not understand how deeply they feared the Morlok's retribution. How much they valued the small comforts that they were given as peasants and soldiers. They took the scraps they were given and held on tight, too scared to lose what little they had. And he couldn't blame them.

Maybe he should have held on tighter to what little he had too.

The harsh cries of the Surtrian King brought Viggo out of his thoughts and back into the sweltering tree palace deep in the jungle of Boai. "It is not enough!" The King's voice boomed, causing Alaia to stiffen. The anger seeped into his words like a syrup of desperation and hopelessness. Jag Agar, King of the Surtr Islands, tried to regain his composure, holding tightly to his dignity. The King wore what was left of his formal clothes, a once elegant and immaculately regal teal tunic that had lost its luster long ago, and the necklace of sea wraith teeth that had been passed down his bloodline for generations, that now appeared to be missing several gems and teeth. He had dark skin and broad shoulders. Like Viggo, Jag Agar was a warrior turned leader. He was muscular and intense and one of the only blood-born royals that Viggo respected in the entire realm.

He was also one of the only people in the realm who was more desperate than Viggo. He had lost the war to Skierka. And they were now losing another rebellion.

Alaia twisted her face in disgust at King Agar's anger and overt display of emotion. The Amicans found anger and yelling to be disgraceful. And as the Empress of one of the most powerful nations, Alaia would not appreciate being addressed in such a manner. "Not enough?" She asked coldly. "I have taken in your people. Opened my lands to them. Opened our schools to them. We have saved your people. And it is not enough?" She spoke smoothly and quickly, just as all Amicans did. She looked to Viggo, seeking his words in support of how much she had already given. Only Viggo himself was having a hard time holding it together.

He wanted to pick up every platter and every cup on this table and throw them at the wall. He wanted to fight and scream. It was not enough. How could she not see what he could see so plainly?

"And who will take in your people, once the King comes for the D'Ami Cos?" Viggo asked. He didn't bother to lift his head from resting on his hand, nor did he bother to sit up straight. "Have you asked your neighboring lands? They are already overpopulated. What will happen to your beloved universities? Your museums? Have you made shelters for your irreplaceable sculptures and manuscripts? Are there enough shelters for your people to hide from the King's fire?" He could feel his death magic rumbling from deep within his bones, swelling into his gut and saturating his organs. He had to take deep breaths to even attempt to still the magic. It rumbled up into his arteries and took over his body. He needed to regain control, before it was too late.

Alaia scoffed. "Your father would not be so stupid as to march upon my lands. He knows of our power." Viggo's eyes narrowed. "Do you forget that I was his General, Empress?" Her brow furrowed as she took in his words. It was a long moment before she responded, breathlessly she said, "You can't be serious."

Viggo let out a laugh, a cold and dark thing, before clicking his tongue against his teeth. "Have you not learned that there is no end to that man's greed?" He kept his temper and voice smooth, but the bitterness and contempt burst through each word like water through breaking ice. Every muscle in his body stiffened as he held his magic at bay. He could feel Skender's cautious and worried gaze as he did all within his power to hold himself together. He was unraveling, and he couldn't afford it. Not now anyways. Not yet.

Alaia bit the inside of her cheek as she considered Viggo. Slowly, her eyes drifted down and back up, reading the tension in his muscles like a book. "I can smell the desperation of you. You have a bleeding heart, Viggo of the North, and you'd say just about anything to convince me to join your forces and save your homelands." She motioned back to Jag and the jungle outside of the palace at the mention of the homelands. Her stance was clear. The D'Ami Cos did not see the Surtr Islands nor Skierka as worth risking her armies for. "Can we still expect you to take our refugees?" Viggo asked.

Alaia took a sip of the blend of juice in front of her, an orange concoction of many of the finest fruits of the islands, including fruits from the farthest ends of the Surtr Islands. "I will take in your refugees, as long as the Fire Monger King does not suspect it. If he was to ever learn of our arrangement, measures would have to be taken to ensure the safety of my people." She dabbed her mouth with a napkin, one of the last pieces of finery that the king—and what was left of his servants—could find and prepare ahead of the Empress's arrival, staining it with the bit of juice that sat upon her lip after she sipped.

As Viggo took in the weight of her words, he couldn't help but wonder if she would appreciate the napkin if it held some fantastic equation or an exquisite sketching. What would it take for the empress to see the value in the effort of several servants who had spent the better part of the week desperately trying to find usable cutlery and fabrics to convince an empress to come to their aid? Perhaps Viggo and King Agar should have combed the island for geniuses in the rough, but there was no time left and so few Surtrians left. Would the mass graves filled with bones have convinced her? The thought of losing potential geniuses and innovators to the dirt?

Viggo doubted anything would have been enough. She knew before she boarded her ship to the islands what her answer was, she probably only came to scope out the state of the rebellion for her own curiosities. And what did she think as she took in the once lavish jungle palace? Built out of a grove of trees, polished on the daily with blessed waters, it sat now dusty and burnt. Vines that were once painted as a tribute to the Gods were now slashed apart to be used as fire kindling to feed the armies. Did she see the sacrifice when she saw the state of Boai, or a lost investment?

The King took a long look at the Empress, pain and despair written all over his face. The king understood that he had nothing left to barter with, nothing left to give—to beg—for her mercy for his people who would now call the D'Ami Cos their home. "If you have made your final decision, I will ask you now to leave." The King spoke quieter than Viggo had ever heard the man speak.

Alaia nodded, taking one last bite of the fried tentacle with a garnish of mixed sweet and hot peppers, dipping it into the sauce of the tentacle creature's own eggs. She made a slurping noise as she ate the creature, an ora oba, only found within the beautiful reefs of the Surtr Islands. "What a shame," she muttered to herself after swallowing the creature.

And then her eyes lit up with thought. "Jag, would you mind if we took a few of these back with us to breed? And maybe your chef who concocted such a brilliant menu?"

Viggo tensed at the insult, to let the King's people die but to save a fish she enjoyed eating. But the King did not erupt. Not as Viggo would have.

Instead he smiled politely, sadness still in his eyes, and nodded. "Of course, Alaia. And you may ask my cooks if they would like to go with you. The choice is theirs. Although I am sure they will be honored to accompany you to your land."

Alaia stiffly rose and nodded a 'thank you' to the king, "I wish you the best of luck." As she turned to Viggo she added, "I was so sorry to hear of your brother's passing. And frankly quite surprised to hear that you've allied with the syrens after they killed him."

Viggo's heart stopped as it tore into two once again. The King, who did not understand nor trust Viggo's alliance with the syrens either, carefully watched his reaction. His gaze a heavy weight on top of his already broken heart. "Yes, well, at such a fragile time in our realm, there was no room for retribution against his killer. The real enemy is the King, and that is something we can agree upon. But believe me, there is nothing I want more than to bring my brother's killer to their knees." Skender, the only one among them who knew Viggo was Raask's killer, stiffened. He could see his jaw tensing at his temple from across the room.

Alaia stopped and twisted her head, watching Viggo curiously, as if he was some kind of experiment in grief. "And will you? Bring your brother's killer to their knees? Will you battle against the Blood-thirsty Queen of the Seas? If you were to win this rebellion with your father of course."

The power of death swelled within his chest. He did not want to stain these fabrics nor what was left of King Agar's palace. He did not want these powers at all. But they begged to be used, they needed a release, particularly whenever he was upset or agitated, his magic would rise in his body like an overflowing pot of boiling water. "Alaia, with all due respect, I do not share my plans with those who are not my allies. Now if you don't mind, King Agar and I have very little time, and you have already wasted enough of it."

Viggo didn't bother to stand as Alaia and King Agar left. Skender stood by the window and watched as Alaia and her soldiers left the palace and headed towards their ship, hidden in a tiny alcove that was not on any Skierkan maps. Skender stayed still, long after the Empress and the King were out of their eyesight. And Viggo, he of course was still at his seat. He allowed himself the freedom to hunch, to cave in on himself as he tried to pull the reins on his magic.

Without looking from the window, Skender asked, "Is that what you plan to do when this is all over?"

"What?" Viggo barked. He was drowning in his grief, in fighting a losing battle. Drowning under the weight of it all.

"To bring Raask's killer to their knees?" Skender's words were tight, filled with worry, but gentle. It angered Viggo, he didn't deserve gentleness or worry from Skender. Everything angered him now. And facing his people—Emir, Skender, Silia and oh Gods especially Mayta—he couldn't do it any longer. What if it happened again? What if he snapped again? He'd already killed the person he loved more than all others. Where was there to go from here?

He owed it to his people to finish this.

Viggo ran a hand through his messy black hair, longer than it had ever been before. The waves of his hair brushed against his shoulders, feeling too hot against his neck, too overwhelmed with life and everything else that had happened.

"Yes. I meant it." His words were short and crisp, leaving no room for argument, or at least so he hoped.

Skender sniffed, still facing the window. "And who will be left to rule Skierka?"

CHAPTER 3
MAYTA

A thick blanket of snow enveloped the Bleached Palace, the capital city of Etra, just below the palace, and the entire mainland of Skierka. Cold. Rigid. Dangerous. Just like the Skierkan people.

Skierka was a frozen wasteland for a majority of the solar cycle. And Mayta, who had watched from the shores of the Dahs as the little greenery along the shore died each winter, was amazed by the plethora of plants still alive and flourishing in the Morlok's royal gardens. She worked each morning in the gardens, assisting the gnomes and goblins and sprites in the maintenance. This week, they focused on the lunar gardens, of plants that flourished under the long nights of the Skierkan winters. They continued to blossom, even throughout the plundering temperatures and the sharp shards of ice that would occasionally fall from the sky like a rain of daggers.

A torno bear and her cub had ventured to the river looking for fresh water and fish. Although they generally avoided people, the massive white bears with great curled horns could be incredibly dangerous if they wished to be. And with Mayta now officially a lady of the court, the Vermilli and the goblins attempted to scare the creatures back into the Gaulic Forest. A few fire sprites and some more goblins stayed with Mayta as she hid within the shadow of the Irridesci tower. No snow fell within a certain radius of the tower. And no natural creature ever ventured close enough to the tower, thus why they had always placed Mayta there whenever anything came crawling out of the Gaulic, in an attempt to keep her safe.

Truthfully, Mayta would prefer being unsafe and further away from the tower. She may look meek, but she could certainly handle herself. The tower was disgusting and made her uneasy, her belly swirled just looking at the damned thing, yet alone being curled up beside it.

Today the bears had come purely out of luck and not from any tugs of Mayta's syren powers, luring them closer to the palace. Mayta did her best to appear scared of the beasts. She widened her eyes just so. A few shivers here and there. It was all so convenient as she cowered, hugging closely to the walls of the stupid disgusting tower. Silently, Mayta sent a prayer of thanks to Loor, Goddess of the Moon and the Wild Things. For Mayta had not been anticipating the King visiting the Irridesci tower today. He was not due to be back from his travels with Selby, the leader of the healers, until the next week.

But his presence was unmistakable. She could feel him, even from so far away. Even as she faced the city of Etra, her back to the palace, she recognized the Fire Monger King. His presence felt like wrongness, much like his disgusting tower. And he smelled of burned things.

She did not like to look into his face. And he did not like his face being looked at, that's why he kept it hidden under the shadows and blinding glare of his fire crown.

He was hideous. His face was scarred and disfigured from his own magic. Like a fool, he had never learned to create a fire that would not harm himself. He was powerful, sure, but what did any of it mean if he consumed himself along with the rest of the realm?

She hated him. He had killed her people. Enslaved entire nations.

She listened as he spoke with Balk, the leader of the Irridesci, whom she also hated. But just as every other time she tried to gather information on them, she couldn't focus on their words. The King's voice was smoke and pain. He had lost his wife long ago. He had lost his son a solar cycle ago, and the other son rallied a rebellion against him the very same month, freeing whom he believed to be his other son's killer.

She could hear the loneliness in the King's voice.

It sounded like hers, when she stripped away the layers of her disguise.

She'd killed that man's son. And nobody would ever know it.

His body was buried in an unmarked grave not too far from where they were at that very moment.

Her heart caught in her chest as she saw it happen over and over again. The dirt falling over the prince. The broken nose. The bashed-in skull. She saw it whenever she closed her eyes. How could she focus on anything else as his body laid just over there? She was much more than a simple lady of the court, that she knew for certain, but she was not meant to be a killer. She was not meant to be a spy. She didn't want any of this.

She could feel blood dripping down her arms, and dirt underneath her fingernails. But none of it was real. She fisted her heavy red fur cloak, feeling the warmth and the softness of reality and not the cold blood and gritty dirt she imagined.

The King and Balk were deep within the tower, far below the surface. And if Mayta was properly focusing, she could hear them. It took her magic a moment to find the two bastardly creatures. She hummed quietly to herself, quiet enough so no one could hear nor wonder about the soft clicks and strange noises she could use to map out the depths of the tower and listen to their conversations.

Balk's voice startled her. The sounds of a hundred cries of despair formed into one creature's horrendous voice. A whisper and a shout all at the same time. "He is not happy with you," Balk quietly hissed.

The King scoffed in agitation. "None of them are." She heard his footsteps as he paced back and forth, foot scraping against the slick stone of the tower's floor. "And how will you fix this?" Balk spat back.

The King's pacing halted. "Is this why you called me here, Balk?" His voice rose with each word. "I am your king! If you are to summon me, it better be for something worth my damned time. You think I don't already know how he feels? I am working to fix it and you summoning me to this disgusting place is wasting time I could spend fixing our problems."

Balk laughed, a cold and phlegmy sound, in the face of the King's rage. "You are not my king, and surely you know that. That was the deal that was made. We live outside of your reign, and in turn, you receive what you need most." Mayta could hear the twisted joy in Balk's words, the smile from whatever kind of mouth hid beneath their veils. "You do not know what you are risking, King Morlok. You have not seen what my kind has seen. If you had, you'd be crippled from the weight of it all," Balk added, the disgust he held for the King palpable with each word.

Mayta listened as the King slammed some door and began walking up the stairs. Balk hissed his parting words, a warning, while the King remained in human earshot, "We have held our end of the bargain. You know what will happen if you don't hold yours, human!" Mayta shivered at the words. A few goblins looked her way with worry on their brow. They had grown to love Mayta, and took their role of protecting her quite seriously.

It was quite sweet, but also far more unnecessary than they would likely ever know.

Mayta did not enjoy killing, nor causing harm of any kind, but she would do it if she had to. She may be a kind and gentle thing, but she was capable of more if pushed.

The torno bear and her cub were still at the water. A couple of sprites had taken to attempting to herd the pair back into the Gaulic

Forest. But the cub seemed to be entranced with the creatures. And the sprites, the little vain things, had taken to playing with the cub instead of herding.

The King stormed out of the tower, leaving a trail of flaming footprints in his wake. Mayta remained tucked into the shadows until the torno bears had left, watching as the flames slowly flickered out one by one.

She considered this conversation, hanging onto each word until late in the evening. At some point in the past few months she had taken to wandering the corridors at night. Sleep, which once came easy to her, was now a luxury she rarely indulged in. Blankets reminded her of cold, black Skierkan dirt. And the inevitable tears would cause her to race to the mirrors to make sure they were not blood. Her own red hair would scare her from the corner of her eye.

Padge, the head cook within the Morlok palace, had taken to leaving her sandwiches and other savory treats for her nightly hauntings. It was there that she had grown closer to the servants, and ultimately the underground scene of the courtiers. That night, Mayta was wandering around the upper parts of the palace, those facing the shores of the Dahs, with great open windows along the bridges between each tower. She came here most often, finding comfort in seeing the Dahs with her own eyes, imagining the sounds of the black waves and her family that lived among them.

She had been staring into the distance, wondering if somehow she could catch a glimpse of her sister's tail, or the spikes of her wraith, for what felt like hours. She finished the spiced turkey leg Padge had left for her that evening and tossed it to the ground beneath the bridge where some creature would surely enjoy breaking the bones between its teeth.

"There was still meat on that," Ilana's soft voice spoke from the shadows behind Mayta. A cold smile crept across Mayta's face. "I was wondering when you would decide to speak up," she commented without turning to face the coquette. Ilana snorted in both amusement and disbelief. Her heeled boots clacked against the stone bridge as Ilana joined Mayta at her perch, overlooking the black seas of the Dahs. "You're here often," Ilana said, flicking her long black hair back and out of her face.

Mayta turned to face her, her eyes lazily looking Ilana up and down, taking in the leader of the coquettes' tight corset and long draping black silk skirts. "I could say the same to you." Accusations and questions hung in the air like the bloody bodies of the rebels hung far below the bridge.

The wind howled as the light of the indigo moon started to give out to the silver moon. Dawn would come soon. And the magic of the Wild Things, the pull of Loor, Goddess of the Moons, would give way to Baldrei, God of the Sun. Creatures like Ilana and Mayta, they were drawn to the moonlight. Gained strength by it even. And the sun, for all his glory, did not offer the same strength as his twin sister, especially not for the Wild Things.

"What do you look for, Princess?" Ilana asked, the silver light of the moon reflecting off of her dark eyes.

Mayta's lips curled in a faint smile. "*Now* you're ready to talk?"

It was not the first time the two had stood at this bridge together, watching the Dahs for all of her glory, looking for people and places that did not exist anymore. Silently, they watched as drops of snow began to fall. Slowly, and then quickly, the snow shot through the sky like arrows, sticking to the roofs of Etra, and the shores of the Dahs.

"I won't tell anyone, you know?" Mayta asked, as she turned to Ilana and watched as a few small snowflakes landed in her lashes.

"Oh, I know, Princess." Ilana turned against the edge of the bridge, allowing her hair to flow wildly into the wind and snow that rushed behind her. "Because if you told anyone, I would have to tell them who you are." Ilana smirked with a smile that was all teeth, before pinching Mayta's freckled nose in a condescendingly affectionate manner. Mayta listened as Ilana's steps faded.

She stayed there until the first glimmer of dawn came cresting over the mountains behind the Bleached Palace. As the black skies gave way to blues and purples, she continued listening until she heard the two short howls from the Gaulic.

Two more days.

CHAPTER 4
RAASK / HAUTH

auth Orn, the former Crown Prince of Skierka, had drank far too much Surtrian liquor and smoked way too much emerald lithe.

His glazed eyes searched frantically over the black waters of the Dahs. Even when out of his mind, he couldn't help searching for her. What would she look like in her original form? He didn't even know. Desperately, he searched for a glimmer of scales. Her wild curls in the wind. The sound of her laugh. Sometimes, when he came to smoke by the shore, he thought he could feel her heavy gaze. He'd search for her. But had not found her just yet. His supposed killer. The creature who changed everything for him. Who broke him. Who made him. He searched for her as a moth searched desperately for the euphoria of blinding light and self-sacrificial burning of a flame.

Hauth listened as the Gray Goblin's quick and loud steps echoed behind him. "Your break is over, get back in here, boy!" The Gray Goblin yelled from the door of his pub. Hauth threw what remained of his emerald to the ground, and stepped on it to extinguish the flame. "Now!" The Goblin yelled, beating wildly against his small gray thighs to hurry him along.

"Yes, Sir!" Hauth hollered back in response. As he walked into the smoke-filled rooms of the pub, all thoughts of her fell back into his bones. He focused purely on his work. Pouring drinks. Chatting with the customers. Serving the occasional stew or sweet. He chatted with everyone, even as a peasant, all liked him. With his hair now icy white, and his eyes the pale blue of a cold winter's dawn, no one recognized him for who he once was. He was nobody. Truly nobody. Hungry. Scared. Betrayed. Hurt. And eventually, Raask became Hauth, a barkeep at the Gray Goblin. He gambled. He drank. He smoked. Made friends with all of the Vermilli, the farmers, the soldiers, the shopkeepers, anyone and everyone.

He had to work to eat. He had to make enough money to pay the rent in the little room next to the Gray Goblin. He was cursed at. Stepped on sometimes too, not on purpose of course, but it happened.

Through it all, his heart continued to ache. And at night, when the light of the indigo moon gave way to the light of the silver moon, he sometimes felt so alone that he was scared he would drown in his own sorrows. But he worked hard during the day, so he tired easily at night and fell asleep right away.

Sometimes he would see glimpses of her out of the corner of his eye. He would hear how she would respond to a certain comment or situation. Somehow, she had become a part of him that he ached for constantly. But Aria was gone. And Raask was too—for all intents and purposes.

When the hours faded into the deep pits of the night, as the last dredges of the silver moon's light began to fade, when even the creatures of the night began to retire to their hobbles and homes, Hauth would wipe the bar down. He'd place a few more logs on the fire, so the Goblin could sleep without needing to worry for warmth. He'd nudge awake the travelers who had fallen asleep under their table, told them to visit the Salty Dogs Inn only two doors down. The travelers, a group of gnomes and sprites, swayed back and forth as they stood. So Hauth packed them a bag of extra loaves of bread and threw in a couple hunks of hard cheese, before walking them to the Inn himself.

Ola, the innkeeper, took the creatures in, along with the roll of emerald lithe Hauth brought her whenever he took her the extras who had stashed themselves within the Gray Goblin. She had known him when he was Raask. She'd been kind, but distant. Now that his golden hair had decayed into a colorless white and his mother's eyes had flattened into ice, she did not recognize him. He watched as she cried at the news of his death, practically a lifetime ago.

"Why do you cry, Ola?" He had heard her husband, Igor, ask. "What will happen to us?" She asked back. "We have always been safe in Etra, we never needed to worry, as long as we followed the rules, we were safe."

Hauth watched and served them both complimentary drinks as they mourned his own death. He had just begun working at the Gray Goblin the night that word of his death had gotten out. The pub was overflowing with mourners and Hauth had a hard time keeping up. But he remembered lingering there, to hear what Igor had said to his wife as he held her hand tightly over the sticky bartop. Igor placed his own on the bottom, so his wife's hand wouldn't need to graze the dirty bartop.

"Ola, my love, we bleed coin on giving shelter to those who cannot afford it themselves. How many of the hungry and sick have died on our stoop while the Bleached Palace holds enough healers and food to feed the entire Arkts?" Igor's eyes grew wild with fear and anger before he remembered himself. He gently rubbed a thumb against the back of his wife's hand. "But we will keep going. Just as we always have. And I will not let anything happen to you, alright?" Igor picked up her hand, gently brushing a kiss against her wrinkled knuckles. Ola nodded and gave her husband a small smile. Hauth watched as she mouthed a small *thank you* to her doting husband. And he waited to hear what she would say about mourning Raask.

Only those words never came.

All night, Hauth listened to the mourners, who feared for their lives and themselves. A few times they would raise their glasses in his memory. They drank his favorite ale and sang his favorite songs. Played his favorite games. But they mourned their safety, and not the Crown Prince who had spent countless nights drinking and dancing among them. It seemed that the loss of his life was barely a thought.

Hauth did not sleep that night. He had grown accustomed to the loneliness that came from his previous life, the loneliness of being raised in power, and the loss of his mother as well as his brother— who had been constantly sent to war by his father.

For a brief moment in time, he wasn't lonely anymore. He had *her*.

Now he truly had no one. Not even the recognition of who he once was, and the symbol and heavy weight behind his name. And sometime, deep into that night, the sorrow and betrayal that had been drowning him lifted into a funny feeling of hope. He truly had nobody. And even better, he could now *be* a nobody.

He laughed and he laughed some more. He laughed until his belly and chest ached with it. His brother and the syrens may have killed him, but they also had set him free. He let go of all of the anger and sadness that had built up in him over the years, because all of the anger and all of that despair did not belong to Hauth Orn, no, that was Raask Morlok's to bear and Raask Morlok was dead.

Hauth had kept the first job he had gotten, bartending at the Gray Goblin, although he made most of his money gambling. He drank and smoked most nights. And worked hard. Hard enough that his feet ached from standing on them all day. His old friends would come in still, but none of them recognized him. They also hardly mourned his death. The only exception was Arthur at the bakery of course, whom Hauth would avoid at all costs, occasionally going so far as to ask children to order his breads and bring it back to him.

News came in, with each pass of soldiers or courtiers, of the wars. The Surtrians were rebelling, being led by his brother. The syrens were putting up a hell of a fight over in the Zojz trench. And Mayta, who hardly came into the Gray Goblin, was presumably acting as some spy for the rebels. How nobody in the Bleached Palace had suspected her by now was a bit of a mystery to Hauth, but he figured it wasn't really his business anymore. And if he were to accuse her, it would most likely draw some unwanted attention back to himself.

He had to remind himself of this, over and over, as Mayta sat at a corner table of the pub, drinking her second glass of Skierkan Strong, a clear liquor made from potato, grain and clove, mixed with sprite-berry juice. Her red hair had puffed from the snowfall, and her eyes were nearly as red as her hair. Either crying or smoking or snorting— or some combination of the three. Perhaps even just exhaustion, it was past dawn when she had come in and now the morning was beginning. Normally Hauth would have kicked her and her friend out by now, but he had been uncomfortable around Mayta ever since she buried him alive.

If he wasn't too proud to admit he was afraid of a creature with delicate features that made a point to always wipe down her table once she finished drinking, or help the gnomes back to the palace, he would have admitted that he was utterly terrified of her.

Her friend was also a pretty intimidating looking guy who he'd only seen a couple of times before. He was large, almost as tall as Raask by the looks of it, but huge. He had long messy brown hair and facial hair that bordered between too much stubble and a full beard. Hauth didn't know the man well, but every other time he had seen him he looked clean faced. So this was an odd sight.

The man ordered an ale that sat full on the table's edge. He and Mayta seemed to know each other well. They spoke in hushed voices that Hauth couldn't hear no matter how hard he strained, and especially not after the rush of night workers coming in after their shift ended.

When Mayta put down her second glass, Hauth walked over, slowly, pouring glasses of ale and water at each table around them as he tried to hear what she was saying. Maybe, just maybe, one of them was giving the other news on the war, and the leader of the syrens.

"You're not understanding me," Mayta's sweet voice sounded strained, hoarse even. "I do think it's a good idea. I just don't think I'm the right person."

The man sighed heavily in frustration. "What are you so scared of?"

Hauth poured a couple more glasses of water at the table next to them, as he tried to continue listening.

Mayta's long nails tapped restlessly against the wooden table. "I am not scared!" She groaned.

"You are," The man responded matter-of-factly.

Hauth finally turned towards them, wanting to watch Mayta to ensure she wouldn't poison or kill this man. Or bury him alive even. He lowered his voice forcefully before asking, "Another drink?"

Mayta nodded in response, she herself looked to be avoiding all eye contact with him too, for whatever reason.

Only the man started to eye Hauth strangely, did he see him listening?

He gave a loud sniff in his direction and furrowed his brow, as if considering the scent of mint in his soap.

"You?" Hauth asked, pointing to the full glass of ale. "Can I get you something else?"

The man shook his head. Hauth felt his eyes on him as he walked back to the bar and mixed Mayta's drink. As the ice rattled back and forth in his shaker, Hauth took a moment to peek back at them. Sure enough, the man was still watching. The hairs on Hauth's arm raised and his chest tightened in anticipation.

It was right at that moment, that a roar, loud and unrelenting came from the direction of the Dahs. Each head in the pub turned towards the door. Silence laid heavy as their gazes. They each stood completely still. Eyes locked on the door that ran parallel to the Dahs.

When another roar, somehow even louder, erupted, the Skierkans did not hesitate to scream.

Glasses and tables were knocked over as the patrons stood up in a panic. They rushed out the back door and the creatures that could climb flew out the windows along the high ceilings. Even the Gray Goblin himself had emerged from his cocoon of an office that sat far above the bar. He swung back and forth on the chandelier, watching the front door.

Mayta and her friend were the last to leave, they did not run out in a panic and instead waited for the reckless and the afraid to rush out before they quietly tucked out through the back.

"You must leave, Hauth. I will lock the windows and the doors." The Gray Goblin cried from the chandelier.

"Let me help you." Hauth insisted.

More screams erupted from behind the front door. Whatever was happening, it was terrible. The Goblin sniffed not once, but twice, in the direction of the roars. "If you care for your life, you will leave. And you will take *that* with you." The Goblin pointed to the ornamental dual blades that hung above the fireplace.

Hauth twisted his neck back to get a good look at the Goblin. "Those?" He yelled, pointing back at the ornamental blades that had been there since Hauth had started coming to the Gray Goblin as a young boy. The Gray Goblin howled in laughter, an outrageous sound when paired with the screams and cries from outside. "Do not let the dust fool you! Those blades will never fail you! But you better bring them back to me!" He cried as he swung back and forth along the chandelier and flung himself to the windows that were opened by the sprites, closing them and boarding them shut.

Unwilling to argue and pumped with adrenaline, Hauth grabbed the twin blades and ran out the front door before the Goblin could barricade it shut. It took Hauth's eyes several blinks before adjusting to the brightness of dawn. And a couple more blinks to sort through the smoke from the building along the Dahs that burned with black and silver fire.

Hauth paused, taking a moment to feel the fear that coursed through his veins. Panting, he tightened his grip on the two ancient swords, swinging them, quickly learning their weight and feel as he watched a sea wraith breathe static fire along the shore of his home city. The creature was massive. Hauth's entire body could fit comfortably within its maw, which at this moment was continuing to spew an endless stream of black flame at his people. Its body was that of a snake with flippers that seemed halfway between a lunar wraith's scaled and muscular wings and the flippers of an aquatic creature. The fire that spewed from its maw traveled easily between the creature's fangs that rivaled in size to the dual swords Hauth now wielded.

A rider sat where the serpent body met the winged flippers, holding tightly along the sinewy tip of the wings, the rider pulled the creature back as it pumped its wings to stay in place over the Dahs. Hauth remained breathless, entrenched in the scene before him, refusing to move until the sea wraith angled towards the lighthouse. A silent breath of relief escaped when Hauth finally saw the rider. A syren, the only ones rumored to ever ride the sea wraiths. But not her. *Not her.*

The words echoed in his head, shaking him more than the smell of burned flesh and entrails. With one more breath in, Hauth emerged from the Gray Goblin's doorway and barreled directly towards the sea wraith.

Heat from his burning city singed his throat and lungs as he raced towards the black waters of the Dahs. He ran as fast as he could, pumping his arms with each beat. Thankfully, most civilians had already cleared out, heading in the direction of the Bleached Palace. Gustav, one of the oldest of the Vermilli, carried a child in each arm. Both were severely burned. Crying. Bleeding. Hauth kept running. The cobblestone beneath his feet turned to sharp black sand. He kept running. Faster. He needed to go faster.

The beast was too large to sit within the shallows and Hauth only had the dual swords to work with, no bow of any kind to hit the creature from a distance. The sea wraith was a nearly limbless creature with only the flippered wings that the syren rider wrapped their humanoid legs around and gripped with their hands. The wings beat on, continuously, seemingly holding up the sea wraith in place over the black waters. The blood magic that Hauth had been burying deep within him snaked out, confirming what he had assumed: between those two wings laid the heart of the beast.

Sharp sand turned into cold harsh waters. Hauth ignored every instinct, every part of his aching mind and body that begged him to run as far away from these cursed waters, and he kept moving forward. The thick black tide of the Dahs was up to his knees by the time the sea wraith turned its massive silver and green eyes to him. The entire massive head snapped towards him. The forked tongue curled out of its mouth before quickly retracting. Shit. Shit. Shit. Shit.

Hauth dove into the Dahs. Tasting blood and metal and salt, he swallowed the twisted waters, choking on it, but remaining beneath the surface, safe from the fire.

Only the fire breached the water. He could only see it when it flashed silver, but it came down into the Dahs itself. He felt the flames hitting his back and his feet as he swam deeper. Swallowing back the screams, he continued diving, abruptly switching his angle to where the wraith did not expect, nor could it see. Burns already began to blossom along his entire back, stinging from the heavy salt of the water.

While Hauth Orn had never been burned, Raask had known the feeling all too well. His father, the Fire Monger King, had been sometimes careless and almost always cruel with the use of his alignment. Burns were a familiar pain. A tolerable one.

Hauth stayed under the black waters, thankful for his increased ability to see in the dark after the incident. His lungs ached from running through the flames to the water, and they throbbed as he stayed under. Searching for the body of the beast.

The burns along his back bled into the water, joining the blood of his people. So much blood. It caused the black waters to shimmer with it. But no... Not that one, a glinting shimmer caught his eye. There. That was not a thick cloud of blood, but the scales of the sea wraith. He swam until he was nearly under the creature. Each movement further burning his scorched lungs.

His muscles tensed, bracing for the moment he would rise. His blood magic, from far below his surface and deep within his bones, began to stir. It was hungry, always hungry lately, and so weak. But with all of this bloodshed, his magic had awakened. He felt stronger than he had in weeks. Ignoring the burns on his body and the currents pushing him further into the Dahs, Hauth settled into an area in front of the beast, where he estimated that the water would come to chest level. Any deeper, he wouldn't be able to wield his swords. Any shallower and he would be too far to strike where it counted.

It had to be here. And it had to be now.

Hauth's fingers tightened against the hilt of the blades before he stood in front of the sea wraith and its rider. His shoulders rose and fell with each jagged breath as Hauth stared down the beast that continued to spit fire across the Salt District, his home for far longer than when he moved there as Hauth.

A clicking sound, deep and guttural, erupted within the beast's throat as it slowly twisted its long neck towards Hauth. With precise movements, the creature twisted its neck in a serpentine motion until the scaled head was nearly within reach of Hauth's blades. The neck twisted as the beast moved its head all around, as if wishing to get a better look at the man who dared to challenge it—within its own waters nonetheless.

As Hauth stared deep into the creature's maw, he did his best to not measure its many large and sharp teeth, and instead to see the creature as he would any dueler, by looking into its eyes. The sea wraith angled its head in curiosity as it took him in. The languid movements of the beast stopped as its eyes scanned Hauth back and forth like it was reading a book.

From within his mind, Hauth could hear the creature's voice in the common tongue, *"A curiosity, you are..."* His eyes widened at the voice of the creature, a female with a lyrical voice that dragged the *s* in curiosity as a hiss.

The sounds of destruction and devastation continued to rage from the shores. The smell of burnt flesh and gore sank into Skierka like a fog. But at that moment, Hauth forgot all of that. This was his moment to find the answer he'd been searching for in every wave and every drunken tale. "Have you seen *her*?" He asked, out loud.

The sea wraith clicked its tongue, but kept it within its mouth where it could not call upon the fire. Suddenly the creature turned its head behind itself to watch the rider, as if the rider had said something to it mind-to-mind. The sea wraith huffed impatiently before turning back to Hauth. *"Whom do you mean, bloodbringer?"*

Hauth swallowed, his throat still raw and burnt from racing through the engulfed streets. "Her. Your Queen." His voice broke into a whisper, "Is she alive?"

The sea wraith studied him. *"Are you?"*

He wanted to beat his fists against the creature's chest until it answered him. Until it told him that she was alive. Until it told him that she was near. If he could not hear from her, he must hear about her. *"You speak of Aria the Ruthless?"*

Hauth nodded, brows furrowed as he searched the wraith's face for some kind of answer, some kind of response. Anything. He needed to know.

"A curiosity you are, indeed. Aria the Ruthless is alive. The drums of war beat to her heartbeat, do you not hear them?" Hauth's heart fell into his gut as he fell back onto his heels. He mouthed a "thank you" to the wraith, which gave a short nod in acknowledgement. "You must leave now. Your war is not with these people. They are innocent and have suffered as you have."

The wraith snickered, a strange clicking sound with huffs of hot breath, *"Sitting in comfort as mine are hunted. There is not an innocent soul on this island."* Hauth watched in horror as the creature extended its forked tongue far past its teeth.

Fire was coming.

CHAPTER 5
ARIA

Aria slipped through the chaos and bloodshed. Cloaked. She kept her head low and feet steady as she stalked through alleys and past Skierkans who bled and screamed, just as her people did.

The familiar smells of blood and scorched flesh filled her nostrils, only this time she did not dread the smell. A hint of a smile, nothing more, crept across her face. *Let the Skierkans bleed*, she thought happily, narrowly avoiding a family running past with their wounded child in hand. The streets of Etra, once nothing more than the land of her enemy, were now familiar. She remembered running through these streets. Drinking with the enemy. Laughing with him even. A shudder ran down Aria's spine as the familiar pit of dread began to squirm in her belly. *He* was no longer. So there was nothing holding her back. She would kill the Fire Monger King. She'd have his head on a stick.

The violent fantasy kept her calm and collected as she kept her face hidden in the shadows of her cloak. Sea wraith fire warmed her back as she rushed through the city. The Vermilli stormed past her in hordes, heading towards the direction of one of her lieutenants and their wraith. The fools were so wrapped up in killing the creature, they did not even stop to consider that more beasts were slipping right past them and into the heart of their stronghold.

Chilled cobblestones turned to snow as Aria reached the edge of the city.

She did not falter. She continued, forward, always forward, as she walked up the icy hills that ran between the Gaulic and the coastal capital of Skierka, Etra. The snow was hard underneath her feet, luckily the military boots that she stole from a cadaver were designed for the icy hills of Skierka. She did not slip.

Aria did not mind the cold, the depths of the Dahs themselves were far colder than this, yet she found the wind to be tedious. It slapped against her face harshly as she traversed the first great hill bordering Etra and the dense forest. She had grown better at walking during her time in the Bleached Palace. But that had been over a year ago now, and each step uphill against the snow felt like a battle in itself. Staying balanced with legs was a tricky skill among her kind, one that was hard to practice. It's why she had sent many of her kind to Viggo, to train among the Surtrians, to learn the skills of land battle. Without that, they would never win this war.

The sensitive skin of her legs prickled against the cold Skierkan north winds. When she finally reached the top of the hill, Aria turned to watch the razing of the city beneath. The wind, while irritating in her climb, had been the perfect aid to the fires, spreading ember across the city. In the distance, Aria watched as a lone Skierkan stood waist deep in the Dahs. The Skierkan's long icy white hair fought against the wind as they prepared to duel the wraith. A courageous fool. The wraith's muscles began to contort from below the waters of the Dahs up through the creature's neck. Fire was coming.

Aria turned around and continued walking to the forest. It was dangerous to linger in the open, where anyone could watch as a lone female trekked up the icy hills. She couldn't afford anyone to follow her. She continued. Each step taking her closer to the Bleached Palace.

The smell of blood and flame had turned into ice. Now the smell of pine overtook her senses. The forest was dense in parts, green needles stuck to her hair and cloak along with clumps of sap. A snake, white with thin rings of red, joined her at some point, slithering along her side. The creature hissed, long and breathy. Aria rolled her eyes.

"I don't know where you're going, but I am heading to the palace," Aria answered.

"But what for, ssssyren?"

Aria debated not answering. Everyone knew snakes were gossipy creatures, and if the wrong snake heard her plan... Then again, the Morloks rarely employed any non-humans. And humans could not speak to animals. Only creatures could speak to creatures. "I am going to kill the King." Her deepest desire, her deepest wish.

Nothing would stop Aria now. She would kill the King. Or she would die trying.

The snake shuddered, clearly startled, before wrapping around her boot and up her leg. "Excuse me!" Aria cried.

"Yesss! Excussse you!" The snake's voice cut in and out as it climbed Aria's torso, popping up out of her cloak and turning its head back to look her in the eye. *"Thiss isss not a good idea."*

Aria was growing more and more exasperated. "And why not?" She was seconds away from grabbing the snake and throwing it against a tree. But it's big eyes blinked back at her, looking similar to the eel she had kept as a pet as a young syren.

"It does not end with the King. There are too many that agree with him."

Aria stilled. Her already stiff muscles tightened as her hand balled into a fist at her side. *"So what? He just gets away with it? He needs to pay."* The words ripped from her throat like a battle axe.

The snake, as if alarmed, twisted its head in curiosity. It stilled for a moment before whispering. *"A hylbra approaches."* Aria could have sworn the snake's eyes squinted before it continued, *"Friendly."* The snake went back into Aria's cloak, making a home in the warm hood.

"If it is friendly, why do you hide?" She whispered back, elongating her human nails into the claws of her syrenic form. The snake only shushed Aria in response. Her nostrils flared in annoyance at being shushed by the forest-floor-dwelling creature. But she kept her body ready for the hylbra. She had never seen one for herself, but knew of them from the tales. Giant canine-like creatures that, like her, could shift between humanoid form and their beast form. An evolutionary advantage that the most ancient predators had developed.

She smelled the hylbra before she saw him. A wet dog with a cologne of warm clove and wood. *"You know now why I hide?"* The snake hissed quietly in disgust.

"You know what, Jor? Maybe I don't care for the smell of your musky scales." The male's voice was warm and rough. A fire in the cold wood.

"How do you know you're not smelling my scales, dog?" Aria asked, raising her voice so that the hylbra could hear her from however far away he was. She still could not see him through the thick pine. It agitated her and even slightly alarmed her to have no eyes on the predator.

The hylbra snorted. "Believe me, I wouldn't mistake the smell of Jor for anyone or any*thing*." Aria stilled, listening closely to determine the size of the creature along with his exact location. Unfortunately, through the howling wind rustling through the pine needles she couldn't hear too damn much at all. "Why don't you come on out from the pine?" The hylbra asked, in a not-so-overtly-threatening way that might not have even been a threat at all. In fact anyone else may have heard the voice as just plain friendly. To Aria, it sounded like a trap.

The hylbra laughed again, a soft sound. He had to be semi-close.

And seemingly standing north from her, the direction of the castle. "You're not scared of me, are you?" He asked.

Aria stilled.

Jor slithered his head closer to Aria's ear and whispered, *"The pine dwindlesss into a grove of assspen just up ahead. He musst be there."* Aria nodded, silently stalking forward, being careful to remain hidden.

"Is he dangerous?" She whispered back to the little snake.

"He seemsss to think ssso," Jor retorted with obvious disdain before adding, *"he helpss your sssisssster. They ssseem to be good friendss."*

At the mention of her sister, Aria barreled forward, running directly into the male's chest before tackling him. The man was large and didn't flinch at the takedown attempt, only that made him too assured, cocky even. Aria flung her knee high into the hylbra's gut with enough power to make him hunch over in pain and surprise. When his arms moved up to hold her at a distance, Aria swept her elbow inwards, hooking his arm into hers, forcing his shoulder and elbow to move far past their limits. She pushed his body against a semi-sturdy aspen with her left hip as she cranked his elbow and shoulder into a painful position. "What do you know of Mayta?" Aria seethed. Jor hissed in what sounded oddly like glee.

"Skullin's Scythe! Will you relax?" The hylbra coughed. "I'm on your side!"

Aria cranked the shoulder and arm further. "What do you know of Mayta?" She asked again, saying each word slowly, allowing the pain to seep into the hylbra's joints. His eyes widened and breaths deepened as Aria continued cranking his joint far past its limit.

"I know that she owes me for coming out here to get you!" The hylbra spat. He looked at her with frantic wild eyes. She could smell the pain on him, the desperation in the beads of sweat. "Aurna! Aurna?"

As soon as she heard the name come from the hylbra's mouth, she let go of him. He must truly know Mayta, if he knew the name, and she must truly trust him to have given it to him. The hylbra quickly backed away a few steps from Aria, rubbing his shoulder and elbow.

"How did my sister know I would be here?" Aria asked.

He rolled his shoulder over a couple of times before grabbing it with his opposite hand and pushing back against the joint. The shoulder clicked into place with a loud snap. The wolfman glared at her, ignoring her question. "You know I heard Jor tell you I was Mayta's friend?" His eyes narrowed.

Jor clicked his tongue against his fangs, *"The dog is right. Did you not believe me?"* He asked offendedly.

Aria rolled her eyes. "I do not know either of you. Now answer my question, dog." The hylbra threw his hands up in exasperation.

"Fen." The dog barked.

Aria's head tilted in confusion. "You've got to be kidding me... It's my name! I am Fen, not *dog*."

This was growing tedious. The dog was wasting her time and she did not have a lot of it to spare. Etra would only remain in chaos for such a brief period of time after the sea wraith attack. She needed to get to the palace. To the King. "Alright, Fen. Is my sister okay? And how did she know I would be here?"

The cold wind howled through Aria's ears, pushing her hair back behind her shoulders and over the little snake that sat perched there.

"The wraith attack. She said no sea wraith would ever disobey your orders. A rogue syren maybe, another syren's clan of course, but she said the sea wraiths answer to you."

Aria felt Jor's body tighten as Fen watched her reaction carefully.

Aria did not confirm nor deny the wolf's statement. Mayta had no business telling the dog their politics. "And she is okay?"

"Yes."

Aria scoffed and walked past Fen, deeper into the grove of aspen. The dog followed close behind.

"She thinks it's a bad idea." He called afterward, voice husky and commanding.

Aria sighed. *"What* does she think is a bad idea?"

"Killing the King." The wolfman stopped in his steps. His shadow cascaded over Aria, blocking the patches of sunlight from hitting her. Aria turned back towards him, her jaw tightening and claws elongating.

Fen's eyes widened, not out of fear or pain, but with what may have been compassion. "She says that they will put you to death. And that she can't do it without you. She needs you, Aria." Her nostrils flared, as she turned to look back at the direction of the Bleached Palace. The home to her enemies. Her home once. "The syrens will not win without you. And if you kill the King now, you'll be dooming us all."

She couldn't breathe. It felt as if her chest was caving in on itself. Her heart stammered and her stomach dropped. The dog was right. Mayta was right. If she killed the King now, one of his *friends* would take his place, committing the same atrocities.

But she couldn't break. Not now. Not ever. "So what am I to do?" She asked, hating the weakness in her voice. Hating the ache in her chest. The sorrow that buried itself so deep into her that it became a part of her very marrow. The rage that fueled her blood, flowing through each muscle and tendon. It was growing to be too much. It was always too much. How much longer was she meant to survive with so much pain?

"You can either go back to your warriors and continue battling or you can act as the queen that you are." Fen crossed his arms in front of him. Watching her so very carefully.

"And what do you believe the syren queen should be doing?"

Fen laughed as if it was the most obvious thing in the world. "It's time to pick the successor to the Skierkan throne, a kinder ruler who will not enslave the non-humans, who will give us rights... And once we find the poor bastard, we'll have to get the Skierkans to choose them as their next ruler, to go to battle for them."

It was logical, but Aria hated it, for she knew who would have been her choice.

Raask.

A king with a kind heart.

But Raask was always just a fantasy, not something that could have ever been. She was supposed to die anyways. He just beat her to it.

With a broken heart, and a bloodlust that would not be sated anytime soon, Aria went off to find a man to replace the one she had loved.

CHAPTER 6
VIGGO

A grief-ridden smile sat upon Viggo's face as he took in his father. The underrealm, Helk, was cold as always. And a deep sadness emanated from the General's brown eyes that appeared black in the nearly colorless realm of his father. The realm of his mother. The realm, now, of his brother too.

The familiar patter of Viggo's dead mother's footsteps against the cold volcanic stone of the Dark Palace echoed, the only warm sound in a world of despair and grief. Kel watched his son closely. The ancient god looked upon his son with the hollowed gaze of grief. Viggo was certain that his father was grieving the man he thought his son was: a decent man, a good one. Viggo was none of those things—not anymore at least.

Kel placed a warm hand onto his shoulder, a comforting gesture. Before Viggo's mother could enter, he quickly and quietly asked, "Is he okay?" His voice was strained, rough with the hoarseness of someone who had been screaming for hours. Kel's eyes crinkled at the corners as he nodded. His long glossy black hair swayed gently with the slow movement.

Viggo nearly collapsed in relief.

It was the first time he had been to Helk since that day so long ago. He couldn't face it. Any of it. Any time he felt his father's summoning, he would fight with all he could to wake. The grief had eroded any decency that was left of him and over time it grew easier to avoid the loving tendrils of darkness that his father would send in his sleep: an invitation and a plea.

Tonight the darkness beckoned him, not warm and comforting, but the all-consuming darkness of the entire night sky. Viggo was being ordered into Helk, and he was a lot of things, but stupid enough to decline a command from the God of Death, Darkness & Destruction was not one of them.

His mother's footsteps were quickening, she was nearly there. "Does she know what I did?" Kel let out a breath from deep within his chest. He rubbed his son's shoulder, sending his shadows to wrap around him in a comforting embrace. His father was powerful, one of the most powerful of the Gods, only matched by his brothers Tsu and Rahn. Not just the kind of power that could level the entire realm into oblivion, but the kind that could tamper the vast well of power at his disposal into small magics, comforting even. Viggo, as a halfling, inherited his father's powers but not enough strength to truly control them. He was a child, constantly at risk of tantrum from his magic. A slave to it.

Kel shook his head, "No." The old god removed his hand from Viggo's shoulder, but kept his shadows wrapped around him in a comforting cocoon.

"He did not tell her?" Viggo asked, his words breaking. His world breaking.

Kel shook his head once more. "Viggo, please. This was not your fault. It is mine. It is why we forbade each other to mate with humans. The power... It is too much even for me sometimes. You must not blame yourself, my child." Viggo grimaced at the words. It was a lovely thought, that it wasn't his fault, but not true of course.

Still, he appreciated that his father was trying. "I love you," Kel said, his shadows warming against Viggo's cold skin.

The smell of dried lilac and cold stone overcame Viggo's senses as the door creaked open.

Viggo's mother, who was nearly as tall as him, stood in the doorway—like an owl who had finally located her prey. She crossed her long slender arms in front of her as she leaned on one leg, outstretching the other towards the roaring fireplace. Her icy blue glare switched back and forth between Viggo and Kel before finally landing on Kel. "How dare you not tell me my son was here?" She stalked towards her husband, the God of Death, and poked him hard in the chest. Viggo knew from experience how painful those long fingers were when poked into the chest. Or an arm. Or a rib.

"I'm sorry, my love." Kel grimaced, eyes widening as he took in Amara Hawthorn's rage. She turned towards her son with the swiftness of a warrior and poked the same finger into his chest. "And how could you not visit me for the past year? Where have you been? What, *the Skierkan Bruin* doesn't have time to visit his mother?" Amara growled, removing the finger from his chest. The glare in her eyes remained as Viggo rubbed the sore spot on his chest that would most certainly bruise. Her once warm blue eyes and golden hair that he remembered from childhood had long faded into ice. Other than that, she appeared almost eerily the same. Her angular face and long, slim limbs seemed suited for her second life as the queen of the dead.

Viggo wanted to tell her what he'd done. He wanted to know why Raask and Kel hadn't told her about it. He wanted to know what Raask had thought about where their mother was, to whom she was married, but the words failed to reach his tongue. It was too much. Perhaps in time, he'd learn. Maybe Raask would forgive him too. He knew he'd never do it—forgive himself. But to see Raask again, even in the underrealm, it would bring Viggo no greater joy. Raask was Viggo's everything. Everything he had done and everything he was, was for his little brother.

But for this moment in time, his mother was angry that he hadn't visited in over a year. And that was enough for him to handle at the moment. "I know, I'm sorry. The war has kept me busy." Amara's gaze pierced through his like a sword. Her eyes were so sharp and accusatory, just like Raask's.

Viggo shook off the memory of the lifeless gaze of his brother.

Amara tsked her tongue against her teeth. "And you think we haven't been busy? We have an abundance of the dead now! We are building more infrastructure at a greater rate than ever before! And the syrens continue to try to sneak into the barracks we've built for the Skierkans, it has become such an ugly mess. It's despicable! Even in death they're still trying to kill each other."

Kel shook his head gently. "Amara, Drakyr is handling it fine. You don't need to worry about such things."

Viggo bit his lip. It was impossible to cause pain or another's 'death' in Helk, but it didn't stop some from trying. His father's guard, the daumans, would do their best to put an end to any fighting within Helk. The humanoid creatures had sharp, protruding bones, black irises, and claws. Some had horns. Some had wings. They had always been very kind and doting to Viggo, but he was certain they were capable of cruelty. Afterall, they were also his father's army.

Amara whipped back towards Kel. "Are you telling me that I am not allowed to rule?" She was a queen in life and would accept no less in the afterlife. Viggo did his best to stifle a chuckle. He knew Kel would not stop his mother from ruling. He also knew that if he wanted to stop her, there was no way he could. His mother's stubbornness and wish to have things her way could outlast even the eldest and most powerful of Gods.

Kel sighed. "No, of course not." He picked up her hand with a great gentleness and brushed a kiss against her knuckles. Amara nodded, accepting the gesture as the apology she knew it was. "Darling, I would like to speak to our son in private. Would that be alright?"

Amara scowled, looking between the two of them. "Why?"

"He has lived through a few too many wars. He is now leading one. I understand the toll that can take and would like to discuss it with him."

Amara scoffed. "What would you know of fighting in a war? You only welcome the dead."

Kel shrugged his shoulders. "There was a time when war had come."

Amara rolled her eyes before hugging Viggo. She held onto him tightly, the smell of dried lilac and cold stone once again filled his nostrils. She was never a warm mother. But she had loved him with everything she had. He held onto her tightly, for only a moment, before they both let go. "You will be back soon, yes?" Amara asked, carefully eyeing every inch of Viggo's face.

He nodded. "I promise." Amara took a deep breath in before departing from Kel's office. She allowed the door to slam behind her in a fashion that was so utterly Raask-like that it brought an ache back to his chest.

Kel waited a moment before proceeding. Viggo knew this gesture to mean two things. One, he could be checking in mentally with Drakyr, the head of the dauman. Or two, the more likely one in this scenario, he was checking to see if Amara was listening by the door. Kel nodded to himself, either way, it was sorted.

"I would like you to find the Sistros."

A tunnel of painful memories flashed through Viggo's mind. That was once the plan. To find them, with his brother. He was to share the truth about his father, their mother, and his treason on that trip. And they would find the three ancient sisters who wove the secrets of the realm into their tapestries at the edge of the world. The ones who had spoken a prophecy of Viggo and Raask—according to his father's spies.

"Why?" Viggo asked, "We already know the ending to their prophecy. Brother kills brother before he leads a doomed revolution."

Kel grimaced. "I don't believe that that is what the prophecy says. And there is only one way to find out." Viggo's chest tightened. His heart rate increased, and his breath quickened. How could his father ask this of him? Especially now, when what little that was left of the Arkts needed him. He needed to finish training the syren. He needed to battle. It was what he was designed for.

"I—I can't. I can't abandon my people. I can't not fight against *him*." Kel remained silent, Viggo could practically see the thoughts and plans constantly formulating and reformulating within his mind.

"I was afraid you would say that, but I'm also proud of you." He scratched absentmindedly at his chin. "Perhaps you can send one in your wake. We need to know what their prophecy has stated. I believe it is imperative for your war." Kel smiled, just the slightest upturn of the lip. "Perhaps, you could ask the syren you have imprinted on."

Viggo shook his head. "No. No for a thousand reasons. Just no."

Kel chuckled as he walked behind his desk and retrieved a glass of liquor from a decanter, and two crystal glasses. He gave them both a generous pour, the deep purple liquor sloshed around the glass as he gave them both a swirl. "Name a few of those reasons, why don't you?" He asked, handing Viggo a glass that was surprisingly cold against his skin in a suddenly overly warm room.

"For one, it's quite a treacherous journey, is it not? I would need to accompany her and as I said, I can't just leave my own revolution." He took a sip from the glass, the liquor was strong yet still sweet and syrupy. The liquor of the underrealm, aycha. Made from the bark of the aycharo tree, a long and spindly white tree that grew in abundance in Helk.

Kel nodded, pursing his lips. "I believe your love is a syren, is she not? And she has been trained by her sister, Aria, whom I understand to be quite a warrior in battle. You don't believe she could hold her own?" Viggo scowled. Kel was, unfortunately, making an excellent point. Aria would not have allowed Mayta to be anything less than a formidable opponent in battle. "And as you can see from your mother and my darling wife, women do not enjoy being undervalued for their skills."

Viggo's grip tightened on the cup. He did not like where this was going. Unlike his mother, Viggo could not outsmart the God of the Dead. "Well she is our only spy within the palace, and with her unique abilities, she is at a particular advantage." That would be it. His father understood, more than almost anyone, how power-hungry the Fire Monger King was.

"And if, say, another spy with a similar skillset could work within the palace? Mayta would be able to fulfill her quest?" *Her quest?* Viggo was stunned. What was he talking about? He had just asked him to seek the Sistros. Now it was *her* quest?

"What is this about?" He asked.

Kel swirled the purple liquor around his cup once more. "I believe you have imprinted on the syren." Viggo's eyes narrowed upon his father's. He had absolutely no clue what he was talking about. He heard him say the word before but assumed it was just an insult—or his father's funny way of saying he had an interest in her.

"And what is that supposed to mean?" He demanded, feeling suddenly angry at whatever the accusation had meant.

"It is an ancient word, long forgotten by the humans. When we had agreed to no longer interfere with human matters, the term eventually became obsolete." Kel took a large gulp from his glass, polishing off what was left of it. "When a God falls in love, it is not a simple thing. It is all consuming. It is not rational. It is dangerous. And above all, it's only given when the Sistros see no other possible outcomes."

The words stumbled out of Viggo's mouth like blood from a wound, "You believe I've imprinted on Mayta?" Kel nodded. "Why would the Sistros choose that? Choose her? Why me and why now?" His powers began to build within him once again. His heart felt like it was damn near about to fall out of his chest.

"I'm not sure. It's one of the questions I wish I could ask them.

Alas, they will not see me, nor any spies that I have sent. They will only discuss matters with those directly involved in the prophecy."

Viggo attempted to calm himself with another swig from his own glass. The harsh liquor burned its way down his throat, giving him something to focus on besides the impending doom that was moving into his gut.

"There is another thing..." Kel's words trailed off for a moment before he continued. "When Gods imprint, we can communicate with our mates across any distance. Across realms even. You may enter her dreams. And you may enter her mind at any time. However, the more you build the bridge between your minds, eventually she will be able to enters yours as well. Particularly as a syren, she is already gifted the magic of mood reading and manipulation. I can only assume it would be easier for her to reach across this bridge than it is for, say, a human."

And there it was. A dagger to the chest. A creak in the night.

He did not just love Mayta, merely a complete stranger, he had imprinted on her. And the Gods knew she didn't feel the same for him. His entire soul and his future were woven into this poor creature, who had already been through so much. She didn't deserve this. It was too much. Too much for him. And certainly too much to put onto her.

He had to center himself again. "If Mayta were to find the Sistros, then I could communicate with them via Mayta, correct?"

Kel nodded. "And I believe there is a solution to your spy problem as well... Would you like to hear it from her yourself?"

He was lost and overwhelmed. He barely knew what he was doing when he nodded. "Great, then you must only think of her and follow that thread of thought, the essence of her that already lives within your soul. Eventually, with more use, it will become stronger and sturdier. To block her, you'll only need to snip that bridge."

Viggo had drank too much of the aycha. He was a complete mess with bags under his eyes and dirt under his nails. This was no state to see Mayta in. But Kel had a way of getting what he wanted, and pushing things forward. "I will help you out your first time and send you to her dream. But do not forget—one of you must visit the Sistros. You *must* question them of the prophecy and your imprinting. Find out what you need to do to win your war. And don't forget to visit your mother."

With that, Kel's shadows pushed Viggo over, where headfirst he fell into the swirling vortex of inter-realm travel.

CHAPTER 7
MAYTA

Like in all of Mayta's dreams, she was underwater, in the cavern she called home. A pit of black and silver flashing syrenic fire lay in the center of the cavern. Innately, Mayta knew that Aria was training their soldiers, and would be home shortly and most likely ravenously hungry.

Mayta was preparing a meal of shark gills and crab legs. She hummed to herself as she moved about the cavern, piercing the shark gills on the bottom of the stalactite that hung over the fire pit. Her tail swished effortlessly between the spikes that shot from the top and the bottom of her and Aria's cave. As the heirs to the Abisian Syrenic throne, her and Aria received a cavern that had more spikes than most. Spikes were a luxury among their kind. A place to cook. A deterrent from other creatures. A way to bleed, which for their kind was the same as prayer. Particularly for royalty. They were to constantly bleed for their people.

Aria bled enough for the both of them.

Mayta felt the water shifting, a disturbance from the direction of the door. She smiled, thinking of how happy Aria would be to come home to the fresh gills. But it was not Aria's long black hair floating in the entrance of the cavern, nor the familiar sound of her tail swishing through the door, but a massive human. A male.

Viggo Morlok, the former general of the Skierkan military, had somehow found his way to her cavern. He stared at her with wide eyes. She could feel his heartrate quickening from the movement in the water. And the fear, the desperation... She could smell it on him. Supposedly, this man was a decorated killer. An apex predator among the humans. So why did he look at her so fearfully? And how on the Arkts could he even get into her cavern?

The realization hit her like a wave. This cavern did not exist anymore. She was dreaming.

But she had never dreamed of the General before... And something was odd about him. She could not smell his... humanness. No sweat. No bodily odors. Only the scent of his fear and despair. "Are you truly here, General?"

He nodded. His chin-length black hair swaying in the water along with the slight movement. His eyes crinkled, grimaced even. "Prove you are not just a part of my dream," she demanded. Somehow, she could feel the truth to his answer. But it wasn't enough. She wanted more.

His voice appeared in her head as if they were her own thoughts or a memory. *"When you awaken, I will speak to you in this same way, and you will know."*

Mayta allowed the words to wash over her before she asked, projecting the thought to him, *"How?"*

She watched as his body stiffened against the current. He steadied himself against a thick stalagmite. His large hand gripped the tip of the spike tightly. *"There are some things that you don't know about me... Things that nobody knows, really."* She just stared at him, waiting for him to answer the damned question. But he looked so pained, growing whiter by the second. She could smell it riling up inside of himself. Mayta floated across the space, over to where he gripped onto the cavern like it was the only thing keeping him in her head. His eyes tracked her as if he was anticipating violence. And when she wrapped her arms around him, she felt him sink into her. The smell of relief, warm and inviting, began to phase into his bitter despair. He felt so nice against her. His strong arms wrapped around her shoulders, his hand gripping the back of her head, as if he was unsure if she was really there too. If this was truly her dream, it meant nothing could harm her here. Nothing in here was real or had any consequences. With this thought, she allowed herself to sink into his touch. She closed her eyes and breathed in the scent of him, smoke and wood. Somehow, he felt safe to her. Like a little piece of her soul recognized him. He had to feel it too, with the way he was holding her, she knew he had to be feeling a lot of this too.

But she did not know him. And she did not want to get wrapped up in the idea of a man ever again. With Raask, she had built up so many ideas of what could have been that she had lost herself in reality. She flickered open her eyes and her body stiffened before she pulled back. Her tail swirled around to give her enough space to look into his eyes. He watched her tail, tracking the constant movement it took for her to stay in place. His eyes seemed to stay hyper-focused on her tail, not in the curious manner of a human, but in a way that insisted he was avoiding meeting her gaze.

"What is it?" She asked aloud, uncomfortable with the idea of the human in her head. When he finally did meet her gaze, her heart fluttered. The training in the Surtr Islands had done well for him. His skin had the faintest tanned kiss from the sun, and his deep brown eyes seemed to have warmed just the slightest. Stubble lined his cheeks and jaw making him look far more rugged than she had remembered. He was built like a warrior, padded with endless muscle, and moved as fluid as her kind. But a deeper sadness was there, a pain that sat between his neck and his shoulders, keeping him rigid and tense.

Gods, even when hurting, he was handsome.

Mayta had been so wrapped up in getting a good look at the

General, that she was completely taken off guard by the words that spilled out of his mouth. "The Morlok King is not really my father. And my mother, she didn't kill herself, well not like how the people say she did." The words started pouring out of him like wine. "My mother, at some point, met and fell in love with Kel." Mayta's brows furrowed at the casual mention of the most brutal and vicious of the Gods. Syrens rarely mentioned his name aloud for fear of his retribution. To die in battle was holy— it was the greatest honor a syren could hope for in their life. But death, without the pretext of battle, was the greatest fear of her people. A disgrace.

"And the King, he didn't treat her well. He didn't treat any of us well, really. So Kel offered to save her. To take her to the underrealm with him, where she would be his queen. He promised her he'd look after Raask and I. She waited until I was old enough to watch over myself and—and my brother." His voice broke at the mention of Raask. She wanted to hug him once again, wrap him in her arms and take the pain away. But maybe he should be feeling this, he'd been the one to kill him. The human he loved above all, he had killed in cold blood. Mayta had to be smart. He may be kind, but he was also incredibly dangerous. And worse, out of control. Apparently, if she was following this story correctly, he was also likely the son of a God.

"Your brother?" She asked.

Viggo shook his head. "He was a product of the King's unwanted advances."

Mayta shuttered at the cold words. And she wondered, if a little part of Viggo resented his mother for not taking them with her to the underrealm.

"Why are you telling me all of this?"

Viggo sighed, his shoulders slumped in on themselves. An utterly and completely defeated man. "Because as a godling, things are different for me than they are for regular people."

Mayta nodded at the obvious remark. The blood of one of the original ancient Gods coursed through his veins. His very matter had divine materials from the God of Death, Darkness & Destruction. He was as different from a human as a sea wraith was to a coral.

"It's why, what happened on that day, happened. I have a lot of power inside of me. Too much. And I just, I just can't handle it all sometimes. It's like I'm constantly at war with myself to control it all. My physical body just wasn't designed to hold the power of a God and if I'm not careful, then I can lose control." Mayta thought back to that day so long ago, when he had mentioned preferring the snowy winters in Etra to the summer, as he didn't have to worry about reigning in his magic and killing off the greenery.

Then she thought back to the day it happened. The day Viggo killed Raask. He had lost control after Raask had found out what she really was. "Do you know how Gods fall in love?" His question pulled her from her memories. It shocked her, as she never really considered how Gods had fallen in love. Aria had always been more religious than her, and Mayta herself preferred the fairytales to the stories of wrathful Gods. She shook her head no.

"It's something out of their control—our control—determined by the Sistros, interwoven into the threads of our realm when considered either dire, or perhaps a perfect match arises. I'm not sure why. But when a God falls in love, it's instant and it's dangerous." Mayta searched his eyes for an answer she'd known for quite a while. Even if she wasn't a syren, even if she couldn't smell it on him... His love for her was an obvious and universal truth, like the blueness of the sky and the warmth of the sun. But Mayta had seen what he'd done to those that he loved.

"You love me?" She had to hear the words from his lips, had to know how he felt saying them. She felt his eyes devouring her, searching for something.

"I don't know," He answered.

Her jaw tightened, disappointed for some reason that this near-stranger didn't admit that he loved her.

"What I do know," he placed his hands gently on top of her shoulders, "Is that I'm not going to force any of it on you. This wasn't your choice. It is not your curse to bear. I need you to understand that, okay Mayta?" His hands dropped from her shoulders and flexed at his side.

"I believe you," She said, although she wasn't sure if it was true. But he seemed visibly relieved just by those three simple words. "I still don't understand why you would tell me this then? Did you just need me to know?"

He chuckled, almost to himself, "No, I wouldn't be so selfish." He rubbed at the side of his jaw before continuing, "My father, Kel, he told me that a prophecy has been spoken."

Mayta gasped. A prophecy at wartime meant only one thing: hope. There had to be a way to defeat the Morloks. "What does it say?" She asked breathlessly.

"That's the thing. He doesn't know. The Sistros will only share it with those who are directly spoken of within the prophecy, and as you and I have been linked by their choosing, we could hear their counsel."

And with that, Mayta understood. "But you cannot leave the war. You are needed. And you have come to ask if I would seek the Sistros? Especially since Aria is now here and can take my place as a spy within the Bleached Palace."

Viggo's head jerked back in shock. "What? Aria is where?"

Mayta stiffened, he did not know. "The Skierkans took back the Zojz. They had fed their soldiers with some kind of lithe that exploded in the water. They know we like to eat our victims, and counted on it. Most of our army, the ones who stayed to fight within the Zojz that is, died in the explosions." The words rang hollow in her ears. She tried not to think of all of the friends and family that died in the attack... The friends and family that died in slavery to the Skierkans... She had already lost so much. If the Sistros knew of a way to defeat the Skierkans, she had to seek them out. It was her duty. She may not be a warrior like Viggo or her sister, but she still felt the responsibility of her people, the call to serve them. Let them fight like brutes, and she would worry about speaking with the ancient weavers of the universe.

Viggo leaned back against the stalagmite. He looked as if he was going to be sick. Mayta didn't resist the urge to rub his back in slow languid circles as he panted, hunched over the spiked floors of the cavern. "And just how, will your sister—the most hunted creature in Skierka—act as a spy?" He asked between heavy breaths.

Mayta laughed, a warm and sweet sound. She picked up his hand and gently led him through the cavern to the fluffy and soft beds of seaweed in the back. "Don't you worry, that's something that we've got covered." He looked at her with uncertainty in his eyes, but he didn't voice any protests. "Now sit down and relax. I'll bring you some fresh shark gill, that by now should be overcooked just as you like, and you must tell me how to find the Sistros."

As Mayta was plucking the shark pieces from the stalactites and placing them on the long flat stones she and Aria used for plates, she looked back at Viggo, just for a second. He sat against the edge of the cavern, sitting up straight. He was watching her. His eyes held an easiness that hadn't been there before. He smiled at her, such a small thing, but it made her heart stop. He was sitting so carefully. Watching everything that she did so closely. Mayta could practically taste the love he held for her. The love he denied, but she knew to be there.

And as they shared their meal together, discussing the treacherous path to the Sistros and the too-spicy cuisine of the Surtrian islands, Mayta couldn't help but wonder what the kiss of a godling would taste like.

Rough hands awoke Mayta abruptly from her dream with Viggo. At first she was startled, to be touched in her sleep and taken from a moment of peace and laughter. And then she recognized the touch.

She would recognize those hands from the deepest of comas.

She'd know her sister's touch when it was gloved. Through a blanket. Through snow and ice and the thick toxic waters of the Zojz. Her sister's hands—or now just singular hand—were as much a part of her as her own. The rough touch of a hand built to destroy—built to cause violence in the most carnal and brutal nature—touching her hair with a gentleness that was foreign to them both. To be loved at all was a blessing, but to be given love and gentleness by a creature who had never received it, was entirely its own beast.

Aria should have been taken care of by her...

They never spoke of their mother. She and Aria had been enslaved by the Skierkans. And Mayta was alone, for the briefest of times. It was long ago, but it was a feeling that never really went away. Something that sat heavy in her chest.

Aria arrived back to their cavern after two nights. Her back had been covered in dozens of lashes, the marks of a whip. She did not say where their mother was, the former queen of a damned people, and Mayta had never asked. She knew what happened to the syrens who were taken, plucked from their breathing grounds at the surface of the Dahs.

Their mother, the queen of the Abisian syrens, made Aria look gentle. There had never been a crueler creature in the Arkts, of that Mayta was sure.

So it was Aria's arms that would wrap around Mayta after she had awoken from nightmares. It was Aria who would brush her hair. Her rough callouses would scratch against Mayta's scalp, her too sharp claws occasionally pricking her ears or neck, but Mayta never complained, for she could feel the lightness of her sister's touch. A touch her sister, most likely, had to learn from the fairytale books she'd stolen from Skierkan ships and villages along the shore. It was paradise. A paradise that she worried she could lose at any moment.

Aria had washed up before bed, and now smelled of the spiced soap Fen kept in his bathing chambers. Slowly, Mayta blinked open her eyes. Aria's body laid right up against her, leaving the other half of Fen's massive bed completely empty. The hylbra had slept on the couch, she'd fallen asleep listening to the sounds of his snoring through the thick wooden door of his bedroom. And Aria... She was staring at Mayta. Her brown eyes rested on her with a gentle warmth reserved only for her. She twirled her long fingers in Mayta's hair, massaging her scalp and tracing words into her head, just as she did when they were younger.

From far away, Mayta could hear a small whisper, a husky voice of honey and rich whiskey, *"I promised you I would speak to you once you awoke, Mayta. I won't linger in your mind, you have my word. But come to me. Come to me if you are frightened. Come to me if you are lonely. Follow this thread and you'll find me."* Her eyes widened as she felt the warmth from the back of her skull disappearing with a *whoosh*. Viggo was gone. And she did not just dream of him.

"What is it?" Aria asked, worry written in her furrowed brows and extending claws.

Mayta couldn't help but giggle. "Nothing, nothing! Oh Gods, Aria! Are you always ready to battle?"

Aria's face relaxed, and even she let out an abrupt laugh. "I'd hope you'd know the answer to that question." Aria leaned forward and kissed her forehead before adding, "I have missed you greatly."

A rock settled its way onto Mayta's chest as it dawned on her that she would have to leave Aria. It had been so long since they'd been together. Her sister, who had been her mother and her father and her best friend, would not like being the one to stay put as Mayta traversed Skierka. But as the heirs, they both understood that their duty would always lie far outside of their own wants. They could not deny what was best for their people. Even if it meant losing the few comforts and moments of love that they could receive. Even if it meant losing each other.

"Ari, there is something I must tell you."

Surprisingly, Aria stayed quiet as Mayta recounted what Viggo had told her. Her only reactions being a few looks of concern and outrage, nothing out of the ordinary for her sister of course. When

Mayta was done, Aria turned to lay on her back. She stared up at the ceiling. Breathing through her nose and out through her mouth.

A slithering sensation from the foot of the bed made its way up between her and Aria until Jor, the snake her sister seemed to have adopted for some unknown reason, popped his little head out from under the blanket. Mayta gently patted his head, tracing the scales along his huge eyes. Jor squinted his face in pleasure at the sensation. "My Queen, if you'd like, I can accompany the princess and keep her safe."

Aria's only response was a heavy sigh. Both Mayta and Jor looked at one another and then back at Aria. Fen's snoring continued from the other room.

Mayta had known her sister her whole life. She was the first set of arms to ever hold her. Undoubtedly, Aria was running through about a hundred different schemes and futures, intricately planning out her best odds of success. Most likely trying to calculate the best way to ensure the safety of their people, and of Mayta. It's what she'd always done: put her people first. Jor seemed to know enough to keep quiet too.

Finally, Aria turned back to Mayta. Taking her hands into hers and holding them tightly. "How well do you know this Fen? Do you trust him?" She asked.

Mayta resisted the urge to give her sister a dirty look. She'd been over this many times the night before. "I told you, if he wanted to kill me or sabotage us, he had plenty of chances by now to do so and he hasn't."

Aria only rolled her eyes at this. "And I told you, that means nothing."

"Why do you even ask?" But Mayta understood as soon as she asked the question. "Wait, do you want him to come as some kind of guard?" Her nose scrunched up. This was so unbelievable and so like her sister. To not trust her to look after herself. It was ridiculous! And insulting!

"What if I do?" Aria huffed. She crossed her arms against her chest. Furrowing her brows, deep in thought once again. "Alright you're right. I will be the one to accompany you."

Mayta sat up. "Aria, you are being ridiculous. You're needed here. A resistance lies hidden in this city. And they need you. And *you* need to choose the successor to the Morlok King and ensure a treaty between their people and ours. It has to be you, Aria." Mayta watched, waiting, to see if Aria had any rebuttals. When she didn't, she continued, "As for Fen, I do trust him. But you'll need him to access the rebel meetings. I'm also worried that the Sistros won't meet me if I show up with someone not spoken of in the prophecy." She wasn't sure Fen wasn't in the prophecy, but it seemed unlikely to her.

Slowly, Aria sat up. Her red hair, big and wild, fell over her face as she offered nothing but a pained smile before taking her sister into her arms. "You will be careful?" Mayta nodded into her sister's hair. She hoped Aria would not feel her tears.

"Am I to join the princess or the queen?" Jor asked from below, he seemed to have slithered his way between them once again. Mayta laughed. "You can come with me, Jor!" She felt bad for the little creature and wouldn't mind the company.

Aria shook her head no. "Unfortunately, Mayta, I believe Jor could be of great use as a spy. Unless you'd like him to prevent you from being lonely." Jor looked at Aria in great wonder. He seemed to like the idea of being a spy.

Mayta was the first to release Aria from the hug. They smiled at each other, silently agreeing that for just that morning, they would only be sisters and not heirs to a dying people, not leaders of a revolution, not the last stand against an unjust king, but just sisters.

So they did just that. Sharing a breakfast of sweet pastries and fatty meats that they made Fen whip up for them. He poured them tawny. The wolf wasn't as good of a cook as her, but he did just fine. He even packed her up a handful of rolls, hard cheeses and dried meats to pack in her bag. Both Fen and Aria took turns packing it, arguing constantly over the best way to pack the bag and if it was too heavy for Mayta or not; neither of them bothered to ask her.

Aria had braided her long red hair into neat braids that she wrapped into a beautifully intricate bun that should stay put through the harsh winds of a Skierkan winter. Fen gave her his warmest fur coat.

Mayta knew that she would feel their stares long after she finally left Fen's warm chambers that sat on the edge of Etra. But what she was not expecting was for the feeling to linger long after she had entered the dense wood of the Gaulic.

CHAPTER 8
RAASK

Hauth Orn once again found himself staring down the kiss of death. The sea wraith, a silvery blue and green creature appearing mixed between a serpent and a lunar wraith, had come to Etra for one thing and one thing only: retribution.

It was a terrifying creature, straight out of a book of nightmares. With sharp sleek scales that shimmered under the light of the sun, accumulating to a row of massive spikes that ran along the beast's spine. Razor sharp teeth sat in perfectly straight rows in the creature's mouth. Massive wings beat powerfully, holding the creature upright in a near floating position above the water. Its long neck, a simple continuation of the beast's long body, moved like a snake. Quick. Powerful, Precise. Designed purely to be an optimal predator. A creature that had never been killed by a human, only washed ashore to be harvested. From somewhere deep within Hauth, a surge of excitement began to rise. The last time he had felt equally terrified and in awe of a creature, he had fallen in love with her.

This time, things would end differently.

Guttural clicks began from deep within the water. They traveled from the beast's gut and up through the long neck, growing louder and quicker as they approached the throat. Hauth wondered if Skullin would keep him this time, or if again, he would bring him back to the realm of the living, a paler and far more desperate man.

The wraith's tongue drew back into the creature's own throat and then extended far past the teeth. Fire was coming. The same fire that had burned his people. All the children that ran bleeding through the streets. The homes that had burned to the ground. This beast was responsible for that gore, for the slaughter of the salt district.

Maybe Skierka had done exactly as the beast said, power-hungry and cruel. But these people, they didn't deserve to die. These people... They didn't deserve any of this.

So he dove back into the black waters of the Dahs.

The fire reached him as the sound of the roar hit his ear drums like a blast. The fire licked the wounds along his back as he swam. For once, Hauth was grateful for the opaque blackness of the sea, hiding him from the beast. He zigged and zagged through the water. Now that he knew which glimmer to look for, he swam directly towards it. He'd given the creature a chance at peace, leaving him no choice but to stand against its attacks. With one steadying foot, then another, Hauth found his footing and rose directly under the beast.

Without any hesitation he stabbed the sea wraith directly through the belly and silently thanked Harik, God of Forging, for the sharpness of the blade. Violet venomous blood spewed everywhere as Hauth yanked the blade from its chest. The sea wraith screamed in anguish and fury. A horrifying sound filled with phlegm and ire.

The syren reached behind her back, grabbing some kind of weapon as she held onto the bucking creature. Hauth didn't stick around to see what she was getting, instead he dove back into the Dahs. The salty waters tore into the burnt flesh of his back with the vengeance of his father. He welcomed back the pain that he had been running away from since he dug himself out of his own shallow grave. The pain gave him purpose, awakened his blood magic to heights he had never felt before. It was euphoric. It was agony. He was a killer. He was a protector. A coward. A showman.

The beast thrashed through the waters creating splash after splash that threw Hauth around like a rock in a can. Desperately, he did his best to avoid the thrashing body of the beast that would surely crush his bones into dust.

Growing nauseous from the turmoil, Hauth desperately dove deeper into the waters, resting his body against the crawling sand dwellers as he did his best to remain still. He had nearly given up and thrown up when the beast's white eye sparkled in the black waters. Gaining a moment of clarity and focus, Hauth raced for it.

He swirled around, gaining as much speed and momentum as he could before he flung his sword straight ahead and directly through the wraith's eye. The roar that erupted from the creature shook the Arkts itself, rumbling deep into the sea and the very soils of the land. But a sword through the eye would not stop a creature of the deep.

Determined and filled with fury, Hauth launched himself out of the water and into the black mist above the waters. Somehow, defying all the laws of the natural world, Hauth jumped higher than should have been possible and slid the blade out from the beast's eye. Eye juice and bits of brain cascaded out of the wound, stinging and blistering the hand that drew the blade. The other, swung, hitting the spiked flaps underneath the jaw on the other side of the beast's head. Another roar, quieter, escaped the beast's mouth as Hauth pedaled his legs, slowing his fall and preparing for a running landing as he hit the waters once again.

The beast coiled and uncoiled at rapid speeds. Blood littered the once perfectly black waters causing rivers of purple to roil with each splash.

The water pushed and pulled Hauth closer and further. But he pushed, with everything he had, he pushed himself to the place he had spotted before falling. The beast's venomous blood had entered into the burns on his back. Stinging as it entered his bloodstream. And the waters, they themselves seemed to have a mind of their own as they barreled down on his head, pushing him further into the depths of the Dahs. He couldn't breathe. And all he could feel was pain.

He was becoming desperate for oxygen. Not able to hold his breath for as long as he could before, the exertion and the wounds and the waves from the creatures thrashing required more from him. The blackness of the waters was beginning to remind him of the blackness of the soil he was once buried underneath. The all-consuming blackness that took over, slowly and then all at once.

Once again, he found himself alone and aching for life.

His blood magic, mimicking the maneuvering of the wraith, coiled and recoiled from deep within his marrow. He felt it learning the rhythm of the sea. The rhythm of battle. The blood magic he once feared. The blood magic he had felt, long long ago, that he pushed deep within himself so he couldn't align, because he was afraid to be a creature of blood and war like his father. He accepted it. And he called it.

The blood magic answered.

The blood of the wraith that had pooled into the Dahs propelled him, pushing him to the head of the creature, pushed him to stand on top of the blood where he could find some leverage, and leap high into the cold air. Hauth flew into the air like the first arrow of war. He swung his body around, swinging the blades in large circles, gaining momentum and speed. He was the air itself. He was the blood of life. He was power.

Just before the creature, in one last attempt at retribution, opened its maw wide enough to swallow him whole, Hauth swooped the blades together from behind, circling them to the front in a scissor motion that cleanly cut the head off of the wraith.

The head, the same size as Hauth's body—if not a bit larger—fell into the Dahs at the same moment as him. The creature's body fell a moment after. With the tidal-sized splashes, Hauth's blood magic had satiated. He felt it, coiling back into himself, wrapping around his spine and liver where it promptly fell back asleep.

When Hauth had emerged from the waters, he looked back onto the shores. A crowd of his people had gathered, open-mouthed and very, very still. Did they recognize the swordplay that was identical to their late prince's? Could they smell his blood magic, potent and rotten and metallic? Would they recognize it if they had? Hauth swam back, feeling not as if he had just ended the threat, but opened up another one altogether.

When he had first began working at the Gray Goblin—the same establishment he had drunk in, gambled in, and debaucher himself within for years on end as Raask Morlok—his greatest fear was that his old friends and the Skierkan commoners would recognize him. His face hadn't changed that much. Truly, he only lost his coloring. His once golden hair turned silver. His bright sapphire eyes were now leached of color and turned to ice. He kept his tattoos covered, which sometimes included some creative thinking. And at the beginning, he went to great lengths to hide his previous identity. This included breaking his own nose with a rock, causing it to stick out at an odd angle.

Hauth had also made a point of not drawing any unnecessary attention.

Apparently that had all been a waste since not a soul had uttered any mention of *Raask Morlok* or *the Crown Prince* instead their whispers sounded a whole lot like *Hauth, the barkeep,* and even several people had uttered the word *hero.*

They only stared at him in awe. Not the fear they would have looked upon him with if they knew who he really was, and exactly whose blood coursed in his very veins.

As for the syren, the rider of the sea wraith that had destroyed the entire Salt District, Hauth had let her go. She fell through the sky, just as his Aria had done, only she reached her home of the Dahsian waters. He watched as she turned to look at her beast's severed head that now floated, leaking an outrageous amount of blood, over to the shores. She looked so sad. What if she knew Aria? What if she had been a friend?

He let her go. Watching as she whipped back around, growing a tail where two legs had one straddled the beast's neck, and swam at break-neck speeds away from Skierka and further into the black waters of the Dahs. He hoped the people hadn't noticed he let her go. Perhaps they didn't. Perhaps they didn't care now that the threat of the wraith's fire had ended.

Hauth panted the whole way back. Adrenaline had left his body with the pain he hadn't felt before. The gray goblin had appeared, seemingly out of nowhere, and took the swords out of Hauth's hands, replacing them with a heavy glass of a dark ale. He drank the entire mug in one swallow, wiped the sweat from his forehead, and nearly died once again when he looked up and saw his people kneeling.

He had no way of knowing how many Skierkans there were. But he estimated hundreds of them, Vermilli and commoners alike. They all kneeled, with their heads bowed low. Many of them shook with sobs. They shook with pain. Shook from the harsh cold winds of a Skierkan winter.

He didn't know what to do.

As Raask, he would wave off the bows and the head tilts and the occasional ceremonial kneeling, laughing them off with a joke and turning the conversation back on them. But this waas unlike anything he had ever experienced.

"Rise," He commanded. Feeling the word that he once dreaded come back to him with a new feeling that he couldn't identify.

And their eyes... There was not one featherweight of fear in them. They were relieved. Thankful even! Once his people, now his friends and fellow commoners, looked to him as if they were expecting something more from him. Something that they had deserved from him long, long ago.

"Do not kneel for me." He projected his voice with the ease of a born-royal. "I am no hero. I am no warrior. I am not the savior that you need." He turned, ready to leave the weight of their stares behind. But Gustav, of all people, had stood and come forward.

"Have you not saved us? Have you not saved your city? Your people?" He asked, loud enough for most to hear.

Hauth turned to the old man, a true warrior who had spent many years training Raask Morlok, praying to whatever Gods would listen that he wouldn't recognize him. "That does not make me a hero, only a fast man with a sharp sword. A hero? A hero would be the one to put an end to this Gods-forsaken pointless war." Hauth had not realized what he was saying until he had said it. But it was too late, the words were out. But the Skierkans, they did not stand up and riot against Hauth. They shared nervous glances and hushed whispers, not a soul screamed in outrage as he would have expected.

If anything, they looked like they agreed with him. Gustav, who was briefly shocked by the open disagreement with the Morlok King, had regained his composure. Hauth knew the laws of Skierka well, Gustav along with any other Vermilli should have decapitated him at that very moment. They should have killed him for speaking against the King.

Instead, they offered him another glass of ale. And together, as one, the people of Skierka began to clean up the rubble that had once been their homes.

It was deep into the night, long after the people had put away their buckets and left the rest of the cleaning and rebuilding to tomorrow, when Hauth slammed an empty glass of ale against the top of the bar. Laughing, he poured himself and Gustav another mix of Skierkan Strong and ginger beer, as Gustav sipped his drink, he smiled at the barkeep, watching him closely. Hauth knew the man well and knew to expect some comment from the occasionally cranky older guard. Only it wasn't a plea to do something correctly as it so often was when he had been Raask, instead, Gustav offered Hauth an interesting proposal: a job as a Vermilli guard. A well-paid position too.

Another glass of ale slid down his throat and into his warm belly. Hauth loved to drink, and out of the corner of his eye he was closely watching a game of Four-Footed Monk at one of the tables in the corner. He loved to gamble too. How lucky was he, that this could be his life?

"I love it here and I'm not interested in leaving."

Gustav smiled knowingly at him, "And who exactly are you serving all of these drinks to every night?" Of course many of them were Vermilli after their shift. Point taken, he could theoretically become a guard and still have plenty of time for his hobbies. "I could never leave him, I owe him everything," Hauth jerked his head towards the Gray Goblin's office high above the bar in a nearly hidden room. The Gray Goblin had taken him in, set him up with his room and offered him a job when no one else would even open their doors to him. He owed the old goblin. And perhaps, if he truly thought about it, he felt a familial sense to the persnickety creature. He had loved him as Raask too.

"And who do you think suggested you for the role?" Gustav asked with a playful smirk.

Hauth looked up to his boss's office, a cocoon of warm blankets and paperwork high above the bar, where the gray goblin peeked through his curtains and down at Hauth himself. When they met each other's eyes, the goblin merely gave a phlegmy laugh and disappeared deep into his office. A bastard if he ever knew one.

Hauth told him he'd think about it. Of course, not really planning to think any more on it. But his thoughts kept falling back to the red cloak. The thought haunted him as he laid in bed that night, unable to fall asleep yet too out of his mind to do anything productive—and it was too odd of an hour for anything fun either.

Restless, Hauth left the warmth of his bed and walked to the shore.

Birds whistled as the blinding light of the dawn reflected off of the snow surrounding his city. Even with a heavy woolen coat, the cold had seeped into his bones. He didn't miss much from his life as

Raask, but his fur coats were certainly one thing he wished he could sneak into the castle and retrieve. He doubted his father nor Viggo had gotten around to clearing out his chambers. They probably sat there unused, growing dust and moths. Hauth shivered, severely underdressed on this treacherously cold morning.

The salt district had acted fast. It was filled with the most resilient of his people, the ones who could not afford to spend time wallowing in misery. Things were already beginning again.

Hauth turned from his people. Walking down onto the black sands, carefully avoiding the sharp shells and pinchers of the sand-dwellers. A chill ran up his spine that he did his best to ignore as he scanned the waves.

He was looking for her. Just a glimpse of her would be enough, he told himself over and over again. Her wild hair. Her onyx eyes, sometimes a deep brown when the sun hit just right. The scales of a tail he had only imagined. A bloodstained claw. Anything. Anything of her. He looked, feeling his heart swelling into his throat at every slight movement. Of course none of it ended up being her.

He didn't know why he came out here so frequently. Whenever his mind refused to quiet or he became lost in the haze of substances, he'd find himself here. Always looking, always searching for her. Gods, why did it have to be her?

The ruthless syren queen.

She was said to be in the Zojz. She probably wouldn't even recognize him if she were here for whatever odd reason. And if she did, would she even be happy to see him? He represented everything she hated. The Crown Prince to the land that had conquered hers. Killed her people. The enemy she had sworn to destroy.

He knew all of that. He really did. But he couldn't stop himself from looking for her.

As time passed, more and more Skierkans started their days. The sounds of hammers and saws drowned out the peacefulness of the birds as the Vermilli helped to rebuild their city. Their swords, still strung to their back, ready to protect if another attack were to happen.

As a loud crow swooped in front of Hauth, clasping a crab's claw in its beak, a terrible thought overcame Hauth.

Once, not *so* long ago, Aria had arrived to these very shores. She crawled onto them, bleeding and crying for help.

What if it were to happen again? Would the Vermilli storm the shores and kill her? They'd have to, wouldn't they...

But she wouldn't be so stupid to do such a thing, she knew she was the most wanted creature in Skierka, perhaps the entire realm of the Arkts.

He couldn't let the thought go. What if she did come again? What if she was too weak to fight?

As if somehow summoned by Hauth's sudden realization, he felt a presence approaching him from behind. Even without the glimmer of a deep red in his peripheral, he would have known it was Gustav. The old guard sat beside him in the wet, sharp sand. The two sat silently for a couple of moments. Only the sound of the sawing against the sea wraith's body called both their attention away from the Dahs. They watched as the leather workers and the butchers teamed up to retrieve both the valuable skin and the meat from the creature. The people of Skierka were hungry. Desperate enough to eat the crooked meat of a sea wraith. It was hard to watch, how desperate the people of Skierka had become. They needed help.

"I'll do it." Neither of the men broke their gaze from the operation of dismantling the carcass of the beast. But Hauth could see the old man nodding from the side of his vision.

"I know." Gustav only commented once the workers had torn a particularly stubborn part of the flesh away from the cords of muscle on the beast's long body.

Gods, Gustav was just as cocky as Hauth remembered. "But I want to be stationed in the salt district, outside of the Gray Goblin. It has to be here."

Gustav nodded once again. The old man started to get up, Hauth quickly shot up to help him up first, stretching out a hand. Gustav declined the help, shaking his head, but taking a while to get up from the sand and up to the cobblestone. "You may have today off, but you're expected to start tomorrow at dawn." The guard called before he was out of sight.

And with that, Hauth left the shore and headed to bed. This time, sleep came for him quickly, where he dreamt the head of the witch that Aria had slaughtered for him screamed in endless terror, shrieking his beloved's name over and over again like the warning cry of a crow.

CHAPTER 9
ARIA

Aria had been born and bred for battle. Everything about her was optimized for bloodshed. As a syren, as a queen, as a warrior. Everything she had done was in pursuit of one thing and one thing only: retribution.

It's what made her such a popular ruler among the syrens. Even those not within her clan of the Abisian syrens had answered her call to war. The eternal drumbeat that echoed her heart, deep within the now-destroyed caverns of the Zojz, all the way to the Rigelus trench. It echoed across the Arkts. She was a perfect predator. A perfect killer. An inspiration among the syrens. Mothers would line their daughters up to receive scars from her. She was a beloved ruler among her kind—who respected and valued brutality above all else.

Aria would never admit it, not out loud at least, but sometimes her violent instincts were not what she needed. Sometimes, they even made things more difficult. Sometimes a queen had to know when violence wouldn't get the job done.

The concept of a task that brutality couldn't succeed in was an odd one for her, she thought it over for months before leaving for Skierka so long ago. But she could only come up with that one plan.

Mayta would have married Raask, the man she loved from afar for so many years, and Mayta would have convinced him to end the slaughter against syrens.

That obviously didn't work out how she'd envisioned. If it did, she'd be dead by now and Mayta would be the queen-in-waiting of Skierka. When that didn't work, when she heard that her sweet sister had been the one to snuff out the Crown Prince, Aria assumed it had to do with the silliness of a non-violent coup.

A ridiculous thing.

But after a year of trying things her way, following each and every one of her dark instincts, listening only to the bloodlust that came so easily to her, Aria had lost so much of the little that she had to begin with. So many of her people died in those caverns. So many of her people died defending the Surtrian Islands. She was desperate. The queen of a dying people... Desperate enough to try anything, including the ridiculous notion that they could cherry-pick the next Skierkan ruler and convince enough of the nobles to accept this next royal—who would have to agree to end the slavery and slaughter of the syrens.

Ridiculous. But it was their last hope. Aria and Fen stood hidden within the shadows of the Gaulic, staring at the Bleached Palace.

The stronghold of her enemy, and once her home.

She had to fight her instinct to stroll into the palace and not leave until she had the Fire Monger King's head on a stick. She wanted to burn the whole thing to the ground. She wanted to paint the white lithe-bleached walls red with Skierkan blood. But that would only prove their words right, it would only fuel the fear of their kind among the humans. If Aria wanted her people, and their children and the next generations of syrens to not have to live in fear of the Skierkans, she needed to reign in her bloodlust. She needed to establish a peaceful relationship between the syrens and the next ruler of Skierka. But this was not her strong suit. She was not a diplomat, but a warrior. Mayta would have excelled in this, everyone always loved her. But her sister had received the call to war in a way that only she could answer. And that left Aria to the ridiculous pursuit of peace talks and treaties. Who in their right mind would agree to peace if not for fear of retribution?

Fen handed Aria a piece of dried lamb. She took it, tearing off bits and pieces with her dull humanoid side teeth. They had been waiting in the cold for an entire morning now. It was the unbearable part of spy work: the waiting. The way her mind raced with anxious thoughts. To the prince who laid buried somewhere within this very wood... He would have known how to do this.

The sun was high above them, providing a whisper of warmth against the ice-capped snow they sat against. Aria closed her eyes, enjoying the sunlight on her skin before it fell past the line of trees. The vibrations of a snake's movement, with a large man's steps following close behind took her from her train of thought. She placed an ear against the ice and smiled wickedly. Jor was back and Aria now knew who the spy within the palace was. She must have been delirious from all of the waiting as she nearly giggled in glee at the sound of the heavy guard's careful tread against the ice. *Walk well on the ice indeed,* she thought.

Steps she would know anywhere. One of the few friends she had made in Skierka. Okay, one of the few friends she had *ever* made. She laughed, imagining his face when Jor appeared at his side with a note tucked between his fangs. He was so scared of snakes, she'd have to ask Jor later how he reacted.

And there he was, through the trees, the outline of Zaries. He walked cautiously, watching all corners of the forest at the same time as he closed the gap between them. It was a dangerous forest, particularly for humans, so she couldn't blame him for his caution. The guard, who had once been assigned to watch over Aria, who had shared books and meals with her, was a welcome sight.

"Aria!" The guard smiled, forgetting himself, and once remembering, he looked around cautiously, hoping no one was there to hear him exclaim the name of the most wanted creature in Skierka.

"Zaries!" She couldn't help but squeal back. Fen looked between the two with his mouth agape. "You two know each other already?" He stared at Aria curiously, head crooking to the side in a canine-like manner. Aria ignored the dog's dumb question.

Thrilled to see the one person left alive in Skierka who had liked her for a time, Aria asked, "How long have you been a part of the revolution?" She had no idea the guard's loyalty wavered from Skierka. From her recollection, he came from a long line of royal guards.

His hand shook nervously as he ran it through his thinning hair. "Er, you see—it started actually after you went missing and the boss told us not to worry about what happened to you. But you know, people talk, so when I heard who you were, well I couldn't believe I'd been so close to an infamous killer!" He laughed, the same choking sound that she remembered. A beautiful sound. Zaries continued, "It was on my mind a lot, and my sister asked me what was wrong, and well, I told her. Not sure if you remember Miss Aria, but my brother-in-law is a wraithkin, his people had faced a lot from the Morloks. And my sister, well she said she was rooting for you! At first I was angry, how could she root against our very land that had always done well by us. But then I thought about it some more, and I realized that Skierka hadn't really done so great by us. His family, now mine I guess, had been attacked countless times. Their land was taken. And I didn't even make enough coin as a guard in the palace to afford the lamb at the butcher, always the chewy mutton."

Zaries's voice trailed off. He looked back at Aria, giving her a little smile. "And after I realized all of that. I realized I wanted to do something right by my family. So it was easy to help Miss Mayta, your sister is a very kind girl."

Aria beamed, "Yes she is."

Fen coughed awkwardly, drawing attention to his presence, "And how exactly do you two know each other? And more importantly, Zaries, why do you seem happy to see her?"

Zaries laughed loudly, then realizing again that they were meant to be in hiding, clamped a hand around his own mouth. "Oh Miss

Aria and I go way back! I was assigned to guard her last year. Truthfully, with her relationship with Prince Raask, I thought she was going to be the next Queen of Skierka. I was kind of hoping to be appointed to her private guard."

Fen's brows furrowed, "Why on D'Aks realm would you ever want to spend more time with her? Do you know when I first met her she nearly tore my arm off?"

Aria smiled at the memory. Zaries smiled too, apparently finding the image funny as well, "Well you ought to be glad she didn't pull it out, we both know she could have done worse if she wanted to. And she's not so bad, got the worst taste in books, but I look past that." They both laughed, Fen just looked between the two, bewildered.

The familiar sensation of Jor climbing up her leg, twisting around her boot then up to her hood caused Aria to jolt. She felt him settle against her hood, nuzzling in the nape of her neck. The coldness of his scales was refreshing against the direct sunlight they'd been sitting in. "So, Miss Aria, what's my first order? Miss Mayta had me put together a list of potential replacements to the King who were well-liked and sympathetic to your cause."

Aria stilled, the muscles of her body tensing against the sudden gust of wind. She swore that even Jor held his breath in anticipation. "Are there any such men?" Aria asked, her voice quiet. She prayed that neither Fen nor Zaries could hear the desperation in her question.

Zaries nodded, "Of course!" Just a tiny slice of tension evaporated from Aria's shoulders. He gave her a small, genuine smile as if he knew the weight of his words, what they meant for a queen who was out of options. "The way I see it, it's between two men: Caden Callady and Lok Ollen."

Fen nodded, idly scratching at his chin, apparently he knew them. "What of Bran Ashter?"

Zaries shook his head, "I thought of him too, but it would never work. He is the heir to the largest fishery in Skierka. An alliance with the syrens would likely take business from his."

Aria's patience was growing thin. "Who are these other men? Caden and Lok? Why them?"

"Well, they're popular. Well liked among Skierkans." Fen answered, even though she had clearly asked Zaries.

Zaries, who didn't seem to mind, nodded in agreement before adding, "Caden Callady is a high noble from both his mother and father's side. So he's well known and already in a position of power within our court. He's also been one of the few to push back against the King's war in Surtr. And his private guard has told me that he thinks it's foolish to put so much of our resources into mining for white lithe. He thinks we should focus on advancing technologies. But of course, he does, his mother's family are weapons dealers, and his father comes from a long line of inventors."

Aria nodded, this Caden didn't sound all that bad, but she knew there were likely more than a few skeletons hiding in this man's closet. "And Lok?"

"His mother's a high priestess in the temple of Freyite." Aria knew that could go one of two ways. One, his family had great respect for syrens since they were creatures of Freyite; syrens had been the offspring of her and Voskulle, God of War. Or, this simply meant she was a very beautiful woman who could perhaps be using it for political power by relying on the inherent respect Skierkans had for high priestesses.

Zaries continued, "Lok's baby sister was taken by the Irridesci when she was born. Since then, his family has been very open about their disdain for the freedom King Morlok grants the Irridesci." Aria ignored the chills that ran down her back, remembering the smell of dust and wrongness that emanated from the twisted slithering creatures.

"His father?" Fen asked.

"Lok *Ollen's* father?" Zaries asked, clearly in disbelief that Fen didn't know of the man. When Fen, nor Aria, nor Jor responded, Zaries shrugged his shoulders. "He's Taug Ollen. The greatest black-smith of the Skierkan army. His word will have say in the military who didn't split with Viggo. I've heard there are stragglers, those who regret not going and those who were too nervous to go and didn't want to risk their families."

Fen nodded. "That's true. There are many who were too scared." Aria didn't understand how Fen knew this, as a hylbra it was unlikely he served in the Skierkan military. Fen caught Aria's curious gaze. "Did you forget? I am a Vermilli, Aria." Aria had never known it to begin with. She knew he was a hylbra of course, that fact was hard to forget with the constant smell of wet dog he carried with him that somehow humans could not pick up on. But a Vermilli? She didn't know. But it made sense. Hylbra fell within the Gaulic Forest Kingdom, he answered only to the Keepers of the Wood, who would want to keep close eyes on the nation their land fell smack dab in the middle of. Aria did not want to admit she was impressed by his ability to sneak within the enemy's stronghold for so long, so she merely *hmphed* in response.

"You know it is possible to hide within the palace without getting caught?" Fen laughed at Aria's snarling response to that.

"You do know that was my plan, right?" Now it was Fen's turn to roll his eyes.

She was about to tackle the dog when Jor stirred against her. "There isss another," He added. Zaries, a human, couldn't understand the snake, so Aria translated.

Fen and Zaries both looked at the little ringed albino snake with furrowed brows. "A hero named Hauth has emerged." Again, Aria translated for Zaries. Fen was silent, though he was obviously deep in thought considering this Hauth. Zaries followed suit before answering, "We don't really know anything about him."

Aria sighed, "What do you know?" She trusted Jor, the creature could hear and sense things most others would miss. And more importantly, she knew snakes were such gossips, that he'd know how the common Skierkan was feeling, who they were listening to as well.

Fen was the first to answer. "He's a barkeep at the Gray Goblin."

Aria recognized the name from Raask's stories. An ache deep within her chest began to swell at hearing the place's name out loud. A place beloved by a man who would never visit again. The grief from losing him struck her at odd times. Like an old wound that had never quite healed right. She resisted the urge to look at what had once been the Prince's tower. The miscolored top of the tower from the faulty fixing after the lunar wraith attack. The space where her left arm once hung began to ache, a distracting pain from the far greater one in her heart. She welcomed the physical pain, anything to distract from thoughts of him.

"He was the one to slay the sea wraith," Zaries added.

Aria remembered, she saw him briefly before she entered the wood. The white hair warrior, who stood alone against her beast.

"Afterwards, he made some comment about how a real hero would end this war. I've heard he's taken a position as a Vermilli, stationed by the Dahs." It was an interesting choice. Jor stirred again, giving Aria chills as his cold scales moved across her back.

"He is beloved by *all*," Jor said.

Fen shook his head. "He is certainly well loved among the Skierkans, but there's something off about the guy. I don't know what it is, but there's a darkness to him." Aria hardly respected the hylbra, but she knew that like her, they could sense things that humans couldn't.

"I will meet with them. Lok and Caden. And then I'll make a decision. In the meantime, let's keep an eye on this Hauth, if he is as well-loved as Jor believes, he could be a valuable asset." The forest behind them rustled. Aria turned to watch, nothing appeared, but the forest grew louder in the howling wind and the chirps of the birds and the songs of the sprites. "Zaries, continue to listen, see if you can find any weaknesses in the King or the high nobles. See if you can hear anything that'll help on the Surtrian front too. We have ways of sending quick messages if needs be." Aria turned back towards Fen, "I'll meet you back at your house. Arrange the meetings." She gave Zaries as warm of a smile as she could, and a departing nod to Fen before turning to walk the path parallel to the edge of the forest. With her heightened hearing, she heard Zaries's parting words, a whisper, an ancient Skierkan saying that she believed to have been outlawed, "Walk well on the ice, Miss Aria."

A fitting parting word from the guard as the forest floor was covered in a thick cap of ice. Spears of it fell at random around them, slicing deep into the snow below with the sound of a whining blade. She had asked Mayta for the directions, unsure if she'd be able to find them in the dead of the Skierkan winter. Maybe it was best if she hadn't found it... If she never saw it...

She kept walking, kept moving. Forward, always forward.

Even in the coldness of winter, buried beneath mounds and mounds of crisp white snow, the decay of the Irridesci tower rang of wrongness. A ring of snowless soil surrounded the black tower. A tumor of horrors in the epicenter of all that was cruel. She kept walking, careful to avoid the sleek parts of the ice. Her balance had yet to fully restore since losing her arm, and she felt it more so when in her human form.

Forward, she trekked. Thankful for Jor's silence as he stayed tucked tightly in her hood. Occasionally the little snake would swipe his tail around the curve of her neck, it felt cold and slimy, but she could sense the creature was trying to comfort her, sensing her distress as he laid on the backside of her heart, feeling every shallow breath and every disturbance in the beat of her life.

And then she saw it. At the base of a great black tree, with roots that twisted and curved even far above the deep snow. A spot of purple blood had burned through the wood, causing the bark to bubble and ripple in the shadow of one of the knots. An ancient syrenic custom. An offering of blood to bring into the afterlife. To satiate the syrenic bloodlust one last time. An offering to Skullin. To bleed with them. Blood was a powerful symbol among the syrens. And Mayta, who hated to kill, who hated to cause harm to any creature, couldn't help herself in marking the grave of her kill. It was a stupid decision, but one that Aria was grateful for.

She crouched before the tree. Sinking her claws deep into the cold snow, reaching for the soil that held him in death's embrace. The soil that coated his lungs in his dying breaths. The last thing he saw. She clawed into it, reaching as far as she could through the snow until she could feel the hard dirt. She scraped it like the wild animal their people saw her as. From far away, she could feel Jor slither down her back and down her arm, out of her sleeve. She felt the dirt caking under her nails as she kept digging. Finally she removed her arm, bringing her nails up to her face where she smelled.

But it did not smell of him. Not the mint of his soaps nor the warmth it used to bring to her. All she could smell was dirt. It was all that was left of him.

She collapsed against the snow, twisting her body, desperate to feel close to him once again. He promised to make Skeirka better for her. He promised her so many things, perhaps not in so many words, but she could see it in his eyes. Why did he let them kill him? He was stronger than them. Perhaps not physically stronger than his brother, although she wasn't entirely sure, but he was a blood-screamer. He could have ended their lives with just a thought, stopping their hearts and then starting them again once he was safely away, just as he did in the first trial.

Why didn't he fight?

She knew the answer. Just as she knew, so painfully knew, that he had been the key to everything. A true prince. A true ruler.

She turned, laying her back against the snow. Trying to imagine what the stars looked like on the night he was buried alive. Without thinking, she reached whatever remained of her left arm, up to the sky. With her other hand, she drew blood on the most sensitive part of her body, where they had to amputate her arm, just above what had been her elbow. She scratched once, willing the blood to change, turning it red. Red as the blood of the girl he loved. She brought her arm to the side, allowing the blood to seep into the snow. She scratched her stump again. The pain tore into her like a wound far greater. The skin was sensitive to even the slightest of touches, and a scratch from her claws was nearly unbearable.

This time she allowed her true blood to drip: violet. The blood bubbled into the snow, burning a hole all the way down to the soil. She placed her left arm back down, hiking the sleeve of her cloak all the way up to her shoulder. She laid her bare arm against the snow and acidic blood. Feeling the blistering and burning all the way down her stump, she kept it there, looking up, still imagining the stars on that night. She did not want him to suffer alone. So she would suffer there with him. It was all she could offer him.

Tears fell down her face, sliding sideways and down off her cheek into her hair. And Aria mourned. She mourned the man who would have been king. The man she had loved, despite it all, despite his heritage, despite his past, she had loved him so fiercely it nearly destroyed her.

And she mourned the Arkts that would have been possible had he ascended to king. For he was everything she was not. She was a killer. Vicious. Cruel. A heart and body made for one thing and one thing only: bloodshed. She had always known it. Always known that she had what it took to take on the Skierkans in battle. She could lead a war. And despite the Zojz, despite the desperation, she still felt she could win the war.

But to lead a nation... Aria was a warrior. And she knew that that wasn't enough to be queen.

CHAPTER 10
VIGGO

The Skierkan Bruin donned his armor. Black metal scaled down his arms. His chest plate, a sturdy piece of steel embossed with the Morlok crest in white lithe, protected his vital organs. Winged spikes, resembling the wings of the raven on the Morlok crest, jutted out from his shoulders. The spikes easily sliced through skin, even muscle—sometimes bone if Viggo put enough force into it.

While Viggo was not a Morlok, not technically, he was a godling, so the white lithe granted him an immense boost in power, and more importantly in his circumstances, control. His helmet was also sharp. A pointed face with small openings for the eyes that stuck several inches above his actual eyes, giving space in case a dagger was slung with precision. His mouth and nose had a large opening, although it was hard to see unless anyone was close enough to see past the black shadows he kept stored in the pocket. Smaller spikes fanned from the crown of his head, resembling Viggo's Skierkan crown.

After seeing Mayta, he had cut his hair and shaved his raggedy beard. He knew he was fighting a losing war, but he felt embarrassed that he had seen Mayta in that state. He did not want her to know how broken he felt inside. Even with the slight grooming, the despair was still written across his face in the tightness of his jaw and the purple rings underneath his eyes that he was beginning to think were permanent.

His armor helped. He trusted his armor, he had always felt powerful within it. But that was before. He now felt like a child in their parent's outfit, too out of place and too undeserving of the beautiful metalwork that was his armor. The white lithe began to hum, reacting to his sour mood, amplifying everything he did including everything he felt. A small push would become a shove with the activated white-lithe against his chest. A spark of anger would turn to rage. And his inferno of guilt and hopelessness had amplified as well. But he had to keep going... Somebody had to, and he believed that someone had to be him.

Although he did not fight for the Morlok King anymore, he believed himself to still fight for Skierka. For what Skierka could be. For the thousands of defenseless Skierkans. He did not fight for the Morloks, but he would gladly fight and die for the innocents of his nation.

The helmet was heavy against his head, particularly under the heat of the Surtrian sun. He had asked the Morlok King, once his father, for modifications to his armor long ago, when they first began to conquer the Surtr Islands. His father declined, for he had already amassed a reputation as the Skierkan Bruin. A beast. The sight of him, his armor, incited fear.

There was power in image. In an icon. He hated when the King was right, but unfortunately, he was.

Two syrens, the watchers from the Surtrian clan, had swum as fast as they could to warn them. Skierkan battle ships were coming. Taura, the General of the Abisian syrens, who acted as the general of all of the syrens, as the Surtrians had lost all of their leaders when Skierka first conquered the islands. The only one left to step up into any form of leadership position was a young girl. A child, really. Alia. Her sister had been the acting queen, who died at the hands of the

Skierkans, at the hands of Viggo, years ago. A death he could not avoid, but he did save Alia. He told her to run, to swim to the D'Ami Cos where they would take her in. She refused.

She would not take orders from Viggo, but she would listen to Taura, who apparently had a reputation among the syrens as Taura the Terrible. The syrenien politics was confusing to Viggo, but he did his best to understand his allies. Taura had been, by blood, a Surtrian Syren who had abdicated to the Abisian Syrens when Aria's mother had saved her. She commanded respect from the syrens of both clans. An excellent choice of leadership on Aria's part.

Viggo could hear Taura's voice from the makeshift weaponry they had kept hidden underground on the edge of the jungle and the shore. However, only the Skierkans and the Surtrians used it.

The syrens preferred to leave their weaponry out in the night, particularly on the clear nights with no rain or clouds. They believed in bathing their weapons in the light of the moon: Loor's Kiss. It rained last night, causing the syrens to enter the battle with far more anxiety than normal. Although they themselves seemed to gain power from the rain, the extra water and all of that, they thought it meant that their weapons had not been properly blessed by Loor, Goddess of the Moon.

Viggo thought that perhaps it had to do with leaving their weapons out in the rain. But he wouldn't dare to say that to any of them. Then again, he was the son of a God, perhaps Loor did bless the weapons left in her moonlight.

As Viggo emerged from the weaponry, sweat immediately began to welt at his neck, beading all the way down his body. The air was heavy and wet on the islands, one of the few advantages that the Surtrians had was the ability to battle in the sweltering sun. Skierkans were pale and used to the bone-aching cold of their land. Even the coldest day in Surtr felt like being roasted for the average Skierkan. Surtrians, with their darker skin and clothing designed to provide airflow, were far more prepared for battle under the heat of Baldrei's gaze.

The sun's rays beamed down onto the white sands, bouncing back up and directly into Viggo's eyes as he left the underground bunker carrying their weapons. When his eyes settled, fear coursed up his spine like a Surtrian centipede. There were so many fewer syrens than there had been before. So few Surtrians. The drums of war continued beating, they said it was an exact replica of Aria's current heartbeat, something they could all hear once a syren queen inducted the call to war. But at that moment, it felt like his own. The drums beat with intensity. Quickness. It was overwhelming and all-consuming.

But Viggo was a leader, he could not let his fear show.

The syrens, as they did before every battle, began to thump their chest. Two thumps came from behind him, one on his left and one on his right. Viggo did not have to turn to know it was Skender and Emir. A similar practice was done by their kind, the Rakkei, native to the Red Peaks of Skierka. Only they thumped their chest at the end of battle, to mark respect to the warriors who had passed. He turned to his men, taking in their famed swords, forged under the mountains of the Red Peaks in prayer to their patron Gods: Voskulle, God of War, and Harik, God of Forging & Invention. They were once princes, until the Skierkans had come.

Skender, with his lengthy build, opted for a massive bow and arrows to accompany his sword. Emir, who was all brute strength, carried one long sword and a battle hammer. They both wore the armor they had been forbidden to wear while in the Skierkan military, the armor of their homeland. A bright red linked metal lay against their skin like an undershirt, as a deeper redded metal sat heavy over their chest and shoulders. Their helmets resembled the brighter red linked metal that lay under their heavier armor. It fell against their heads like a wig, draping along the back and the sides and to their brow in the front. The red was metal infused with blooded lithe, it gave the wearer greater speed and strength and was said to even increase ruthlessness.

An orange sash was worn in place of a crown among the Rakkei.

The original sashes that had been passed down by their ancestors lay in the Morlok vaults underneath the Bleached Palace. Emir and Skender had been gifted a makeshift sash from King Jag Agar. Emir had sobbed at the gift. He sobbed again when Silia had brought them their armor when she dropped off weapons and food.

Like the Surtrians, the Rakkei were better suited for heat. Only they were accustomed to fires. Forges and wraithfire alike. The Rakkei had long lived with the wraithkin, Silia's people. They formed a relationship that started as a business deal. The Rakkei would arm the wraithkin. And the wraithkin would provide their wraiths for fire as needed. Their scales too.

Their lashes were thick. The skin of their palms and fingers were naturally far heavier and rougher than a Skierkan's. And their skin was tanned, not quite as dark as the Surtrians, but darker than the pale alabaster skin of the Skierkans. Viggo did not understand where the dark palor of their skin had originated, as they had lived among the wraithkin in the Red Peaks—who were naturally as pale as the Skierkans—for as long as was recorded in their history books.

Skender's gaze, heavy in his observations of Viggo, fell against Viggo like an extra layer of armor. Skender noticed too much, always aware of his surroundings. Emir, the other half of the Twisted Twins of the North, had an equal heaviness in his eyes. Only his came with a puffed chest of pride. It meant a great deal to him, to represent their homelands, even in a losing war.

They thumped their chests along with the syrens. To mourn, as their people did? Or to bond, to fight as one, as the syrens did? Viggo was not sure.

"You understand your role?" Viggo asked his men. They nodded. Silia had yet to arrive with the next tow of weapons. With more food. The desperation and hunger was as palpable on them as the sweat on their aching bodies.

Viggo took one long look at them. The men he had fought with, the men he had committed treason with, and immediately his heartrate slowed. No longer panicked. He looked at them, wearing a sash that they should have been wearing all along. In *their* armor. The brothers who stuck by Viggo from the very beginning. The ones who saved the Surtrians at every chance, learning ways to hide the refugees. They were, in a way, Viggo's family. "Vittai santito," He whispered their blessing, their wishes of good luck back to them in their own language, just as he had before every battle. They smiled, hearing their native words while wearing their own armor, fighting under their own flag.

Viggo knew that they understood what he didn't say. He loved them. And though he didn't deserve them and their loyalty, he had it. And he would fight for them. Fight for their people. Fight for the Surtrians. Fight for the syrens. Gods, he would fight for the Skierkans too.

He'd give it all up for his people. It was all he could do.

With a pat on Skender's back, and a nod to Emir, Viggo walked towards the shore where the syrens were waiting for him. The thumping against the chests had ended, but the drums of war continued on. As they would until Aria took her last breath or until the war had ended.

Viggo dragged the small boat from the shore with the help of Taura and a handful of Abisian syrens. The waters surrounding the Surtrian islands were a beautiful teal, clear enough to see the vibrant coral underneath. The cool water felt like a brief moment of paradise ahead of the bloodshed that awaited ahead of him. He tried to enjoy the relief from the heat, and before he jumped into the boat he splashed the water into the inside of his armor to cool his body down. He would always overheat while using his powers. And in Surtr, it happened far more frequently and far more easily.

The waters turned from the vibrant teal to the all-consuming blackness of the Dahs abruptly and not gradually. It was normally an hour ride from the shores of the Surtrian Islands to the border of the Dahs. But with the Abisian syrens towing his boat at incredible speeds, it at least passed far quicker.

He felt it the moment they let go, departing to their battle formations. Their hands against the boat, even the occasional scratching of their claws against the wood, were in a way comforting. For he was not alone. Now the sensation of another, of being watched, had left. He knew they were around. But with no one else visibly near him, as he floated alone in the terrifying waters of the Dahs, the feeling of loneliness crept into his heart, accompanying the fear and guilt that had taken harbor in his organs, fusing until it all became a part of him.

They were coming. He knew that. And for the moment, all there was to do was wait.

Far enough away from the islands, and with the syrens rallying beneath the surface, there was nothing but emptiness and the unbearable heat from the sun that was beginning to feel like a punishment from Baldrei himself.

He didn't used to mind the waiting. He used to enjoy the moments before war, the sense of calm before the storm. The rallying of his power in his gut, finally being able to siphon off some of the magic that fought to consume him.

But he did not enjoy it anymore. Guilt and despair had twisted themselves into his very cells. A constant distraction, that he could not afford anymore. It was one thing to wallow in his misery when he was alone, if nobody needed him. But now, too many relied on him.

He could not be this creature of misery, not if he wanted Emir and Skender to go back to the Red Peaks as the rulers they deserved to be. Not if Skierka were to ever be free of the blight of the Morloks.

He was the son of a God. It was time to start acting like one.

The drums of war grew louder underneath the too-still black waters. Only this time, it did not feel like a taunt, a mirror to his own fear, he felt the drumbeat for the battle cry it was. Without thinking, Viggo beat his fist against his chest in time with the drums. Then suddenly, hands, more than he could count, beat against the bottom of his boat in time with the drums. Viggo laughed, a cold and cruel sound that he almost didn't recognize.

Battle was coming.

Gods, for the first time in a long time, he felt ready.

The Morlok crest, piercing the air like a sword, was the first part of the ships to appear over the horizon. Three of them, the largest ships the Skierkans had. The black raven, with wings spread, rested against the red background of the flag that flapped against a nonexistent wind. They must have been using silver lithe to push their boats along faster. Only the top trained members of the Skierkan military had access to lithe. Knowing that they had the aid of silver lithe, Viggo assumed they had also snorted copious amounts of blooded lithe for the boost of ruthlessness, speed, and strength. Found deep within the mines underneath the Red Peaks, particularly the mountains with temples to Voskulle on top, the lithe appeared like tiny droplets of blood. In early stages of Skierka, blooded lithe had been overused and overmined, causing it to be an incredibly expensive rarity now.

For whatever reason, the Morlok King must be just as desperate as Viggo was.

A cold smile fell across Viggo's face. He imagined them, a scene he'd witnessed himself, the Skierkans would smash the blooded lithe against their foreheads before snorting the rough chunks. Almost always, they would scream from the immediate adrenaline kick.

The boats grew closer.

Still Viggo waited for the signal.

Everything had to be just right. And Gods, he knew none of this was easy. He had to do his part right. All else counted on that.

Finally, from the Dahs itself, the static of flashing black and silver syrenic fire shot into the air. Arrows immediately shot towards where the syrenic fire erupted from the black sea. But the syrens were smart enough to not be where they had commanded the fire.

More arrows came from the Skierkan ships, falling into the water at random intervals. The way he had trained them to do, long ago.

It was the last thing he saw before he commanded the skies.

Viggo threw his arms out as he brought darkness upon the realm.

Darkness. It seemed to rain from the skies as Viggo pulled it down, blocking the sun and all the light. It came from the marrow of his bones, all of the power, rallying at the chance to be used. He was half of the darkness, it was just as much a part of him as his liver or heart.

And the Abisian syrens, they were creatures of the darkness. While it didn't run through their veins, it was their home. All they knew came from darkness. The light, so bright and glaring, was a discomfort for them. They hunted better in the dark. As did Viggo. The Abisian syrens could see through the blackest of nights and the darkest of waters. Something that none of the Skierkans could do. It was why Emir and Skender stayed behind, and the Surtrians and Surtrian Syrens too. They would defend their island, their makeshift stronghold from anyone who penetrated through the valley of darkness that Viggo had summoned.

It was only him and the Abisian syrens at the front lines.

If all went right, that was all that they would need.

Torches lit aboard the three Skierkan ships. Just as they expected. And if Viggo wanted, he could have sent his shadows aboard their ship to snuff out the flames. But he allowed them the small light of their fires. Let them think they were somewhat safe. Let them think they outsmarted him.

The waters beneath his tiny boat began to stir, the creatures believed it to be night already. Like the syrens, all predators of the Dahs hunted better in the dark hours. It was a show, entertainment for Loor, Goddess of the Moon, from Rahn, God of the Seas, who had loved her since the dawn of time. Loor loved bloodshed, and Rahn loved to see her happy. His creatures happily obliged. Another thing they had counted on. Mist rose from the black sea, a gift from the syrens as they commanded the waters to distort the surface. A miraculous display of magic on their part, commanding that much water to rise in hazy droplets, was like keeping several plates spinning on top of slender sticks.

Now, using his magic, Viggo amplified his voice so that the Skierkans aboard the battle ships could hear him as he offered them their final chance for salvation. "As your General, it was my job to protect you. To guide you." He did not want to kill the Skierkans, just as he did not want to kill the Surtrians all those years ago. "I am still your General, if you choose. I am giving each of you the chance to join our ranks. To fight for a free Skierka. We will protect your families." He paused, allowing his words to reach past their ears. "If you'd like to join us. Jump from your ship now. The syrens will protect you from the Dahs and bring you to safety. But do not see this as a way to get close enough to kill. You will be in their waters. And you will not stand a chance against a vengeful syren, of that, you have my word."

He waited, holding his breath, praying, praying to Gods knew who, but to one of them, that some of them would choose to fight for freedom, for a better world. Several heartbeats passed, measured by the drums of war that echoed from far beneath the waves.

And then there were splashes. Viggo nearly collapsed in relief. He knew of the goodness that existed in the Skierkans, the wish to do good, to end the corruption of the power-hungry king. But it had been so long since he himself had seen it. The Skierkans he had seen in the past year had predominantly been the ones who came to battle. Not many had opted to his side in the beginning.

Too many splashes to count. So many of the Skierkans dove into the darkness, the harsh toxic waters of the Dahs, leaping for a chance to join the right side of history. He wanted to cry, filled with the hope that had bloomed within his chest at the sight. But to rain darkness, to snuff out the sun itself in a vast open area above the Dahs was no easy feat. He had to focus.

He had armed each syren with as much crystal lithe as he could. He now worried it wasn't enough. He felt the water wooshing by as syrens dragged the Skierkans who chose to join their ranks. A laugh, from so far away, a place he forgot existed, erupted from his chest as, through the darkness and mist, he witnessed the Skierkans holding on for dear life on top of the spikes of the sea wraiths that the syrens commanded. The very beasts the Skierkans were the most fearful of, the massive serpents of the sea, they now rode onto for safety.

Blindly, they held onto the spikes of the creatures they did not know had a consciousness, at tumultuous speeds they rode on to join Viggo's army.

Viggo watched as the splashes began to fade. Enough time had passed now. Enough soldiers had taken the opportunity to allow for any stragglers to fall into the passions of a crowd. It was time.

"And now for the rest of you who have chosen to fight, those who see you as nothing but pieces on a gameboard, for more lives within their hordes to command control, may Kel have pity on your souls."

Viggo could swear, from the corner of his eye, he saw Taura, with her waist long braids and her nostril pierced with a purple gem, smiling, the glint from her white fangs rippling across the water. For Taura the Terrible, she was strong. And cunning. Quick too. But what really made her stand out among the syrens was the sea wraith she had bonded. The largest of the wraiths, twin to Aria's he had heard—although he had never seen Aria's elusive wraith—was a brutal beast. Dragna. With her pearlescent purple scales that secreted a flesh-burning poison and her gigantic size, nearly half the length of the Bleached Palace, Dragna was one of their greatest weapons and greatest secrets.

She was also quite finicky, with not wanting to leave her home of the Rigelus Trench. Luckily, they were able to interfere with the Skierkan war ships before they had left the heavy black waters of the Rigelus. And even luckier, Dragna was hungry.

Her purple scales, so dark they were nearly black, erupted from the Dahs. Straight into the air, she launched her long body that just kept going on and on. Screams erupted from the ship, for even though they could not see what beast awaited them, they could feel the massive waves that rocked their warships back and forth from the power of her leap.

Finally, after reaching the sun itself, or at least it felt like she had, Dragna flopped her entire body over the three Skierkan warships. A sickening crunch of bones and wood echoed across the Dahs. Dragna wove her head back, underneath the ships, so her body formed a loop around them. As her head popped back around where her tail was, she opened her maw wide and breathed syrenic flame onto the ends of the ships that stuck out of the Dahs. More screams. Even from this distance, Viggo could smell the burnt flesh and hair. After thoroughly soaking whatever was left of the ships in her flames, Dragna constricted her body, tightening around the ships in one last fatal move. More cracks. More sounds of spines snapping. Dragna released a roar that sounded peculiarly like a laugh, before releasing the ships from her grasp.

Viggo gave Dragna a few moments to return to the darkness of the trench. And when he finally released his darkness, he collapsed onto the boat. Sweat soaked through his entire body as he laid his back against the rough splintered wood. His pants, deep and heavy, rocked the boat as he stared up at the bright blue sky above. This morning he had awoken with a nearly vanquished army with bands of warships coming. Now he had replenished his ranks. Killed many of the King's fiercest soldiers. Again, Viggo could hear a laugh that he vaguely recognized as his own.

He had commanded darkness. Brought an entire sea into the night. Extinguished the light of the sun, even for a few brief moments. Clawed hands scraped under the wood of his boat. He felt them tapping in beat to Aria's heartbeat, to the drums. As one, they pulled Viggo's boat back to the Surtrian islands.

CHAPTER II
MAYTA

Mayta brought her red, furred cloak closer to her chest as she walked through the cold wood of the Gaulic. A layer of thick, heavy snow blanketed the forest floor, snuffing out the greenery of the wood, causing her to stick out against the whiteness of the snow and the blackness of the strange dark trees. They were tall and thin. From far away they appeared to be purely black, but upon closer inspection, Mayta saw that veins of a deep blue ran along the bark, along with tiny beetles.

She ate a few as she walked, enjoying the crunch to keep her from the boredom of trekking alone through the forest. Occasionally she would see sprites, usually air sprites, as they swam through the wind currents as if they were warm waters on a hot summer's day. Sometimes they would wave to her, a few pinched her butt as they snuck past. She mostly ignored them. While wishing for company, Mayta knew better than to entertain a sprite. They were troublemakers at heart and trouble was the last thing she was looking for as she continued her quest to find the Sistros.

A lot of people were counting on her.

It was not something she was used to, but she felt proud for undertaking such a quest. Also, a little part of her was hoping that Aria would shut it down before she left. And the fact that she hadn't meant that they were truly desperate for Mayta to be successful in finding the Sistros.

Gods, the last time she was left to her own devices she'd gone to the Bleached Palace and snitched on her own sister. But to be fair, she had planned on freeing her the next day. Aria expected Mayta to snoop in and protect Raask.

Hah! How well that'd turned out.

The loneliness was beginning to get to her. Mayta had never been alone too much in her life. She always had friends and caretakers. It wasn't that she couldn't take care of herself, she was a syren after all, it was more that she didn't really want to. She liked to be taken care of. She liked gossiping with her girls and making meals and staying warm and safe. But she was not just any syren, no, she was a part of the royal family. She had a duty to her people. In times of abundance, that meant she could do whatever she wanted. But in the dire times in which they lived, it meant she had to step up.

She savored the crunch of the beetles. Taking a while to chew each bite. She only wished she'd thought far enough ahead to pack salt. She even checked her bags, but no luck. Of course not, Aria and Fen packed them. No salt. No spices of any kind even. It was mostly weapons and a couple of outfits and some bandages. Oh Gods, she really should have checked her bags before she left.

Her round cheeks turned red in the harsh winter winds. In the depths of the black wood and the white snow, Mayta was a burst of red. Her black cherry red hair. The blush of her cheeks. The reddened fur cloak from Fen. And the rings around her eyes as she silently cried. She would constantly go back and forth from pride in undertaking such a mission to an overwhelming feeling of loneliness. It hadn't even been a full day since she'd left and she was quite the mess already.

Mayta sniffled, wiping her nose against the sleeve of the red cloak, grateful that nobody was there to see such an unhygienic act.

But of course, neither Aria nor Fen had thought ahead to pack her a handkerchief.

On her left, a patch of the dark wood was unnaturally dense. It appeared almost like a mass of blackness and shadow too dense for even her syrenic eyes to pierce. It was from behind this patch, right after she had walked past, a voice emerged. "Why do you cry?" The voice sounded male and ancient, with a hollowness to the voice that Mayta recognized as nonhuman.

Mayta quickly wiped away the tears from her sleeve, double-checking to make sure it wasn't the one covered in snot. "Why do you ask?" She answered, searching for who could have asked her. The voice was too deep, too large to come from a sprite or another small creature. But she couldn't imagine that a large creature could come through the dense pocket of wood. To Mayta, it appeared as a spill of blackness against the white and black speckled forest.

The being, whatever it was, seemed to think for a moment. She could hear its breath—so whatever it was could breathe—but it took a while to respond. "Because I seek to understand," it finally answered.

At that, Mayta couldn't help but to laugh. Fair enough.

"Now why do you laugh?" The creature asked, clearly exasperated and confused.

"Because it's a silly answer to a silly question," Mayta answered. "Where are you anyways?"

Like drops of ink, an image began to form in front of Mayta's very eyes. Only the drops seemed to fall upwards from the forest floor, and not down from the skies. Slowly, more drops began to rise until the creature became visible. He was tall. Taller than any humanoid creature she had ever seen. Taller than herself even in her syrenic form. He wore a cloak, long and black, that billowed and creased with the abundance of the thin fabric. His face was covered by the shadows of his large hood. "You're not an Irridesci are you?" Mayta asked. She hated those *things*, they reeked of wrongness and sin.

This creature did not have that smell though. He smelled similar to Viggo. The sweet smell of death, an alluring scent to a syren. The creature's hood tilted towards Mayta before he answered. "We do not claim that kind nor their barbaric sacrifices."

Hm, so not an Irridesci. "So who are you? Or what are you?" she asked.

The creature tilted its head to the side, as if considering some riddle, "I will answer your questions if you tell me why you were crying." Mayta thought about it for a moment, and figured she had nothing to lose by answering his question.

"I was crying because... Well, I was given a task to do, and I'm scared to fail." A shiver ran down her spine as more wind somehow channeled its way through the thick wood. "And I'm cold," she added. Then after a beat, "And I'm lonely."

Then the creature did the oddest thing. It lifted its cloak from its fingers, pulled it off from one hand, and then off his back and off his other hand. Beneath his cloak, remarkably, was another cloak, only thinner and a faded black that had turned to a dusty gray. This one was a little shorter on the fingers revealing that the creature wore a pair of long black gloves made of some leathery black hyde that Mayta did not recognize. His fingers appeared to be unnaturally long, although not sharpened to claws at the end. A scythe, with a long black handle carved in a language Mayta did not recognize either, and a bone white blade sat against his back where it had been previously covered by the overflowing top cloak.

The creature reached its hand out to give the cloak to Mayta. "Thank you, but will you not be cold without it?" The creature merely shook his head no.

"Well, thank you then." She said, taking the cloak carefully from his hands and wrapping it around herself. It took a while before she found the belt, and she had to get creative with it so she could walk in the endless blankets of the fabric. It was thin, but somehow quite warm. It smelled of Viggo, and for whatever odd reason this comforted her.

"Now, I answered your question, who are you?" Mayta asked as she tied a bow into the two ends of the belt around her waist. The creature tilted its head again to the side. His second cloak remained large enough to keep his face hidden in shadows. With his gloved left hand, he merely pointed to the scythe along his back.

Mayta laughed once again. "Yeah, I kind of figured, but didn't want to be rude and just assume." Standing in front of Mayta, the princess to the Abisian syrens, in the Gaulic forest by a spill of black trees clustered far too close together, was Skullin. The creature, perhaps the man once, who carried souls to the underrealm. Suddenly, Mayta's large green eyes widened. "You're not here to take me, are you?" She asked, in nearly a whisper. It couldn't be now. She had so much to do. To find the Sistros. To reclaim her kingdom. To find love. To perhaps, be a mother one day if Freyite blessed her enough. It could not be her time. She'd run from him. In that moment, she knew she'd run as fast as she could away from death's grasp.

The creature, Skullin, shook his head no. For whatever reason, Mayta believed him. Why would he lie? There was an honesty in death, a cosmic truth, and Mayta knew that. "If you are not here to bring me to Helk, then why are you here?"

"I heard your crying. I grew... curious." Mayta nodded, understanding the feeling. She could be known to be nosey herself. But the smell of Viggo lingered in her nose. "Did Viggo send you? I thought he said it would be best for just me to see the Sistros."

Quickly, Skullin answered, "No. He nor Kel know that I am here with you." Mayta's eyes widened. The superstition of mentioning the God of Death by name brought a cold river of air down her spine.

Mayta leaned in closer to the harbinger of death, and whispered, "Why? It's a secret?"

Skullin leaned in. She could feel his breath, but still could not see his face. "I am not supposed to interact with the living. It is a rule, created in the agreement of the ancient ones." The ancient ones: Tsu, Rahn, and Kel. The three oldest and theoretically most powerful of the Gods. Mayta's stomach grew uneasy, hoping that they could not see whatever was happening here.

"Will I get into trouble if they find out?" She asked. She could not afford the wrath of a God, not now at least. Not when so much was relying on her. Skullin shook his head no. "But you will?"

He did not answer, but Mayta understood what that meant. "Why risk the wrath of the Gods to ask me why I cry?"

Skullin's breaths rasped in and out. Again, he delayed in answering. "Do you know of Aashi?" Mayta shook her head. She had never heard of such a creature. "Aashi was the daughter of Svati and Voskulle. Their only daughter, for her death had brought a great sadness to Svati, the Goddess of Kindness. And when she died, as godlings do, Voskulle couldn't bear to see Svati in such pain. So he attempted war against Kel."

This Aashi would have been a distant cousin of Mayta— as syrens come from the original union of Freyite and Voskulle. The tales say this was before Svati was born, before kindness had become a thing of power.

Skullin continued, "Aashi was unlike any I had ever met, or seen before. Some had called her the Goddess of the Home, for she created a home wherever she went, a sense of belonging to all those who wandered. You remind me of her." Mayta wasn't sure what to make of Skullin's words. She could see that this Aashi meant a great deal to him. But she did not understand death in the way that he did. Did he love her in death? Did she remain in the underrealm? Mayta did not know enough to understand the weight of his words, she could only feel them for the truth within them.

"She sounds lovely." It was all Mayta could think to say. Skullin merely nodded in agreement.

"You said that you cried also because you were lonely? And overwhelmed by your task? Perhaps, I could travel with you," Skullin offered.

Maybe it was because one simply didn't deny the requests of a being as ancient as the carrier of death. Maybe because Mayta *had* been lonely. Maybe because for some odd reason, this dark creature seemed to have a sense of longing that Mayta could feel in her own heart, a mirror to hers in some strange, twisted way.

Mayta nodded and accepted Skullin's request to join her on her journey to find the Sistros. She smiled up at the strange creature. "I'd really enjoy that." She took his hand, holding it tightly in her own, not in a feeling of romanticism but in a feeling of friendship, partnership, as she would travel with this creature to the destiny of herself and her people. She led death's harbinger, death's voyager, death's guardian, along with her deeper into the Gaulic forest in search for answers.

As Mayta and Skullin walked side-by-side, lighter than air and quicker than Mayta could understand, they ran into a horde of strange and smelly creatures. They looked remarkably similar to dead humans, with their rotten flesh and odd gait. Smelled like them too. Only these creatures foamed at the mouth. And when a creature of the wood—a sprite or even a toad—would startle or move, they'd dart towards them at staggering speeds and rip their heads off, tilting the blood and bile directly down their throat before munching on whatever little meat they could get off such small creatures.

Mayta looked on in horror as they barreled past her and death, seemingly not noticing them. She looked up at Skullin in confusion. "Do they not see us?" She asked.

Skullin shook his head. "As long as you are wearing my cloak, no one can see you unless you will them to."

Mayta continued to stare at the dozens of odd human-like creatures.

Skullin walked closer to one of the creatures as it feasted upon the corpse of a toad. The slimy mucus of the toad skin ran down the creature's face, mixing with blood and toad guts. The creature made these awful noises as it ate the toad, as if it was slurping down a great big pot of noodles and broth. Mayta was nearly sick just watching the whole thing. But Skullin crouched down, and got very close to the creature, almost like he was inspecting it. "What are these things?" Mayta asked, hoping that Skullin would answer and they would continue walking as far away from them as possible. Mayta could hear Skullin's sigh from several steps away, through the awful noises of the feasting creatures and the howling wind of the wood.

"These are how the Morlok King plans to win a war far greater than the one that you fight, my dear." Skullin stuck his hand out towards the creature. He placed his thumb upside down against its forehead and it disintegrated into ash that quickly became lost in the wind. Skullin turned towards a shadow of one of the black trees, speaking a language that sounded itself like the howling of the wind. The tree's shadow vibrated and moved, zooming towards the direction Mayta and Skullin had just left.

At that odd interaction, that left the wood with a shadowless tree, Skullin stood. He reached back towards Mayta's hand. Quickly, she grabbed his hand, and they continued through the Gaulic forest. Two creatures who were meant to journey alone, now forever intertwined into each other's destinies at the disapproval of the Gods.

CHAPTER 12
RAASK

Several weeks had come and gone since the wraith attack against Etra. Whispers of a slaughtering in the Zojz kept Hauth awake at night. At the Gray Goblin, the soldiers would ask each other if they thought the syren queen had died in the attack. A brutal attack, one that sacrificed many Skierkans. The king had created some kind of monstrosity, a form of lithe that exploded under the waters, hours after ingestion. And the syrens, who were known to eat their victims, they said they'd been blown to pieces. The syren army that had conquered the Zojz, now lay dead in a trench.

Nobody had seen their queen in the weeks since the attack. A few of the syrens that fought within the Zojz had been seen, so it was clear they had not all died. But where was their leader? The soldiers would ask as they drank endless mugs of ale. Some of them asked in fear, as if she was a demon of the night, a creature who would sneak into their house in their sleep and gut them. Some asked out of a source of pride, their old squadmate had sacrificed themself for the attack, their brother, their neighbor... Word went around that the

King had paid the families of those who sacrificed themselves with the explosive lithe handsomely.

Hauth could see it. He saw it in the gold coins, once a commodity in a pub and gambling den like the Gray Goblin, now a regular occurrence on the tables of Four-Footed Monk and other betting games.

Hauth drank with them each night. Even when his bones could hardly hold himself up from rebuilding the Salt District as a Vermilli, Hauth would find himself at the Gray Goblin. Eating. Drinking. Gambling. Singing. He kept friends with those who had visited him as the barkeep. Occasionally he would even head behind the bar to help out the new barkeep who easily became overwhelmed by the massive amounts of ale and spirits being ordered each night. He needed to stay connected to the people. Some part of him, that had either been ingrained from his grooming or was innate, felt a need to be among his people. To hear them. To search for their greatest needs and fears and rectify them.

Another part of him, maybe too large, just needed to hear if there was any news of her.

Everything he did, had been in search of her. The houses he rebuilt had all had a front row seat to the shores of the Dahs. His outpost, just outside of the Gray Goblin, on those long shifts just watching the shore, was in an optimal position to catch a glimmer of her. She could not be dead, of that he was sure. Somehow, he knew that he'd feel it if she died... The sea wraith had mentioned the drums, beating to her heartbeat... Sometimes Hauth could swear he could hear them. When the night was quiet, and the people had gone to bed. When there was nothing and nobody—but the light of the silver and indigo moons— to keep him company as he stood watch, he swore he could hear the drums. She lived. She had to have lived.

His sixth mug of ale went down like a slug. He had cleaned up the table of Four-Footed Monk and bought everyone in the Gray Goblin another drink with his winnings. Two Vermilli who had rebuilt the same houses that week sat on his left on the circular table, and three soldiers sat on the right of Hauth. The Vermilli, including Hauth, kept their cloaks on. The fire roared in the fireplace behind him, but the Gray Goblin had a nasty draft that crept through the roof of the old establishment. He rolled another cigarette of emerald lithe in the thin smoking papers he borrowed from Alko, one of the Vermilli he had been stationed with the most. Alko was a few years younger than Hauth, perhaps nineteen or twenty years in age. He had a thick moustache and long brown hair he kept pushed back from his face with hair gels and creams. Along with smoking papers and emerald lithe, Alko always kept on his person a miniature comb for his moustache and a larger comb for his hair.

Hauth and Alko got along well. The other Vermilli at the table were Ofte, Alyks and the sisters Roia and Jana

Two of the soldiers Hauth had known from his time as Raask. They were semi-high ranking in the military. Alyks, the one he didn't know, had Rakkei blood in him, it was apparent in his tanned skin and thick lashes. He was an expert at working a bow and somehow an even better Four-Footed Monk player. He also carried around some of the best emerald lithe that he had ever smoked. Even Alko agreed, and the man knew his smokes. Even Ofte, who was quite picky, would smoke his stash. Sometimes he even took some home for his wife to bake into a sweet that he'd bring out at lunch the next day.

The last two soldiers at the table were Roia and Jana. Sisters with ghostly white skin and red hair. It was their brother who had sparred with Aria last year, and later hurt her when she was chained in the dungeons. Roia and Jana wore their military coats on top of their tight fighting leathers. The black against their alabaster skin was striking, but they made up for it with the mean look they seemed to always carry around. Alyks had changed from his uniform into a yellow tunic with a white detail around the trim and loose white pants. It was odd to see such bright colors in Skierka. The yellows and oranges were almost always worn by those with Rakkei blood. Skierkans preferred more muted colors, mostly blacks and grays, with the occasional red of the Morlok crest.

Hauth brought the rolled emerald up to his lips and took a long drag. "You're not supposed to smoke in here," Roia stared daggers at him. He met Alko's pointed look and swallowed a bout of laughter.

"Don't worry, Roia. The Goblin loves me." She continued to stare at him, as if expecting him to put out his cigarette just at her word. "Would you like some, Roia?" Her eyes widened. Briefly, Hauth remembered how it felt to look at the sea wraith before it began to spew fire at him.

"I am a soldier. I command respect where I go. I cannot be seen smoking emerald." She nearly spat in his drink with the force she used to push out each word. Jana only sighed, her position on the matter was unclear, making it very obvious that she didn't mind the emerald. Not to mention that Hauth had smoked with her before they entered.

Ofte carefully looked between the two, taking another swig of his ale. "It's okay, he used to work here." Roia stood abruptly from the table and slammed her palms against the gray wood, nearly cracking the old and weathered table.

"You used to work here? And now you serve as a Vermilli? This is why our nation has gone to shit." This time, she did spit. A hunk of it landed on Hauth's chest, dampening the spot just above the raven's head in his Morlok crest tattoo that remained hidden in his cloak and leathers. Roia stormed out of the Gray Goblin, letting the door slam shut behind her. The silence from her outburst lasted only a moment. The Gray Goblin had seen much worse, even earlier that night.

Jana reached her hand out to Hauth, he passed her the rolled emerald. Lighting a match for her, he only shrugged when their eyes caught. "I'm sorry about that, she's been moody since our brother's passing." Jana said the words from the side of her mouth as she took several long drags of the emerald.

Hauth wasn't aware that their brother had died. He saw it then, in the redness of Jana's eyes and the sagging in her chest. She was a born soldier. To sit or stand in a non-perfect posture meant something to her. "I'm sorry to hear of your brother."

Both Alko and Ofte repeated their apologies. There were no strangers to death in this entire nation. Not as a land at continuous war. Hauth leaned back in his seat, taking a tobacco cigarette from the table. He lit the match against the rough edge of the wood and enjoyed the familiar scent of burning and smoke that filled his lungs and nostrils. Like a reminder of a home that he hated, but was still a home.

"How did he pass?" The smoke lazily fell from his mouth along with the question.

Jana looked towards the door, towards the Dahs. "He volunteered to take the lithe."

Hauth nodded, he figured as much. The man hated the syrens. "You know he told me he scrimmaged against their leader? He said he beat her ass. He said the Crown Prince was so stupidly in love with her that he couldn't see what was obvious. He showered her in gifts and then she killed him. Why even come? Why didn't she just kill the Prince and the King on her first night?" She shook her head in disbelief at the memory and the questions that seemed to bother the people of Skierka.

He continued smoking, rubbing the cigarette between his thumb and finger. Hauth was there, and that wasn't exactly how it had happened. Aria had actually kicked her brother's ass. And Aria was not the one to kill Raask. Though she took the credit for it.

But the rest was the truth, Hauth supposed.

"I met him once," Ofte's words caught Hauth by surprise. He knew of Alyks by name only, and remembered meeting with Roia and Jana. But he did not remember Ofte. He supposed he didn't remember everyone he had met, and as the Crown Prince, meeting him was a bit of an ordeal. It'd been a long time since Hauth had felt that shame. Not remembering the names of those who knew him, who knew his life so well. It haunted him.

"What was he like?" Hauth asked, although his voice sounded foreign to him.

"Pompous," Jana said. Her voice as bitter as the burnt tobacco smoke against his tongue. Then after a beat, she added, "And nice. He helped me wrap my knee after I took a nasty hit training one day."

He remembered that day. Her knee had swollen to twice its size. Her brother and sister had laughed at her, and she'd laughed it off herself, but he could see the pain in her eyes. He heard the crack her knee made at the impact. Hauth grimaced at the memory.

Ofte sort of smiled at himself, the memory of something kicking up the edges of his lips. "What?" Alko asked.

"He tried to pick up Teigha." Teigha was Ofte's wife. He continued, "Right in this very pub. Right over there actually." Ofte pointed with his mug at the edge of the bar. Hauth only knew of Teigha from Ofte's stories. And he quite frankly had no clue who she was.

Alko laughed, loud and boisterous, "Yeah?"

Ofte idly scratched the spot on the back of his neck. "Teigha and I had only been going out for a couple of weeks. I was already crazy about her. And I swear to God I almost punched out the Crown Prince of Skierka over her." The whole table erupted in laughter, even Jana, who was properly intoxicated by the rolled emeralds and the ales. Ofte was anything but a violent man. He was around Hauth's age, with short blond hair and big eyes that made him appear constantly startled. His wife was a baker, and he would always bring the other Vermilli sweets and breads from his home. Hauth reckoned that Ofte would rather be working the bakery with her, but he came from a long line of Vermilli, so the decision was made for him before he could even walk.

Hauth smiled, lighting another tobacco cigarette. "And what stopped you?"

"Teigha politely declined his offers."

Alyks nodded at this with a thinking deeply kind-of-look on his face. Ofte chuckled to himself again. "I just remember thinking, that poor bastard could have anything in the world he wants, but not my Teigha." He took a final swig of his ale and motioned for another to the barkeep, "I proposed to her a couple of weeks later."

Hauth didn't know what to make of this. "What, just because she declined the Crown Prince? I'm sure there were a couple of women who declined him over the years." There were. Maybe more than a couple. Perhaps several.

"No, of course not, I knew I would marry Teigha the moment I met her. I just remember feeling bad for the guy."

Alko snickered. "Why, Teigha's that good, huh?"

Ofte playfully, maybe a little too hard for playfully, hit Alko's bicep. "I just felt bad for the guy. I mean can you imagine getting everything you ever wanted?"

Alko flipped his hand and scrunched his brow in disbelief, "Can I imagine getting everything I ever wanted? Yeah it doesn't sound so bad."

Alyks looked thoughtfully at Ofte. "Yeah, I know what you mean."

Alko kept laughing as he rolled another emerald cigarette. Hauth stayed quiet on the subject. Did he get everything he ever wanted? Was that what his people thought? Perhaps it was important for the people to think of their ruler's children as being spoiled, it meant their land was prosperous.

But Raask had no mother. No father, not really, at least not one that would teach him swords and hug him goodnight. His brother had tried to kill him. His love, whom he hadn't seen in over a year, was leading a war against him and his people. That was if she was still even alive.

He spent his life moving alone from room to room in a palace constructed of a dark powerful magic. Learning the languages of the realm. Battle strategies. Trade agreements. History. Learned to channel his magic from the torture of dark creatures in an even darker tower.

He may have had nice jewels and extravagant furs and a personal carriage, but Raask would have traded it all to have been born among them.

And he did.

"Do you think he would have supported this war?" Alyks asked, dropping his voice low so no eavesdroppers could potentially over-hear and report the conversation. Simply asking the question was treason. Questioning the monarchy was dangerous, particularly in Skierka were the Morlok King had established a reputation for burning alive those who even hinted at a disagreement with his regime.

Jana snickered. "Like it would matter? He wouldn't be brave enough to fight for the rebels, even if he did believe in their cause."

Hauth crooked his head to the side, looking Jana up and down. The way she phrased it, it sounded as if she could possibly believe in their cause. She caught his gaze and shook her head. With too-large pupils, she withdrew a blade from her side, and sliced a light cut down the line of her forearm. "I bleed Skierkan Red, Hauth, a loyalist through-and-through." She wiped her blade against her leathers. "What about you? I heard what you said after you killed the sea wraith."

Raask may have been too scared to stick up to his father.

But Hauth wouldn't be afraid of the King.

He looked around the room, and with a commanding voice, said, "Oh I'll bleed for Skierka. But not for the Morloks. We fight and we die all for what? An endless pursuit of more. More land More power. More people to control. We starve and die of infections and diseases with cures just sitting up in that palace, going to waste." He felt the heavy gaze of every single person in that room.

A table full of soldiers broke out in laughter, one of them raised his hand, "Alright, alright, just get me another ale, barkeep, alright?" Alko and Ofte stood, their chairs scraping against the wooden floor.

The soldiers stopped laughing and reached for their swords. From the corner of his eye, Hauth could see the Gray Goblin getting ready to swing to the chandelier from his office and onto the floor, either to kick them all out or to stop the fight. Hauth gave him a strong nod, indicating that he'd handle it. The Goblin squinted his eyes but remained in the window.

Hauth lifted his hand to Ofte and Alko, stopping them in their place, as he walked behind the bar. He began pouring several mugs of ale from the tap. "I'll pour you your ale. But why don't you tell me, do you like losing your friends? Do you enjoy going to battle for the right to enslave our friends to the sea and the islanders?"

"Our friends to the sea? They killed our Crown Prince. They attacked us!" The one who originally spoke up and asked for the ale was the only one to speak up again. He was a large man with a long beard and the Morlok crest tattooed along his neck in plain black ink.

Raask nodded, still pouring ales. "Have we not hunted their kind? Have we even considered a peace agreement? We respect their seas. We respect the islands as their own nations. And we all just move on."

Several of the soldiers scoffed across the pub. "And a syren would respect a peace treaty?"

Hauth brought the ales over on a large wooden serving board. He began handing them out to the entire table. "I think they just want freedom."

A quiet woman, sitting in the back of the pub at a table filled with women dressed in finery, spoke up, "What about the white lithe they mine? Don't we rely on that?"

Hauth nodded. "And we have plenty. I'm sure if we needed more, we could pay them handsomely for their labor. Do you know how much this constant warring costs us? This money we spend on losing our lives and killing, endless killing, could be used to feed our people. To invest in our agriculture. To invest in our schooling."

"So what? We'll leave our country unguarded? The D'Amicans will swoop right in. Or Gods forbid the heartless soulsuckers in the Morrills."

Hauth felt exasperated. And his courage was beginning to wane. Maybe Jana was right about both Raask and Hauth when she called him a coward. The people had been led by a bloodthirsty king, and of course they felt protected under his reign, but did they not see that they could flourish without the constant warring? He didn't know how to get them to see what he could so plainly. And why was he trying so hard to make them see? Isn't this exactly what he was escaping from? He wanted to live a quiet life. Help rebuild the Salt District. Protect Etra as a Vermilli.

Hauth just shrugged his shoulders. "I'm not saying that. I'm just saying, perhaps it is time that we invest less in blood and more in our own people."

The original soldier who spoke up rolled his eyes. "We'll call you over when we need another ale, alright? But maybe less chatter next time." A couple of them snickered. Many did not.

Feeling defeated, Hauth looked up at the Goblin and nodded. The Goblin understood this to mean that Hauth would be leaving without paying, but he'd get him back. Before leaving, Hauth looked back towards his friends and shook his head slightly.

Hauth was the first to walk out, but he could hear his friends following close behind. When Alko caught up, he looked Hauth over, "You really believe all of that stuff?"

They walked towards the edge of the shore, Alko passed Hauth the rolled emerald he was smoking when they abruptly walked out. "Yeah, I guess so," Hauth answered. He felt like a fool. What was the point of all of that? He'd been attracting too much attention lately.

Jana's voice came from behind, "You just made yourself a target, Hauth. I'd think about your next move." Her eyes were still red with grief, but Hauth could have sworn he saw fear in them too.

"You're not going to report him, are you?" Ofte asked.

Jana shook her head. She would not, but that didn't mean any of the others in the pub would not. "Goodnight," she called as she turned to walk back into Etra, most likely to the apartment she shared with her sister Roia in the military housing. Alyks, who worked closely with the two sisters, sighed. "I'm going to go check on her," he said, rushing off to walk with his squadmate.

The three Vermilli stood silently, passing the lithe between themselves, for a few more minutes. They turned towards the houses and businesses they'd been working on rebuilding. "Tomorrow, I think we move to that one," Olfe said, pointing to the next one in the long row that they'd been rebuilding. The three of them were responsible for clearing out the debris before the others would come in and actually rebuild. Loose brick and stone still littered the streets. Black burns marked the edge of the houses. Most of the inner parts of the Salt District had finished at least the exterior rebuilding, it was only this last row left. The most dangerous section, the one closest to the Dahs.

From behind, Hauth could hear the heavy door of the Gray Goblin, opening and closing. Two women, short and curvy, walked towards the three of them. They had been sitting with the woman who asked about the white lithe. One wore a fine black furred cloak and the other had a cloak of rich wool. The one with the furred cloak had large silver earrings going down her entire lobe that shined under the light of the indigo moon. The other wore a lip stain of a dark red that accentuated the small gap between her two front teeth.

The one with the heavy jewelry handed Hauth a small orange coin bag. "You left this inside." He was about to argue, he would not carry such a thing, orange was never his color, especially not now that his hair had turned a cool silvery white. But he saw the look in her eyes as he was about to decline. For whatever reason, she wanted him to have the bag. He took it, feeling how light it was, empty of coin, but he could feel something between the thin fabric of the bag, some kind of paper. Once Hauth took the bag they smiled politely and left, heading back into the heart of Etra.

Alko shook his head, "That's not yours, why'd you take it? It's probably Alyks's."

But Alyks, who had been a fantastic Four-Footed Monk player and held a high position in their army, would not carry such an empty nor cheap bag for coins.

"It seemed like they really wanted him to have it," Ofte

commented. He would usually notice little things like that, gestures or looks were something he was very in tune with. "Open it," Ofte added.

Hauth obliged his friend. And within the cheap coin bag laid a folded-up piece of paper.

We believe in a peaceful Skierka. We meet at the crematorium tomorrow when dusk turns to night.

CHAPTER 13
ARIA

Fen was being absolutely ridiculous.

He refused to comply with any of Aria's plans. Refused to grab her the cinnamon nut breads from Arthur's, nor any other. Refused to allow her to sneak into the Bleached Palace. Refused to even let her run. He lived on a diet consistent with that of the dog he was. Constant beef. Duck. Goat. Mutton. Any cheap cut of meat in large quantities, the creature would eat. Occasionally he'd throw in a baked potato, but rarely.

Aria couldn't live this way. She needed sweets. She needed to run and battle and swim.

But the ridiculous dog was anxious, he was convinced Aria wouldn't be able to hold her disguise for long enough. Fen sat at his table, opposite of Aria. He was massive as a man, and refused to turn in front of Aria for her to see how large he was as a dog. He had shaggy curly brown hair that flopped with each movement and a strong nose that highlighted his full lips. The man was all muscle. At first glance, she assumed he lived to train. But she hadn't seen him train once! Not once in the week she'd been cooped up in the apartment. He mostly only left for his shifts as a Vermilli. He didn't seem to have much of a social life except running out to meet with other rebels. Most nights he would stay at home reading books.

Aria liked to read too. But after being in the tiny apartment, it was the last thing she wanted. And whenever she tried, she felt as ridiculous as Fen. There was a war to win! It was just not the time to be lounging and reading.

But the one night Fen took Aria out with him, for just the briefest of moments her disguise had slipped. He took her past the Gray Goblin where they had to give a couple of women directions to the next rebel meeting. And when she first laid eyes on the pub, for a brief second, her magic wavered. As a syren, Aria's magic mostly centered around reading and manipulating emotions, and sensing desires. The strongest of her kind could hold what was called a veil, where anyone who saw her would not see her, and instead see a person that they saw as the most beautiful combination of features. Not a person they knew or anything, just a composite of all of the traits that individual found the most beautiful. Fen said he saw her as a tall man with dark skin and broad shoulders. He said her voice sounded like a mixture of honey and danger. Aria rolled her eyes at that.

She stayed out of the Gray Goblin, unable to enter. And apparently when Fen came back out from passing his message, he had 'left a gorgeous man and come back to a mess of a woman.' It only happened for a second, when her mind wandered to what once was, but it happened.

Nonetheless, when Fen left for his post, Aria would sneak out. She was sure Fen knew it, but she didn't want to rub it in his face. He was annoying, but kind. He looked out for Mayta when Aria couldn't. And even if he didn't, he was the closest thing to an ambassador the Keepers of the Wood had. She needed to ensure that if they ever did pick a side in this war, it was hers and not the Morloks'. So it was better not to piss off Fen.

Aria had just come back from a run when Fen entered close behind. Just to be safe, she would generally only run through the

Gaulic. And she was careful to keep her hood up and over her face when walking through Etra, and her left shoulder tucked in tightly to try to hide the lack of her arm. Fen loudly sighed. Clearly smelling the pine and snow of the Gaulic on her. "Would it kill you to stay put?"

Aria's jaw tightened, "Maybe not me, but it could kill you." She withdrew the daggers she took with her and laid them out on the table. Preparing for a bath, she continued to undress, beginning with her cloak and then she took her hair out of its braid. Fen laughed. "Just because you're not out there with a sword doesn't mean you've left the cause behind. What we're doing is far more important." He went to his sink and filled a glass with water. Fen's kitchen was small but functional. It was an old and rundown apartment filled to the brim with books and notes and drawings. The wall was a red wallpaper that had faded into rust. Several scratch marks tore at the wallpapering, revealing the sad gray wall behind it. His glassware was all mismatched, as if he had slowly taken enough from the restaurants and taverns he had visited to create a collection.

Fen sniffed the air around Aria, she groaned knowing what was coming. "Now hurry on up with your bath, we're meeting with Caden for dinner." Aria had hoped that today would be the day she'd finally meet one of the prospects for the next King of Skierka. They'd been trying to arrange this meeting since the day they had met with Zaries. Aria grabbed one of the towels from the closet off of the kitchen and headed into Fen's washroom.

Before she shut the wooden door she yelled, "Oh Gods, Fen, what will you do if Caden serves a vegetable or a grain? What if the whole meal isn't just a pile of meat?" Aria could hear Fen's chuckle through the thin door, and the distinctive sound of him heating a pan on the stove, prepping for what had to be some kind of meat.

Like his kitchen, Fen's washroom was small and functional and impeccably organized even though it was a bit of a mismatch of decor. The towels were all different, some were blue-and-white striped, some were all white, some were even fluffy. Those were Aria's favorites.

The soaps smelled lovely, and the oils felt tingly and pleasant on her sore muscles. It was not a bad home that Fen had created with the very little that he had. It was not easy to make a life from scratch in a new place.

Aria jumped into the hot bath before it was even halfway filled. Quickly she cleaned her body, taking extra care to scrape away the grime from the forest left on her scalp and hair. She exfoliated with a big heavy brush Fen had gotten for her, it left her skin raw. Pink and fresh. It somehow had a way of making her feel new.

After thoroughly washing, scrubbing, and drying, Aria basked in the aroma of caramel and pistachio. She wouldn't like to admit it, but she did miss some of the more luxurious parts of living in the palace, including the hot baths at the ready and the nice soaps. It was one thing that the humans had gotten right. Fen must have thought so too, or else he wouldn't have kept his washroom so well-stocked with the luscious scents and potions. She put on a thick robe that matched the fluffy material of her favorite towel and headed to the mirror. It was old and cracked with an ancient, bronzed edge, but it worked well enough. Aria took a moment to inspect her features. Caden would not be seeing her as herself, but she wanted to feel put together.

Such meetings were not her strong suit. Perhaps if they met while hunting or sparring, Aria would feel more at ease. But this would be staged as a diplomatic meeting between the rebel party and Caden, a high-ranking noble in Skierkan society. She was a princess once, and now a queen, so she could handle politeness and manners if need be. But so much of her fate was in the hands of this human. So much of the fate of her people rested in the hands of others, and she just didn't like it. She wanted to control it all. Beat everything down into submission until she got what she wanted.

But that didn't work, so now she was left with this option.

She took a heavy breath in through her nose and out of her

mouth. Carefully, Aria brushed her hair, removing any tangles from the voluminous mess of black waves. She added the pistachio oil to her hair, giving it a nice shine. That was one thing about the Skierkans, they loved a shiny look. Their leather shined. Their jewels shined. Their hair and faces shined.

Aria placed a drop of the oil on her fingertips and worked it onto the skin of her face, massaging her facial muscles that often became sore whenever she had to make nice and try to smile. Then, with the same oil that seemed to be working well enough, Aria smoothed the hairs of her thin brows, ensuring they all faced the way they were supposed to.

Aria left the washroom in her robe, smiling at the smell of a decadent goose leg, knowing Fen had probably left one for her. On the bed where Aria kept a tangled mess of sheets and furs was a shiny long red dress with a hole beginning at the center of her hip that closed in the space between the breasts. The material was softer than even her robe, but it was incredibly tight. The sides of the dress seemed to be crafted to hold her breasts up snugly, pushing them high and together. It was beautiful. And she looked beautiful in it.

Only she looked like a beautiful Skierkan. Which was the point, really, the tight shiny fabric designed to push breasts up, it was a popular fashion in Etra. Unlike the syrenic clothes which cupped the breasts, but not high enough to meet the skies as the Skierkans did. Syrenic clothes flowed in the currents, and often mimicked the scales of their tales.

The fabric of the red dress was thin, clinging to her toned arms and legs, and the hole in the middle showed off her slim torso. She hoped that Caden kept his house warm, because this outfit did little to provide any warmth against the cold Skierkan winter. Just as Aria was leaving the bedroom, she noticed the red fur hanging on the back of the door. A large coat with a triangular collar and trim that—while warm—managed to keep her torso exposed. It was nearly a match to the one Fen gave to Mayta, only this one had a cropped look where that one was long and far thicker.

Maybe she would be dressed as a Skierkan, but at least she'd match her sister.

Fen, who laid out the outfit for Aria, had made his message clear. Aria was to appear wealthy. Powerful, not in the way of danger or violence, but in the way of a member of high society. Powerful enough to only travel to warm places in the cold Skierkan winter.

The nerves for the evening were beginning to give her a stomachache.

She had to stop thinking of this as *their* territory, as *their* game. Aria grabbed the stockings she'd left on the floor, they ended at the top of her thigh, the perfect place to store a small dagger.

Caden may have an upper hand in the arts of diplomacy, but Aria was a warrior. She was the creature to fear. She would be the one to decide the next King of Skierka.

With that thought, Aria opened the door to find Fen, dressed in a fine embroidered cloak and wide-legged leather trousers, sitting on the couch waiting. "You clean up nice," Aria commented with a smirk, walking towards the table and taking a bite out of the goose leg Fen had indeed left out for her.

The grease coated her fingers and ran down her face as she took another big bite out of the leg. She let out a groan. Fen had used a spice combination of cinnamon, clove, ginger, and a lot of pepper. It was an uncommon combination of spices, one she had never tasted in her time in the palace, but she loved when he used it in his cooking. When she asked where he learned to mix such spices, he said he'd made a friend from Luru, in the southern continent, who taught him all he knew of cooking. He left it at that. "So you *did* decide to eat before our dinner?" Fen asked, from the couch.

Aria snorted, "I scared myself a little too much wondering if they'd only have vegetables." She grabbed a cotton napkin, rough with gray, white and blue stripes and wiped her face. "Do you think they'll have dessert?" She asked while chewing on a hunk of grizzle.

Fen shrugged, looking over a few sketches that looked like crude maps of the palace. He had his glasses on, big and round, so whatever he was doing, he must have been focusing. "I'm not sure, but if there is, keep in mind we're trying to appear regal. Not like animals."

Aria finished the leg, "But we *are* animals."

Fen dropped the papers, looking at Aria over the tip of his glasses. "Don't ever say that again."

Aria's claws elongated as they always did when she felt attacked or defensive. Often it was a needed bodily precaution, at times like this, it was a little too telling of how she felt.

Fen's eyes dropped to her sharp claws that grew out of the still human and unwebbed fingers. "That's what they think of us. As animals. It's why they capture us, and chain us, enslave us. We're not animals. Yes, we're not human. But we're not animals either. As a queen, and a leader, among the non-humans, it's important that you know that. That you're an ambassador to not only the syrens, but the other *creatures*. If they see that you're sticking up for them, they might join our ranks. And that could be the difference between a failed rebellion and a revolution. We're trying to change the maps here, not just be a footnote in history."

She didn't appreciate the lecture, but she allowed the words to sink in. To think of the treatment her kind had endured at the hands of humans, and Fen was right. They *were* hunted like animals. Chained like them too. She wiped her hands, cleaning her claws before allowing them to retract as she thought a bit more. "Who do they think I am?" She asked in between bites of the leg bone. It crunched in her teeth with a satisfying snap.

Fen shrugged. "They don't know who you are, just that you're powerful within the rebel movement and have a say in who the rebels propose as the next king." He stood, grabbing his cloak from the back of the couch. "Are you ready?"

Aria nodded, wiping her face one last time. She grabbed a fistful of mint leaves from the jar by the window and slipped on her pointed black boots. Leather, of course, that appeared to have been shined recently.

The cold air stung Aria's face, starting from her nostrils and traveling all the way down to her lungs. It was a long walk from Fen's apartment by the edge of the Gaulic, to the Callady Estate, that lay nestled on the outskirts of the military housing, just under the hill where the Bleached Palace overlooked. The main building was made of gray and black stone and had a massive iron gate that enwrapped the entire multi-building property.

Green vines wrapped around the gate with 7-pointed leaves. Aria was about to run a hand across the leaves, testing the level of sharpness with an innate curiosity and attraction to anything that could hurt, when Fen grabbed her hand and stopped her. He gave her a look that said, *don't*, which made Aria only want to touch it more. Fen sighed, "It's dauman's ivy."

Aria looked at him bewildered, did he truly expect her to know each plant? She came from the deepest pits of a black sea. "It's poisonous to touch. Just one touch, and you'll instantly break out in blisters and boils that'll spread across your body and down your throat until you die of suffocation." Aria yanked her hand back and mindlessly wiped her hand against the hooded cloak she wore over her red fur.

"You must come back at night when they bloom." The voice came from the other side of the gate. Through a narrow gap between the ivy leaves, Aria glimpsed the whites of the man's eyes. He was looking directly at her with eyes the luxurious brown of an aged whiskey, that crinkled into a smile when they caught her gaze. "They bloom into these tiny white petals with silver tips, under the moonlight. It looks like there's millions of them, like a moat of stars." He spoke quietly, whether he was muffled from the vines themselves or was just a soft-spoken man, Aria was unsure. She saw a flash of movement, his arm, beckoning them to continue walking towards the gate on their left.

The snow around the estate had been shoveled away, causing Aria and Fen's steps to click loudly against the stone streets. The entrance gate to the estate was peculiar, in that no vines grew on it, giving Aria a complete view of the property. Large statues of the

Gods littered the edge of the pathway to the front door, which was huge and carved with intricate designs against the black wood. The man stepped into view a moment after Aria and Fen had reached the gate, blocking her from being able to scrutinize the artwork of the door.

Everything about the man reeked of wealth. He appeared to be around Aria's age, somewhere either in his late twenties or early thirties. His hair was an ashy blonde that seemed to match the golden accents of the statues against the overall grayness of his estate. When he smiled at Aria, he looked boyish and untroubled, and his teeth were very straight and white in a way that irked Aria. He was a little bit too perfect. Too well groomed. Too attractive, as if he were a doll of a king.

Aria resisted the urge to run a hand through her hair. For a moment she worried that she'd left her hair too messy, but then she remembered the magic veil. She wondered what the man saw when he looked at her.

He opened the gate wide for them and as Aria stepped through, she saw what she didn't before. Behind each statue and across the fence in hidden locations, guards stood at attention. They each had a long sword at their hip, a variety of daggers across their torsos, and crossbows slung across their backs. They did not wear the Skierkan military garb, nor the red cloak of a Vermilli. These were privately sanctioned guards wearing very expensive weapons that were decorated with blooded and bronzed lithe that did nothing when adorning weapons other than waste valuable assets. She wondered how well trained they were, or if they were merely enough of an image to stop any criminals from even trying to enter.

Fen walked through first, he smiled at the man. "Caden, what are you doing answering your own door?" Fen laughed.

Aria snapped her head towards Fen, hearing a joyfulness to his voice that she hadn't heard before. And his smile... It was huge and unnerving coming from such a serious man. Aria resisted the urge to sigh, Gods, even Fen was better at this stuff than her. She mustered a smile and once again she caught Caden staring at her.

Caden chuckled in response. "I fear I was eager to meet you and your guest, you mentioned some rather tempting things the other day." His voice trailed off as he continued to stare at Aria. As if snapping back into place, he added, "But first do come in. Let's not talk business on an empty stomach."

They followed closely behind Caden as he led them through the great door and into a large dining room just to the right of the entry room. The estate was just as beautiful on the inside as it was on the outside. A servant, a tall and sharp woman, took Aria and Fen's cloaks. And Aria's prayers for a warm fire were granted, the dining room contained not one but two large fireplaces that were roaring away. One of the long rectangular tables made of a warm dark wood had its place set for four guests. Aria looked at Fen, the question written across her face.

Caden snickered like a boy.

"Is that my cue?" The sound of another man came from just behind the doorway to where Aria assumed to be the kitchens. Nobody answered, Caden only began to pour the wine in all four glasses. A dark red. Fen, who must have recognized the voice, appeared slightly agitated, his fake smile becoming just a tad tighter.

Then the speaker erupted through the doors, shoving them open with great force as if relishing in the grand surprise entrance he had created for himself. Like Caden, he was draped in wealth. Caden wore a spotless array of a perfectly pressed black silken shirt that had quite a deep v and a tight pair of black leathered pants that appeared to have been oiled. This man wore, what appeared to Aria as, equally fine clothes that had been through the rough.

He wore wide-legged leather pants that looked similar to Fen's, only this man's had quite a few stains and was significantly lacking in the shine department. On top he wore a tight black top with a high collar and ripped frays where the sleeves should have met the body. Where Caden had the lean look of wealth, of living a life that didn't require any hard labor or threat of danger, this man looked like he trained hard and often. They both had nearly identical haircuts, short yet long enough to look vaguely boyish and wavy. Only Caden's was the ashy blonde and this man had hair as black as Aria's.

"Raia," Fen looked at Aria, in a subtle reminder of the name he had given her, and then back towards the man who had erupted from the kitchens, "This is Lok Ollen."

The other candidate to be king.

Aria looked back at Fen, eyes widened. But this couldn't be it. These were two boys. They played an impractical joke, they grinned widely, they did not look like they had suffered enough to be a ruler. Her heart beat quickly in her chest, and from some deep primal connection to her clan, she swore she could hear the drums quicken alongside her.

Lok laughed wildly before grabbing the glass of wine Caden had just poured for him and drank the whole thing in one loud gulp. "How does she look to you, Cay?" He asked his friend, who now sat across from Fen, also drinking his wine. "To me she looks like a hot red head, what about you, Lok?"

Lok poured himself another glass, staring at Aria in a mockery of a squint, "Yeah, she looks like your sister to me." Caden smacked his elbow.

Aria felt like she could erupt in a storm of claws and teeth. This was a mockery. They were acting silly and worst of all they had bested Aria and Fen, since they obviously knew who she was, and how her magic worked. Any pretense of a smile evaporated off of Aria's face like steam from a kettle.

She looked between Caden and Lok with the heavy gaze of a predator. Her head tilted forward, beckoning them to feel her anger, to see in full force the snarl that revealed her too-sharp teeth. They did not reveal their fear through any physical changes, but Aria could smell it on them, like the intoxicating scent of blood in the water. She dropped the veil, like Lok, she too could enjoy a theatrical reveal.

"You know who I am, and this is how you choose to greet me?" She asked, grabbing the glass of wine in front of her. She drank the whole thing in one gulp as she leaned back into her seat, feeling her body smack hard against the wooden back of the chair. After swallowing the wine down, a bit too bitter for her taste, she licked her lips with great exaggeration, making sure to reveal the tips of her sharp teeth once again.

Fen coughed awkwardly, obviously in a hopeful reminder to Aria that she was supposed to be playing nice. "I hope you understand why we needed to obviously keep Aria's identity a secret. But now that it's clear that you know who she is," His voice broke off for a second as he looked towards the door in which they'd entered with the servants, "You trust your staff to keep things under lock?"

Caden and Lok merely shared a glance and broke out in laughter once again. "Yes, I'm afraid that they've seen much worse than a rogue syren queen. They will not tell on you nor your friend," Caden winked in Aria's direction. Almost as if on cue, four servants came out of the kitchens carrying what looked like four plates of salads. Aria resisted the urge to look at Fen. Salads in the cold season of Skierka were one of the greatest indicators of wealth, for no fresh fruit or vegetable could be found on the entire island in this season. Vegetables had to be imported this time of year, and as Skierka was often at war, not many nations opted to trade with them.

Meaning, Caden Callady was either wealthy enough to pay the exorbitant prices from a sanctioned exporter or he had illegal connections. Aria was sure both were true, but she was guessing his kitchens received their produce illegally. He was, after all, hosting her.

Aria poked the lettuce and strawberry with her fork, thanking D'Ak silently that there was at least a sweet vinegar and a sweet berry to accompany the plate of vegetables. Lok watched her with great amusement in his smile, "I'm sorry, Caden is usually a much greater host. Would Aria the Bloodthirsty prefer a glass of fresh blood? Perhaps a human's? Or what about a human arm or leg? Which do you prefer?"

Aria could feel Fen's body tensing from next to her. This was not how he wanted this to go, not at all. For his sake, she swallowed back a biting comment and did her best to smile. "The only time we eat humans is after they've attacked us. Your meat is far too sour to be eaten out of choice, only as tradition after battle." She thought she was saying the right thing, but the look on Fen's face said otherwise. Caden and Lok wore similar faces of shock and discomfort.

Nobody said anything else for the rest of the salad course. Which, thankfully, didn't last long. Four more servants came in, the same as before, and grabbed the salad plates and silverware. Moments after they left, another set of four servants entered carrying plates of what smelled to be smoked herring and boiled potatoes. It was a dish she'd eaten often in the palace. One that she enjoyed.

Aria felt Caden and Lok's heavy gaze as the plate was set in front of her. Lok piped up as he speared a large chunk of the fish on his fork, "We assumed you'd like to eat fish. But we were worried there was also a chance that it could have been a relative. Did we guess right?"

The humans were toying with her. They had to be. Aria bent her fork as she tightened her fist in anger. "She eats fish. Syren are not related to fish. And this is delicious, so thank you." Fen commented, taking a massive bite of it. She heard the bones crunching between his teeth and enjoyed the show of him pretending to enjoy the taste of fish.

Caden, who appeared perhaps a bit kinder or at least more well-mannered than Lok, spoke up, "Would you like to ask us any questions?" He directed his gaze to Aria.

Aria nodded. "Why are you both here? Don't you both want to be king?"

Caden and Lok stopped midbite. Clearly shocked by her question, for some reason Aria couldn't figure out. Wasn't it obvious what they were doing here? Lok eyed Aria with a different look now, he looked her up and down not as a creature, but as if he were truly sizing her up. She could smell the desperation on him, on all of them really. Times were dark. Even the elite were desperate.

Caden looked as if he were about to speak, but Lok cut him off. "Yes. We both want to be king." He said the words almost breathlessly, like a prayer or a curse.

Caden nodded, putting his glass of wine down. "We want to know how you will decide who you would back as king. And we want to know how you'd protect us—and our families—if this rebellion fails."

Aria sat back and continued to eat, being mindful to not chew the bones too loudly. This line of questions was all Fen. He was probably drooling to talk about the political strategy.

"Deciding who we will back as king will not only fall upon Aria and I, we will also take into account General Viggo's opinion and most importantly, the opinion of the people. We will choose who we believe the people will go to war for. And who we believe will be able to unite a kingdom divided." Fen spoke with the precision of a courtier's son. Once again, Aria found herself curious as to the wolf's background.

"And our families? Us? What will happen if we lose?" Caden asked, his voice wavering slightly.

Lok looked at Aria and Fen, motioning to the grandness of the Callady Estate's dining room, "We are risking a very high position and very comfortable lives. Do you understand that? You are risking nothing. You have nothing to lose. We have everything we could ever want."

Aria carefully looked at Lok, seeing the sincerity in his eyes. He was scared. *They* were scared. She stood, pushing the wooden chair back with a loud squealing scrape. She'd seen enough. "Aria," Fen insisted.

But she saw all that she had to see. "Come on Fen, we are wasting our time. They are not ready to be king."

Fen quickly stood, grabbing Aria's arm. "They are our best

chance," He said, quiet enough for only Aria's preternatural hearing. "Our only chances," He added. She could feel his sweaty palm on her arm, feel the truth to his words, his dislike of Caden and Lok too.

If this was the best Skierka had to offer, they were screwed.

Caden stood too, "Please Aria, stay, we just want to know if there are any protections you can offer if we lose the war." Aria couldn't believe they once again asked how she would protect them if she had lost the war. Couldn't they see it?

If Aria lost the war, it could only mean that she was dead, along with everyone else she had ever cared about. So if she did lose this war, and her bones had finally turned to ash and she could rest in the underrealm with her ancestors, her duty to these men would be done. There would be no safe soul left in the Arkts if they lost.

CHAPTER 14
VIGGO

Viggo had slept for two days and two nights after he had blocked out the light of the sun. He would have slept for longer if Skender and Emir hadn't woken him, worried that he'd never wake again.

He'd never used power like that before. For once, he was not afraid of holding himself back. He allowed his darkness free reign, and it consumed the daylight. To clean off from his slumber, Viggo walked to one of the many bathing pools in the Jungle Palace and kept going until he found one unoccupied. The pools were large and used to be pumped with fresh water twice daily, but that was when there were enough Surtrians around to complete such a task. Now the water changed once every couple of days.

The Jungle Palace was high above the shores of Boai, past the rainforests and deep in the jungle itself. Lucious vines with beautiful pink and purple flowers grew along the outside of the palace. And the inside was filled with almost as much greenery as the jungle itself. The walls were carved from the trees themselves, a pale tannish wood that smelled of fresh salty waters and smoke. Everything in the palace was open to the elements, including the bathing pools. With beautiful teal water that was constantly warmed from the heat of the Surtrian sun. Viggo stripped his clothes off by the edge of the pool, leaving them in one of the many woven-leaf baskets laid out, and opened the stopper from one of the many wooden pipes that crept over the edge of the roof that ran along the open-air pool.

As soon as he pulled the rope, water began to pour out of the pipes and over his body. Unlike the warm waters of the pools, this water was kept shaded in the wooden pipe and was a bit cooler to the touch. It shocked his body as it ran down his hair and down his back. He used one of the soaps left by each of the pipes, scrubbing away the grime from his two days of sleep and the sweat he accrued from using all of that power.

Once he was properly scrubbed, he tugged on the rope again, closing the lid to the pipe and dove into the middle of the bathing pool. This particular one was deep. Once at the bottom, he turned around and looked up to the top of the pool, where the sun was shining directly ahead. He stayed there for a moment. Perhaps it was the feeling of the water against his skin, or the feeling of the warmth of the sun, but for a brief moment his thoughts led him back to her. He enjoyed being in her dream. He enjoyed feeling her close, even if it wasn't necessarily real. It felt real enough to him.

He sank into the feeling of her, the feeling of light and happiness that sat in the dark corner of his mind, constantly calling out to him, like a lighthouse against dark and stormy waters, her consciousness was his salvation. The thing he held onto now, when he needed something to center him.

He could feel her through that little bridge in his mind. He didn't dare to sneak into her mind, although he was quite tempted, but he could sense that she was happy. Mindlessly, Viggo reached up to the sunlight that cascaded through the waters all the way to the bottom of the pool. His hand grappled with the sunlight, feeling the warmth against his skin, even through the miles of space between the sun and him. Through the air. Through the water. He felt the sun, just as he had felt her. And it was enough for him. It would have to be enough for him, to feel the aftereffects, the echoes of her soul that reached the back of his mind.

Viggo pushed off of the green tiles and swam up, breaching the water still thinking of her.

"I was beginning to worry, I almost dove in after you," King Agar's rich voice reached Viggo's ears, tugging him immediately out of any thought of Mayta. It had been a long time since he'd heard the Surtrian King speak with anything close to humor. He must have been pleased with the new Skierkan soldiers. As he should—Viggo had trained most of them himself.

"What stopped you?" Viggo asked, pushing his wet hair back and off of his face.

Jag had entered the bathing pool at some point while Viggo was at the bottom. His dark ebony skin glistened under the sunlight. For the first time in many months, perhaps even years, the king did not look sullen. There was a lightness in Jag's smile that hadn't been there in a very long time. Viggo wondered if he was thinking the same of him as he himself laughed, feeling lighter than he had in many moons.

Jag smiled, "I wasn't even sure if you could die." He winked and dove into the water. When he emerged, he floated on his back. Viggo, a born and raised Skierkan and therefore not as comfortable with nudity as the Surtrians and even the syrens, averted his gaze. He took the time to study the tiled walls enclosing the sides of the pool. Like the bottom, they were a deep green that matched the plants that grew along their edges.

It was not the first time his mortality had been questioned. His magic was dark and familiar to humans as a natural part of the life cycle. It felt like death. An old friend to some. And something to fear for others.

Viggo would live a normal human life span. This had been confirmed to him by his father years ago.

"The syrens are getting better on their legs." Jag commented as he continued to float aimlessly around.

Viggo silently agreed. "How are the new recruits getting along?" He knew that the King understood that he was asking how the absconding Skierkan soldiers who had leapt into the Dahs to join them, were getting along with the Surtrians and the syrens, who were once their enemy and now their allies.

In the beginning days, there had been many fights they'd had to break up. A mutual distrust. A mutual hatred. But nothing bonded the two warring factions better than a mutual hatred towards the Fire Monger King. A part of Viggo often worried that if they were successful in killing him, if they would all just go back towards their hatred of one another, and eventually back to war. Skender was right to worry over who would rule upon their success.

"Your men keep asking to see their wraiths again," Viggo could hear Jag's smirk in his voice.

Of course they were. They had been taught to fear the wraiths. To fear the syrens. To fear all non-humans. Viggo was unsure if it had ever occurred to them that these creatures would be more than something to fear. Something, possibly, to even admire, or even enjoy. A lot was changing.

The two rulers floated in silence for a few more minutes before Viggo muttered a goodbye to Jag. Viggo dried off with one of the many towels left by the edge of the pool, wearing the towel for the short walk to his rooms. There, while still a little damp from the pools, he put on the light fabric that the Surtrians wore—loose billowy pants that would still allow for movement, and no top. The same outfit he had been opting to wear while training for the better part of the past year.

Before his quarters, which he kept extremely neat and tidy, with his sheets and blankets tucked in tightly to the edge of the mattress and his clothes always neatly put away and hung up, Viggo stopped at the mirror within his room. He removed a long blade from the table in which he had been sharpening his weapons before the battle, and cleaned it off in the sink using hot water and soap. Carefully, Viggo shaved his face. He'd been at war his entire adult life and for a considerable amount of his life as a child. It wasn't the first time he'd use a dueling blade to shave, and it most certainly wouldn't be the last.

The blade felt warm against his skin. After he finished shaving his stubble, he took a moment to inspect himself in the mirror. He'd trimmed his hair a week or so ago, removing the general look of shagginess that happened too easily while leading a revolution on a tropical island. Instinctually, he made a quick decision to cut off all of his hair. With precise movements, Viggo held his hair up, and began to slice it off. He left a little bit of it, mostly to protect his scalp from the intense heat of the Surtrian sun, but it was a dramatic change.

His shorter hair made him look a bit rougher and less like a Skierkan. Skierkan men, and women for that matter, tended to keep their hair long. Hair meant warmth in the winter. And a display of wealth and power in the warm months. They didn't have to worry about becoming overheated, or hair falling in their face too much as they labored.

Viggo may have been born the son of a king, but by blood, he was the son of a God. A God of Death & Destruction. His short hair showed off the scars that ran along his scalp from his helmet. And more noticeably, it showed off the burns from the Fire Monger King.

When Viggo looked into the mirror, he saw not the Skierkan Bruin, but the leader of a revolution. Not a man at war with himself, but a man at war against an unchecked cruel king.

He grabbed his sword and walked to the training grounds. He felt the eyes of the servants and the soldiers as he walked out of the Jungle Palace and down the long path to the shore. His men bowed their heads in respect as he walked past. Keeping a straight face, Viggo continued on his path, not stopping until the dense forest floor transformed into packed light soil and again into the airy sand of Boai.

They were taking a break, eating lunch. Syrens, Surtrians, and Skierkans. All together. Laughing and chatting. The smell of freshly fried fish and fluffy flatbreads lingered in Viggo's nose as a sense of great joy erupted from his heart. This. This was exactly what he had been fighting for. This was what they had to lose.

"Looking good, General," Taura called from the water. She sat half in and out, allowing the tide to coat her legs. At her yell, the soldiers all turned to Viggo and hollered. Viggo couldn't tell if it was because he had won the battle, or if it was for his haircut, but he was enjoying it all the same. After a couple of seconds of clapping, he threw his hands down, settling the crowd down.

"I leave you to yourselves for a couple of days and I come back to not a single one of you training. Just feasting, huh?" A couple of laughs floated across the group, but mostly, the soldiers quickly finished whatever food they had left. They knew what was coming next would require all of the energy they could muster. "Alright, we've got a war to win, let's run a lap." He caught a couple of the syrens looking amongst themselves. "That's right, we'll run a lap. And then we'll all swim a lap."

Viggo was the first to take off down the shore. Taura caught up in no time. Even in human form, she was a beast. Skender's light tread followed closely until he caught up. And last was Emir's heavy foot-steps. As Viggo promised, they all swam a lap after completing the run around the entire island. By the time they had finished, the skies had turned from clear blue to shades of peach, fading to a haze of pink by the horizon. He rested against the shore, sitting as Taura had earlier, half in the water and half in the last remnants of the day. The cooks had brought dinner out that evening when the soldiers were most exhausted. They ate barrels and barrels of shellfish that the syrens had caught on their lap around the island. Some of the Surtrians and the adventurous Skierkans ate fried lizard that smelled salty and fatty.

Moments before the sun would disappear behind the horizon, encompassing the islands in natural darkness, a horde of black clouds climbed across the sky. A horde with wings.

Viggo stood. Silia was not due for another week or so. But *there*, at the front, on the lunar wraith with horns that curved around its head like a ram, was Silia and her mount. The lunar wraiths were long, scaled creatures with four legs and massive wings. Unlike the sea wraiths, that looked like massive sea snakes with wings and enormous heads, the lunar wraiths had stockier bellies and more muscles around their shoulders. Long ago, the first Skierkans had called them *dragons*. But the name had been changed when the common tongue had evolved.

Soldiers yelled, whooping with excitement and perhaps a little bit of fear. The sea wraiths they had met, and understood to be controlled by the syrens who had fought among them. Lunar wraiths were another thing entirely. Lunar wraiths caused havoc across Skierka. Although he did warn them that the wraithkin had joined their side of the war, it was another thing entirely to see a horde of them heading their way, just as Loor's moons began to settle along the night sky.

Emir stood next to Viggo, watching as the wraiths flew at great speeds, coming remarkably close to their shore in a matter of minutes. "I thought Silia was not coming for another week."

Skender, who of course was not far from his brother, said, "She wasn't."

Viggo could feel more than see, Taura's careful eyes on his, assessing how he felt about what was happening. Aware of his emotions being scrutinized at all angles, Viggo was careful to keep his face straight and not move a muscle.

Silia was the first to land, along with her sister who had lost her wraith to Aria over a year ago. Something that all of Viggo's inner circle had agreed to keep quiet for the sake of better relations between the wraithkin and the syrens. Her lunar wraith landed with a loud thud against the sand. The usually graceful creature appeared exhausted. His tail, long and scaled with a sharp point at the end, twitched like an agitated cat above the sea. Silia ran towards Viggo, finding him quickly among the crowd. Her sister stayed tucked under Silia's wraith's wing.

"What is it?" He asked, voice low, unsure if he wanted the soldiers to hear whatever Silia had to say. Her long blonde braids, normally impeccably neat even after riding, were frizzed and had partially fallen out in chunks. She was a small woman, but she commanded each eye as she strode across the beach with the presence of a warrior. There wasn't a soul in this army who wouldn't recognize her long blonde braids. Silia was, perhaps, one of the most fearless and vicious among them. And there was an unmistakable fear written across her bloody face.

Silia's eyes were wild. Flashing back and forth across the group before finally resting on Viggo's. "They came in the night."

CHAPTER 15
MAYTA

It took Skullin's shadow three days before it reappeared. By that point, Mayta and Skullin had exited the forest and now walked towards the Red Peaks.

The shadow appeared as they walked through an empty snowy valley. It zoomed across the white snow, in broad daylight, before meeting Skullin. It appeared excited, vibrating back and forth and rushing around in circles once it approached Skullin, who did not notice the shadow. Mayta merely cleared her throat pointedly, causing Skullin to look down and see the buzzing entity. He lifted his long, cloaked arm, extending his knobby gloved fingers out as if beckoning the shadow to his hand. Obedient, the shadow climbed on.

Skullin nodded and added a few *Hmmmms* as he apparently listened to the shadow. Suddenly, he looked back up at Mayta, his cloak still covering his face in shadows. "It is just as I have feared, young one." Skullin turned back to the shadow, which spun around his arm at increasing speeds before catapulting back in the same direction from whence it came.

Mayta watched with a mixture of amusement and awe. She

wondered if all shadows were sentient, or if it was a gift Skullin had to grant them consciousness. But realizing something important seemed to be afoot, she focused her questions on that, "What do you mean?"

At this point, Mayta was very comfortable around the creature of death. And quite frankly, it was a blessing to have him on the journey with her. He didn't sleep, so he could stay on guard as she slept. His cloak granted her invisibility, so she was relatively safe from most threats besides disease or the cold, but the cloak did help a lot with the cold since it was so thick and warm. He also didn't need to eat, but could find animals to hunt with great ease.

Essentially, he was the best travel companion Mayta could have asked for.

"The creatures we saw, the ones who reeked of rot and aggression, I have seen them before. Long, long ago," Skullin's hood moved as the creature looked back towards the direction that the shadow had come and gone from.

Mayta continued to walk. Again, she had grown comfortable with Skullin and had learned his ways. The creature spoke slowly, and would often get lost in his own thoughts. Seeing as they had quite the long journey ahead, Mayta saw no need to rush him. He would continue speaking eventually, he always did, but sometimes it would take a great while in between and Skullin would act as if no time had passed since he had begun his statement and finished it.

Aria would have hated it. She was impatient, and hated the dramatics. Mayta found it quite wonderful. As they walked she would imagine what wild things the creature of death would finish his sentence with, and he never disappointed.

They had entered a village and still, Skullin had yet to continue. It was a small village with many farms on the outskirts and perhaps more sheep than people. The village appeared to be pre-dominantly human, as things were in Skierka after years of persecution against the non-humans, but a few soil sprites ran across the dirt in search of mischief. In the distance, Mayta could see the silhouette of a family of trolls working among the sheep. She wanted to ask Skullin if the trolls were enslaved, just as her kind was, but she wanted to hear about those odd rotting humans more and she didn't want to risk his next sentence to be an answer about the trolls over the rotted humans. She'd ask about the trolls some other time.

The houses seemed to be made mostly of stone, but a few huts were crafted of wood. Each house held a chimney with a steady stream of black smoke pouring out, warming the families that lived within each home, and the guests at each post. The town, like most of Skierka, was various shades of gray and colourless, besides the occasional pop of red or the Morlok Crest which flew outside of each building. Unlike the people of the capital, who dressed in shined leathers or great furs over top of extremely tight outfits, the people here seemed to wear mostly black and gray cloaks. Despite the great number of sheep, the few people she did see on the streets appeared to be extremely thin, with graying skin and sunken eyes. It was a look Mayta knew all too well. The unmistakable look of famine.

A feeling of regret and shame overtook Mayta, for when she first saw the smoke of the village she was looking forward to stealing a few bites, taking advantage of her invisibility. But upon entering the decrepit place, she knew she couldn't stomach it. "Is there anything we can do for these people?" Mayta asked, risking losing Skullin's answer regarding the rotted people.

Skullin's cloak angled in her direction as the creature of death looked upon her. "Not I, but perhaps you." This time, Mayta was a bit frustrated with his lack-of-answer answers.

"What do you mean? What can I do?" She asked, her voice wavering in the cold wind.

Skullin continued walking, a silent reminder that they had a great ways to go. Mayta walked along death's side, awaiting his answer. "It is not just the syrens who would benefit from a greater ruler in Skierka." Mayta thought his answer over as they walked out of the village, following the main road to exit from the town into the direction of the Red Peaks. The snow over the makeshift road had been trampled into slush by the horses and occasional carriage marks.

Again, it all seemed to come down to the war. To win the war, they would free their people from enslavement. Free the other non-humans. Free the Surtrians. And perhaps bring a kinder rule to Skierka, one who would not flood his friends with wealth as his people starved.

The pressure that Mayta felt when she first set off on her journey settled back into its familiar spot in her gut. There was a lot riding on Mayta and whatever the Sistros told her. Mayta picked up her speed, Skullin easily matched her pace. She swore she could hear the creature chuckling from underneath that hood as she hurried her footsteps. She couldn't even see the Red Peaks at this point. And by the time she got there, climbed Mount Disparadi, and requested to speak with the Sistros, even if they took her in immediately, it would still take so long to get there. Mayta prayed that there would still be people to fight for by the time she reached the Sistros.

"Would you like to get there faster?" Skullin asked. His voice sounding both ancient and young— eerily similar to the Irridesci. Only Skullin didn't feel like wrongness, he felt like a part of her that she could recognize in some primal manner. Death was, after all, only natural.

Mayta groaned. "Are you kidding me? Obviously!" She was panting now. The cold air coated her throat and stung her lungs as she did her best to walk at a faster pace. But she'd been walking for so long now. Sleeping on the forest floor. She was beyond exhausted, and her body was aching for rest.

"And you seek the peak of Mount Disparadi? Where you hope to meet with the Sistros and hear their prophecy in hopes that it reveals how you will win your war?" Skullin asked, recapping basically Mayta's entire life and the situation she had been offloading onto Skullin for the past several days.

Mayta sighed, not bothering to mask her frustration with the creature, "Yes. That's the whole ordeal."

Skullin's hood rippled in the way it did when he nodded. Did he not get this? He seemed to be very smart, but also distracted, as if his mind was constantly wandering. As if he was constantly in many places.

"Do you fear flight?" Skullin asked as Mayta returned from relieving herself behind a thicket of berry pushes that ran along the edge of the road. Mayta squinted as she looked up at Skullin who stood directly in front of the nearly setting sun.

She put her hand on her hips, wondering where this was going. "No, I don't believe so. At least not on Olla, my sea wraith, but she glides not too high above the water for only short periods of time. Why?"

Surprisingly, Skullin answered immediately. "Do you know what an abberack is?"

Right away, Mayta shook her head, no. She breathed a sigh of relief when she saw that he kept looking in her direction, hopefully not losing his train of thought. "They are similar to the lunar wraiths and sea wraiths that live upon this side of the realm. But they herald from Helk."

Mayta's throat began to run dry. It had never occurred to her that there would be creatures native to the underworld, but she supposed Skullin himself had been traveling with her. "They are like you?"

Skullin shook his head no. "I do not originate from Helk, young one. But they are similar to my current state, I suppose. They will be invisible to all except myself, my shadows, and you as you wear my cloak. And of course anyone else who has been kissed by death or have it in their veins." Mayta bit her lip in thought.

"So you can summon an abberack here? And we could ride it to Mount Disparadi?"

Again, Skullin shook his head. The scythe on his hip wobbled with the dramatic movement. "They can bring us halfway up the mountain. But not all the way. The Gods would be able to see them should they venture too close. And they are not allowed to leave the underworld."

"And the Gods won't see us riding it on the way there?" Mayta didn't understand the powers of the Gods past their specialties. She was unsure if they could always watch and see everything, or if they walked upon the realm like mortals. It seemed that they kept it vague on purpose. But what did she know of such things?

Skullin crooked his head to the side, "The ones who would be troubled by their presence remain on top of Disparadi."

Mayta dropped her hands from her hips and jumped up in excitement. She swung her arms around Skullin and hugged him deeply. "Let's do it! Thank you! Thank you!" Skullin stayed stiff as, well a corpse, before finally sinking into the hug and bringing his arms around her. He was not cold as she thought he would be. If anything, he felt hot. Almost feverish.

When Mayta let go, Skullin wasted no time before raising his arm up, fast and powerful. He held his hand out with an open palm before suddenly dropping his hand into an outstretched fist.

While her surroundings did not change, Mayta could hear voices. The roars of what must be the abberacks. Crackling flames and screaming. Was this the underworld that she was hearing?

A pool of black began to form in the center of the road, as if a trough of oil had begun to bleed onto the snow. A roar, far louder and closer than the others erupted from the pit. Like Skullin, the roar seemed to screech at a pitch both high and low, causing Mayta's eardrums to ache and a rush of chills to fall down her spine.

Wing beats came next. And a claw, as large as Mayta herself, gripped onto the edge of the black pit.

CHAPTER 16
RAASK

"It's not a trap," Hauth said, swinging a sledgehammer to remove the bits of damaged wall against a house of goblins that was damaged in the wraith attack. He hoped that the waver in his voice would be accredited to the physical labor and not the doubt behind his own words.

But Ofte was too smart to fall for such things, and too distrusting to believe in a note from two strange women outside of a pub. "Maybe they use notes like that to trick rebel sympathizers. They show up and then they never leave," Ofte mimed a sliced throat motion with his thumb.

Alko rubbed his moustache as he considered Ofte's words before taking a drink straight from the glass bottle that one of the goblins of the house brought out that morning. Ofte groaned. He hated when Hauth and Alko drank straight from the bottle and greatly preferred when they would fountain it from above their mouths. Hauth could hear Alko's gulping through his own panting and the swinging of his and Ofte's hammers against the thick stone wall. "But if that's the case, couldn't we just say that we were there to arrest the rebels. We are Vermilli, that is kind of our job anyways."

Ofte snorted. "Yeah, like logic has ever stopped the Morloks from killing first and asking questions later." His big eyes widened, carefully he looked all around to make sure nobody else was close enough to overhear.

To that, even as Raask, Hauth had no rebuttal, for it was his own brother who had killed him after all. As Alko picked up his hammer, Hauth put his down against the snow and took a few loud gulps straight out of the bottle. "Really?" Ofte demanded, thoroughly annoyed by this point in the late afternoon. Hauth only responded by drinking faster and louder.

After finishing that bottle, Hauth looked out at the shore. It was almost an involuntary tick at this point. He was always searching for her out of the corner of his eye. A glimmer of scales. A lock of wild black hair. Maybe the rebels would know about her. Where she was and how she was doing. A pit, deep in his chest, opened at the thought of her. Like an old wound that never healed properly, or an aching joint on a rainy day, thoughts of her brought him right back to his last year as Raask. The greatest year of his life, even with the whole being buried alive thing. If he could do it all again, just to see her, just to meet her, he'd do it in a heartbeat that he didn't have.

"I think I'll go. You two don't have to, but I will. I'll tell you how it went tomorrow."

At this, both Ofte and Alko stopped their hammering and looked at Hauth. They saw the seriousness in his face, his tense jaw and lost gaze. "And if you don't come tomorrow?" Ofte asked. He saw the worry in his friend's face and somehow it only added to the pain in his chest.

But Hauth only laughed, a light laugh that didn't manage to reach his eyes. "I'll do as Alko says if it's a trap, I'll just pretend like I came to arrest them." Truthfully, Hauth wasn't sure if he could be killed. He also wasn't sure if he was really alive right now either. So he figured he'd be relatively safe.

Alko didn't respond. Instead he just began to swing his hammer faster. Picking apart the stone wall piece by piece, careful to not allow any of the breaking pieces to land on their feet. "You're not going to say anything?" Hauth asked.

"Yeah, get to work," He bent down and threw Hauth's hammer to him. He caught the handle, staring curiously at Alko, who was not exactly a man of few words. Alko saw the look on Hauth's face and rolled his eyes. "I want to bathe before we meet with the hot rebels, so we need to at least finish tearing down this wall within the next hour if we're going to make it all the way to the crematorium by dusk."

Hauth smiled warmly and began to swing his hammer once again. The three of them finished the wall in record time and placed a large tarp around the gaping hole that used to be a burnt hole of jagged stones. Tomorrow the masons would come to start rebuilding. The goblin who had brought the glass bottles out early in the day came out just as they were leaving. Tears ran down her small, pointed nose. She thanked each of them, insisting on hugging them each for far too long as she sobbed into their Vermilli cloaks. With a container of bonchos in each of their hands, the three of them hurried back to Hauth's apartment, which was the closest one out of all of them, to bathe and get ready for their meeting. It was the first time Ofte or Alko had seen his living space.

Hauth's apartment was small and nothing but one large room with a tiny kitchen, the smallest fireplace he had ever seen, a bed, an eating table that came with two chairs, and a cramped bathroom. The building was old and ran along the Dahs. The smell of salt wafted in with the cold air at all hours. And the drunken yells from the salt district could be heard all day and night. The apartment itself was the picture of cheap and dirty living. However, Hauth did fine for himself working at the Gray Goblin and gambling. His furniture was all fine materials. Dark and polished woods. Luxurious furs and leathers were thrown across every space and overfilled his small hand-carved wardrobe. And because Hauth couldn't quite shake

Raask, most everything was a dark shade of gray or black itself, with an occasional pop of red.

Alko made himself at home immediately. He sat at the table in the kitchen space and opened his box of bonchos from the goblin. The bonchos, a sweet buttery cookie mixed with nuts, seeds, and dried fruits in the shape of a pyramid that was a staple in any goblin's house, only added to the pile of crumbs that Hauth had been meaning to wipe off of the table.

Ofte was the first to bathe. Followed by Alko and with Hauth going last. By the time they finished, all three boxes of boncho cookies had been eaten. As they walked to the crematorium, rushing as the sky turned golden in the light of the setting sun, Ofte commented, "You know if you sold some of that really nice furniture and clothes, you could probably afford a nicer place and get out of the Salt District." Hauth merely grunted a response. He knew what he could afford. He also knew what he wanted.

The crematorium was a large building, longer than it was wide, made of black stone. It sat on its own in a long clearing of snow just a ways out of the capital city itself.

They would have thought the building to be closed if not for the pumping of the black smoke barreling out of one of the chimneys. The smoke was what caught Hauth's attention. It should smell much worse. That was the whole point of the building being moved to the outskirts of the city. Hauth remembered being young when the issue was raised and brought to the palace. It had been debated for weeks before the seemingly easy decision was made.

This smoke did not smell of blood. It only left his blood magic hungry in anticipation. And his belly, even hungrier, as the smell of barbequed meat wafted into his nose like a thick syrup. Ofte and Alko both made sniffing noises. "I didn't expect humans to smell so delicious," Alko said, stopping in his tracks along what appeared to be a well-walked path in the snow.

In front of Hauth's eyes, Ofte turned from his tan, slightly pinkish, complexion to a pea green. He rubbed a circle in his friend's back. "I don't think that's a human roasting in there."

Ofte took a few deep breaths in and out. "Gods, I hope it isn't." He said quietly before puffing up his chest and continuing to the door. Ofte was the first to enter, surprising both Alko and Hauth who followed close behind. The only light in the windowless space came from the few torches alighting the hallway, forming a path straight towards the back of the building. When they reached the end, Hauth attempted to open the last door only to realize it was locked.

"Do you think it was just a prank?" Alko asked, trying the door himself. Obviously, it was still locked.

As if hearing Alko's question, a door that seamlessly blended into the stone opened just a crack. A cloaked figure peaked their head out, they looked between the three of them in their Vermilli red cloaks. Dropping the hood, one of the women who had passed them the note, the one with the gap between her two front teeth, smiled up at them. "I'm glad you decided to come," She squealed, opening the door wide enough to reveal a dark stairwell leading underground.

"Of course, we were quite interested to hear about this," Ofte commented quickly. Hauth resisted giving him a strange look until he realized why Ofte had been eager to come after initially being so against it. He wanted to keep the charade up that they were there to arrest the rebels if it did turn out to be a trap. And he did not trust Hauth nor Alko to commit to this ruse.

Hauth only smiled at the women and introduced himself. "I know who you are. Everyone does after the wraith attack. I'm Kili." The woman, who was leading them down the stairs, turned back towards the others. Alko introduced himself easily, Ofte hesitated and then said his name very quietly.

The stairs smelled of smoke and mildew and were lit by a great many torches that undoubtedly added to the smoked smell of the entire crematorium. Ashes littered the ground like snow, showing the footsteps of the well-traveled steps with ease.

Another cloaked figure appeared at the bottom of the steps. By the size and gait, it appeared to be a very large man. Hauth swallowed, feeling his throat drying in the smoky space. "They're Vermilli?" The figure asked Kili.

She nodded. "They're alright, trust me."

The figure turned towards them. Hauth recognized him immediately, it was one of his old personal guards from within the castle. Zaries. His heart quickened, a thousand worries raced across his mind, each looking like the millions of moments he had with the guard as his former self.

"Are you Hauth Orn?" Zaries asked. The guard looked as if he'd lost a considerable amount of weight and added it back in muscle. Hauth wondered how long Zaries had been a member of the rebellion, if he had been when he was still Raask or if this was a new thing. Was he really naive enough to miss one of his closest guards being an enemy? This time, Aria's beauty couldn't be to blame, but only his own stupidity. For his own sake, and maybe mostly pride, Hauth hoped Zaries turned sometime after his death, somehow that lessened the blow.

Hauth stared at Zaries, slightly slack jawed. Sensing Hauth's awkwardness and hesitation, Alko spoke up, "Yeah he is." Zaries laughed joyously, an odd sound in such a damp and dark dwelling. Immediately, the sound brought him back to a life that wasn't his anymore, a life that wouldn't be there waiting for him either.

"Everyone knows who you are! We were hoping you'd find us after word spread around about what you said after slaying the wraith." Hauth managed to nod, albeit stiffly. Zaries merely looked around at them and shrugged before opening the door.

The space underneath the crematorium was large, far larger than the crematorium itself. It would have been dark and cavernous if not for the abundance of torch light and the fire pit in the center. Above the pit was some kind of vent that must have led to the chimney that they had seen smoking as they walked in. Familiar with silver lithe and the sweet lemony scent of it, Hauth could tell at least a couple of people within the cavern had been controlling the air, directing the smoke up and through the vents. Silver lithe was not a rarity exactly, but it was hard to acquire and as all lithe was, it was controlled by the crown. The use of the silver lithe was telling to the strength of the resistance and who exactly was involved with it.

Hauth walked in, his boots clicking against the stone ground. As he walked further into the room, he saw what was sitting above the fire pit and dared a look of amusement directed back towards his friends. A fat boar, roasted to perfection, sat above the fire. A look of relief flashed across Ofte's face at the sight of the pig.

Around thirty people littered the dark cavern. Many of them drank goblets of fine wines and short stacked cups of what smelled to be Surtrian sugar liquor. They each looked up at Hauth and his friends, curious over the newcomers and more than likely to scrutinize if they were trustworthy. Interesting enough, it was not all humans, but a variety of species.

Goblins, sprites, and even a witch sat in the back corner. The humans were also diverse, many Rakkei with their tanned skin and thick lashes and even a couple from Surtr with ebony skin, stood hunched by the roaring fire to keep warm.

This was not a couple of people, powerless and desperate. There was wealth in this room. Wealth in the whole roasted pig. The silver lithe. The shined leathers and the jewelry and the smell of quality liquor. The resistance was in Etra, and it was not some desperate prayer from those with nothing to lose. Hauth recognized some of the people from the palace, nobles with high rankings who had sat in meetings as they discussed defeating the resistance. They had offered battle strategy to conquer more land and more territories, to capture more slaves to mine for more lithe, to use for experiments from the Irridesci, just to say that Skierka could. How long had they been a part of this resistance? Did the cruelty get to them overtime? Or had it always been an act? Hauth felt speechless. One again glad for his new identity that was not required to always make a statement.

Hauth heard Zaries's heavy steps, steps he knew instinctively, as he approached him from the back, clapping a light hand on his shoulders. "Welcome to the resistance, son!" Like a spell had been lifted, everyone stopped staring and went back to their drinks and company. Was this how they planned to win a war? By drinking and eating and gabbing?

Hauth was feeling a wave of emotions rising within him, and with it, his magic's hunger. Alko placed a glass of Surtrian sugar spirits into his hand, Gods knew where he got it from, but Hauth slugged it back.

Ofte took the goblet Alko had gotten for him, a thick Skierkan wine, but did not drink. "*This* is the rebel movement?" He seemed to echo Hauth's thoughts.

Zaries chuckled, shaking his head, "It's a part of it. But we haven't started the meeting yet. We're waiting."

"For what?" Ofte asked, holding his goblet stiffly in his large hands.

The door slammed open behind them, reverberating as it bounced hard off of the wall. The man who had been sitting with Mayta in the Gray Goblin entered. He wore shined wide-legged leather trousers and had the gait of a man entering the battle field. Everyone stopped talking as he moved through the room with the grace of a warrior and the command of a leader. Silently, the people on the outskirts of the room fell into a ring around him.

"For those who don't know, I'm Fen del Gaulic." He said, looking at a group of other Skierkans who must also be new. His eyes scanned the room with the focus of a predator, they paused on Hauth. He too, must have recognized him either as the Gray Goblin's barkeep or the man who slaughtered the wraith. Perhaps both.

Fen continued, "I'd normally like to take a moment and individually speak with each new member. But today I must be brief. The Syren Queen and I have been meeting with prospects of who we would like to appoint as the official leader of the Skierkan revolution. The meeting is going long, and my presence is needed. But I didn't want to leave you all waiting here." Fen started to leave, walking back towards the same door he came in. The only door in and out. But none of it mattered, because this man had implied that he had just left a meeting with the Syren Queen. She was here. In Etra. His heart raced as he struggled to breathe properly.

Zaries yelled out, "That's it? No other updates? We're sitting with our asses out here, the least you could do is give us more information." A couple murmurs of agreement echoed across the cavern.

Another yell, coming from one of the Surtrians, "Do we have no say in who our next leader will be?" Again, but louder this time, echoes of agreement flooded the room like a tide. Hauth was grateful for this uproar, hoping that it masked the reason for his sudden stiffness.

Fen seemed to be considering these words with a great seriousness. "The decision depends greatly on who the Syren Queen will back. Along with myself, as speaker of the Gaulic forest, and Viggo Morlok who commands our army." More uproars of disagreement, loud enough that Hauth almost missed the faint change in lighting and the sound of the door opening behind them. Someone must have been late. He wouldn't have even looked back to see the newcomer if not for the dirty look Fen shot their way, and the distraction from his thundering heart.

Half out of curiosity and half out of need for a distraction, Hauth turned his head to see who had entered the room.

But this was no distraction. Nor did it help his anxiety.

In fact, his heart felt like it stopped entirely, missing not one, not two, but three beats.

In the corner of the cavern, covered in waves of shadows from the flickering torches, was a mess of long black hair. Eyes that rang with intense power. Sharp features. Cool arrogance. Beauty far greater than anything Hauth had ever seen before, and would ever see again. A beauty that haunted his every waking moment and the dreams that tormented him each and every night.

Aria leaned against the back wall. A wraith among wolves. A

killer of killers. And she was looking at Fen, giving him nothing but a shrug in response to his dirty look. Others looked, but they did not react. Did they not recognize her? Her posters had been plastered across the entire capital. Quickly, Hauth looked away and prayed that Aria would not look in his direction.

CHAPTER 17
ARIA

Caden chased after Aria, catching her before she could fully storm out of the house. He called over to one of the servants, who upon seeing Aria and the look on Caden's face, promptly went to another room and came right back out with a long box wrapped in a red bow.

By this point, Fen and Lok had followed them out into the great entry room. "Don't leave, but if you do, at least don't leave without this," Caden said, handing it to her.

The box was heavy and clanked loudly. Unable to grab it in one hand, Aria opted towards untying the ribbon, letting it fall to the floor, and lifting the lid of the box. Inside, on a bed of a soft black fabric, was a metallic arm. Black with ripples of white. Aria swallowed, looking up at Caden. Fen had said Caden came from a line of inventors. It was obvious what it was, but it didn't stop Aria from asking out of shock. "What is this?"

From the corner of her eye, Aria saw Lok roll his eyes at the obvious question. "It was built for you. Designed by Raask. But I had finished it a couple of days before you..." His voice trailed off, probably out of politeness but it annoyed her, before she was sent to the dungeons. "It's some of my best work and honestly, I didn't want it to go to waste." He paused, and Aria could feel his heavy gaze.

The gift was kind and generous, but she hated it. A wave of nausea overcame her just at the sight of it sitting on that soft fabric. She could see him in it, the elegant curves and the intricate workings of this arm. He must have spent a great deal of time designing this.

She wanted to throw it at Caden and run away. But he was right, it would be a shame to allow it to go to waste. "Would you like to try it on?" It even had fingers and a thumb. But she didn't understand how it would work, how it would respond to her mind's commands.

Instead of asking, she just nodded. Caden placed the box on the ground and carefully lifted the arm. Aria lifted what was left of her arm towards him. Ever so carefully, he placed the cold metal against the fragile skin over the end of her upper left arm. It hurt a little when he was moving it across the space, like a great pressure was forming. Suddenly, with a whoosh, Aria felt it seal against her stump. And from there, it just dangled.

She felt silly. A small part of her had hoped that it would truly work as her arm once had. Her nose crinkled as she tried to hide her foolishness. She should have known better than to hope.

But Caden was not done. He pulled a leather strap out from the top of the arm and wrapped it around her shoulder. Two more straps were wrapped tightly around her shoulder and around her bicep, holding the metal securely in place. Aria coughed, uncomfortable, and now just hurt by the disappointment of it, wanting to get it off. She looked at Fen, but he was just looking at the arm. He didn't seem disappointed. Maybe he was thinking that she'd be a better symbol of the revolution with at least the partial image of being whole.

Lok was also staring at the arm. But he seemed mesmerized by the thing. Aria couldn't understand why, it seemed to just be a very pretty hunk of metal that would probably annoy her with the constant clanking all of the time.

When the leather straps were properly secured and looked over once again by Caden, he stepped back and looked at her arm in awe. "Well, what do you think?"

Aria shook her head. "It's nice of you, Caden. But—" He looked at her with such a look of bewilderment, obviously confused as to why she wasn't more excited. Then he had a sudden realization, jolting his body and eyes widening. He reached into his pocket and pulled out a vial of a powder, the same black and white combination of the arm itself.

"What is that?" Fen asked. He stepped forward, placing a hand on Aria as if to hold her back. As if she was stupid enough to just down some strange powder from a Skierkan noble.

Caden looked between the two. "You don't know?" His eyes settled on Fen, as if this revealed something about him that he didn't know before. Fen took the vial from him. He swirled the powder around and held it up to his eye before sniffing loudly. As he did, Aria caught Lok and Caden glancing at each other. They must not have known Fen was a hylbra, and could easily sniff through a closed vial.

"Is it twilight lithe and white lithe?" Aria asked. Recognizing the blackness of twilight lithe as a pain treatment and a numbing agent, and white lithe from her time mining it in the Zojz. The white sheen of it, instantly recognizable. But she knew it wasn't those things. White lithe smelled of sweet ocean rot. And twilight lithe just smelled sickly sweet.

This was a strange smell. Salt and wet stone.

"It's metaled lithe." Caden answered.

Out of the corner of Aria's eye she caught Lok fidgeting. They were hiding something. Finally Caden continued, "The Calladies have kept a secret from the Morloks for generations." He nodded, directing his eyes to the vial that sparkled from the light of the setting sun.

"There is a summer home, that we go to in the warm months. Along the northern coast of Skierka, not too far from the shores by the Zojz." Aria knew the area well. She nodded along as Caden spoke. "There are caves on our property. Water rushes in them, charged with the power of the white lithe within the trench, but diluted enough for us to walk through without harm. That's where you can find the metaled lithe. In its natural state it is the perfect metal. It shapes well and is strong once it is reformed. It can be sharpened like a blade. Or built into nearly impenetrable armor. And when consumed, you can shape it to your will. Push it. Pull it. With training, it can become like another limb."

Lok smirked. "How do you think his family became such famed metalworkers and inventors?" Lok threw back another glass of wine, Aria had no clue where it came from or when he had grabbed it.

"And the Morloks have no clue?" Fen asked, his voice hoarse.

Caden shook his head no. "But before you get any ideas. There isn't too much of it. And definitely not enough of it, or Calladies, to form armor or weaponry for an entire army." This was directed at Fen, but Aria herself was thinking of it too. Sensing Aria and Fen's distrust of the powder, Caden poured a tiny amount of it onto his palm and snorted it up his nose. Suddenly, Aria's metaled hand began to move. The fingers flowed like a regular hand, drumming back and forth. Caden made her cross her arm and uncross it. Lifted it high above her head and then patted her own head. His message was clear. One, the powder was not poisonous and did in fact do what he said it did. And two, Caden would have control over her arm as well.

"But Raask designed it? While this powder was secret?" Aria asked, unable to understand.

Caden nodded, "Raask knew we could make a working prosthetic, and even match his design, but he did not understand nor seek to understand how it would work." Aria resisted the urge to scoff. How many rulers went about ordering things to work that they didn't understand? How many other Skierkans kept secrets right under the noses of the Bleached Palace?

Aria didn't know whether to feel excited or anxious. Dread and hope tumbled around in her insides, knocking around every organ leaving her breathless. The thought of so many powerful nobles and families within Skierka who had hidden their own small rebellions from the Morloks, combined with the hope of having two working arms again, both crippled and excited her.

"Can we go back and finish our meal now?" Lok asked, leading the way back to the dining room. Fen's gaze caught on the waning light from the windows high above. He quietly cursed. "I need to go. But I will be right back."

Aria could have tackled him. He couldn't go, definitely not now. She was panicking. Too much was happening. And she could not be trusted to remain diplomatic with these two. Fen moved closer to Aria. Strangely, he moved as if he was going to hug her goodbye.

Strangely, that's exactly what he did.

Only when he pulled her into an embrace did she understand; Fen was close enough to whisper into her ear, "Everything will be alright. Work with Caden to learn to control your arm, if that's what you want. Ask them questions. Try to figure out who you'll back as King." He pulled away, and said out loud for everyone to hear, "I'll be back."

And with that, Fen left, leaving the room far colder and emptier than it was before. Her heart beat wildly. Lok leaned against the wall. "Did he whisper to you who his choice for King was?" He winked and laughed.

Caden was already sitting down at the table. Aria ignored Lok and took her seat across from Caden once again. The metaled arm hung limply at her left side, clanking with every step. With her right hand she quickly lifted and swallowed the entire glass of wine in one gulp. One heartbeat. Two. She looked up to see both Caden and Lok carefully watching her every move. Caden gave her a small smile that looked like pity. Aria swallowed the anger that rose as a gut reaction to the look of his pity. She wanted to argue and fight with that look, but she knew she shouldn't. She couldn't, not if she wanted to win this war. She needed one of them to be successful, to save her people, to become the next king.

"Would you like to try?" He stretched his hand out, offering her the vial of metaled lithe. Aria snatched it out of his hand and held it up to the light to inspect further.

She twirled it between her fingers. "Who else has access to this?"

"Only my family and Lok."

Aria nodded. "And if I need more, where do I go? How much do I take and how often?"

"A pinch a day should be enough. But you'll have to see how it reacts to your body. We've never tested it on a non-human so the dosages could be different. I'm not sure."

She pocketed the powder, not wanting to use it for the first time in front of them. "A 'thank you' would usually be in order." Lok looked at her expectantly. Syrens didn't bother with thanking. It was a very human thing to do.

Abruptly, Aria stood. "I must go with Fen, but we will be back." Caden and Lok shared a look, but Aria was already storming out of the room before she could linger on any thoughts of what they were thinking. Before exiting out the main door, she looked back quickly, making eye contact with Caden, she said, "Thank you. I'll be back with more questions." As quick as she could, she untied the straps holding the metal arm to her, quickly catching it with her right hand before placing it on the dinner table.

With that, she stormed out of the house. Following Fen's scent, she easily tracked his footprints and his smell all the way across town and into a deserted crematorium. Careful to keep her veil up, Aria walked into the pork-scented black stone building and all the way down the hall. She could smell and hear the people below her. But it took her a few minutes to figure out just how to get down there.

Sniffing, she could tell where the slight gaps in the back stones sat. Then, after repeatedly hitting at it in random spots, the door eventually popped open.

It wasn't until Aria had slunk through the second door that she realized where she was. This was a meeting of the rebels in Skierka.

Sticking to the shadows, and double-checking that her veil was intact, Aria dodged a dirty look from Fen as she silently listened. The rebels were demanding to know who they were considering appointing as king, the symbol of their revolution. And if they were successful—their next ruler.

Aria didn't understand why Fen wouldn't tell them. If anything, their opinion was what mattered most. Whomever they chose, it would need to be the one that the Skierkans would rally behind. The one who had the power to unite them. To inspire hope in the desolate and hungry people of Skierka.

So it was their opinion that Aria wanted more than anything. Lok or Caden, she didn't care much for and she'd much rather the choice be out of her hands. She just needed to pick the right one. And they —the actual people of Skierka—would know better than her who they would fight for. Who they would die for.

She kept her gaze low and listened intently as Fen revealed the two contenders. There was support for both parties. Those who hated the Irridesci and the lack of morals under the current crown tended to side with Lok, who ironically didn't appear to Aria as the picture of high morals. And those who seemed to push towards progress and technological advancements of Skierka, seemed to root for Caden. Fen listened to each opinion. He didn't rush or cut people off, even when they were taking forever to make a point or just repeating what had already been said. He made everyone feel heard and seen.

But enough time had passed, and Aria wasn't sure how long was appropriate to leave Caden and Lok waiting, but it seemed to be nearing.

She looked at Fen, knowing that he was still seeing her as the tall, dark and handsome man. Fen gave a slight nod, unnoticeable to everyone else in the room. He allowed one of the Surtrian women to finish speaking before telling the group that he had to leave but they would take their thoughts into account. A few people called out asking when they would meet the Syren Queen. Aria took that as her cue to leave.

She quietly snuck out the door and up the stairs. The smell of Fen, clove and forest, filled the stairwell only a moment after she had entered. He must have sprinted right out. Hearing the quickness of his step, she walked faster.

"Are you worried they're going to follow us?" She asked, wondering if there was a reason for their fast speed or his distrust.

He shook his head. "No, but with you here I'd rather keep it safe. I'm guessing you ditched Caden and Lok and followed me here." Aria didn't respond, which was answer enough. Fen sighed, now leading the way out of the door to the crematorium and back out into the cold. "Well we better get back quickly. It would be rude to leave them any longer."

Aria ignored the obvious bitterness of his tone, figuring it was slightly owed due to her behavior. But especially after seeing what Fen had left for, she didn't regret running out of the Callady Estate. It was obvious that—for whatever reason—both Lok and Caden were well respected among Skierkans, at least the rebels. From what Aria saw, either of them could be chosen and well-backed by the people.

Fen and Aria walked the path twice as fast as it took Aria to get to the crematorium from the estate. The sun was down, and the air was cold. They were walking through the business district, where most occupants had left once the business day had ended a few hours ago, so there were very few torches to light their path in the darkness. Aria was a creature of darkness and could see fairly clearly through pure blackness. Fen couldn't see so well in the dark. And Aria could only see what she paid enough attention to.

A gloved hand covered her mouth.

A silver blade shimmered in the sliver of moonlight from just above the horizon. Aimed directly towards her chest. Aria was fast, but she had not been prepared. Her thoughts were elsewhere. Too distracted.

And now her people would be left without a ruler. Mayta without a sister. All because she hadn't been thinking, allowing her thoughts and disgusting endless feelings to take over.

She should have known better than to hope.

As if the whole world had slowed, Aria saw exactly how everything had played out. Her last moments. She saw Fen turn around—fear clouding his eyes—he began to move. But he was too slow.

Would they bury her bones under Skierkan soil? Would her skull sit on the back of the Fire Monger King's throne, forever engulfed in his orange flame?

Fen's eyes moved from the glint of the knife. Aria wanted to move. She wanted to strike back. But her thoughts were on her flaming head impaled by the Morlok throne.

Too distracted. Too many feelings. Too many fears.

Aria would pay the price for losing her focus. And into the arms of her ancestors, who would no doubt feel ashamed of her for her loss, she would fall. Perhaps it would be peaceful, to enter a realm that didn't fall upon her shoulders.

Red blood sprayed upon the snow. The heavy metallic scent filled her nostrils as the man who had tried to kill Aria laid lifeless on the murky streets of Etra. Recognition flashed in Fen's eyes as he looked just behind Aria's shoulder. She turned.

Her heart stopped.

It was like all the life had been sucked out of her and her heart laid in a perpetual floating catatonic state. Everything hurt inside of her. She wanted to scream. To cry. To throw up. Was this some cruel joke? Was she really the one who laid dead? Was this paradise or was it the realm of the damned?

For the Crown Prince of Skierka, Raask Morlok, stood behind her. His knife was bloody. His eyes, wild from the blood lust. His shoulders lifted up and down heavily as if he was using a great deal of control and exertion when all he was doing was staring at her.

"Thank you, Hauth," Fen said from somewhere so very far away.

Hauth? Her brows raised quizzically. But neither of them broke eye contact. So much time had passed. So much grief. It laid heavily inside of her like a tumor. It twisted around her very insides like a barbed wire spoiling her entrails and turning everything into rage.

Raask was here. But there was still this heavy grief of him that had become as much a part of her as her rage at the Morlok crown.

Hauth. She recognized the name. He was the one who had killed the sea wraith. The distraction.

Hauth. The one that the Skierkans already looked up to. Who was well-loved among their kind. Enough for both Fen and Zaries to consider him in the running for king. Of course. It wouldn't matter what name he took. It wouldn't matter that his golden hair had faded to a cold white. His eyes, once the color of a warm summer sky, froze into ice.

He would always be a ruler. He'd always be loved, and looked to as a leader. It was as much a part of him as the endless pursuit of revenge was for her. Intertwined in their DNA. A genetic curse. A genetic gift. It's what it meant to be an heir. To inherit the powers, good and bad, of every ruler before. It was what it was to be Raask Morlok. He was loved. By all. Just as the sky was blue and trees grew from the ground, Raask Morlok would be loved by all he had met. Including her.

"Hauth?" Aria asked. Her voice broke as she whispered his name. But she was too mystified to feel embarrassed. Raask nodded.

Fen continued. Aria had no clue if he was aware of the entire oceans of emotion that had overtaken her, or if he assumed it had all been from the attempted assassination. "Thank you for saving my cousin. They're visiting from the North." Fen didn't want to take any chances on what gender Hauth was seeing through Aria's veil. But the way he was looking at her. He knew who she was. And he knew that she knew who he was.

Fen was the only one left in the dark. Aria could hear Fen digging through the pockets of the assassin. He wore the same uniform of the guards outside the Callady Estate. Raask's eyes dropped to Fen. She saw him swallow, his throat contracting. He was the same. So much the same. How did Fen not recognize him? How had no one recognized him as Raask?

"That looks like one of Cadan's mercenaries." His voice was the same too. Smooth and enchanting. A rumble of thunder through a green wood. Alive. He was alive.

It did not surprise Aria that Raask recognized Caden's guards. But it seemed to have surprised Fen. "Did you piss off the Callady family?" Raask asked, now only eyeing Fen, completely avoiding Aria. And she didn't mind, because *he was alive.*

Fen grunted out a no. "You came from the Callady Estate?" Aria followed Raask's eyes to the thorns sticking onto Fen's cloak. She forgot how smart he could be. Observant. "He must have followed you. Caden assumes loyalty a little too easily."

Aria felt those last words like a knife. Raask was once too trusting with her. Was that why he had assumed this fake identity? Was he scared that she would come to kill him?

Then she could see it in him. In his shoulders, he rolled them back, shifting his gait between his legs. He was about to leave.

But he had just come back to her. "You saved me?" Aria asked. She sounded weak and she hated it. This was why she almost died. Why she needed to be saved. She was becoming too weak. Too dizzy. Too heartbroken. Too *broken.*

Fen looked at Aria with his jaw dropped just the slightest. He heard the weakness too. It was unlike her. Even in the face of death and gore. If anything, the violence made her feel more herself than what she felt now. Love was foreign to her. Something that she reserved for Mayta. It did not come naturally to her to love. For how would she know how to love, when it was not something she had ever been given?

Creatures like Aria were not meant to love. Especially not a Morlok.

Raask only nodded. Why would he save her? It was her fault he was buried alive. Maybe it was all a ruse. Raask would pretend to save her, only to gain her trust once again and then betray the rebellion and kill her. It was a brilliant plan.

That had to be it. He had always been so clever.

Aria straightened, trying to put herself back together, piece by broken piece. "Hauth?" Aria asked again. This time he did not nod. He just looked at her with that damned look. The same one she saw in the mirror when nobody was looking. He was as haunted by her as she was by him.

"How do I look to you?" She asked. Needing to hear it, for some Gods-known reason, she wanted to hear him say it.

He was taken aback. She felt Fen tensing from behind her, he'd want to throttle her for the question. He barely trusted her veil and he had no clue if they could trust *Hauth*. She knew she couldn't trust him, but she didn't care. Not right now.

"You know what you look like," His voice was quiet. Pained.

Desperation seeped in his words like a thick syrup. A syrup she wanted to stuff her face into. A mess that she was as equally terrified of as she was exhilarated by.

This was dangerous. But she couldn't stop herself. She was stumbling in her motives and her feelings, jumping back and forth from anger to resentment to relief that *he. was. alive.*

She wanted to tell him how badly she missed him. She wanted to run into his arms and act like none of this ever happened.

But this was no fairytale. And Aria had learned to not trust hope.

"You know each other?" Fen finally asked. She was surprised it took him this long. Yet again, she was surprised he couldn't see Raask Morlok standing in front of him.

"Do we know each other?" Raask looked between them, a dangerous laugh fell out of his mouth and into the streets. "Before she broke my heart." He placed his hand back into his pocket and retrieved a crushed cigarette of emerald lithe. He spoke from the corner of his mouth as he lit the cigarette, "You know, the other time she was visiting from *up north.*"

Fen looked at Aria for confirmation. He was not stupid. And possibly, Fen was one of the most cautious creatures Aria had ever met. He would not dare reveal her identity without absolute certainty that *Hauth* knew who she really was.

She thought her options over. And gave just the slightest nod to Fen.

Hauth knew who she really was, alright. He knew perhaps better than anyone else. For his soul was a mirror to her own, only where she had been sharpened into a weapon, he had been born to dominate war rooms, dictating strategy over spilling blood. Perhaps Mayta's children would have the luxury of learning such skills, not needing to become a monster to save their people.

Aria couldn't hold it in any longer. She wasn't sure if she wanted to reveal Hauth's identity. Wasn't sure what the right thing to say or do was. But she knew what she wanted: answers. "How?"

Hauth took a drag from his emerald cigarette. He didn't turn his gaze. Instead he held on, making sure Aria felt every word like the attack it was. He wanted her to hurt. "I looked for you. For a long time." He threw the lithe on the ground and stomped on it. Flashes of fire crinkled onto the snowy street, a mere couple feet from the dead body.

"Whose idea was it for you to take credit for my death?"

She may not have poisoned him, or beaten him, or buried him alive, but she had orchestrated the events around his death. "Was it not me?"

"I guess in some ways it was you that killed me." He shrugged as if his supposed death meant nothing to him.

Raask began to finally leave. A shudder of relief and fear—both due to his absence—made its way down Aria's spine like a bucket of spiders. Fen saved Aria from embarrassingly stopping him. Because she would have. She would have tackled him to the snow to stop him from leaving.

Fen placed a hand around his bicep, stopping Raask midstep. It was not enough to hurt, but enough to make it clear that Fen believed he could hurt him. Ridiculous, but Fen didn't know who he was dealing with.

"I need to know what you're talking about right now. You heard a lot of things tonight from our cause. I need to know that information is safe if I'm going to let you go."

Hauth rolled his shoulder back, shaking Fen's hand off of his arm. "And how would you like me to prove my loyalty?"

That was the problem with loyalty. It was always easy to fake. And Fen knew it.

Aria saw no way out of this. She looked at Raask, "Fen can keep a secret."

Raaks's eyes narrowed on Aria. He didn't want her to tell him. "They were considering you," she added. He looked at her, not understanding the weight of her words. "They were considering backing Hauth as the leader of the Skierkan rebel movement. To be the next king."

Raask laughed loudly into the night. It was not a joyful laugh, but one of apprehension and thinly-concealed anger. Even in this fake reality Raask had constructed for himself, he could not escape the throne that was so clearly destined for him. "Absolutely not."

The words were barely out of Raask's mouth before Fen, quick as a wraith, smacked him on the side of his head with the handle of a dagger. Raask fell to the snow unconscious, leaving Aria and Fen to deal with both the dead body and the unconscious heir to the Morlok throne.

CHAPTER 18
VIGGO

"They came in the night." The shore shook with the weight of the wraiths as they began to land. With fear in their eyes, the Skierkans and Surtrians brought the wraithkin skins of water and food. The syrens, familiar with their own wraiths, dragged the carcass of the boar, severing it up into various pieces and feeding it to the lunar wraiths. The wraithkin were covered in grime and blood and burnt flesh. They must have set their forest on fire. Their houses too. Viggo wondered how many of them were left behind. How many bodies were left out to weather the fires and elements. When there wasn't enough time to bury the dead, things like that would often haunt survivors.

Silia fell into Emir's big arms. In all of their shared years of warfare, Viggo had never seen her so vulnerable. Emir rubbed circles into her back as she cried into his shoulder. Silia was a warrior. Highly respected within the Skierkan military. She had saved their asses too many times to count. To see her cry, to see her break, it was a significant sight for the army.

And Viggo, he would console her too. Hear her story, whenever she was ready to tell it. But for now, he let her, and her people eat and drink and rest.

But the image of some of the most feared warriors in the entire realm so broken down haunted him for days. Weeks.

✧

The coast had been quiet since the last attack and Viggo took advantage of it. They ran drills daily. Drills that trained their bodies and minds for war, but also bonded them to one another. They had all hated one another not long ago. It was one of the difficult parts of reigning over an army composed of different species and nationalities. They'd been taught since birth to either fear or hate one another. Usually both. Now they needed to entrust their lives with one another.

It was not an easy task, to rid their hearts of the beliefs they'd been taught since birth. To teach them to trust each other. Not an easy task, and not one that Viggo took lightly.

He had been in the war room when he got the news. Ships were in the distance. Flying the flag of Luru, a baby blue, orange and white striped flag. One of the Surtrian syrens spotted it first and gave the signal. A couple of syrens had run all the way to the Jungle Palace to tell Taura, who had been in the war room along with the other leaders: King Agar, Viggo, Silia, Emir and Skender.

They'd been planning an attack on Etra that Viggo had been stalling for weeks. He wanted to wait until Mayta had heard from the Sistros, not wanting to risk any more lives if it wasn't necessary. But this wasn't public knowledge. He also wanted to avoid any needless killing of the civilians of Skierka, a stance that was not popular within the war room. Each of the leaders had lost many to the Skierkans. They wanted to bleed the nation.

Taura looked to Viggo immediately upon hearing news of the Luruvian ships. Viggo had the most experience in dealing with the other nations, and understood their customs and stances far more deeply than the rest. But even he was confused by the news.

The Lurus worshipped Svati above the rest of the Gods—Svati, Goddess of Kindness, and wife to Voskulle, God of War. Because of their values of kindness and moral goodness, they had abstained from all other wars. And without any lithe deposits within their lands, or vast weaponry, Skierka had left them alone except occasionally relying on them for agriculture in the cold Skierkan winters.

Luru was a hot land, filled with jungles not unlike in the Surtr Islands. The people varied in their coloring, the ones who resided in the west had tanned skin and were often short and curvy. The ones who resided in the eastern part of Luru were generally pale, living high up in the mountains, with eyes that slanted upwards. Luru had once been two different nations—Lu and Ru—but merged into one as a precaution against conquerors. A decision that had indeed saved them many times over in the past few centuries. The Luvians and the Ruvians now lived peacefully among each other.

Perhaps that was why their ships had come. To offer advice in merging different cultures under one banner, under one flag. Viggo gave a comforting nod to the room, he did not believe this to be an attack. King Agar's shoulder's sagged upon Viggo's nod. His bright green and yellow tunic had been mended, filling the rip in the arm that had been there at this morning's sparring session.

The King saw Viggo eyeing the patched-up section, the golden thread that held the once-fine tunic together. "We should all get dressed. We do not know who is in that boat, or what they have come for. We will meet them as a representation of our lands, so dress quickly, and meet me by the shore." His deep voice flooded the room with the ease of a born king. He hesitated at the door, and looked back at Taura. "Can you meet them out there first? Or send scouts to ensure this is a friendly visit?"

Taura nodded, her long braids shuffling with the movement and swaying back and forth as she quickly left the war room to race to the shore. Taura was a fast runner and even quicker in the water. He didn't like that the syrens, so often, had to be the first line of defense of the Surtr Islands. But they were creatures of the sea. It was only logical. And it came with the understanding that once the war progressed to the point of primarily land warfare on Skierka, they would be relying heavily on the Surtrian Islanders, the Skierkans, and the wraithkin.

Viggo quickly left and dressed in the black cotton trousers he had been wearing for any formal events in Surtr, along with a black tank top. The island was far too hot to wear his leather Skierkan formals, and to wear his armor would give the wrong impression. The light top would show the white lithe-infused tattoos that swirled across his chest and arms, all the way down the sides of his legs. And because he knew King Agar would be annoyed that Viggo didn't want to wear those damned leathers in a meeting he deemed formal, Viggo wore his leather boots.

He met Skender and Emir in the entry to the Jungle Palace, an open patio-like area on top of the trees that held the palace. From here, Viggo could see all the way to the beach, where King Agar was already waiting. He stood at attention as servants brought out cold drinks and platters of fruit.

Skender and Emir had worn their orange tunics and sashes. A sight that Viggo would never get used to, nor the warmth it brought to his chest. The wraithkin had brought only a handful of Rakkei back with them. But neither Emir nor Skender seemed worried about the ones left behind in the Morlok fires. "We are born among the fires. Our kind know how to survive such things." That was all they had said. Silia looked knowingly at them. So Viggo took their word for it, trusting that they would continue their armories when they could.

Silia came last. She wore a bodysuit made of her wraith's shedded scales, a tight thing that sparkled, luminescent under the Surtrian sun. It was the same outfit she had worn when she first landed on Boai, only it had been cleaned and shined. Typically, she wore only the bodysuit, which ended in shorts and began by the neck. Now, she wore a purple wrap skirt she must have borrowed from one of the Surtrian syrens or one of the Surtrians themselves. Her long blonde braid was wrapped around itself forming a thick bun at the back of her head.

She was beautiful. But what Viggo enjoyed even more than the sight of her, was how flustered Emir had been the second she popped onto the patio. Skender and Viggo shared a look as Emir approached Silia a couple of feet ahead of them.

Giving Emir and Silia some privacy, Skender and Viggo began to walk the jungle path towards the shore. They heard Emir and Silia walking not too far behind them, but far enough to keep their conversation private. Viggo stole a couple of glances back, watching as Silia smiled for the first time in weeks. She loved the Luruvians. But he suspected that wasn't why she was smiling so brightly.

Viggo turned back and caught Skender's smile as he watched his brother and Silia, and then he actually halted in place as Emir picked a large purple flower from off a dense vine and tucked it behind Silia's ear. For whatever reason, Viggo assumed she would slap it off. He'd never seen Silia so much as look at a flower. But she smiled, no not smiled, *beamed* at Emir.

Viggo and Skender's gaze caught again, passing a hidden smile among themselves like a secret. They didn't say anything to each other the whole walk to the shore. By the time they got there, a large spread of delicious fruits and smoked fish had been spread out on the tables usually used for weaponry. They had been cleaned and had a covering of woven jungle leaves and flowers covering the scratched and stained tables. King Agar, even in the darkest of times, always knew how to throw a party.

A Surtrian singer, dressed in a flowing gown in a similar yellow and green as the King, began to set up along the sand. Her skin was nearly as dark as the King's and her big brown eyes eyed the approaching ships with a great curiosity. Due to the syrenic drum-ming coming from the Dahs, there would be no drumming accompaniment as was customary. This caused quite a few problems when the syrens first joined the island.

The singer warmed up as Viggo fell into place behind King Agar. The smell of a fine scented oil drafted in from the sea breeze as it passed the Surtrian King: coconut and lime. Viggo laughed, "You really think she'll be on the ship?"

Jag turned back towards Viggo with a playful smirk that he hadn't seen the once-lighthearted king wear in ages. As the large ships crept in closer and closer, a handful of Surtrian syrens took a small boat out towards the ship. As the syrens guided the boat from under the water, from a distance, it looked as if it was magically floating over to the ship. But in these teal waters, Viggo was certain that the Luruvians could see the syrens clearly.

To Viggo's surprise. She was on that ship. *And* she got onto a boat being directed by syrens.

Diya Latifi was always easy to spot. She wore a long red skirt that flowed into the wind as she climbed down the ladder onto the small boat, after only two of her guards had already reached the boat. She had a golden headpiece with what looked like many beautiful coins that created a beautiful sound in the wind, and a matching band around her waist which was bare as her top ended high above her belly button. Her skin was similar to Emir and Skender's—a dark and golden tan.

Behind Diya was Mei Gao. She wore the same colorings as Diya, the national colors of Luru, red and gold. Only Mei wore a dress with a high collar that clung all the way down her lean body. Mei was tall, possibly even taller than Taura in her human form. She wore a large straw hat, and when a gust of wind threatened to take it, she quickly smacked her hand down on top of her head to hold everything perfectly in place.

Viggo was quite frankly shocked that the two rulers of Luru had hopped onto a tiny boat being steered by syrens, with only two guards.

Taura emerged from the shallows first, ahead of the boat of

royals. Two Abisian syrens, with long black straight hair that fell to their waists, were waiting with a black wrap skirt, similar to the one Silia wore—answering the question of where she had procured such a thing. Taura kept her top that she was wearing in her syrenic form, a fishing net style top, woven with beautiful shells and gems. Now in her smaller human form, it fell against her like an oversized sheath dress.

Taura walked quickly to stand beside Viggo. "From what I can tell, this seems to be a peaceful visit. But we should stay on the ready."

Viggo nodded. "I'll warn my people, as should you." Taura snorted in response.

"I don't need to warn mine to stay vigilant, General." Viggo rolled his eyes before sending a look down to the members of his armies that were closest to the commotion. His eyes were sharp, and he gave nothing but a gentle nod of the head. His soldiers nodded, understanding the silent command. *Just in case.*

"Do they have any magic?" Taura asked.

Again, Viggo shook his head no. "They are human. And there are no lithe deposits that we know of on the southern continent." But he wouldn't be surprised if they had been keeping a trove of lithe secret. They were a peaceful nation, but far from stupid.

The syrens pushed their boat in with ease and efficiency. They chose to stay in the water in their syrenic forms and merely pushed the boat the last bit until it was shallow enough for the royals to step out of the boat. Their dark tails swished in the water as they turned to go back towards the boats. A precaution, but necessary, to keep a close eye on the foreign ship.

Viggo had been watching the syrens swimming, darting through the waters like an arrow, and by the time he had looked back towards the Luruvian royals, King Agar was already wading in the water, helping the royals step out of the boat.

Diya stomped through the clear warm waters, holding her flowy dress up high to keep dry. Mei, with her more form-fitting dress, simply walked through the water, allowing the fabric to get wet. As Jag had focused on helping Diya out of the water, Viggo went in and offered a hand to Mei, who gingerly accepted.

"Is all of this food for us?" Diya asked, an air of excitement ringing in her voice. "Jag, you shouldn't have! You didn't even know that we were coming!" Mei sniffed the air, her eyes scanning over the table of sweets as she said, "I'm sure some of their allies alerted them of our arrival." Mei turned her gaze to Taura, now fully in her human form, as she spoke, before continuing to look around.

Taura stood stiff as a soldier and gave a curt nod. "We did."

Mei's ever-wandering gaze halted on Taura. After a moment of an odd silence where the two women merely smiled at one another, Viggo cleared his throat. "It was quite a surprise to hear that your boats were found in the Dahs, let alone heading over to Boai. What brings you?" He asked, wanting to skip pleasantries and learn why they had travelled all this way.

Diya and Mei shared a look, jaws tensed, and shoulders hitched. Oh, something was wrong. Of that, Viggo was certain. But Jag, who had never been one to skip pleasantries, merely hushed Viggo, and took a moment to introduce everyone properly. Viggo couldn't resist rolling his fingers on his pants as he waited anxiously to hear of their news. He never cared for the ridiculousness of court formalities. They had traveled all the way from Luru, and on the Dahs, where time didn't travel quite so normally, so it could have taken anywhere from several weeks to several months. And the Luruvian royals, they almost never left their homelands, nor their palace on the border of the once separate nations.

Despite Viggo's annoyance at the games of courtly politics, they were unfortunately necessary. Luckily Jag was a master at such things. As he stood back, allowing the others to get to know the Luruvian royals with whom he already had a friendly relationship with, he thought of Raask once more. Raask had always understood patience and the power of charm. He could convince a crocodillo to not bite him, charming the scales off of the beast even. Raask was the one who was meant to be king. And Viggo was always meant to be his weapon.

He was playing a part that wasn't his, and was never meant to be. A dangerous game, with even higher stakes. A wave of shame overcame his body, settling into the pit of his stomach. He was playing the part of Raask, the one person he'd meant to save above all.

He'd lost control. And with it, the last trace of family he had left on this side of the Arkts.

But it had happened. And all he could do now was try to lead the way to a peaceful Skierka. And he'd do just that. He'd kill an entire army, rain darkness from the heavens once more and doom all those that stood in his way. All to clear the path, for a Skierka of peace and abundance. Of hope. He would not be the one to lead that new Skierka though. For it was never meant to be him. And it couldn't be him.

Viggo was a killer. Not a ruler.

And this was beyond evident in the day that passed before Diya and Mei revealed their intentions in coming to the Surtr Islands. King Agar had no problem providing endless entertainment and feasts. He asked the right questions, made the right introductions, all without pushing the royals to speak before they were ready. Skender would pop in and out as well. Taura and Mei seemed to be hitting it off as they spent most of the feast huddled off on their own table; while Diya took a great interest in Viggo's entire inner circle and all of the other leaders of the revolution. Viggo's heart raced the entire day. He kept jumping at every odd noise.

It wasn't until after the massive feast the next evening that Diya and Mei came together to finally share why they had come. Viggo knew it was coming when he saw Diya's eyes darting around to ensure that nobody else was close enough to hear. She spoke in hushed words, asking if they could speak to the leaders somewhere privately. Jag only stood and led them all to the war room, which had already been cleaned and prepared as another hosting space.

The war room was large with an open ceiling and vines that clawed their way around the columns. Tables of more fruit and sweets sat out and a table of Surtrian sugar liquors and juices sat upon the ends. A servant poured everyone a glass before quietly leaving them to their news. Viggo had to stop himself from pouring the glasses and plating for everyone himself just to get things moving faster.

Eventually everyone had settled into their seats. Diya and Mei stood at the front with only the two guards that had come onto the rowboat with them originally, standing on guard at their flanks. Diya turned to Mei, she breathed deeply in before relaxing with her exhale. Mei nodded, a silent agreement between co-rulers. It would be Mei who would reveal their intentions.

"Svati has sent us a message." She looked around the room, making eye contact slowly with each of them. Svati, the Goddess of Kindness, was the patron Goddess of Luru. She was married to Voskulle, God of War. Besides Viggo's conversations with his father, he had never heard of one of the God's sending a message to the human world. It'd been centuries since they had left this side of the realm. It was also considered a break in the Gods Agreement that stated they would not interfere with humanity nor the other creatures on their side of the Arkts.

"She came to us in a dream," Diya added. Mei only nodded in confirmation to this before continuing. "She believes that Voskulle has been meddling with humanity. She has seen some things... Heard some things. Terrible things that are happening in a dark tower overlooking a white palace."

Everyone in the Arkts knew of the white lithe-infused bleached palace, the stronghold of the Morloks, located in the capital of Etra. And all those who had been there, the majority of the group, recognized immediately the reference to the Irridesci tower. Viggo knew that they were supposedly communicating with the Gods, but he never believed that they had actually succeeded.

"What things?" Viggo asked, his voice rough. His entire body was at alert.

At this, Mei stared at Viggo with a hollow look of disappointment in humanity. "Terrible things. Did you know, General?"

Viggo shook his head, he felt the heavy gaze of everyone in the room. But it was the truth. The Irridesci had always been out of his purview. They sat above Skierkan law and were protected by the Morlok crown. Viggo only knew of the twisted methods they had used to teach magic. Unlike Raask, Viggo had mastered it on his own quite early and didn't need to keep visiting the Irridesci. He left that part of his life behind him, never once stopping to look back at the twisted people that ran around the palace like they owned it.

Another, very costly, mistake.

But this alone was not enough to explain the intervention by the Luruvians... At least not why the two royals would come themselves. Torture, unfortunately, was not only a Skierkan practice. "What else did she say?" Viggo prodded.

Mei continued watching him, looking for more signs of his knowledge of the Irridesci's practices. "She believes that Voskulle has partnered with those in this tower. Aligning with their goals." The whole room looked at her in a mixture of confusion and fear.

It was Diya who asked, "Do you not remember the War of the Gods?" Only King Agar nodded his head. None of the Skierkans, nor the syrens, were familiar with this war. Diya inclined her head in an invitation for Jag to answer, "When Aashi, their daughter, died— Voskulle attempted war on Kel." Viggo's entire body tensed even further, at this point it was remarkable he hadn't snapped one of his own bones. How did he not know this?

Taura looked at Jag, furrowing her brows. "That is ridiculous, how could one fight death? As soon as you kill someone they enter into his army." That wasn't exactly how it worked, but Viggo didn't interrupt. Jag himself didn't seem to know the answer to the question, everyone in the room turned back to the two women in the front.

Mei answered. "Voskulle figured a way to create an army that was not living, nor dead. He created a blood curse that trapped the life in a body while leaving the soul paralyzed. These creatures would kill anything in their path, in an eternal state of hunger and blood lust that existed here on this side of the realm and doubled in the underworld."

Viggo's eyes widened. He knew the creatures she spoke of. He had run into them with Silia last year. They had killed an entire group of them. Viggo and Silia shared a brief look of horror. "How?" Silia asked. Curt and straight-to-the-point.

"He partnered with the first Morlok. It's how your line has such an affinity for magic and power," said Mei.

Skender finally spoke up. "But what does this have to do with the Irridesci?"

Mei and Diya looked to one another. "We are not aware of an Irridesci."

Skender explained to them of the dark cloaked creatures that stalked the Bleached Palace. Diya grew several shades paler as she quietly listened.

"So Voskulle, for whatever reason, has started his war against Kel again. And he's partnered with the Morloks, somehow through the Irridesci?" Viggo asked, summarizing the news, feeling insane just saying the words. A God's war. If they weren't careful, this could become another war of the Gods.

The room grew quiet as everyone thought over the implications of fighting an already losing battle that had just been tipped so insanely far into the Morlok's favor. "Who could win a war against a God? Let alone against the God of War." Emir asked. His cheeks had flushed, and his eyes kept darting to Silia.

"Another God." Silia answered, eyeing Viggo carefully.

Jag slammed his palms against the table, hard enough for everyone to jolt upright. "Your island holds the mountain to the Gods, does it not? Mount Disparadi is what you call it, no?" Silia's eyes remained on Viggo as everyone listened to Jag. His voice was taut with determination, he would not give up on his people. "You will have to venture to the mountain and climb it and beg for a favor from the Gods, or perhaps they will be outraged enough by Voskulle breaking the Gods Agreement that they will at least stop him from joining sides with the Morloks." He side-eyed Viggo at this last bit with a look meaning, not you.

Silia stood. "I'll take my wraith. We should be able to make it to the mountain within a couple of weeks' time. I can leave within the hour." Emir went to stand with her, to volunteer to travel with her, but Viggo placed a hand on his shoulder.

Viggo interjected. "We already have someone travelling to Mount Disparadi."

All eyes turned to him. To travel to Mount Disparadi was not a task to take lightly. The Gods did not like to be troubled by the humans or any other creature from their side of the Arkts, not after the Gods Agreement. And they did not make it easy to climb the mountain.

He did not worry about sending Mayta there as she would only have to travel half the mountain to be able to communicate with the Sistros, who did not reside with the Gods. But to travel all the way up, to seek a word with the Gods, that was another thing entirely.

Viggo watched Taura carefully. She was close to Mayta, he could see the worry in her eyes whenever she had been brought up. She was as protective of Mayta as she was of Aria. Mayta, so lovely and kind, held a special place in the hearts of the Abisian syrens. They saw her as someone to protect. They saw the lives they wished for their children in her. The ability to not have to be vicious to survive. The choice to be kind, if they so chose. To not be hardened by cruelty. It was a powerful image. And an unfair one to place on her, in Viggo's opinion, for he knew that she was indeed capable of cruelty if needed.

Taura saw it in Viggo's gaze, the softness and worry. She snarled. "No." Her teeth grew into fangs. "You did not send Mayta the Precious to Mount Disparadi."

Mayta the Precious. It was the first he had heard the title. His heart ached as the title repeated itself over and over in his brain until it had scratched itself into his skull. He felt it settle on the bridge between their minds. She was fine, he could feel it. He was sure of it. But he was not ready to reveal how he knew. And he wasn't sure if Mayta would ever want anyone to know. It really wasn't his decision to make. He swallowed, his throat dry in the heat of the jungle. "She was going there to seek word from the Sistros. My shadows have heard of a prophecy being spoken. We had hoped the key to the war would be within it." That was fine, that was enough for them to know.

Taura looked like she was about to lunge across the table and beat Viggo with a glass of Surtrian sugar liquor. He wouldn't stop her if she wanted to. Gods knew he would deserve it for everything he'd done, everyone he'd failed to protect.

Jag, on the other hand, looked like he could kiss him. "That is perfect! We will just ask her to travel to the top to meet with the Gods!" Taura turned to Jag. There was a war promised in her eyes. The terrible noise of her fingernails turning into claws, a harsh pop and a sinister sliding noise, filled the otherwise quiet room. "Mayta will not be travelling to the Gods Summit."

Viggo and Jag shared a look. Taura saw it, her nostrils flaring.

Skender, always calm and rational, placed what was meant to be a comforting hand on Taura's back. Taura flinched at the touch. "Perhaps it isn't necessary for Mayta to speak with the Gods. Maybe we have another way to communicate with one." He stared at Viggo.

Viggo already knew he'd have to visit Kel to discuss Voskulle. To learn of the past war. To learn what he was doing about the creatures that must be wreaking havoc on the underrealm. But he wasn't ready for the room to know. For the world to know.

Godlings didn't get happy endings. They got lives of sacrifice and violence, designed to build a legacy. Their prophecies were never kind to them in their lives, only in the words about them once they had already died. He knew he was condemned. He knew it in his bones.

But it was another thing entirely, for the world to know that he was condemned.

And another thing entirely, for the world to know that his mother had not been faithful to the king. He didn't want anyone to speak the words he was sure they would, hearing she had a child with another while in a marriage. His mother was far from weak and even further from needing his protection, and yet he couldn't help but feel protective of her and her legacy.

But Skender had put Viggo in a corner, one he'd done a decent job of avoiding up until now. Skender was the calculating one. The smartest man Viggo knew, and he trusted him. If Skender believed it was imperative for them to know who he really was, and for it to be now, Viggo would trust his word. They would not win this war if they couldn't trust one another.

He took a deep breath in, feeling it expand his lungs, before exhaling through his mouth. Taura watched him closely, her eyes like daggers.

"Skender is right—about many things—but this especially. We do have another way to communicate with at least one of the Gods." Taura sat back down, Viggo saw the promise of confrontation still in her gaze, but she would hear what he had to say.

Viggo had fought in countless battles. Travelled across the Dahs too many times to count. Helk, he even dove into the damned Dahs. But he had never been more afraid than he was right now, telling the leaders of the realm who he really was. A godling. Destined for a life of devastation. Destined to be a story, and never meant to be an actual person with a life full of gentleness and love.

CHAPTER 19
MAYTA

The claw was as black as the oil-like substance bleeding from the ground. The talon was shiny and smooth. The knuckles flexed, rippling the black and gray scales as the creature tried to get a better grip on their side of the Arkts. Some of the snow seemed to fall into the pit along with the frozen dirt that rested beneath it.

The terrible sounds of screaming and roaring continued, but all Mayta could focus her hearing on was the laborious breaths of the abberack trying to climb out of the underrealm and the scratching of its claws against the Arkts.

Another claw erupted out of the black goo. Quicker than Mayta thought any creature so large had the right to be, it gripped onto the Arkts before pulling itself out of Helk.

First came its mouth. Endless rows of large, serrated teeth. Then its eyes, huge and milky. Mayta took a step behind Skullin. She could have sworn he laughed at this movement, but only the Gods knew as she was focusing everything she had on the movements of this obscenely large and terrifying creature.

The abberack seemed to struggle to raise its shoulders through the tight fit of the portal. Deafening pops of the creature dislocating its shoulders to raise itself into their realm caused Mayta to stumble even further back. More pops as the shoulders somehow went back into their socket. Next were the wings. The abberack had to hold them tightly against its body to squeeze through. It looked to be painful, but nothing about the creature indicated that it was in pain. Could a creature of death even feel pain? She wasn't sure. But a wave of sadness overcame her at the thought. If the abberack could feel pain, it was feeling it because she had asked Skullin to summon it for help on *her* quest. A selfish thing to do, really.

Skullin had turned his cloak back to Mayta. She felt his heavy gaze through the shadows of his hood. "You are sad, again?" He asked, no trace of frustration in his voice, only pure confusion and curiosity. Mayta shifted on her feet uncomfortably as she watched the abberack stretch its wings out. They seemed to secrete some kind of black goo that sizzled when it hit the snow.

She nodded, her only answer to Skullin's question that she was willing to give for now. She may feel bad, but she also didn't want to turn her gaze from the creature for one second. Finally, after far too long and far too many bones cracking, the abberack had pulled its wings out of the portal and lept into the Arkts. Skullin flew his hand out, the leather of his gloves just visible at the end of his long and draping cloak, and slashed his hand downwards into a fist. With the movement, the portal closed, leaving no traces of the deathly black goo that had been bubbling across the snow.

In its place stood the abberack, landing on the ground with a thud that caused the bushes and trees to bend. It looked similar to one of the lunar wraiths that Mayta used to watch with her sister from afar. With long wings, claws, and horns—although the abberack's horns appeared more similar to antlers now that Mayta got a better look at them. And this creature was far larger, almost the size of Taura's sea wraith. Its eyes a foggy milky white that caused Mayta to shudder. "Is it blind?"

"*She* is blind." Skullin said, striding toward the beast. "Almost all abberacks are blind. Only Kel's personal flock has the ability for sight." The creature sniffed, drawing in a good and long breath at Skullin's approach. Its long, spiked tail started to wag.

Skullin placed his arm out onto the creature's snout and began to pet it, working his way to scratching underneath its chin. It rolled onto its side, shaking the bushes and trees once again, leaning into Skullin's scratching before starting to purr.

Everything was vibrating in rhythm with the creature's purring. And then a thought came to Mayta, pulling her out of her fear and sympathy for the creature. She took in the sight of this giant monster of death that wiggled along the ground enjoying being scratched and Mayta began to laugh. Loud and joyous. For if this creature could disrupt the realm with its purring and the wagging of its tail beating down a tree, Mayta could laugh. Perhaps there could be room for joy in a world full of pain. Maybe joy, in the face of misery, could be just as radical as the lifting of a sword.

The abberack tilted its head towards the sound of Mayta's laughter, still rolling into Skullin's hands as he scratched at her scales. "You were just sad, and now you are laughing?" Skullin asked.

At this, Mayta laughed even louder. "How can you not?" She asked him back, finally settling down. Her steps were quick as she closed the distance between her and the abberack. Seeing this wonderful terrifying creature so full of love, she couldn't help but plant a fat kiss on the creature's scaly cheek.

A sound seemed to rumble from Skullin. The abberack twisted upright and leaned closer to him, as if investigating him worriedly. Mayta too, turned to him. Only she realized quickly that the odd sound was a laugh. Skullin, the bringer of death, was laughing. And by the way the abberack was reacting, Mayta got the impression that it was not a common occurrence.

"Now you get it," Mayta placed a hand on the abberack's chin, scratching where Skullin had, to calm the creature down, providing her some reassurance that everything was alright. Or at least it would be. "Doesn't it feel good?"

Skullin nodded. He gave the abberack one last pat, a light smack just above the nose, which the creature seemed to understand was a signal to get serious. She straightened up once again and lowered her belly closer to the ground. Skullin took Mayta's hand, leading her to just below her wings. "You're lucky she seems to like you. She doesn't like anybody but me. And I guess you."

Mayta stared at Skullin, wondering what exactly his plan would have been if she didn't 'like' her. Images shot through her head. Being swallowed in one piece. Beaten down by her thorny tail. Pierced by her talons. She tried her best to shake off the image, glad that it did seem to work out. Skullin climbed onto the ridge of her lowered shoulder, turning back to offer a hand to help Mayta up. She climbed easily onto the abberack and settled into the spot where her wings connected, behind her long, long neck.

It was different than riding her sea wraith. Oh how she missed her. Syrens had a special bond with their sea wraiths. They became one another's family. Sharing a connection that was unlike any other. Mother and child, both wraith and syren feeling the responsibilities and love that came with both identities. It felt odd riding on another's mount, but also just plain odd as this abberack was shaped so differently. When Mayta rode her girl, she laid against the skin as flat as she could so as to not disrupt the currents. To ride the abberack, she'd have to sit upright, especially alongside Skullin. It felt odd and engaged more of her core where she was used to using her legs.

"Does she have a name?"

"Nio." She alerted at the sound of her name, twisting her head around to get closer to them. "Nio, fjor!" Skullin's voice boomed the command. At once, Nio's head snapped forward and she began to run, her four legs trampling bushes and trees like they were nothing but twigs. Her wings began to beat, slow and powerful.

And then she leapt.

The wind smacked against Mayta's face, her long red hair flew freely behind her, going at such a fast speed with the current of air beating against her, she was reminded of swimming impossibly fast in the Dahs. Zooming through the waters as she now did through the air with Nio. Such a privilege, and such a lovely thing to be able to race through the realm. She loved going fast, seeing the world blurring around her.

Mayta had been holding onto Skullin's waist as they took off, as she sat directly behind him. But once they hit the air, she couldn't resist but to hold her hands out, a sin in the water, but in the air where all she had to do was hold onto Nio, it felt like ecstasy. Skullin's hood turned as he looked back at her. And when he turned forward once again, he too lifted his arms up to feel the wind in his bones.

Nio was climbing into the air, even though she was so large and impossibly heavy, she made the ascent look easy. Full of joy and life, Mayta let out a yell that echoed across the Arkts. She could feel the power in Nio's muscles as she began to show off. She would climb and then dip down. Straight through the clouds which felt cold and wet but were so fun to travel through. Nio was preparing to do a loop in the sky, Mayta could feel it, just as her sea wraith would do in the waters. Again she yelled into the winds. This time Nio and Skullin joined her. With the cloak she had borrowed from Skullin, and his own magic, no one could see them, nor hear them. And they were free.

But a little tug at the back of her skull took her out of the magic.

Viggo.

The tug, almost like a gentle knock, like he was asking to be let in. Nio turned her head back to Mayta, somehow sensing something was up, as she continued flying forward. Even Skullin let out two large sniffs. "You are speaking to Viggo?" He asked.

Mayta couldn't smell anything, only felt him waiting on the other end of whatever magic had connected him to her. His presence felt like a warm darkness, like the kind she would share with Aria back in their cave. A home in the darkness. Something about him felt so safe. "How did you know?"

Nio, who seemed to somehow understand, turned her head back

with a little huff through her nostrils. "Viggo has a trace of the ether in him. It is visible to us," meaning him and Nio, "and it's a faint smell of home."

She wondered what the underworld smelled like, and what it meant to have it as a home. Was it that terrible screaming and suffering she heard through the portal? Or were parts of it as safe and lovely as her and Aria's cave had been?

She let Viggo in, somehow knowing how to do it without instruction, like opening an old chest that had long rusted over under the sea.

His voice flooded her consciousness, rich like a fine wine. *"You feel so happy,"* it was both a question and a statement. She wondered if he could feel it himself when he was in her head, or just the awareness.

"Can you feel it?" She asked, dropping her arms and wrapping them around Skullin, not wanting to risk falling off while she spoke to Viggo. Gods knew how much he could distract her.

She felt his *"Mmmhhmmm"* like the purr of Nio, it vibrated against her consciousness like a cat basking in the warmth of her happiness.

"Can you see what I'm seeing?"

"I can if you let me, but not without you pushing it towards me."

Mayta thought this over. Then she thought of the image of what she was seeing and pulled the thought back into the corner of her mind where she could feel Viggo's darkness. *"Mayta, are you flying?"*

Mayta couldn't help but to giggle at that tension she could feel, the warm darkness of his presence in her mind turned into a ball of anxiety. It didn't exactly seep into her, causing her to feel anxious, but she was aware of its presence. *"Mayta, is that Skullin?"*

"Yes."

"You're flying. On the back of Nio, with Skullin, the bringer of death, and you're giggling?" She could hear the sound of him scoffing in disbelief. *"Unbelievable."*

This only caused her to giggle out loud. Nio tilted her head slightly at the noise and began to beat her wings a bit quicker along with the gentle wagging of her tail. *"You're completely fearless, aren't you?"* Viggo asked.

The question took Mayta off guard. Fearlessness was always associated with Aria. And rightfully so. But maybe she was brave too. With Viggo in her mind, feeling what she felt, she could feel a certain clarity in her emotions as they came over her. Maybe it was nothing but self-consciousness at the vulnerability, but she was utterly aware of the pride she felt in receiving the compliment.

Reacting to the surge of pride that burrowed into her heart, Viggo's darkness relaxed, *"Good."*

"How are things going over on the islands?" Mayta asked. She may have not known Viggo for very long, but she could sense that there was something he wasn't saying. A reason for his knocking on her mind. More than a check-in, although she wouldn't mind if it was. She was no longer lonely, now that she travelled with Skullin and his abberack. But something about Viggo's presence was so comforting to her. He wasn't from home, but somehow he was a reminder of safer times, or at least times that felt safer to her.

"We're holding it together, May, but I have some bad news." Her entire body stiffened, instinctively she held on tighter to Skullin. Viggo told her of Diya and Mei's arrival, and the information they brought along with themselves. Voskulle's possible alliance with the Morloks. And the creatures that were dead and undead at the same time.

But Mayta had already suspected all of this. She had been a spy in the castle for over an entire sun cycle, of course she would pick up on these things. She assumed Viggo had known that the Irridesci were obviously colluding with one of the Gods. They were religious figures, and they reeked of blood and misery. Mayta thought it was Kel, but Voskulle made more sense now that she thought about it. As for the creatures. She took a moment relaying what Viggo said to Skullin, and what Skullin said to Viggo.

Then the quiet. They were not unalike, Viggo and Skullin, they were both quiet but comforting presences. They preferred to think over speaking. The only problem was that Mayta liked having answers and usually one had to communicate to give those. Or at least throw the question out to one another.

Both out loud and in her head, Mayta said, "I'll do it, I'll go to the top and seek counsel with the Gods." Nio let out a huff through her nostrils. Skullin didn't say anything. And Viggo immediately tensed in the back of her mind.

"Let me speak to my father first. Hopefully you won't need to do that."

"I will if you need me to, though."

"I know."

Mayta smiled. She was about to ask Viggo for any updates on Taura and the other syren when she saw a blur of red in the snowy fields below. Moving. *"And if we kill them in this realm, will they die in the underworld?"* Mayta asked.

She felt Viggo tense even further. *"Skullin would know better than I do right now. But why?"*

Mayta asked the question out loud. Skullin followed her gaze to the world below. "They did in the times before, but I'm not sure about this new breed. Shall we find out?"

"Can Nio breathe fire?"

Nio responded by puffing a large black flame directly into the air below them. Mayta couldn't help but laugh at the abberack's response. *"Viggo, let me know what your dad says. But I've got to go take care of some things."*

"Be safe, alright?"

"Always." She felt Viggo leaving her mind as Nio dove to the fields below. Her stomach flew up into her throat as she descended. Mayta let out another cry of excitement and joy at the sensation. They didn't get close enough to the undead creatures to really take note of any details, but Nio's flames did the job alright. Mayta could feel as Nio prepared to breathe more fire, the muscles in her body all tensed

before she erupted the pure black flame that immediately turned the undead into ashes that floated in the wind, leaving behind nothing but their red gory tracks.

CHAPTER 20

RAASK

For not the first time in his life, Raask woke up unaware of where he was.

Immediately, the years of training and survival skills kicked in. He fought the instinct to open his eyes, not wanting to announce his consciousness before he was ready. Not when the last thing he remembered was *her*.

She was more beautiful, somehow, than the ghost who haunted his dreams and the corners of his mind. The one person he had silently begged for, pleaded for, prayed for, the first one he thought of when coming back to life and crawling out of the grave. The only creature he would ever crawl for. The only one he'd beg for, too, but that had been long ago.

But now she was here. He could smell her. Salty and sweet. She'd either been here or was here. He was on some kind of soft surface, a couch if he had to guess, with his hands tied in front of him and his ankles tied together with a soft fabric, tight but comfortable. Was she the one to bind him? His breath caught in his chest at the thought of her so close. Exhilarating and frightening.

She was the answer to his prayers. But now that she was within grasp, he didn't know if she was truly what he should have been praying for. She had plotted against him. She was a *known liar*. A known con. He couldn't trust her.

He thought of her hands, delicate despite the violence they'd endured and the violence they procured. Did she choose a soft tie to bind him? Or was it just the thing that was closest to her at the time? Did she care that he hurt? That he ached? Did he haunt her dreams as she did his?

He couldn't keep his eyes closed any longer, any nightmare he could endure from awaking couldn't compare to the endless possibilities and questions he held by keeping his eyes closed. No torture could be worse than the eternity he spent looking for her.

And there she was.

Silent. Sitting across from him on a stiff wooden chair. Her legs were crossed, and her hands were neatly tucked into her lap. The bringer of his death. The bringer of his destruction. And she sat there so stoic, as if she wasn't the most dangerous creature in the entire realm.

His irrational heart wanted to reach out, to feel the smoothness of her skin, her wild hair in his fists. But his mind only felt the ache that burrowed into his chest grow, intensifying with every blink of those big brown eyes. Oh Gods, it hurt. He couldn't trust her. He knew that. He knew that with every fiber of his being. So why was it her arms that he wanted?

He was a masochist, and she was the flame he'd follow to his death. Of that he was certain.

She was careful to keep her expression blank, or maybe she just didn't feel anything at all towards him,and it wasn't hard for her to keep her emotions in check. He fiddled with the bindings of his wrists again, feeling the soft fabric as he tested how strong the hold was. The ties wouldn't budge.

He saw her swallow and couldn't help the slight tilt at the ends of his lips. "Are you hungry?" She asked him, her voice was raw, as if she hadn't spoken in quite a while.

"No." He was, but the thought of her feeding him made him feel too weak, too pathetic. Wasn't it enough that she'd broken him? Was it not enough that she had killed him? That now she would need to be the hand that fed him as he laid broken and tied up? There was only so much humiliation that he could take.

Aria pursed her lips and gave a short nod. "I didn't tell him who you are." Raask did his best to keep his face blank. If she wasn't going to show her hand, he wouldn't show his either. "He's not here by the way," She added. But he already knew.

"Why am I here, Aria?" He asked, channeling the cruel voice of the cruelest man he knew—his father. It was small, but he saw the flinch, the stiffness that traveled down her spine at the tone. Good. Maybe it was her turn to hurt.

"Fen was worried that you were a leak."

"And you're not? You don't believe I could be a traitor?"

Her eyes narrowed on him. He didn't back down, he kept his gaze on her and his chin up high. "I think that if you were looking to fight for your father, you'd do it proudly. You'd be in battle, stopping the rebels' hearts without a second thought. Instead you're in hiding. Attending a meeting of the rebels, from which I understand, was your first. I think that death, and I still don't understand how you are breathing, but nonetheless, I think that death changed your allegiance. Or maybe it was living among your people, and seeing their hunger. Feeling their rage. I guess I don't know what changed what side you would fight for, but I can see it has changed."

She didn't know what changed him?

He wanted to tell her to look in a mirror to see. But it would have only added to his humiliation. "Where is he anyways?" Raask asked, desperate to move the conversation away from him.

"He's questioning Caden's guards."

For a brief second, Raask remembered the guards he had executed for her. He could still hear the sound of their blood dripping into the wind as their bodies swung back and forth, high at the entrance gates for all to see. He'd let the world know what he would do for her. And she'd killed him in return.

He didn't want to make the same mistakes again. But at the memory of the guard trying to kill her, a flicker of rage ignited within him. She was brilliant and lethal. But she was acting sloppy. She should have heard him, should have sensed the attack in some way. "Take me to him then. I'll question them too."

At this, Aria looked surprised. "And you think this will prove your loyalty?"

Raask bit the inside of his cheek as he thought it over, truly he just wanted to question the guards to make sure no others were planning to stab Aria in the back. But he couldn't admit that, and she wouldn't believe it anyways. "Did you not say once that the greatest display of loyalty was that you didn't kill me when you had plenty of chances to?"

She had said that to his brother. He remembered hearing it and thinking how funny that was, that to her, trust came down to the choice to kill or to not kill. At the time it was hilarious and intriguing, but now he saw the truth within that kind of thinking. The harsh reality of a life where most things would come down to kill or not to kill. To kill or to be killed even.

Aria smirked. "That didn't exactly work out last time, did it?"

"No, it didn't." He couldn't help the sadness that anchored in his voice at this confession. Without breaking eye contact, Aria leaned over and slid a dagger from her long-sleeved black leather bodysuit and slit the ties around his ankles, and then his wrists. She stood now and Raask got a good look at her. She had more curves and muscles, that much was evident through the skintight bodysuit, typical training wear of the Skierkan military. The left arm of the outfit was hemmed and held a button holding the leather closed around the end of her humerus. His eyes lingered there, in the memory and the fear he felt watching her fall through the sky. She once felt so small and so broken to him.

Foolish of him to ever think that a creature like her could break.

She would keep going, keep battling, even in death, she would do whatever it took to avenge her people. And she wouldn't rest until it was done.

So what did it mean that she fell through the sky for him? That she lost a piece of herself for the heir to the kingdom she hated more than anything? Aria valued strength above all else. She was Aria the Ruthless. Aria the Fearless. Aria the Bloodthirsty. And she risked her life for him.

And now... Knowing everything she had done to him, and for him, Raask couldn't get his mind to settle until he himself questioned the guards at the Callady Estate.

Raask looked for too long at her missing limb. And Aria, she quickly grabbed a black fur cloak and wrapped it around her body. She rushed past him and headed towards the door, just to the left of the couch that he was sitting on. At this movement, he finally took a moment to take in the space. Red wallpaper. A spill of maps and notes and books. A fireplace with blankets and pillows laying in front, as if someone had slept there while he laid unconscious. Finally, he stood, feeling a rush of dizziness and a sudden need for water and food that he only slightly regretted turning down before. Aria must have sensed this, or had been aware of how long it had been since he last ate. He himself had no clue.

She walked towards the kitchen space, and grabbed a piece of bread and a hunk of hard cheese from the counter. She tossed the bread first, then the cheese. Raask caught them both and took large bites out of them. The bread was salty and stale. The cheese—sharp and crumbly—was undoubtedly from a sheep. The duo would do well with a glass of dark fine wine and a roll of emerald. Perhaps a heaping mug of hot tawny.

But his life as Hauth would have to wait. At least for now.

Aria was silent as she moved, but she was already out the door, assuming that Raask would follow her. She was right of course. He would follow her anywhere. And he hated himself for it.

Raask recognized the area of Etra immediately upon exiting the stone multi-home building. Tucked by the Gaulic, the real estate was cheaper here due to the risk of creatures occasionally venturing out of the wood seeking their next easy meal among the Skierkans. It made sense that a leader of the rebels would live there, an easy escape and an easy entrance into the heart of Etra. It had snowed since he'd killed Caden's guard. A fresh layer of untouched white powder heaped across the forest floor reaching up to Raask's chest.

The streets of Etra were not plowed per-se, although some of the wealthier districts and areas like the Callady Estate would clear all of the snow and ice from their grounds, but the streets were busy enough that the snow rarely piled high within Etra itself.

The sky, the vibrant cobalt of a winter's morning, had cleared but the wind persisted. Raask silently hoped that it had only been a night since he had been knocked unconscious, figuring he would have been hungrier if it had been longer. He thought back to the salt district, and the friends he left behind in the meeting of the rebels. They must be worried. He'd need to send word to them as soon as he could.

Raask followed Aria, choosing to stay behind her and not walk beside her. He watched as her hair bounced with each purposeful step. Her stride, long and unbroken against the uneven snow. How did no one recognize her? Morning light fell across the city. Wind pushed into their faces, preventing her hair or cloak from blocking the view of her face. How could she hide so plainly in the heart of Etra?

Maybe she was wondering the same of him. People would see what they wanted to see, yes, but also they would see what they were told to see for the most part. The wind kissed Aria's skin before blowing onto Raask, carrying with it the scent of her.

He did his best to not get swept up in the memory of her in his arms. Cold nights in the palace made warmer. Brief memories of passing moments where he didn't feel so alone. A piece of his soul found within another. He would recognize it anywhere. All that he felt and believed and loved, he could feel that she felt it too. Silly to think he could trust her, when she was made of the same as him.

They were silent the entire walk to the Callady Estate. The blooms had already closed up from the sunlight streaming in over the Dahs. The gate was closed. Raask was unsure of Aria's plan, the guards certainly saw her, but nobody was moving to let her in.

Then the front door slammed open forcefully. The rebel leader, Fen, moved through the yard in several powerful strides. Raask had been trained to notice all the details, and since finding his magic's alignment, he'd become all too aware of bodies and their inner mechanics. Immediately, Raask realized two things. One, Fen was not human. He didn't notice it before, probably too wrapped up in thoughts of Aria to think straight enough to feel what was now obvious. His bones were all wrong. His blood pumped far too fast for any human not going into some cardiac episode. Two, Fen was livid. His knuckles were pale, eyes bloodshot.

He reached the gate, not opening it, and just stared menacingly at Aria. "Are you kidding me?" He growled. "You brought him here?"

Aria, being Aria, did not back down and stepped closer to the iron gate. "Yes. He will be useful in your interrogation."

Fen turned his gaze from Aria and looked at Raask over her head. He could feel Fen's scrutinizing gaze, not unlike Aria's. It was moments like this where he wished, very briefly, that people knew who he was. It was tedious to wait to be admitted. He wanted to question the guards. Ensure Aria was safe, at least from these untrained savages the Calladys insisted on hiring. And then head back to the Salt District to help Alko and Ofte.

"Why would I trust him?" Fen grunted, more animal than man. Perhaps he was.

"Because he has been untied with me all morning and he could have easily killed me." Aria put her hands on her hips. Although Raask could not see her face, he knew exactly what face she was making. A pointed look, more likely with her brows raised in defiance. He had to do his best to bite back a laugh. He did not envy Fen's role in this revolution for many reasons, but mostly because he must be on the bad end of Aria's moods more often than not.

A horrible thought occurred to Raask in that moment. He straightened and carefully eyed Fen's reactions. Aria seemed to be staying at Fen's apartment, Gods knew she would never leave her own place so cluttered. Could they be together?

A flash of a memory, the blankets and pillow by the fireplace, far too cramped for this massive man to sleep in. Instantly he felt his shoulders slouch again, his breath returned to normal. He prayed they weren't aware of the panicked state he had just been in.

Fen seemed to agree with Aria's terms on his loyalty. He at least did not kill Aria. And he was obviously aware of who she was. The iron gates opened, and Fen watched Raask carefully as they walked into the estate and into the Callady manor.

It was exactly how Raask had remembered. Large. Dark. Gaudy. And empty.

He didn't dislike Caden, if anything he felt bad for him. He was a smart and good kid. Perhaps a little too good. It always aggravated him when other kids of the court would refuse to drink or party, and focus instead on studying or working. Caden and Lok, like most kids of high nobles, were just about as lonely as Raask had been. Only they didn't dive into drinks and gambling and girls, they instead focused on doing what was 'right.' At least Lok would sometimes go out with them and have a little fun. Even though Lok's fun could be cruel and at other's expense, it was better than Caden who was never cruel and only focused on studying.

He felt their eyes on him as soon as he entered. They looked at him with curiosity in their eyes. He knew immediately that they did not recognize him as Raask, instead they saw him as Hauth. The slayer of the sea wraith. For once in his life, Raask saw respect in both of their eyes as they looked upon him.

"Why have you brought him into my home?" Caden asked. He didn't sound accusatory, more curious. Again, he was studying him. Studying them and their inner mechanics like they were a contraption to take apart and put together again. He didn't know why, but he found it so unbelievably annoying.

Fen, who looked like he was about two seconds away from throt- tling them both, stopped in his steps. Looking between Hauth and Caden and Lok who were staring at each other. Sizing each other up, he must have thought. Maybe they were.

"He will be useful in my interrogations."

Fen continued, walking straight to the back of the house. Raask followed, giving a nod of a hello to Caden and Lok who continued to stare at him. Curiosity in Caden's moving eyes, and judgement in Lok's hard jaw. Fen took a left, heading towards the library. It was maybe a quarter of the size of the library in the Bleached Palace, which given the size difference of the two estates was rather impres- sive. The Callady library was one of the most famed in the Arkts, known to carry scripts in technological innovations and histories that were missing across many other esteemed libraries. It was not uncommon for diplomats to request to visit or to bring back a certain script. The Calladys never allowed for the books to leave the premises, but Raask had escorted many diplomats himself to these very libraries. That's why it was particularly shocking when Fen went to one of the many sliding ladders, lifted it at an angle, and pushed it into the wall above.

Across the library, Raask heard the sound of moving wood. A piece of the floor had moved, revealing a dark hole with a ladder inside.

How many of these hidden underground chambers laid in Etra without his, or the Palace's, knowledge? If he was still Raask, this would be beyond annoying. An insult even. But now that he was Hauth, none of this was his concern. He just wanted to make sure Aria could do her scheming—or whatever she had been doing to get the rogue guard's attention—and then get back to work with Alko and Ofte. Gods, Ofte must have been worried sick.

Alko probably was too.

These were the thoughts he had as he followed Fen down the

dark hole in Caden's library. It smelled musty. And the wooden ladder was partially rotten, slick in Raask's hands. Aria went last. Effectively sandwiching him between the two of them.

He never used to be afraid of tight places. Or being underground.

But being buried alive had a way of leaving a lasting fear of dark, cramped spaces that smelled of dirt. He did his best to control his heart. His hands grew unbearably sweaty. He wanted more than anything to trample over Aria and get out of this Gods-forsaken hole in the ground. People didn't belong underground, of that he was sure. But he had to do this, he knew he did. He couldn't rest worrying about Aria. Who would watch her back? She was so tough and strong, no one would think to worry for her. She was invincible, at least that's what everyone thought. But she was just as much flesh and bone as anyone else. She could break.

He'd seen it himself.

So he continued down the ladder, into the darkness, with no goal other than to rest assured that Aria would be safe.

Skullin's scythe, how stupid was he to be so worried over Aria's safety, the very creature had plotted against him...

The stupidest man alive probably. Or dead. Or whatever he was.

Compacted soil of the ground jolted Raask out of his thoughts of doom. The underground cavern had a surprisingly high ceiling and ventilation, not unlike the other bunker under the crematorium. Only this one smelled of blood. His magic roamed over the room, trying to find the blood, looking to feed on the violence. Only there was none that Raask could see.

He hated being underground. It was slightly better than the small tunnel with the ladder. But still, it was deep underground. Just terrible. He sighed. Taking an excuse to heavily pant out some of his worries.

One-by-one, Fen brought in each of the guards. Raask could sense a lie, or at least the tell-tale signs the body gave when lying. Quickened heartrate. The increase of blood pressure. The way the blood moved in the brain when lying and telling the truth was just, well, different. He didn't know how to explain it, only how to feel it. It was probably why he had always been so fantastic at cards, even before he had realized his alignment. It had always been there. Only chalked off to observational skills and gut feelings, but it was his blood magic. Attuned to the body. Control of it, even—if he wished.

Fen must have been annoyed as he questioned the guards. Raask stayed quiet, waiting to hear someone lie. Aria stood beside him. Again, he smelled the salted caramel of her skin. He wanted to reach out and wrap his arms around her and pull her into him. Feel her body against his. She was only a step away from him. The air between them felt electric.

A distraction. She was nothing but a distraction from his current life.

He thought of the distance between their shoulders. Could he close it without her thinking anything of it? Perhaps just a brush of her shoulder against his would be enough... He knew it wouldn't be... Gods, nothing short of a life with her would ever be enough.

He'd thought it was possible once. But he knew better now. She was a true ruler, who would put her people above everything and anyone else. Exactly as she should.

And he was only there to make sure that she wouldn't be stabbed in the back by Caden's loose wrangling of his mercenaries. He knew he wouldn't be able to rest unless he secured it himself.

So there he was, ensuring no other guards were acting against the rebels. Once he did just that, he would leave. That was it. He was Hauth Orn now. And he no longer had any business to do with the rebels or the Morloks or any sort of politicking. He had no business being so entranced by a creature who wanted nothing more than to kill him.

Again, his thoughts drifted to the air between Aria and himself. He felt magnetized by her presence. Like he simply had to hold her. He wanted to reach out, and oh he was just about to, when the next guard was brought down by Fen. The guard's blood pressure was unusually high. Raask snapped his head in the guard's direction, eyeing him carefully as Fen led him to the deteriorated stool in the center of the room where they had been questioning each guard. Several torches lit the space, and a pit of fire sat directly behind the stool. It put the guard in the shadow of the flame, which wasn't ideal for interrogation, but it also put the scorching flames directly at their backs. Putting them both in a sense of false comfort by the shadows, and pain by the proximity to the heat. Raask was initially surprised to see the configuration that Fen had been using to question the guards—it was typical in a Skierkan interrogation—particularly for higher nobles, not usually done on those trained in combat.

The guard appeared to be Luruvian, from the western side of the country, with his tanned skin and large brown eyes. This in itself was peculiar. Luruvians were peaceful people and relied on the protections of the D'Ami Cos. He was a large, very strong man, so much so that Raask was a little surprised to see that the stool took the weight of him. He had a long beard that was kept well-groomed and a shaved head. Half of his head was covered in tattoos that looked to be infused with blooded lithe, enhancing his ruthlessness, speed and strength. It could have been the blooded lithe that Raask had sensed —that would certainly elevate blood pressure. But there was something else odd about this man other than the blooded lithe tattoo and his Luruvian heritage.

"Name?" Fen asked.

The guard looked Fen up and down in disgust.

"Name?" He asked again.

"Vikram." A lie. Raask stepped forward, getting a better look at the tattoos. They were written in a language that Raask himself did not know or recognize. Again, peculiar, since Raask knew just about all of the languages spoken on this side of the Arkts. The script was interconnected and filled with a combination of long dashes and swirls that Raask couldn't make any sense of.

Fen watched Raask as he got closer to Vikram. His eyes were on Raask as he asked, "And who are you loyal to?"

"Whoever pays." Vikram answered, jutting out his jaw in annoyance. Again, this was another lie. And it wasn't the blooded lithe on his skull, this was certainly a lie, Raask felt as the blood in his brain pooled into the sector responsible for creating, not remembering.

Raask stiffened. Fen moved on. "Do you know who this is?" He pointed to Aria.

Vikram shook his head. Another lie.

"Do you know who I am?"

Vikram shook his head no. Lie.

Fen pointed at Raask. "Him?"

At this, Vikram nodded. Finally a glimmer of truth. "Hauth, the Slayer and Protector of Etra." It was the first he had heard such a title. So much for keeping a low profile at his new chance of life.

He couldn't help but smirk at that and look back at Aria. She rolled her eyes, but he could see the tiny smile she tried to stifle.

She may hate him and have tried to kill him, but at least she still found him funny.

"Do you care about this war between the Morlok crown and the rebels?"

"Not in the slightest." A lie.

"If you were to pick a side, which would you choose?"

"Whichever one Mr. Callady told me to."

Lies. Lies. Lies. But none of it was enough to confirm if he was secretly aiding the King. He could be lying and still have a preference for the rebels. That was the difficult part in sensing lies, it didn't really tell what the truth was, just that the lie wasn't it.

But then Vikrum turned to Aria. And he felt it. Rage and lust.

And it was enough proof for Raask.

With nothing but a thought and a snarl he couldn't suppress, Raask stopped Vikrum's heart.

CHAPTER 21
ARIA

Aria knew immediately that Raask had killed him. And some part of her knew that it was for her. It was a selfish and self-absorbed thought. For he could have just been protecting the rebels, whom he seemed to have gravitated towards.

But it wasn't.

He did it for her. She knew it as true as she knew the taste of blood and the feeling of the sun.

She knew him intimately, the way his magic and his mind worked, so of course she knew it was by his magic that Vikrum was dead. What she didn't know was how Fen seemed to know. He looked at Raask, eyes wide and jaw tense. Assessing a predator. A threat.

Aria watched Fen, she had gotten to know him well enough in this time to know his mannerisms. And the way in which he scanned Raask, it was more than the primal fear of witnessing a touchless and thoughtless kill. Fen, somehow, had begun to recognize Raask.

"Aria," His eyes snapped towards hers. There was anger in those eyes. Betrayal, too. It was a look Aria knew well. "Tell me that you didn't know."

She swallowed, not out of fear, but at the discomfort at being caught in her stupidity. And that's what it was, stupid. To trust a Morlok? To bring him into their plans? Stupid, stupid, stupid.

Fen let out an aggravated sigh. He kicked Vikrum off of the stool and took a seat on it himself, placing his forehead in his hands as he just kept shaking his head. "How?" He asked, still not lifting his gaze from the floor.

Aria herself wanted to know the question that she had been too afraid to ask. She turned from watching Fen, to see Raask's eyes, still watching her. And for some odd reason, she couldn't help but smile. And when he smiled back at her, it felt like the first rays of sun after days of endless storms and harsh winds. He was the last piece of warmth in her cold world. And she was tired of pretending like she wasn't so unbelievably relieved and happy that he was alive. Enemy or not. She craved him, leaning towards his light like a plant towards the sunshine.

Fen's annoyed drawl sliced through the moment like teeth into bread. "For Keepers' sake, you love each other, don't you?" His head was still in his hands, but he had been watching, he saw the moment they'd shared. Caught. The smiles slipped off of their face just as fast as they arose.

"No." Raask answered. Any trace of that moment had disappeared. Of course he didn't love her anymore, she had lied, schemed against him, taken credit for his death, and rallied troops against his kingdom. The one-word rejection sank into her. Burrowing into the endless knots of grief and despair that fueled her anger. She hoped none of it showed on her face, but one look at Fen told her that he could see it now. He understood now, what he was dealing with in terms of her heart. He could see her weakness.

Shame crept its way across her cheeks and added to the tornado of emotions in her gut. Shame that Fen could see her weakness so clearly. Shame that her ancestors, who had fought with everything they had to kill the Morloks, were somehow seeing this, seeing her weakness too. She wasn't meant to love. She was meant to lead her people to glorious retribution. Love was never a part of her destiny.

And she knew that.

But it didn't snuff out that tiny flame of hope that she couldn't let go of.

Fen looked back at Raask. Thankful for the brief levity from his heavy gaze, Aria allowed herself a moment to sink into herself, to regroup, remember who she was. Fearless. Vicious. Bloodthirsty. Cruel. The words that once felt like compliments now tasted sour against her tongue. She was tired of it. How much longer would she have to fight? And if they did win this war, could she finally let go then and rest?

But she knew there was no rest for her. Just as there was no love or family outside of Mayta.

"How are you here, Prince?" Fen nearly spat out the title. Oh, he was pissed. She was very used to his annoyance and aggravation, but rarely did he look so completely mad. It was almost a little refreshing as she felt mad just about every second of her life.

"I don't know." Raask's voice was quiet, quieter than she had ever heard. Hollow too. "I remember being buried alive. And then I remember waking up, choking and coughing on the black soil. I remember digging myself out of the grave. Crawling into the woods where I stayed until the morning." He was looking at Fen as he spoke, and Aria wanted him to look at her. She wanted him to tell *her* how he had survived. About how scary it must have been. She wanted him to seek comfort in her arms, even though the Gods knew she didn't know how to give it. How badly she wished she understood how to love, it tormented her far more than she wished to admit. A piece of her, a part of her foundation, wished so desperately to not live a life of great retribution and violence as she was designed for, to not be the savior of her kind, and instead to live a gentle life with the only person who ever really saw her. But she was not meant to be a person, but a weapon. Somebody had to save her people. And it had to be her.

As Raask continued, Aria could picture his words so clearly, as if she was seeing the scene for herself. She braced her heart with pieces of cold stone, enforcing it and hardening it to ensure it wouldn't break at his words.

"And when I went back to the castle, looking for someone who was no longer there, nobody seemed to recognize me. Nobody knew who I was. And at first it was horrifying, like a nightmare I couldn't wake up from. But then I got to thinking about it, and I realized it was a gift. I didn't have to be Raask anymore. I could live a life free of the burden of the Morlok crown. So I became Hauth. I got a job at the Gray Goblin as a bartender, and now after the whole sea wraith thing, I became a Vermilli. What you saw at the crematorium, that was my first time seeing the rebels. I guess I was curious."

Fen absorbed his words, the anger was written in the tightness of his jawline, the exhaustion in the slump of his shoulders. The war had already been complicated. Messy. And this just added a whole new level that he hadn't been aware of. One that Aria herself wasn't sure she understood, nor wanted to.

"Are you still curious about the rebels?" Fen asked. Aria wondered if she was grouped into the rebels, was he still curious about her? Did he think about her? Gods, she felt pathetic even thinking the questions. It was an endless agony constantly being pulled in a hundred different directions with a hundred conflicting emotions. And she felt each one so strongly. It was her greatest gift and her greatest curse.

Raask was hesitating to answer. He was not one to mince his truth to protect feelings, so if there was something he was hiding, it was to protect himself.

Maybe he did think of her. The thought was instinctual, hopeful even. Still, it made her want to puke.

His next question surprised her. "You now know my greatest secret and I still know nothing about you."

Fen lifted his head from his hands, and shrugged his shoulders in a look that seemed to say, *fair enough.* "Ask me anything you'd like."

Immediately Raask rattled off questions. "Who are you? Where are you from? How have you gained power in the revolution? How do I know I can trust you? And what is your relation to Aria?"

Fen leaned back, not afraid to feel the lick of the flames against his back. "Fen is my real name. I'm from the Gaulic. I've been granted power by the Keepers of the Wood who have appointed me as their liaison with Skierka. You don't know you can trust me because I don't know which side you're on. And the syrens, including Aria, are unofficial allies of the Gaulic. Unofficial because the Gaulic has not officially taken a side in this war. If we choose to fully enter this war, that will be at my say with the Keepers' approval."

Truthfully, some of this was a surprise to Aria. She didn't know they were unofficial allies. She just assumed that the Gaulic had no army to offer. She also noticed that he conveniently left out the fact that he wasn't human. "And why aren't you offficial allies if you seem to believe so strongly in this revolution?" Raask asked.

Aria didn't miss the annoyance springing up on Fen's face at the question. "I can't divulge that information. Certainly not to the heir of the Morlok crown. But I can say that while my kingdom isn't offi-cially at war with yours, the rebel party has my full support along with many other creatures of the wood."

"Yes, well, I didn't want to be rude but now that you've brought it up, what exactly *are* you?"

"A hylbra." Raask's eyes narrowed on Fen, seemingly assessing his anatomy.

"Can you change?"

Fen stood, taking great offense at the question. He closed the space between himself and Raask in one quick step. "I am no parlor trick. I will not change for your entertainment." Raask didn't back down, but he did not repeat his question to see Fen in his dog form. Aria herself had asked the same thing, Fen had refused then too, but not quite as aggressively. Still in Raask's face, Fen huffed, "Now, will you remain a coward? Hiding from the problems of *your* kingdom? Or will you join the rebels?"

Aria wanted to step between them. Raask may be able to stop a heart with a thought, but Fen was as quick and as dangerous as they came. But she stayed put, frozen in place by Fen's question. Wasn't that what it would all come down to anyways? Unlike her, Fen had no qualms and no fears with asking the questions they needed Raask to answer. He was unclouded by the torturous feelings that made everything so much harder for Aria. Maybe this was her chance to hear what she needed to hear without having to be brave enough to ask.

But Raask... He didn't step up. He didn't grunt back. Instead he shrank in on himself, looking to the ground instead of Fen's eyes or Gods-forbid even hers. "I'm here to help you weed out any traitors in Caden's guard. But after this, I go back to being Hauth."

Rage flashed across Fen's face at the same moment that Aria felt the last little bit of her cold heart breaking. Maybe the man she had loved did die. Or maybe he was never who she thought he really was.

"Understood," Fen responded, stepping away from Raask. Aria avoided the assessing look he gave her. She wanted to scream and throw things, demand that Raask step up. She knew that he was the answer. That he could be the king to bring peace to the Arkts.

Oh, how the people flocked to him? How they looked to him no matter his name or title? He was a born ruler. And he was going to waste it all away on what? To gamble and drink as the realm went to shit? To live a normal life? The one thing she secretly craved, but knew she could never have. It wasn't right, she knew it, he knew it, and he knew she knew it.

Her heartbeat quickened, and she prayed to the Gods that as the drums across the Arkts quickened with it, her people would think she was doing something courageous and not falling apart at the seams.

Raask stayed with them as they questioned the rest of the guards. It took all day and into the night. He killed three more guards. Caden, nor Lok, never said anything as they dragged their bodies out of the cavern. Aria didn't say anything else to Raask that entire day. She stood on the opposite end of the cavern and when they had finished interrogating all of the guards, she waited a few moments before following him up and out.

She considered asking him to eat with her and Fen. It was late and they hadn't had any food all day, he must have been starving. But then Caden brought out that box with the metal arm and Raask stiffened.

Aria had forgotten that it was Raask who had commissioned the limb for her. She felt his eyes land on her as Caden helped fit the metal arm back on. Instead of ripping it right off or even refusing Caden's gift, she let him put it on her. And she watched Raask's face as Caden brushed against Aria's skin, looping and tightening the straps against the piece of her she lost by protecting him. She tasted his anger as he watched Caden's hands carefully. It tasted just like hers.

Caden offered them all a meal. But Raask was already out the door. It closed sharply, echoing into the night. "I guess Hauth won't be joining us." Lok commented, taking a long sip of some dark spirit.

"No, he won't be." Aria turned back to the dining table, and without waiting for the others, cut off a piece of turkey leg and ate it with her hands. Fen, who was equally exhausted, sat beside her and took some of the buttered peas and rolls onto his plate before cutting off a big hunk of ham that he ate carefully with a fork and knife. She knew he wanted to reprimand her for eating like this, and it annoyed her immensely that he didn't, for it meant that he was pitying her.

Silently all four of them ate. It wasn't until the plates had been long cleared that Aria realized she should have been asking them questions, and figuring out which one of them she would back for king.

But too much had happened. And she was too emotionally exhausted.

Fen handled the niceties, and arranged another time for the four of them to meet. Sometime later that week. Aria wasn't listening to them, instead she kept hearing the clanking of her limp metal arm as

Raask's footsteps walked away from her. It was like she was somehow stuck in that moment. The sounds of it on a constant loop, always starting at the beginning again and ending with the slamming of the door.

Fen and Aria went home immediately after and went straight to bed. And things went back to normal over the next week. Fen would go to work and Aria would pretend she wasn't sneaking out with her veil on while he was away. She would practice using her new metal arm every morning. Starting with things she felt should be simple like picking up a cup or braiding her hair. But it wasn't so straightforward.

Everything she did, she did too hard.

She broke many glasses and forks. Every day she got a little bit better though.

The time moved slowly. And nothing felt real.

Her people were fighting a losing war. And she was stuck in Skierka, playing politics when she should be leading the battle front. That's where she belonged, it was silly to even play at this. Fen could handle it. She would back whoever he chose. And Mayta, she would be alright. At least if she joined Viggo in Boai, she could communicate with her through him.

She had this conversation with herself every night as she tossed and turned in Fen's big bed. His snoring from the couch in the other room would occasionally snap her from her spiraling thoughts, but never for too long. Every night she promised herself she would leave in the morning.

And then each morning, when the sun rose and the warmth hit her face, she realized she couldn't leave Etra just yet. She didn't want to be too far away from him. Even if the *him* that she loved was long gone. She felt like she was anchored there, too scared to drift away and lose any chance of Raask waking up and choosing to take his throne. Too scared to drift so far away from the sun and back into the cold dark waters.

It was the morning they were supposed to meet Caden and Lok

for dinner. Aria had travelled to the Salt District to purchase more glasses and another bow to practice with as she'd snapped the last one that morning.

She saw him there, in that red Vermilli cloak. He was working with two others, and they were laughing as they helped to rebuild a small house with a broken wall. She hid in the shadows of an alley further down the shore from him.

She understood how no one had recognized him as the crown prince. He looked lighter. Happier without the weight of the kingdom on his shoulders. He didn't move with the careful movements of a warrior or the required charm of a prince. He looked free.

She could never do what he did, turn her back on her people. But she understood it, maybe better than anyone else. The weight of an entire people should never fall onto one person. It was an insufferable and unbearable burden to put on anyone. But somebody had to do it.

And she would not abandon her people as Raask had.

She hurried home, carrying a massive box of glassware and cutlery, and left Fen a note saying that the syrens would back any king that Fen chose. Not needing to pack a bag, Aria left the small apartment and headed towards the Dahs. As the sun was still shining and the Salt District was filled with people at this hour, she would have to head towards the Gaulic to dive off one of the cliffs. Too wrapped up in her own mission, Aria forgot to build her veil.

CHAPTER 22
VIGGO

As a godling, the realm of the Gods was always at Viggo's disposal on a technical level. But things were never as easy as they were in theory. It was one thing to be summoned to the underrealm and follow the swirling currents that would drag his consciousness into the other planes of existence, but to get there on his own was a different beast.

It didn't help that Viggo was hyper-aware of how much relied on him speaking to Kel, which of course relied on him getting into the underrealm in the first place.

He tried to summon the whirlpool portal of feelings on his own, but none of it worked. Every time he tried to clear his mind, he kept feeling himself falling back to the door of Mayta's mind.

He leaned back against his bed. Beads of sweat from the concentration, frustration, and the simmering heat that penetrated even the darkest parts of the nights in the Surtr Islands ran down his body. He was beyond sore from all of the training. Running. Swimming. Sparring. Teaching. And just being so damned tense for the past year. Helk, he'd been tense for as long as he could remember.

He'd spent his life always trying to protect someone. First his mother from the King, then Raask, then the entire nation of Skierka, and then of course he'd added just about every other innocent soul in the Arkts. He felt the realm on top of his shoulders. And if he relaxed just the slightest, or slipped up at all, people would die.

People *had* died from his lack of control.

More than Raask. Too many people who he would never forget. Long after their tombstones would have crumbled back into dust, he'd be remembering their names in the underrealm. He shuddered thinking of seeing them. It's where he was trying to go after all. Shouldn't he want to see Raask? He loved him more than anything, but that didn't mean he was ready to see him after what he'd done to him.

Wishing to think of anything but Raask, he went back to thinking of his mother. He had promised to visit her more.

He would never admit it out loud, but she wasn't the same since she'd left the world of the living. Her skin grew cold, her hugs, once so important to him as a young boy, had felt stiff and just so damned cold. But at least she was safe. And much happier without the constant fear of his father's moods. And the coldness, a shock to the touch always, did at least suit her better. She loved him and Raask. But Amara Hawthorn was the furthest thing from a warm, loving creature. She was a ruler, cold and cunning, and she loved them as best as she could.

It was these thoughts that allowed Viggo to feel his mother's presence. A cold spindle of thread, as deep a purple could be before turning black, smelling of dried lilacs. It tugged at his gut, a visible thread, pulling him downwards in a coursing rush of waves.

When Viggo opened his eyes, he was in his mother's chambers in the underrealm.

She sat at a desk, her back to him. Her body facing the empty fireplace, hunched over as she furiously wrote away. The sound was as familiar to Viggo as the sound of swords clashing or his father's favorite whip. His mother had always been writing long letters— both orders to be distributed across the realm and journal entries for her records. She was nothing if not diligent. Detail-oriented. She was not cruel in a violent manner, but her cruelty did exist in these writings where people were often reduced to nothing but numbers.

Viggo had appeared on the opposite side of her bed, between the large black ornate bedframe and the stone walls of the palace. It was a large chamber, but fairly empty. Only the bed, and Amara's desk, occupied the room. Doors rested on either side of the fireplace, one leading to the bathroom, the other to the closet. In order to leave, they would have to pull up the latch on the floor, and travel down a long ladder.

Kel was elsewhere. Viggo had never materialized in the under-realm not in the presence of his father. Maybe because he had never followed the thread to his mother before. He took a moment to watch her as she furiously wrote, line after line, using a quill and ink.

"Letters or records?" He asked, voice rough from the interrealm travel.

His mother, the most elegant in any room, did not jump at his voice, no she was too proper for such a reaction. She did, however, stop her scripting. The scratching noise of sharp metal imprinting ink onto paper, quickly began again. She did not turn towards him. She was a queen, and she always insisted it was not her duty to move her eyeline. Others would need to move into hers.

So Viggo walked across the chamber, stopping beside her desk, taking a look at what she had been working on. It was in a language he did not know nor recognize. He was certain that if it were, she would have quickly hidden it away. She remained silent as she scripted away. Only when Viggo recognized the formatting of a letter's closing, and her signature underneath did Amara look up at him.

She ignored his question, but she did smile. Her pale blue eyes crinkled as she took him in. She may have never made him cookies or rubbed his back after a bad dream, but she loved him in her own ways. It was clear by the way she looked at him, even going so far as to turn her head to look at him carefully.

"You've decided to finally visit me?" She asked, her words biting, but her tone as warm as she could be.

"Yes, I'm sorry it took so long." He leaned down and kissed the top of her head. Surprisingly, she brought him in for a cold hug. She held him tightly, and he could have sworn she even smelled him.

"And where is Raask?" She asked, looking at the back of the room as if Viggo had been hiding him back there.

Only Viggo didn't understand the question. "Is he here?" He asked, eyeing the doors to the bathroom and the closet. He didn't hear anything, but maybe he was staying quiet, not ready to talk to Viggo the same as Viggo wasn't ready to talk to him. He swallowed, his throat dry as Surtrian sand.

Amara looked at Viggo with confusion. "Why wouldn't you bring him to visit? He doesn't know his way around here as well as you." She chastised.

Again, Viggo did not understand. Wouldn't Raask know the underrealm better than him at this point after living in it for over a year? Did Raask not tell her that they hadn't seen each other since the incident?

No, not an incident, the murder. Maybe Raask had been protecting him, and had told their mother that he visited often. Gods, it would be like Raask to do something like that. But he couldn't do that though. He couldn't lie, not to her.

"I haven't seen him since... since he died."

Her head snapped back towards him. "What do you mean? It's been over a year. Who has been watching over him?"

He swallowed again. Only his mouth was too dry to provide any relief. "I hoped you would watch over him." His voice was quiet and everything hurt.

"How can we watch him and protect him from down here? For Gods' sake, aren't you at war together? You couldn't watch him?" She stood and began to pace back and forth in tight circles.

But she wasn't making sense. "I don't understand, isn't his soul here?"

Her pacing stopped. She looked at him again, only her eyes weren't sharp with ice but soft like snow. "You don't know, do you?"

The shadows around the desk began to gather around her. They piled up, wrapping around her in a cocoon of warmth and darkness. Piece-by-piece the shadows formed into Kel. He held onto her tightly, tucking her head into the curve of his neck. His hand, clawed in a protective manner, held the back of her head steady against himself. "He doesn't know, my love." He whispered, loud enough for Viggo to hear.

He didn't want to hurt his mother. But Viggo was growing impatient, he wanted to know what he didn't know. "Why didn't you tell him?" He heard his mother's voice, too soft and fragile, asking him. He didn't like hearing her sound fragile. She didn't break against the King's fists nor his whips. She didn't break as ruler of a desperate and angry land. But whatever she knew, was breaking her now. It was too much for him to handle.

"It was not my place to tell him." He whispered back. Kel held onto his mother for several long moments. Without words, he lit the fireplace with a warming fire. The room quickly grew warmer from the heat of the flame and the shadows Kel commanded to cocoon Viggo in a comforting darkness, just as they did for Amara. He felt his heartbeat slow, and his anxiety halt.

When they pulled away, Amara looked at him with such wide sorrowful eyes, Viggo had to stop himself from hugging her. He wanted to hear what she had to say, and didn't want to risk holding up the information any longer. "Raask is not here."

Viggo shook his head, not understanding. "Your father sent his soul back."

Still, Viggo did not understand. He didn't think this was possible. And if it was, it was certainly a break of the Gods Agreement. "He's alive?"

Amara was still, but Kel shook his head. "Not exactly. He is neither dead nor alive. If anything, his soul is frozen in a state between the two."

"Like Skullin?" Viggo asked. Kel gave a short nod to this. "So that is what Raask will become? Another Skullin? Is that the plan?"

"No." Amara answered this, "When Raask's body ages to the point of human death, we will unfreeze his soul and we will bring his soul to rest with us. As was always planned. As is planned with you as well."

This meant that he was in the same body. How had the crown prince of Skierka remained so long in hiding? And more importantly —why? Was he so fearful of Viggo that he hid? A wave of shame and nausea overtook Viggo, causing him to sit back on the hard bed.

"Where is he?" Viggo asked, his voice raw and filled with pain.

"He remains in Skierka." Kel answered, he kept the shadows hugging Viggo. The weight of the eyes of his parents was too much. Raask was alive. Or... He was out in the realm of the living at least. The shadows that clung around Viggo in warmth suddenly shattered across the floor. Shadows darker than the Dahs stained the dark room, shattering from him like shards of his heart and soul. Tears coursed down his face, he hung his head into his hands as he sobbed.

Feelings of relief and terror overtook his entire body. He felt the bed sag with his mother on his right and his father on the left. They rubbed his back silently as he shook. Overwhelmed with the shame and guilt for what he had done and the relief of Raask being back in the realm of the living with him swirled inside of him like an impending tornado. He was feeling everything all at once, a storm of emotions that he felt like he was going to drown in.

But the funny thing was—he didn't.

He didn't know how much time passed, but it must have been a while. The tears stopped, his shaking stopped. The dark menacing and sharp shadows he had summoned disappeared. The only noise came from the sound of his parent's rubbing his back, their cool hands rubbing slow circles against him. He expected his mother to chastise him for his tears. She raised him to be brave. Fearless. The Skierkan Bruin.

But there was no disappointment in her eyes, only pain. She had softened in her time in the underworld. The unconditional and abundant love of Kel tamed some of her sharper edges. She was not afraid to show love or kindness as she once had been. A small part of Viggo's heart that hardened long ago softened at this knowledge, by being soothed by his two loving parents. It was something he didn't think about often anymore, but perhaps it was something he needed to heal some deep part of himself that cracked long, long ago.

Taking a deep breath in through his nose and releasing it through his mouth, Viggo then shared the news from the Luruvians. Both Kel and his mother remained quiet as he shared the updates from the war, and the risk of this becoming a God's war.

When he finished, his mother lifted his chin and turned it towards herself. "We know this already, son. We have been preparing for this." Her gaze turned towards Kel with a tight smile.

It seemed that his parents knew a lot more about what was going on in his realm than he did, and he wondered why they hadn't thought to share it with him until he had brought the news to them himself.

"Voskulle first brought war down to my kingdom with the help of Bjor Morlok. It's his power that runs in your brother's veins and all of the previous Morloks before him, starting with Bjor. Voskulle and Svati were heartbroken when their daughter died. And Voskulle, he needed something to release his emotions. So he began a war. With the help of Bjor's blood magic, they sired the first Creati, the beings that you speak of. The Creati resurfaced a little over a year ago. We suspect that the king has petitioned Voskulle to bring them back as an act of revenge against me, for freeing your mother from his wrath. And perhaps, as a way to try to reign over the underrealm in death."

Viggo took a moment to consider his father's story before responding. "So Voskulle is at war in the realm of the living, but not with the rebels, with you?"

"Yes." His father answered.

"Why haven't you told Tsu and Rahn that Voskulle is breaking the Gods Agreement? Surely they'd put a stop to it." Viggo watched as Kel's eyes darted to Amara. Filled with enough warmth and love to fill oceans with, his eyes crinkled as he took in his mother. Kel reached across Viggo and held his mother's hand in his, squeezing gently. How different would life have been if he had been raised with this kind of love? Was his lack of control learned from the King's insatiable need for power and cruelty? Or was it as much a part of him as his fingertips or his magic?

Of course Kel could not tell Tsu nor Rahn of Voskulle's partnership with the King. For then they would know what Kel had done, and then they'd know of the newly appointed Queen of the Underrealm, and Gods-knew what they'd do with her. Kel would never allow anything to bring harm to Amara. He'd battle every other God and every creature that had ever existed before he'd let them take her.

No. They would have to handle this amongst themselves. A small wave of relief fell down Viggo's back as he realized this meant that Mayta would not have to petition with the Gods now, only the Sistros. Still risky, but not nearly as much.

"So what do we do?" Viggo asked, feeling exhausted and overwhelmed by the emotions of the night.

"For now, we have been putting the souls of those in limbo down here in massive pits. They're locked in together and can't cause any harm from there. But it's not right to keep those souls locked up like that, stuck in eternal damnation without any rest. The ones that you killed in Skierka, however, were released from their torment and have been reunited with their families who have already passed." Amara shivered as she spoke, letting Viggo know enough about the state of the poor souls that the King had mangled the humanity out of. Amara may have softened slightly in death, but she was not afraid of brutality nor gore. The state of these creatures must be something truly dreadful to elicit such a reaction from her.

"So if I see them, kill them?"

At this, Kel smirked.

CHAPTER 23
MAYTA

Nio's black flame spread among the gory creatures like warm butter on toast. As they erupted in flames, their bodies turned to a silver and red ash that fell apart in the wind.

Mayta watched the whole commotion from the back of Nio, sitting between her two massive shoulder blades, in a divot in her musculature. Her thick scales and clever manner of breathing the fire protected Mayta from the heat of the flames. It looked similar to syrenic fire, but felt much hotter.

Nio began to fly away from the valley of ash and snow. Her powerful muscles beat slowly as she began to climb back into the sky. From the excitement of the gore, or maybe the flying, Nio let out another roar, a long sound filled with joy that echoed across the entire valley. Skullin patted her on the back, happy with the carnage she had so easily caused.

It was probably a blessing to kill those creatures, taking them out of their misery. But Mayta couldn't take her mind off of the empty valley. How easy it was for Nio to kill them, and reduce them to nothing but dust in the wind. Was anyone out there mourning them?

Looking for them, the way she looked for Aria when she disappeared without a note in pursuit of some insane scheme she'd so desperately concocted?

Mayta knew what it meant to mourn.

She knew what it meant to care for those who never got any answers, any definite closure to the hope in order to fully move into grief. Silently, Mayta prayed that these souls found peace and that the ones who love them found peace without the closure she and Nio took from them.

Her mind wandered to the thoughts of these creature's families for quite a while. On the back of Nio, where she was safe and waiting to be delivered to the Sistros, she was free to think. Something Aria would love, time to really think and scheme, but something that she herself hated. She liked being distracted. Finding purpose. A wandering mind often found stories, and the way her mind worked, the stories she found were often sad. People who needed her help. Creatures who needed hope.

When the Red Peaks rose into view, any swirling thoughts of despair instantly vanished. In all of her life, Mayta had never seen something so magnificent. Nio flew well above the line of clouds, and still, the mountains towered over her line of sight. The range was long and expansive. She couldn't see the end of the mountain range, nor the beginning. Aptly named, they were mostly made of dark stone with what began as a light red marbling at the base that became more and more concentrated till the peak—which was composed of solid blood red stone.

Temples to Voskulle, the God of War, and Harik, God of Forging, littered these mountains. The homes of Viggo's friends, Emir and Skender, the heirs to the Rakkei people and Silia, a wraithkin whose clan partnered with the Rakkei, were hidden somewhere in these mountain ranges.

Mayta looked all around, but she didn't see any lunar wraiths or even columns of smoke from the Rakkei forges, famous among the entire Arkts for their craftsmanship. She knew they had been hunted, even more so because of the rebellion, but always. She hoped they remained in hiding and had not all been killed off.

The sky began to darken, moving from a pale buttery light to a deep peach before ending in a dark lilac. Just before the light of Baldrei was about to fully give to his sister, Loor, Goddess of the Moon, Mayta saw Mount Disparadi. There was no doubt in her mind which one led to the realm of the Gods. It was bigger than the rest with not a single piece of foliage on the entire mountain. Black, and somehow shiny, the mountain felt ominous to Mayta, reminding her of the dark tower of the Irridesci that rested against the backdrop of the Bleached Palace like a tumor.

Disgusting and wrong. The mountain looked like a vile insult to the beautiful mountains around it. Her grip tightened as she held onto Skullin's waist. He stiffened at first, almost surprised, before sinking into it. "You are scared?" He asked. His voice, an endless infusion of high notes and low, each word a chord and each sentence a melody. Beautiful and terrifying—exactly what she expected of Mount Disparadi.

"Yes." She answered.

Skullin's cloak fell further on his face with his single solemn nod. "It is better to see the Sistros under Baldrei's light than Loor's. We will camp, and meet them in the morning." Mayta didn't understand, she wanted to see them as quickly as possible. The fate of their realm could very well sit on their shoulders. They needed answers, that much was for certain, but she trusted Skullin too much to argue with him. He'd done right by her so far, so she would trust his opinion. It helped that the thought of meeting the spiritual sisters that wove the destinies of each person, and the futures of the entire realm for that matter, during the night was terrifying enough to stop Mayta in her tracks if she was the one currently flying them.

Thankfully she wasn't. And Nio seemed just about as fearless as Aria.

She slowly descended into the spot where two of the smaller peaks met. Mayta slid off of Nio's back and onto the red ground below. The rough scales scratched Mayta's skin as she slid down and onto the stone mountain. Her feet slammed against the rock, hard and slipperier than she anticipated, causing her knees to lock and a jolt of pain to course through her body.

Mayta began to set up camp, or at least tried to. The mountain was barren, not a tree nor a bush to be found, and colder than the currents of the Rigelus trench. She looked all around, for something, anything, to create a camp, to create a fire, to build something that could resemble a home for the night, but nothing was to be found. Nio let out a loud cry, not a harsh or aggressive one, but two short ones. Skullin seemed to understand. He nodded his head in Nio's direction, who then took off. Mayta looked to him in question.

"She will retrieve food for you and herself." Mayta nodded, it's what she hoped the abberack had been saying. Tired and sore from the long travels, and worried about what tomorrow would bring, Mayta sat upon the red stone, inclined in a way that she could rest against the steep edge of the mountain. Even wrapped up in Skullin's robes, the cold penetrated the fabric and hit her directly in the bones. She felt silly now. And weak. So reliant on warmth and food and all the comforts. Who believed she would be the one to act as herald to the Sistros?

Looking back, she was the one who believed it. And she still did, but as the sun set and darkness began to ascend, it was easy to regret. Easier to feel meek and too little for such a daunting task.

Skullin silently sat down next to Mayta. Close enough that he could drape part of his robes across her as a blanket. "Have you met the Sistros before?" Mayta asked, curiosity getting the best of her.

"Once." His voice didn't trail off, nor did he look away. But Mayta could sense there was more to the story, just as she could sense that Skullin would not be sharing it. Not now at least.

Powerful wing beats came from the south. Nio was back with a lamb she had found, Gods-knew where. Nio charred the lamb in her black flame, which Skullin insisted was safe for Mayta to eat. The outside of the creature was blackened, and the inside was raw. Mayta began at the leg and ate her way up to the belly, bone and all.

They slept that night under the protection of Nio's great wing. The creature snored, her belly moving in and out with each breath like a great warm tide. Mayta didn't know if it was the exhaustion or fear or the comfort of Nio's wing, but she fell asleep quickly. When morning came, it seemed to Mayta that she had just closed her eyes, even though the night had come and fallen in the time that she slept.

Skullin, who did not sleep, remained quite still and sat upright the entire night. He never complained about the hours Mayta spent sleeping. And Nio, whose snoring had ceased, must have woken up already. Mayta catalogued each of these details before she opened her eyes. The worry that she evaded the night before had finally come to her in a paralyzing way. Once she opened her eyes, she'd be stuck fulfilling the other tasks of the day.

But now was not a time to be afraid. Her people were counting on her.

After too long pretending to still be asleep, Mayta moved her red curls from her eyes and stretched her arms out as long as she could. Sensing the movement, Nio mimicked the stretch with her wing before tucking it in safely along her back. The sun was bright, but still cold against the Red Peaks. Mayta wondered why, if they were so close to the Gods themselves here, that Baldrei's warmth didn't penetrate the air of the mountains? If she was closer to the God of heat and life, shouldn't she feel warm?

She didn't ask Skullin this question. He was busy holding the rest of the lamb out in front of Nio who puffed small clouds of flame over the animal in attempts to reheat it for Mayta's breakfast. A kindness, from both a creature of death and a creature who had become death. Although truthfully she didn't mind eating meat raw nor cold.

"Thank you!" She yelled, before instructing them to stay turned the other way and create noises so that she could go pee as far away from them as she could safely go.

After eating the head of the lamb for breakfast, savoring the pop of the eyeballs against her teeth. She finally gathered the courage to ask Skullin how they would find the Sistros, and what she should expect from them. Skullin remained quiet long after she asked the question, but his hood stayed facing towards her, a good sign.

"They are older than the universe itself. Older than the first Gods even. They will not stop working, and they will permit you to ask questions as long as they deem fit. They are not terrible, but their dwellings are... difficult." She wasn't sure what he meant by difficult, but she was sure it would be ghastly. Mayta caught Nio's milky eyes angled in her direction. She knew she was blind, but somehow she gathered that the creature could sense her, if not see her in some way.

While the rest of the realm was busy in warfare and starvation and slavery, neither Skullin nor Nio rushed Mayta as she prepared to meet the Sistros. She braided her hair back, not once, not twice, but three times before deeming the braid suitable to meet such esteemed creatures. She splashed the little water she had left onto her face to bring some life back to herself and rubbed the grease of the lamb onto her lips to keep them glossy and hydrated.

She wanted to take off Skullin's robes and see them as herself, but every time she tried, she shivered until she ended up putting them back on and quickly wrapping herself up in the warm fabric. She hoped they wouldn't see it as weakness, but maybe as a sign that even the underworld saw her as somewhat worthy.

Finally, as the sun reached the peak of the sky, Mayta deemed herself as ready as she ever would be. Skullin was the first to climb onto Nio's back, reaching his cloaked hand down to Mayta, where she gripped his black leather gloves and hopped onto Nio. As they settled onto the divot between her shoulder blades, they both pet and scratched at her back. She purred in response, and stretched her long neck out against the ground. The strength of the purr was monumental and Mayta laughed at how hard the creature vibrated with joy. At the sound of the laugh, Nio lifted her head up and gave a few short roars, sounding like her own attempt to mimic Mayta. At this, Skullin gently patted her shoulder blades once again causing Nio to shake her butt, arching slowly against the ground, before taking off into the cold air.

Nio's wingbeats thrummed against the wind, reminding Mayta of the echoed drumming of her sister's heart. Cold air whistled in her ears, coursing through her wild hair, as she held on tightly to Nio. No more cries of joy or laughter, not now, not when she was about to meet the Sistros. The ancient sisters. Weavers of fate. Craftsmen of time. There would be no running away from whatever they would tell Mayta. Their words would ring truth and only truth.

She had been so certain, on the trip to the Red Peaks, that the Sistros would whisper to her secrets of how they would win the war. To give her faith in hope and faith in the future of the realm. But what if they didn't have any soothing words to offer? What if their prophecy was only one of pain and despair?

Her fingers tightened on the grooves of Nio's scales, and her throat dried. If Aria was here, she would remind her to move forward, always forward. No sense in hesitating. And no sense in the fear that was beginning to settle onto her skin with the cold. Fear was nothing but a waste of imagination and endorphins.

Mayta had to be brave.

They approached Mount Disparadi. A tall and wicked thing. Nio, who had been climbing the sky at a steady pace, swooped her body down low and angled herself to climb at a far steeper rate. The mountain was sleek and dark. She had no clue how she was supposed to climb it if Nio hadn't arrived, or Gods forbid, if she hadn't had met Skullin in the Gaulic.

Mayta had no idea what they were looking for, nor how they would know when they were in the correct place to meet the Sistros. She remained silent on Nio's back and at Skullin's side, entrusting them with her quest as she mentally prepared to meet the bringers of her fate. The harsh winds stung her eyes and the cold and the fear began to penetrate past her skin. Intense nausea and dizziness came over her. Somehow sensing her distress, Skullin held his gloved hand over hers. A gentle reminder that she was not alone. Was death always so comforting? Would he bring her again, on the back of Nio, one day? Would they meet again as old friends, or would he be strictly all business when it was time for her soul?

Was that why he brought her now to meet the Sistros? Was she destined to die upon hearing her future? And Skullin would save time by bringing her straight to Helk?

She didn't believe these questions, not fully, but they raced around her mind like an eel against the kelp forests. All she wanted was to be home. In the comfort of her own room, tucked under the blankets of seaweed, among her collection of pearls and human jewelry she had taken over the years.

"Skullin?"

"Yes?"

"Will you tell me when we arrive?"

His hood turned towards her, but she quickly shut the world out. She lifted the cloak far over her head, like how she used to as a child, hiding under the blankets. Immediately she was warmer and more secure. From far away, she heard Skullin's answer, "Of course. Rest."

She leaned her head onto his shoulder and closed her eyes.

Sleep came to her, even though she was certain it wouldn't.

She awoke to a gentle shake of her shoulders. By the stillness of Nio's back, she could tell that they had landed. Either Nio landed extremely gently, or Mayta had been far deeper asleep than she had realized. With one deep breath in, and a long exhale out of her mouth, Mayta lowered the hood back and looked around her.

They were higher now than all of the other mountains surrounding Disparadi. But not high enough yet for the stone to turn from the deep gray to the red peak. The mountain was not quite as steep as it had been closer to the base, and Nio found an area to land that was as close to flat as such a monstrous mountain could get.

Directly ahead of where they landed was the opening to a cave. The blackness of it seemed to creep out onto the mountain like the flicking tail of a mischievous cat. The cave entrance was approximately double her height and wide enough for three or four people to enter side by side.

Nio's long neck doubled back, looking Mayta in the eye as she rested on her back. A long and pained moan escaped from Nio's closed mouth, a sound of worry, a warning. Mayta reached her goose bumped arm out towards her and Nio closed the gap, allowing Mayta to place her hand on the bridge of her snout. Gently, Mayta rubbed the scales. Giving sweet Nio a small pat before turning to slide down her scales and onto the mountain beneath. Just as before, the ground felt hard as she slammed her feet flat against it. A wave of pain coursed through her body from her knees, but what Mayta noticed above all was the lack of sound coming from Nio's other side. Skullin had not followed her off of the abberack.

When Mayta turned around, she saw that Skullin remained mounted on Nio. His arm, with his long cloaks draped below, extended and pointed towards the cave. Without words, Mayta understood. This was her duty. Skullin would remain outside of the cave if she needed him. But this was her quest to take.

Mayta bowed her head, her red curls falling across her face as a gust of wind pushed from the cave and directly onto her. With wild eyes, she turned back towards the cave entrance, seeing that the gust of wind had come with black shadows. They wrapped around her on the mountain, not yet becoming a dimensional object, but remaining an outline against the dark stone of the mountain.

It was time.

With heavy steps, Mayta followed the beckoning of the shadows. The air was cold and unforgiving against Mayta's face. She continued on, bracing for the impact of the strong wind pushing out from the cave. Only as soon as she entered, the wind stopped slapping against her. Yet she could still hear it whistling out behind her.

There were some dark strange magics at play on this mountain.

The cave fed directly into a long and tight chamber. Impossible to enter with an army. This cave demanded solitude. Demanded bravery. And for any human or creature without excellent eyesight in the dark, a torch—or at least fire magic.

Mayta could see the cave clearly. Black walls with veins of deep purple that sparkled. Occasional dropped weaponry like a sword or a bow were scattered here and there. Some looked ancient and rusted, others still shined, reflecting the purple iridescent veins in the cave walls. It smelled damp and ancient. Again, reminding Mayta of the Irridesci tower so very far away. Like fungus and blood and ancient tomes.

There was no question of which path, only one hall stretched ahead of her. She walked it for what felt like at least an hour, regretting not packing any snacks or water. But Skullin had walked this path before, and he would have given it to her if he thought she needed it. So she must not have been very far.

Dropped weaponry stopped, and in its place began the piles of bones. Mostly human. A femur bit in half. Skulls cracked open across the top, as if whomever had killed this poor human had drunken from their brain like soup from a bowl. Most were long dead, fully decomposed with nothing left but meatless bone and dust. Some were fleshier. She couldn't imagine what kind of modern human would have the guts to take such a journey.

A dark thought fell across her mind. Perhaps they had not chosen to enter the cave, but had been dragged... Gods, they could even have been called to the cave, like a moth to a flame. Humans did not understand ancient magics. Particularly not the Skierkans, who had banished the knowledge from all of their schools. Burned the books. Burned those who taught it anyways. They did not understand that some creatures could create a sense of longing, a psychic trail for the victim to follow desperately. Did the Sistros eat? Did they have this kind of magic? Mayta didn't know, and her usually curious mind was not in such a hurry to find out the answer.

The bones kept growing in numbers. Piled in neat stacks. Some bitten in half and thrown as if in a tantrum. The recently deceased body of a sprite lay in a pile of dried blood. It couldn't have been the one she accidentally killed last year, on that night that Viggo lost control, the night she buried a crown prince, but it looked identical. The same blue and green swirls across the wings, with the same dots of black along the edge. The same burn spots, from where her blood had landed on the poor creature.

Overwhelmed with grief, Mayta kneeled in the dirt. Through the thick fabric of the cloak she could feel the sharp rocks piercing the skin of her knees and her shins. With shaking hands, she lifted the creature into her palms. Inspecting it closer.

It was the same.

She didn't know how, but it was the same.

Tears instantly welled at the corner of her eyes. She couldn't wipe them away, not now, not while holding this little life that she took. The life of an innocent, lost from her carelessness. Her tears dropped onto the cavern floor with plopping sounds that didn't quite match the size of her tears. It sounded larger and denser than was possible.

She cried and cried as she held the little life that she took.

She cried and cried as she considered all of the lives that she'd taken.

Overwhelming grief and shame hit her like a rogue wave. Penetrating deep into her bones and into her soul. She was always considered the kind one, the sweet sister... The syren of hope and love... Mayta the Precious. A title she loved, one she thought she had earned.

She was no more Mayta the Precious than she was Aria the Ruthless.

She wanted to be soft and loving, and she could be, and she was happiest when she was... But there was a part of her that was capable of such cruelty. Such violence. Whether or not she wanted to take these lives, she had. Want didn't matter much to the victims, did it?

A hand, cold and bony, gripped her shoulder like a hug.

Another creature mimicked the motion on her other shoulder.

A final pair of hands sat against her back, still shaking under the weight of her tears, providing comfort and reassurance. Mayta was not alone. But she was also not afraid.

"You understand, don't you?" The one directly behind her asked. Her voice was not as Mayta imagined, not the same layered sound as Skullin nor the Irridesci. It was sweet. Pure. The voice of her mother, from the one memory she had of her being kind. Brushing her hair, being gentle on the knots instead of pulling to make them hurt more.

Did the Sistro mean to conjure such a sweet memory? Was it a trick or was she truly trying to comfort her? Mayta knew she had to be weary. But she did understand, and with that understanding came the unbearable weight of shame. The bodies were not the victims of the Sistros, nor any other beast that lived in this cave.

They were her own.

Mayta was not built of the same stuff that her sister and mother were. Slaughter did not feel righteous to her. It felt like she was damning her own soul. The memory of each kill had imprinted itself on Mayta's mind, painful wounds and scars that would never heal. She tried to ignore them. And often she was successful. But seeing them all like this...

Mayta understood. "Yes." She answered, her voice weak when she knew she should be pretending to be strong. "Why? Why do you show me this?"

The one on her right side answered this time. "You come to us asking for your future, yes?" Her voice sounded eerily like Aria's. Cruel and cunning and wise and sinisterly sweet.

"Yes." Mayta answered, again, not forcing the illusion of strength. The Sistros saw her for who she was. Mindlessly, she rubbed her thumb on the body of the sprite in a comforting manner. The sprite was not there to feel her comfort. But it assured her, hoping that somewhere, somehow, the sprite would somehow sense the love she was passing on to the poor creature.

Now, the one on the left spoke. Her voice, both a ghost and a prayer that sounded nearly identical to her own as she spoke those last words to Raask. "How do you expect to accept your future, if you do not accept your present nor your past?"

Mayta placed the sprite back onto the ground. She gently placed the creature on its belly, arranging the still pliable body so that the sprite looked as if it was merely sleeping. Wings uncrushed, standing straight up in the air, perhaps in flight wherever it laid dreaming, wherever it rested its soul.

"Is this what you want from me? Ask whatever you want. Demand whatever you need. Just please... Please... My sister, my people, they need this. If my cruelty and my violence is to be worth anything, please, allow me to hear the prophecy. I'll do whatever you ask of me. I swear it." Mayta lifted her arm up above her head, allowing the sleeve of her cloak to bunch by the shoulder, revealing the skin of her arm. Silently, she conjured the claws of her syrenic form. Painfully, she dragged the claw of her index finger down the middle finger of her left hand all the way through the palm. Then the thumb. Then the pinky. One for each sistro. She fisted her left hand allowing the purple blood to smear all over and placed her hand on the floor of the cave thus sealing the blood promise she had made to the Sistros. She would do anything to hear the words of the prophecy. Good or bad—she needed to hear, to bring it back with her.

Called by the feeling of pain from her bloody hand and the agony of her grief, Mayta became aware of Viggo. He knocked against her mind, a gentle rap of the knuckles. Did he know she was with the Sistros? She was supposed to call him, allow him to take this journey together. But now that she was here, what she'd forgotten to do—to share this with him—now became an active choice. This was *her* quest to take.

She felt a well of strong emotions towards Viggo. Admiration and respect. A trace of longing too. But she was not ready for him to see these parts of her. Not yet.

So she turned Viggo away, not allowing entrance to her mind. Going back on her deal with him. With the man, the godling, who had only protected her and saved her since he came into her life. This was private. But also, a test. Would he fall into a rage at the rejection? At her declining his request to enter her mind? Going back on their deal? She needed to know what kind of man he was, if she did not give him whatever he wanted. She had learned to not be as trusting and to say no.

Mayta summoned thoughts of stalactites and stalagmites at the corner of her mind that bridged his and hers. Pushing a wave of dense Dahsian waters to hold him out should he try to force himself in. She did not think he would. But just in case. She needed him to know that while she was soft and lovely, she was not incapable of violence.

She felt his presence disappear from the door of her mind. The warm comforting darkness left her good and truly alone with the Sistros.

Looking back down to the cavern floor, Mayta was surprised to see that her bloody handprint had disappeared. And with it, the body of the sprite, and the presence of the Sistros at her back.

Slowly, the cave began to crumble all around her. And while the dark stone fell apart, the image of a grand room began to fall in its place.

CHAPTER 24
RAASK

The sun shone high above Hauth's head as he ate his lunch. If not for the strong sea breeze from the Dahs, it would have been one of the warmest days of the winter. Beads of sweat fell on Raasks's sandwich. Dark rye, thick cheese, and smoked pork that Ofte had packed for them from home. Alko picked up a couple of ales at the Gray Goblin. And Hauth provided a couple of butter cookies he had paid some kids to pick up from Arthur, his old guard, and the closest thing he had to a father other than his brother.

He had yet to see Arthur. Several times he had walked all the way to the heavy big green doors before turning around and rushing away. He was too much of a coward to face him. Arthur, who knew him better than anyone, was one of the first to see him as more than just the spoiled child of a powerful man. He shuddered, considering what Arthur would see when he looked at him now.

Arthur would see through Hauth in a second. He'd see what he had been hiding from himself, that it was not a wish for a life without responsibility, but fear that drove him from his old life. And Arthur, who was so righteous and kind, it was his shame that Hauth could not face. Arthur was one of the first to instill some of the values of the rebels into him. To see the value in people as people, not to merely see them as numbers or parts of a war game. Arthur was the first truly kind man he had known. Maybe the only kind man he had ever known.

He took a bite out of the sandwich, flavorful and juicy as it was, it slid down his throat like a rock. It was bad enough that Aria had seen him like this, he couldn't handle it if Arthur saw him now. He was supposed to be king. To create a better Skierka, not by rebuilding brick by brick, but by leading and changing the core of his very nation. Placing values away from power and greed and back into the welfare of their own people. There was so much he was supposed to do as Raask.

Hauth, Ofte, and Alko sat together on a small, completed area of rock wall. Silently, they watched the wind blow through the dense pine in the Gaulic and the black waves of the Dahs. Hauth did his best to avoid looking at that green door of Arthur's, it beckoned to him like a constant reminder of his deepest secret and biggest shame.

He took a swig from his pint of ale, hearing both Alko and Ofte follow suit. "You made this bread?" Alko nudged Ofte. Hauth turned towards him and caught his smile.

Ofte answered between chews, "Made it last night, so it's still fresh." His wide eyes crinkled from pride.

"It's insane. Incredible. I don't know how you go from breaking your back all day to going home and baking bread, but I'm happy that you did." Hauth joked, popping the last corner of his sandwich into his mouth.

Ofte seemed to consider this as he swirled the ale around in his mug, taking a moment to smell it before answering. "It makes me happy. I get to go home and see my wife, and create something with her. I don't want to go home and just wait until work tomorrow. I—I want to live for something more."

Alko nodded knowingly. "Yeah, it's like, there's got to be more than this, you have to have something to live and work for, I guess."

He took his moustache comb out of his pocket and mindlessly ran it through his moustache, straightening out any loose hairs or crumbs from the meal.

Alko's answer surprised Hauth. The two used to go out drinking and smoking late into the night. Lately, he hadn't seen his friend at the pubs or smoking as much emerald. Hauth retrieved his bundle of cookies from the deep pocket in his cloak. He carefully unwrapped it and handed it out to his friends. "And what are *you* doing?" He asked when he handed Alko the butter cookie. Some of the crumbs from being packed tightly in his pocket fell as he passed it. At that same moment, the wind began to pick up and swept the crumbs away and towards the opposite end of the shore towards the cliffs of the Gaulic.

Tracing the crumbs' path through the air, Hauth noticed movement up on the cliff all the way on the opposite end of the Salt District, across from where they now sat. Without thinking, he stood to get a better look and knocked over the cookie that sat on his lap.

A figure was barreling through the forest. As the pine was particularly dense in that area, he could only see it through the occasional gap in the trees. Red Vermilli cloaks followed behind. Darker than the deepest of red wines and faster than a wraith, the Vermilli were closing in on the creature.

Hauth sensed Alko and Ofte standing beside him. "What's going on?" Ofte asked, the worry and concern tangible in his voice.

"I don't know," Alko answered.

Somehow, deep in his gut, Hauth knew. He'd know her from across a battlefield, recognize her in the blackest of seas and the darkest of nights, sense her from six feet under and flock to her regardless of her intentions with him. She could kill him for all he cared, engulf him in her flames or bury him alive again and again, but he couldn't help himself. He'd always go back. There wasn't a single place in this entire realm that he wouldn't follow her, crawling if he had to.

There she was.

She left the line of the forest. Running, faster than he'd ever seen her. The Vermilli were gaining on her, Hauth held his breath, unable to watch and unable to look away. Instinctively he reached for his blood magic, but they were too far. He could barely see them as more than blurs in the forest.

She dove off of the cliff and into the water. Good, that was smart, they couldn't follow her there, into her domain. For the second time in his life, he watched as she fell through the sky.

Down, she fell. Not as high as her fall from the wraith, and this time the waters would accept her as their own. She would not break against the soil. She'd live. She had to live.

And she would have, if the Vermilli were not armed with arrows.

They pierced through the sky, and stopped Raask's heart.

He watched as they tore through her. As purple blood fell through the sky. As she landed into the water, unmoving.

He didn't think as he ran towards her. He kept his eyes locked in on her location, he couldn't lose her. His feet stamped against the shore, faster than he had ever moved. Sharp sand turned to cold waters. He kept going. When the water reached his thigh, he dove, swimming towards her. He pumped his legs and his arms in the water, so cold against him, yet he could swear the sun shone directly onto him keeping him from risk of hypothermia.

He was still far away, but he could sense her now, her violent and poisonous blood seeping into the water. As he swung his hands to the front of him, pushing the water back, he did his best to command her blood to switch into the red of a human's, just as she did so long ago. He'd need her blood to make the change so he could get close enough to grab her without burning his skin off.

He'd never done such a thing, changing blood, but he felt his magic rising from his core. Bringing newfound energy into his body as they sang in glory and celebration, his magic that he had neglected since killing those people at the Callady Estate hungered for more. Perhaps because his magic was eager, perhaps because he was desperate, he wasn't sure how, but he was sure that it worked.

He could feel the change in her blood as it leaked into the oil-like waters. No longer acidic and heavy, her blood now leaked red and metallic as a human's.

But it was too much. She was losing too much.

The closer he swam, the more he could sense her injuries. Three arrows pierced her. One in her left shoulder. Another on her right thigh, piercing from the left side of her quadricep and out through the right. The last punctured her gut.

As he lifted his head he heard the cries from the Vermilli guard who had shot her. They screamed and cheered for him, thinking he must have dove after her to ensure she was captured. As he drew a breath in, he lifted a hand towards them, and stopped their hearts, killing his own guard.

The tide was dragging her body further out into the Dahs, and Raask was not the only creature in the Dahs who could sense blood from great distances. As he moved deeper into the water, he could feel the waters stirring against his skin. Perhaps he should have waited til he got closer to shift her blood to humanic. But it was too late, terrified that another creature would be driven into a frenzy from her blood, he pushed himself harder. Faster. Giving everything he had and everything he didn't to reach her.

And then he was there. He gripped her body, gently wrapping his arm around her torso, carefully avoiding the arrows. Spiked by the looks of them. These would not be simple to remove, nor to heal.

Her body was slick with blood and cold, far too cold. He gripped her tightly against his side, careful to keep her head above water so that she could breathe.. As he towed her through the water, she carried easily on top of the Dahs. So small. For such a dangerous creature, she was so small as she lay unconscious. It was too much for him.

He didn't know if anyone would recognize that he was the one who had killed the guard. But he prepared for a fight when he reached the shore. He didn't want to kill any more Vermilli, but he would if he had to, if they threatened her, he'd do it without question.

He was still too far from the shore, and he could sense more creatures. Unable to see through the Dahsian waters, he could feel them as they swam against him. Small creatures, by the feel of it, glided past him with ease as he panted, swimming as fast as he could. The creatures nestled themselves against his side and underneath Aria, helping to propel them forward much faster than before.

Arrows began to rain down upon them. Raask continued swimming, continued pumping his arms and his legs, his lungs screaming from the distance he'd covered and the magic he had used. More arrows, they'd decided he was an enemy to Skierka, or at least decided it was safer to treat him as an enemy. An arrow came close to hitting Aria's head, Raask threw her head underneath his shoulder, protected by his body, at the same moment that an eel with gray spiked bones sticking out of its scales leaped out of the water, taking the arrow for Aria.

Every time an arrow would get too close, one of the creatures would leap into the air, taking them for not only Aria, but also Raask.

He reached the closest point of the shore that wasn't encompassed by a cliff. Anticipating a fight, he summoned his blood magic to just under his skin. Again, he felt it sing, vibrating in his core like a cat's purr, hungry with anticipation.

His feet landed on the bottom of the Dahs, quickly he swept Aria into his arms. She rested limply against his chest as he carried her across the threshold of where water met land. The same place, the same shore, she had crawled out of what felt like a lifetime ago.

He'd carried her then too. To what he thought was safety, he'd thought he had saved her that night, instead he had welcomed his doom into his home with open arms. But it wouldn't matter what she put him through. It wouldn't matter because he would always come back to her. Always save her when she needed him. For she was everything he wished to be. A fire in the darkness, warm and all consuming.

She would do anything for her people. Where he ran away from it all, she ran directly into the arms of her enemies just at a fool's hope of saving her people.

Her cold blood soaked his arms, causing a shiver down his spine as he prepared for whatever was waiting for him on the other side of this shore.

But it was not as he expected. Two bodies stood with their backs to him. Two Vermilli cloaks, standing swords out and angled, pointed at the horde of Vermilli trying to get at him and Aria.

His friends. Alko and Ofte stood between him and his love, and a horde of Vermilli. With no mask and no protection of identity, he wished they didn't. They didn't know of his magic, that he could kill these Vermilli with half a thought. Because he had kept himself a secret from them, they would now lose everything.

He could see the recognition in the Vermilli's eyes; they knew Alko and Ofte. And so Raask had no choice. If he were to temporarily stop their hearts, they would still remember their faces. Their names. Their families. Making a fist in his hand that held up Aria's legs, he felt his magic settle around their hearts. With a squeeze of the fist, they each fell across the black sand with several loud thumps.

Ofte and Alko turned to him with wide eyes. Did they know who he carried? Did they understand what had just happened? He panted, catching his breath. He had not trained his magic in far too long and using it felt like a relief, but he had drained himself quickly.

They needed to move. Get out of sight. "Cover your faces with your cloaks." Alko and Ofte shared a look with one another. Alko immediately shoved his hood over his face, careful to fully cover himself. Ofte hesitated, he was stiff and dazed as he looked back at the dead Vermilli, and then again at Aria as she continued to bleed in Raask's arms. He sped past them. Taking a quick look at his location, Raask silently cursed his luck. He wanted to bring her back to Fen's apartment. He trusted Fen with her, knew the apartment was safe and secure with only one entrance and the only person with access was Fen himself.

But it didn't make sense. To get to Fen's apartment he'd have to cross busy streets as Aria laid bleeding out. She was too recognizable, and they were too much of a scene. So he'd have to take them to the Caden's estate. It was a far more private path. And Raask was nearly certain that they would have a healer on hand.

Raask's hurried steps rushed to the edge of Etra. He could hear Alko and Ofte following behind, their footsteps just as quick and light as his own.

Aria's breathing turned troubled. Her quiet breaths became loud and pained. He began to run. Not caring who would see or hear, just knowing that he needed to get her help. Whoever came after her, he'd take care of it. He ran from his responsibilities as prince, but he could never run away from her. The one who shared the same darkness, the same weight on her soul, the same bits and pieces that had made him him and her her. He could be awful and cruel and selfish and savage. She could too. And he had to protect her, he *would* protect her. He'd throw himself into her flame just to fuel her fire. Let her burn the world down, him included, as long as her fire burned.

The iron gates, twisted with heavy vines and closed buds, loomed high above. The sun that was so bright as they ate their lunch seemed to have dimmed, even though no clouds masked it in the sky, as if Baldrei himself attempted to hide Raask and Aria from the eyes of Etra. He reached the gate, shoulders rising and falling as he desperately waited for one of the guards to come let them in. When none of them moved, he grew desperate. "Caden! Get out here!" The guards littered the estate, eyes forward and unmoving, not even to tell him to get lost.

"CADEN!" He screamed. He angled towards the side and threw his shoulder against the door to the gate. The cold iron sent a shock to his system as he slammed himself over and over again into it. Ofte's hands, large and gentle, pulled him back by the waist. Silently, he carefully took Aria from Raask, holding her as tight and gentle as a newborn. With Aria out of his arms, Raask beat his fists against the gate. "CADEN CALLADY!" He beat his fists and his body against the gate like the drums of war. Alko joined him in his screaming. "HEL-LO?" Alko cried, eyeing the guards who stood immobile.

When desperation was about to give away to hopelessness, the front doors to the manor flew open. Caden strode down the pathway in swift long strides. He was wearing his glasses, and his hair was ruffed up. Raask knew the man well enough to know that he must have been studying or working on one of the Callady projects. If he was in the library or their workroom, they were on the opposite end of the estate. They must have sent someone to alert him. Why didn't they run? Couldn't they see her bleeding out on the entrance to their gates? A pool of thick red liquid stained the cobblestones. Raask looked at it and back to Ofte. "We did our best to wipe off the blood trail as we followed behind," Ofte answered, eyes on Aria's grotesque wounds.

Caden, who had walked quickly but seemed to have taken his damned time, heard the end of Ofte's comment. He turned to one of the guards closest, "Handle the blood trail." He opened the gate. Ofte was the first to go through, he carefully avoided bumping Aria's head or her feet on the edge of the gate, and followed the path to the house where another guard had let them in. Caden looked carefully at Raask, his gaze lingering on every feature of his face as he shut the great door to his manor behind them.

Aria was already on the dining table, laid out like a feast of blood and gore. His heart nearly stopped as he saw her, wounds and all, laid out and open. She would hate this if she was conscious, knowing that so many people saw her so vulnerable. He wanted to bark at them all to stay away, but he needed them to fix her. Oh Gods, why had he never practiced healing with his magic? Why had it never occurred to him before to use his magic for something more than violence?

But even at the thought, his magic recoiled as if appalled at the thought of being used to heal instead of to break. Why did it not matter what he wanted? Why did his magic insist on harm? He felt trapped, cursed, from the destructive magic he'd inherited.

Healers worked on her, carefully inspecting her wounds and her blood. "What happened?" Caden asked. Alko and Ofte stood over Aria, as if they were her royal guard. Had they figured out who she was?

Raask's breaths continued to labor. His heartbeat was racing, growing out of control. She was there. She was in front of him. He was covered in her blood, could smell it and feel it coating his body like a waxed skin preventing him from breathing, encasing him in his own horrors like a cage. Arrows pierced her. Did she feel them? Was she scared? Was she hurting?

He was losing his mind. Panting with such force his lungs felt like they would explode. The room was beginning to spin, and he was too hot, why was the fire roaring so high? He ripped his cloak off, needing to cool down, needing to release himself of the cage of her blood, the reminder that he had failed in protecting her. Alko was in front of him, he had no clue when he had moved from his post beside Aria but he was in front of him. His eyes were mere inches from his. "It's okay. She'll be okay. People survive arrows all the time." Alko grabbed him by the shoulder and dragged him to a chair that he must have placed in the corner of the room as he walked towards him.

"You need to breathe." Alko commanded. Raask nodded, it was all he could do. Alko turned towards Caden and said something he couldn't quite hear, causing him to leave. He came back quickly, and threw him a pair of light pants—no top. Nonetheless, Raask stood from the chair and peeled off all the leathers he wore underneath the Vermilli cloak. He put on the pants that Caden tossed to him and felt a little bit better to be out of the bloody and cold leathers. He placed his head in his hands as he listened to the sounds of the healers working on Aria. Alko stayed at his side.

But as Raask's wave of panic was beginning to subside, he sensed a tension in the room. He looked up, peeling his face off from his fingers, and caught Caden staring at his exposed chest. At the lithe-infused Morlok crest tattoo.

"Raask?" Caden's voice was tense, betrayal written across his face. They'd been boys together. Whether or not Raask was ready for his identity to be known, it now was.

Alko's gaze followed Caden's. Ofte looked over too. The guards and the healers all remained focused on their duties. But he was sure they heard him.

"Actually, he goes by Hauth." Alko walked closer to Raask as he spoke, placing a hand on the hilt of his sword. Raask looked to Ofte who had followed Alko in placing a hand on his own weaponry, except he walked closer to Aria. To grab her, he realized, if things went south.

Raask turned back towards Caden, who was a contender to become king in Raask's absence. Would he try to kill him to ensure Raask didn't come back for the throne?

Caden looked at Alko. "You think I would hurt him? I've known him my whole life. If anything, he is one of the few to understand... One of the few who could actually bring an end to this war too." He turned his gaze back to Raask. "I may not be an heir to a nation, but I am an heir to an enterprise. I understand why you ran. And more importantly, I will not stand in your way of living life as Hauth." He looked back at Aria and then back at him. "I won't allow your secret to leave this room. But for whatever it's worth, I would gladly follow you as king."

Raask nodded. His entire body was stiff and sore. His soul too. Too much had happened all too fast. "Thank you," He muttered. Alko relaxed, dropping his hand from his sword, but not backing away from his closer stance to Raask. Ofte remained rigid as he stared blankly at whatever the healers were doing to fix Aria. He wanted to take them aside, thank them for what they'd done for him, ask them if they had just found out now, or if they had known all along. But now was not the time.

Caden sighed before pulling a chair up beside Raask. He leaned back in the wooden chair, resting his head against the wall behind them as Raask sat at the end of the seat, leaning onto his spread knees. "Are you going to tell me what happened?" Caden asked.

Grief, heavy and wet, sank onto his chest. He didn't want to go through this. Not out loud. And not to Caden. He turned his gaze, feeling the weight of Caden's judgement. "I didn't mean with you. I meant with the queen." He jerked his head, motioning to Aria.

He swallowed. Once. Twice. Every time he reached for the words to explain what had happened, he felt pieces of himself falling apart. He stood up abruptly, moving with uneasiness and an abundance of anxiety, he walked closer to Aria. The healers were working quickly and efficiently, barely speaking to one another, each somehow knowing their role, what needed to be done and when. Their movements seemed mechanical and precise, almost like one of Caden's machines. Raask stood by Aria's head, a hand on either side, leaning over her to carefully watch their work.

Alko was the one to finally answer Caden. "We saw her jump from the cliffs. She almost made it, but the Vermilli were chasing her... And Hauth rescued her. Then brought her here." It seemed cut and dry the way he told it.

Caden seemed confused. He joined Raask at Aria's side, analyzing her body for some kind of answer. Raask had to resist. "She was running towards the Dahs?"

Ofte shared a look with Raask, he'd undoubtedly pieced together who she was—if he hadn't recognized her by sight. Neither of them understood Caden's confusion as the Dahs seemed an obvious destination for the queen of the syrens.

Caden blew out an exasperated breath. "We were supposed to meet this evening." He massaged his temples, clearly annoyed with Aria. He turned towards one of the guards at the edge of the room. "Find Fen, bring him here."

The guard left immediately with a, "Yes, sir."

The healers worked on Aria until the sun dampened into the deep blue of dusk. At some point Caden had fetched Raask a black leather top with sleeves that flared at the end, rendering it relatively useless for sparring, which was what leathers were meant to be worn for. As the heat from his panic had left him hours ago, he thanked his old friend for the change of shirts anyways. Alko and Ofte took seats and ate. Ofte would often look out the window in the direction of his house. The guard who had left in search of Fen had yet to return, nor the one Caden sent to retrieve Ofte's wife upon hearing about her existence. Neither Raask nor Alko had anyone else for his guards to send for.

The fire roared in the pit and Ofte had taken to pacing in front of the windows, checking for his wife. Raask stayed glued to the spot by Aria. He sat in the same chair as earlier, only now it was dragged to be next to her, as he idly played with her hair. The healers had finished their part hours ago and only came in to monitor her healing and spray her wounds with numbing twilight lithe and dab her gums in cyan lithe for the anxiety. The same combination she received on that night so long ago, when she had crawled out of the Dahs and into his arms.

The same combination when she had run towards him during the lunar wraith attack, after she fell through the sky, after she had been crushed by the weight of her own killing.

Why did they keep living through the same events?

Were the Gods giving them chances? Were they getting something wrong, and the Gods would keep doing this until they got it right?

He shook his head physically, hoping the endless questions and thoughts would spill out of him with the movement. The Gods didn't care for the humans, nor the creatures of this realm. If they did, they wouldn't have let it get this far.

There were no Gods coming down to save them.

The thought rattled through his head. Over and over again. Carefully, Raask looked up from Aria and at Ofte. His wide eyes and hands built for kneading breads. Then at Alko. His unease in staying seated, stuck in one place, who always eyed the horizon, and with a couple of ales in him would speak about the other parts of the realm he'd read about and wished to see for his own eyes one day.

And Caden. His slender fingers and darkened eyes. The most brilliant man in Skierka, perhaps the entire realm. And he had chosen to fight against the king, even with so much to lose. He saw each of these men, each of his friends, and saw them for who they really were. And more importantly, for all they had to lose at the hands of a greedy and cruel king.

Aria stirred, letting out a moan of pain. Immediately a healer came to spray her injuries again. Raask watched as her brief expression of pain sank into an easy look of rest.

She would keep going until she had killed the King or he had killed her.

With each breath until that showdown, she would keep throwing herself into danger, she didn't care if she got burned by her own flames, as long as she hurt him. She would happily burn herself alive if it meant she'd hurt him. She'd do anything for her people, or the ones that she loved. And Viggo, Aria's ally, who had killed him when he supposedly loved him above anyone else, would not bat an eye at putting Aria in danger. Mayta probably loved her, but she did turn her own sister in, even if she had plans to release her that night, she still betrayed her to the Skierkans for a fool's hope and a pipe dream.

It had to be him.

Oh Gods, it had to be him.

CHAPTER 25
ARIA

Calloused hands played with Aria's hair, moving from her scalp all the way through to the ends. The smell of spriteberries wafted through her nose as she listened to the oil being dropped into palms and then through her hair once again. She sank into the gluttonous pleasure of being doted on, taken care of for once, allowing herself a moment where she wasn't the queen to a dying people, where the fate of the realm didn't rest on her shoulders.

Just one moment, how much could that hurt? To live in a dream while the world burned away. Isn't that what Raask had chosen?

Oh.

It was his hands which worked expertly through her hair. Memories from deep within her subconscious erupted into the forefront of her mind. It was not the first time he comforted her when she was vulnerable.

The last thing she remembered was being chased by the Vermilli and leaping into the Dahs where... where she was shot by arrows...

She would have thought she was in paradise, but she knew

better than to think she'd ever make it. Tsu only accepted the greatest into his Kingdom of Paradise. When she died, there would not be a warm awakening for her, but the cold despair of the underrealm.

With this thought, she fluttered her eyelids open. Raask. His pale blue eyes were looking down at her, smiling sorrowfully. "Aria." Her name sounded lovely coming from his tongue. The ends of her lips curled upwards at the sound of his voice. "Does it hurt?" He asked.

She shook her head no, unable to look away from him.

A man of the sun, so warm and full of life.

The one who could make her laugh through anything. The one who saw her for all that she was and did not run away in fear. Whenever she thought of Raask she resented the feelings that bubbled within her, but not now, not anymore. Aria had so little joy, so little love given to her, so little love to give. She would not abandon her people. But she would also no longer deny herself love. She just couldn't, not anymore. She basked in his light, soaking it up like a flower.

"This explains a lot." Caden's voice, dry and fatigued, cut through the moment like a blade. Whatever he was commenting on, his voice also answered a few of her questions. She finally looked around, now conscious of the fact that she lay in Caden Callady's formal dining room with a horde of his guards and the two Vermilli she recognized from working with Raask when she had watched them that morning. When Aria started to sit up, Raask's gentle hands met her shoulders, keeping her laying down.

"What?" Raask growled at Caden.

"You love each other, don't you?" Caden asked.

Aria started to sit up, and when Raask placed his palms against her shoulders again, she gave him a look that told him he'd regret it. "Oh please, don't bother denying it. Anyone can see it," Caden added with a smirk.

Aria's fingernails grew into claws.

"Why is she so upset? This is wonderful. We will kill the king, you two will get married, and unite our kingdoms." He said it as if any of this was simple.

She crossed her arms defensively, feeling naked and vulnerable to have been seen not only on the brink of death, but worse, as a creature in love.

Healers with blue ribbons across their biceps hurried into the room. Armed with twilight and cobalt lithe. They began spraying her wounds as Caden continued, "Is it *not* a great solution to our troubles?"

Aria's jaw tightened. It was one thing, to allow herself moments of joy, but another to give her people away. It would always come down to her people. If Aria wanted to be weak, if she wanted to take orders from some nobleman's kid with a mind for creating gadgets, then it wasn't just her pride on the line, but the future of her people. Her people... who had been enslaved and hunted for far too long. No matter what, she had to be strong for them.

"If Aria chooses to marry me, it will not be for the purpose of uniting our kingdoms." Raask's voice was cold and deadly. His words left shivers down her spine. If she chose to marry him, as if it were her choice. But how could it be hers, when the last she spoke to him he wanted to remain Hauth? She was a queen. The most wanted creature in all of Skierka. Perhaps the realm for the ransom on her head was a pretty price. Anybody who married her, would never live a life of normality, but a life of the very danger and responsibilities he was trying to run away from.

"Are you saying that as Raask or as Hauth?" Aria spat the words out like venom. Raask turned his gaze from Caden back to her. Their eyes met, sinking into each other's fires.

"I'd like the room." Raask commanded, keeping his eyes on her. Aria didn't waiver as she listened to the hordes of people moving towards the back of the house and what sounded like two people moving out to the front yard.

Aria turned around, still sitting on the table, only now facing Raask who stood between her and the fireplace. "Well?" She studied him closely, his broad shoulders and long arms, tense as he gripped the edge of the table.

And then he crashed into her, his lips upon hers like a wave. His hand gripped the back of her head as they collided. His knuckles sank into her hair, gripping her roots as he held her against him as strong and certain as the wood beneath her. He tasted of salt and mint and smoke. Everything she desired and everything she had wished for. They had slept against each other so many nights, sparred together, trained together, she knew his body as well as she knew his soul, but it was a different beast now that they had opened the dam and allowed the flood through.

His hand moved from her hair down to the bottom of her back, pulling her to the edge of the table and into him. His hands made their way down to her hips, where his thumb grazed her broken skin. She gasped, unable to hide the pain from her wounds. Immediately he pulled back, searching her eyes. "It's okay," she said, desperate for him to fill the gap between her lips and his.

But he stayed there, too far away. The air was cold against her skin without his face pressed against her. A familiar coldness that settled onto her for the year that he was playing dead. "Why did you run away?"

She watched as he swallowed, his eyes moving from her and to the edge of her face, where he gently tucked a piece of hair behind her ears. "You know why." And she did. She did understand, maybe she was the only person in the entire realm who would understand. They were heirs. Heirs to violent nations at constant war. He was a man of the light, charming and beloved by all, with a secret will and hunger for violence. She was a creature of darkness and sadism, she'd eaten her first human as a mere toddler, bones and all. And in her heart, the deepest pits and corners, there was a small light, filled with love for her sister, her people, and now him. They were each other's opposites. The other half of the stars from which they came.

They'd known it. Felt it. But their lives were so short, already filled with the responsibility of an entire people, never meant to have anything for themselves other than pain and sacrifice.

"I looked for you," His confession fell into her ear like a trail of kisses.

His eyes were back on hers, holding a year's worth of longing and a desperate hope.

"I looked for you," He continued, "In the Dahs. Under each wave. I'd search for a glimpse of you. In every shadow, in every dark alley, in all of my nightmares and my dreams too. I would question every soldier and every sailor and merchant that came through the Gray Goblin to hear if they knew anything about the Syren Queen. I let go of everything in my old life and didn't look back once for any of it— except you. I couldn't let go of you. You were the one thing... The one thing that I can't, that I won't, let go of."

One second she was looking at him, watching him, and the next she was wrapped up into his arms. They kissed each other hungrily, desperate for their salvation. Passion and fire erupted as he began to kiss her ears and down her neck. Aria leaned into his touch, lapping it up like it was a pocket of oxygen as she lay drowning.

He carefully avoided making contact with her wounds and stitches, settling on a moment of stolen kisses. They'd have more time to fall into each other. All the time in the world to explore one another and fall hopelessly and desperately in love with each other. "Raask?" She asked between kisses in her gasps for air. He pulled away only a hair's width, but enough for her to see his eyes, the clarity and intention behind them as he answered.

"Yes." He answered. Confirmation that he was done with playing Hauth. Done with his year of running.

"What happens now?"

He kissed her neck and ear, whispering the words that she ached to hear above all else. "Now? We kill the king."

A river of laughter poured out of her mouth. It was like every-thing she had ever wished for was coming true. For just one moment, Aria felt on top of the world. Raask was back. He was ready to take on the king and assume his throne. He would end the war. Her people would be free. It was all over. It was finally all over.

Aria was filled to the brim with so much hope and adoration and love that for a brief moment she felt the shackles of her anger and despair loosening around her soul.

But Aria, oh, when would she learn better than to hope?

The whistle of an arrow sliced through the air in the front of the Callady Estate. Another whistle. Two thuds. More arrows sounded. Aria could hear far better than any human, turning her head towards the wall between them and the slaughter. Her eyes widened. Raask looked at her in confusion, unaware of the attack.

When the sound of swords clashing began, Raask stood. "Stay here," he ordered, rushing to the door. Aria was getting up, looking for some kind of weapon, when Caden came out of the back with a horde of guards. "Do not open that door." He yelled. Aria looked between Raask and Caden. She saw the feral look in Raask's eyes. She knew the power that lay underneath his skin, and felt its familiar thrum. The hunger for blood and retribution. She tasted it on her tongue like a sweet.

"Lock the door after me, get her healed and get her safe." He spoke to Caden as if he had any control over her. Claws descended out of her fingers, ripping apart her nailbeds. Fangs replaced human teeth. She would not sit back as Raask went into battle.

But Caden nodded and Raask opened the door to the slaughter. The stench of blood and bile crashed into the room like a wave. Acting fast, Aria sprinted after him, a couple of guards moved to hold her back, but Caden held a hand up to stop them. Maybe the human wasn't so bad.

Skierkan soldiers had surrounded the estate. They could not make it over the gates, although she could tell a few had tried by the gutted bodies that rested on the other side. The soldiers were forced to use arrows to hit Caden's guards as they tried to push through the single opening in the gate at the front and center. A blood bath.

But she could not find Raask in the brawl.

Movement towards the side of the house caught her attention.

He was there, holding on to the bodies of the two Vermilli she had seen him working with that morning. He kept shaking them, tears rushing down his face, screaming at them to wake up. But his friends would not wake up, not on this side of the realm. Arrows punctured their bodies. And unlike Aria, these landed with far more precision, puncturing their throats. Blood covered their hands and the entire front of their bodies, leading to puddles of it that Raask kneeled in as he shook them, begging any God to bring them back.

A painful and slow death. The Vermilli who shot them wanted them to suffer for their actions. Aria did not know these men, but she saw the pain in Raask. Putting the pain she felt for Raask and his friends in a pocket far away from her consciousness, she descended into the battle.

Aria smiled, wicked and cruel as she stalked into the chaos. She lifted a sword from one of the bodies, going for one of the shorter guard's weapons, still needing a lighter sword to work with her single arm. She lifted the blade, swinging it behind her, gaining momentum and speed as she barreled towards the opening of the gates. She cut into the Vermilli's throats as an artist painted on canvas, as a dancer moved across a stage. She moved expertly, efficiently, anticipating each movement from her enemies.

Her wounds hurt, but in the heat of the battle, she could not feel anything but the thrill of the kill. She let herself sink into her instincts. Killing was muscle memory for her. It required no thoughts and only instinct.

How lovely it was for her to kill again.

Red cloaks in varying shades stomped through the bloody snow as she moved like a ghost through them. She was quicker than any human. Stronger too. She didn't take the time to relish in each kill as she did when she hunted. Instead she moved as swift as a current and as strong as a riptide through the mass of bodies. Dropping them to their knees. Penetrating their throats. Slicing their heads off. She cut. She saw. She stabbed.

A couple of Vermilli worked in a team as they tried to sneak behind her. She sashayed a couple of steps closer to the madness of the gate's opening and turned to them, simultaneously slashing one's gut allowing for his intestines to fall out of the wound as she bit the throat out of the other. Another came at that moment, knocking the blade out of her hands. She spun around, gaining momentum and slashed her claws down the woman's face. Lifting her knee up into her as she collapsed forward, clutching at her bleeding eyeball, she heard the crunch of her nose as the woman shot backwards, falling to the ground beneath. This woman was smaller, her sword lighter, more manageable with Aria's one arm. She took it and impaled her onto the cold snow and the hard soil beneath with her own weapon.

More and more red cloaks came. And each one, she shot down. It was the rhythm of war. A primal and beautiful thing to a syren. She began to hum the songs of her people as she let herself loose on them. Reveling in the bloodshed. In that moment, she was free.

She hummed the songs of battle. The songs of committing holy bloodshed. The songs of beasts. It was glorious, to kill those who had hurt her and those who had hurt the ones she loved.

Aria rained her fury and bloodlust on the Callady Estate, easily slaughtering those who tried to infiltrate at the gate. And when the couple of dozen attempting to enter through the front gate had been slaughtered, she moved onto the ones who remained at a higher vantage point. Their arrows made it easy to find them. On top of the roof of the neighboring estates. On top of the trees that laid behind the property. Aria removed one of the arrows from a corpse. Unable to use a traditional bow since becoming one-armed, she opted to throw the arrows like spears. She ran a couple of steps before launching one, hitting the Vermilli in the chest.

She leaned over picking up another and another. She threw another, watching only for a second as the red cloak fell through the trees and onto the white snow beneath. She was distracted by the chorus of moans and the decadent smell of carnage. But it was enough.

A heavy boot kicked her while she was bent over. Purple blood spilled onto the snow beneath, bubbling and sizzling, as her stitches split open. Cold snow and hard soil collided with her side as she fell, clutching her wounds. Above her was a Vermilli. More had come, they were quieter, disguised in the melody of the injured and her own war songs, she did not hear them approach.

Smirking, he lifted his sword high into the air. His mouth was filled with blood, covering his yellowed teeth in a thick film of red. Aria's entire core tensed as she tried to gather the strength to kick, to roll, but she was beginning to feel what she had not before. Her injuries came to her all at once. Weakening her in the moment she needed to be strong. She saw the sword descending for her. It was a quick movement, but made slow by her thoughts. If this was how she would die, maybe it wouldn't be so bad. Raask would become king, Mayta would be queen of the syrens. She had done her duty. Maybe, it was time she could rest. Maybe death's embrace wouldn't be so cold, but a warm welcoming, to hear from her ancestors, to be with her kind in death. She would join her family, knowing that her people would be taken care of by Mayta.

But the man stopped, suddenly losing the strength needed to push the sword into her and instead dropping it to the snow beside her hip. It fell onto her abdomen, not a deadly injury, and a weight that would normally be unnoticeable, but a devastating pain as her wounds bled.

Red blood spots were on her belly. Had she accidentally commanded her blood to become humanic in her last moments? She looked up and saw that it was not her own, commanded to transform by her magic in a last moment of desperation, but from the Vermilli. Blood rushed out of him from every hole. Tears of blood welled out of his eyes. Splurted out of his nostrils and careened out of his mouth.

It was not just him, but every guard and every Vermilli on the lawn of the estate was now bleeding to death. Aria turned her head where she saw Raask, still kneeling over his friends, but his eyes on her. His hand, outstretched in a claw shape.

He had saved her..

Bodies hit the ground in countless thumps as she lay panting. "Are you alright?" He asked her, his voice hoarse. He had used too much power today. She could see it in the hollowness of his eyes, the rise and fall of his chest. Too much magic, all too fast, after most likely not training it for a year. He would need to rest. Aria nodded, she was alright, but he wouldn't be if she didn't get him to safety now. If he didn't allow himself the rest he needed, his body would take it without his permission.

She got up, clenching the wounds of her belly. "I'm sorry about your friends." She said as she walked to him. He gave one final look at them. There were memories in that look. She knew it well, after saying goodbye to many of her people over the years. It was not something he would recover from now, but nonetheless, they needed to move. "We need to get Caden and leave. More Vermilli will be on their way." She tried to speak gently, providing some kind of comfort, but her words were rushed and laced with pain and worry. He placed a palm on his friend's chest. And then the other one. A final goodbye.

He stood slowly, and as he turned his body to leave, his eyes were the last thing to pull away from them.

Her legs took her to him without conscious thought. Her hand, wet with blood, met his. She held on tight, letting him know that she was here with him. That she knew, oh Gods, did she know, how he was feeling right now.

But they were in danger here, out in the open. The guards were all dead. And Raask, he was exhausted. He would need time and rest to restore his magic. She led him to the front door, she tugged on the large ornate door handle. The door wouldn't budge. Looks like they remembered to lock it after them. She banged on the door with her fist. "CADEN! LET US IN!" She screamed. Not worried to be drawing any attention, they were already coming for her.

There was no answer. They were most likely hiding out in the bunker in the library. A decent hiding spot, but not great if the Vermilli knew about it or found it. No exits.

Caden. The arrogant annoying bastard that dreamed of a better world. She began to worry. They had to get in there and warn them. More were coming, they had to get out of there. Raask leaned against the door, watching her as she continued to beat on it. She looked at him, his skin, tanned from the sun, had turned a few shades lighter. He wobbled against the door.

They were running out of time. She wouldn't be able to carry Raask. He was too big, too heavy, and she was one-armed. The windows in the estate were high up to prevent somebody from breaking them and entering. A safety precaution she'd only seen done by those that could afford manors of this size. Aria took one look at Raask, grabbed his hand and led him to the nearest statue, the one depicting Baldrei, the God of the Sun. She patted the snow underneath the statue, motioning for Raask to sit down under the safety of the statue, hidden from view from most angles.

Then she ran to the door, hoping for a running start. Her feet skid against the snow and the blood resulting in a sloppy jump—but not exactly ineffective either. She drew her claws midair, fingernails ripping off and strong sharp claws pierced her fingertips. She slammed her claws into the stone wall, praying that five claws were all she needed to hold herself up.

For once, her prayers were answered.

Her claws penetrated the stone like a blade through a heart. Her feet scrabbled against the wall underneath her until they found tiny points of texture to hold onto. Aria looked down, only for a second, and immediately closed her eyes. She'd leapt higher than she realized, and the ground looked much further away than she thought it would. One breath in, one breath out. She had to keep going. Forward, always forward.

After her feet were steady enough, she leaned onto them, removing her claws from the stone and jumping up before piercing the wall again. Again and again she made this jump. Three times in all until she reached the windows. She went to break the window with her fist but hesitated. Red. The floors of the Callady Estate were covered in red.

Her eyes widened in horror as she realized what exactly she was looking at.

Caden Callady, perhaps the only man, besides Raask, who Aria could see as king of Skierka. The one who gifted her an arm. A fixer. A good man. He laid in a puddle of his own blood. Eyes bursted. Ears and nose bloody. A good man laid dead in his own estate. Along with his guards. His servants. And anyone else who was on this estate when Raask used his magic—besides her.

She couldn't look any longer.

Aria slid down the side of the estate, her claw running through the bloody trail that she left as she climbed. Raask did not look up at her as she walked to him. He sat stiffly in the snow. Pain and despair had slipped off his face, leaving nothing but an empty look as stiff as the statue he rested against. "They're dead, aren't they?"

Aria draped the cleanest Vermilli cloak she could find over his shoulders. She lifted the cloak over his head, ensuring that it shadowed his face. She kissed him gently, before whispering, "I'm sorry." His eyes met hers, glazed over. Tired and confused. Ashamed and buried by grief.

"It's okay. It'll be okay. But we need to get out of here." Careful to enact her veil. Aria led Raask through the streets, making sure to avoid the busier sections. They remained silent all the way to Fen's apartment by the edge of the Gaulic.

"Do people not recognize you?" Raask asked, his voice quiet and dry, as Fen's building came into sight. Aria looked around to ensure that they were good and truly alone. Some God must have been on their side, for they were.

"No, I'm wearing my veil."

"No, you're not." She suspected it when he recognized her from the rebel meeting. But he just confirmed it. He saw her as herself. A smirk crested her lips. She knew she was beautiful, of course, she was the queen of the syrens who were born from Freyite, Goddess of Beauty, and Voskulle, God of War.

Arrow wounds littered her chest like the drops of blood in her hair. Their friends had been massacred. And they were the most hunted people in the entire realm. And somehow, it his words still made her blush.

"It's not a physical veil, but a magical one. The strongest syrens, we can wear a thin layer of our magic, it makes us appear as the most beautiful version of a person, to anyone who sees us when we wear it." Raask's laugh rolled out from the hood like a crack of sweet thunder in a spring storm. She forgot how his laugh brought butterflies to her stomach. Countless nights she spent trying to remember the exact cadence of that laugh.

So much was going wrong, but she couldn't bring herself to feel broken, not when he was here. He was alive. And after he rested, he would be physically well again. And eventually, he would grieve. Become king. End the war.

Things would be okay.

Aria opened the door to Fen's apartment. It opened silently. The apartment smelled of Fen, woodsy and spiced. He was not home, but the note she left him was missing. In its place sat Jor, the albino snake she had met in the Gaulic. He picked his little head up, staring at Aria with his big eyes and twisted his head as he curiously assessed Raask.

Raask looked right back at Jor. "Aria, do you and Fen have a pet?"

Jor hissed. "I am no pet. Jusssst asss you are no human."

Aria scowled. "What do you mean by that?"

Raask nearly fell backwards. "Did that snake just speak?" Aria's head whipped towards Raask. Humans did not typically understand the language of animals. Reptiles in particular had a difficult language to grasp for humans, even those who understood most animal communication after years of study could hardly understand a few words of snake. And Raask, well he just spoke in a hiss.

Jor rolled his eyes. The image would have made Aria laugh if the snake hadn't been evading answering her question. "Did you *really* think that you'd been brought back from death by Kel with no change to yourssself other than a new hair color and lightened eyessss?"

CHAPTER 26
RAASK

A snake was speaking to him. A small, white snake, with impossibly large eyes. A cute little thing if snakes could be cute. Was. Speaking. To. Him.

Gods, he needed to sleep. Deciding it was a good place as any other, he collapsed onto the chair in front of the snake. Slumping into the back of the seat as the snake continued talking. And after losing his two best friends in the world, it was really the last thing he cared to deal with. His heart felt heavy with grief, they were there because of him, and they died because of him. Raask wanted just a couple of moments to feel the enormous weight of what had just happened, but instead he was now talking to a snake.

How did Aria know this snake, anyways? He didn't know whether to believe the snake's words, claiming he was no longer human, Raask knew exactly who he was. But Aria seemed concerned.

He snagged the other chair at the table, bringing it closer with the heel of his foot. Aria immediately sat as she stared at the snake like he, or it, held all of the answers to the universe. She was still too far for his liking, so he pulled the chair until she was pressed against his side. Her smell of salt and caramel filled his nose as he felt the familiar weight of her sinking into his side. At this point, he didn't care what the snake had to say, as long as she stayed against him. As long as he could have a break from all of the death.

For so long, he didn't think he'd ever feel her touch again, and if he did, he was certain it would have been a killing blow. So feeling her settle against him felt like a stolen moment, one he wasn't worthy of.

"What do you mean, he's not human? He smells human. He looks human. He bleeds as a human." The snake seemed to scoff at this, a strange sound coming from a snake, but he hadn't interacted with enough to really be familiar with their noises, nor their communication styles.

"Because if it looks like a human and appears to bleed as a human, it's a human?" The snake asked sarcastically. Raask laughed, the snake got her there. "How did you do that?" He asked Aria under his breath.

Aria looked at him out of the corner of her eye. "We can change our blood to match our human form too, Raask. We just usually prefer to keep our syrenic blood since it's superior in every single way." Then Aria, the creature he had longed over for the past year, shared an exasperated look with a snake over his lack of understanding of syrenic magic and anatomy. Unbelievable.

The snake sniffed the air. Looking towards the front door. "The dog and a human approach." Either fortunately or unfortunately, the snake was correct. A moment later, the door handle turned, and Fen halted in the doorway. He looked at Aria, and then Raask, and then the snake. When his gaze fell onto the snake, a clear look of annoyance flashed across Fen's face. He walked into his apartment, leaving the door wide open for Lok Ollen, Caden Callady's best friend and an old friend of Raask's.

Lok's hollowed eyes and slumped shoulders told Raask that they knew about the massacre at the Callady Estate. Fen would have recognized his magic, did he tell Lok? Lok shut the door behind him, sighing loudly as he took a seat on Fen's couch, while Fen started a fire. He threw logs into the pit, allowing them to slam loudly onto the stone tile. Nobody spoke until the fire turned from a faint crackle to a blaze. "I'm assuming you already know about Caden?" Fen asked, poking at the fire with an iron poker.

"We were there," Aria answered, saving Raask from having to answer. Lok's head whipped around to look at them.

"How did you survive and Caden Callady died?" He asked. Lok was loud and brash. One of the only other kids in the upper class that could keep up with Raask when he was in his most hedonistic of moods. It was harrowing to see him grieving so quietly. Even worse to remember that it was his mistake that killed Caden. Another old friend. "Aren't you some barkeep? I get that you got lucky with that sea wraith, but to survive an assault from a horde of Vermilli while Caden Callady died? How?"

He realized that Lok still did not know who he was. Fen and Aria glanced nervously at Raask. He was so damned tired, and he didn't want to deal with this, not right now. And Lok... he was smart, smart enough to figure out that if he was Raask, a blood screamer, then what happened at the Callady Estate must have been by his hand.

But Lok deserved better than a coward. He had been his friend for many years. He deserved the truth. Raask sighed, gathering what little strength he had left before speaking in a low voice. "Lok, when you were ten years old you snuck into the Irridesci tower looking for your sister and instead found the Prince hiding behind a desk sobbing. You took his hand in yours, and led him out of the tower through the same small window that you came in through. Then you both sat by the Incarno river for the rest of the afternoon, avoiding the tutors, and playing in the river. Whenever either of you had a fresh set of bruises or scars from whippings, you would meet each other in that spot."

Lok stared at Raask, his brows furrowed, looking almost angry for such an intimate secret to be shared with someone he thought he didn't know. The moment that Lok realized who he was became obvious. His face softened. Anger replaced by sorrow. Which after another moment, melted into a mask of indifference. "Did you kill Caden because they were going to back him as king?" He asked, motioning to Fen and Aria. He felt Aria tense at his side, her muscles straining as she was about to stand and do Gods know what. Raask placed a hand on her thigh, this was his mess to sort out.

She shot him a look before settling back into her chair, clutching at her wounded belly. He looked around the apartment, searching for some kind of medical kit, anything to help her. Fen gently placed a large tin in front of the couch Lok stood behind. Raask stood, taking Aria's hand and leading her to the couch. Lok kept a close eye on Raask.

"It was an accident. I meant to kill only the Vermilli." He forced Aria to sit down and lay on her back. The fact that she did any of this while in the presence of Lok could only mean that she was in worse pain than he had realized before. He silently cursed himself for not looking after her the second they made it into the apartment.

"And I'm supposed to believe that?" Lok asked, passing him the spray of twilight lithe. The mist landed on Aria's wounds and immediately she relaxed into the couch. Raask pulled the medical string and needle from the kit and began reclosing her wounds as he spoke.

"It's the truth. If I wanted to be king, I wouldn't have had to kill Caden for that right. And now that I've decided to come back, I will be at a severe disadvantage without him." He carefully sewed Aria's skin shut on the first wound on her thigh. He liberally sprayed more twilight lithe onto the area. He then turned to Lok, "Caden was a good man. My friend. His death will stay with me for the rest of my life. And I'm very sorry for it." He swallowed, unable to look at the pain on Lok's face for too long, and moved on to sewing the wound above Aria's hip.

Fen brought a wet handcloth, placing it on Aria's forehead.

Lok moved one of the chairs from the table to sit behind Raask. He gently, almost silently, placed the chair on the ground. "Did you know who he was?" He asked, voice still stiff from his loss.

Raask had no clue which one he was asking, but it was Aria who answered. "I knew the moment that I saw him." She turned her head away from the ceiling and towards Lok. Her big hair cushioning her head, and getting in the way of her sight. Raask tucked it under her head as he placed a pillow there, holding her head up. Her skin was warm and slightly feverish. Worry surged in him. Was she developing an infection? A fever? Could it spread to her blood or her brain?

He didn't know the first thing about healing a syren and only enough about healing to patch up a battle wound. He needed Selby, the lead medic of the palace. She would know what to do and she'd have the right tools to help her. Finished with sealing her wounds, he misted one last layer of twilight lithe onto her, allowing the black liquid to seep into her skin and deep into her muscles. Numbing the pain, it was all he could do right now.

He reached for her hair once again, tucking it behind her ears, carefully stroking her cheek. She turned back to Raask and smiled. His heart ached at the sight of it. He would do anything to keep her smiling at him like that.

"Skullin's scythe, you're in love aren't you?" Lok asked, a chilling joyless laugh spurting out of him. A desperate and hopeless sound. Raask did not look away from Aria, and she did not look away from him.

Fen's heavy and exasperated sigh came from the kitchen. Raask heard Lok erupt from the chair and begin to pace around the room. His heavy steps bounced from corner to corner and back again. "And what are you expecting exactly? What's the end of this love story? You think that because you two are in love that both nations are just supposed to join together? Humans have hunted syrens for centuries, and syrens have hunted humans for longer. You want everyone to just hold hands and forgive each other for years and years of endless slaughter just because you two love each other?"

Beyond exhaustion at this point, Raask sat at the end of the couch, lifting Aria's feet into his lap. His shoulder rested on the couch's arm and his head fell into his hand. He was barely holding himself together here. "Forgive me, Lok, but I haven't quite figured out all of the details. I'm a little preoccupied in figuring out how to end this war. After that, we will figure out how to unite our people."

"And how do you plan on ending this war?" Fen asked, rifling through the pocket of one of his cloaks by the door. Finally finding whatever he had been looking for, Fen brought it to Raask. The snake on the table recoiled into a tight ball as he passed. When the smell of creamy brine and ocean rot hit his nostrils, Raask understood. He looked at Fen, "Are you sure?"

Fen nodded. "I got it for you, just in case." Raask grabbed the hunk of white lithe that Fen had somehow smuggled. He crushed it into his fist and rubbed it into his gums. Immediately the exhaustion sizzled out of him and power—pure, raw, power enveloped him. He felt the effects take over his body like a bolt of lightning. As a Morlok, he had a disposition to white lithe. The stone would give raw power, enhancing magic, strength, speed and wit— all at once—to anyone who consumed it. But to the Morloks? White lithe increased their magic, giving them a nearly limitless supply of power. It was why the palace was bleached in it. As long as a Morlok defended the palace, with that much white lithe, it would be impenetrable.

This hunk of stone. This resource of the Arkts. Found in the Zojz trench. This was the reason for most, if not all, wars in the Arkts. Everything revolved around it and the power it granted. They said long ago that the non-human creatures ruled the realm, and the humans were enslaved. When white lithe was discovered it changed everything. Giving humans power and magic that once only belonged to the creatures. Humans, who were industrious where the other creatures were consumed by the arts and pleasures, turned the white lithe into the great equalizer, and eventually the power that made them higher up on the social status than the creatures.

Aria sniffed at the smell of it. Her eyes widened.

This hunk of stone was the reason her people were enslaved. Hunted and grabbed when they would surface for air, forced to mine for white lithe until they died. Whipped and hurt every time they surfaced from the Zojz without white lithe to give to the Skierkans.

Aria lifted her palm from her belly, reaching for the lithe. Illegal for anyone besides a Morlok to use, he was surprised that she reached for it. As he passed her two nails of the powder, and she snorted it up her nose, he felt the white lithe in his tattoos begin to vibrate. Power called to power. It reacted just as his blood magic did in the presence of blood, excited and hungry.

"I hate to break this lovely moment up, but I would also like to know how you plan on ending the war." Lok retorted.

"I'm going to kill the King." The words felt lovely on Raask's tongue.

Aria sat up, glaring at him. "No, I will be killing the king." Despite himself, a light laugh slipped out. She looked so cute when she was angry, he didn't hold back, taking her face into his hands and kissing her. She tasted of salted sweets.

"Whoever has the first clear shot at him can kill him?" He offered a whisper between kisses. She pulled away, not too far, but just enough to speak.

"Fine," She answered breathlessly.

Lok laughed again, another joyless and hopeless sound. "Are you kidding me?" He turned around the room in disbelief, and when his eyes fell on the snake at the table, he threw his hands up in the air as if the snake set him off again. "You think you can just, what, march into the Bleached Palace and kill the King?"

Raask caught the snake looking at Fen and hissing, "Why'ssss he mad at me? What did I do?"

Fen chuckled quietly.

"That's exactly what we will do. We will sneak into the palace and kill the King." Aria leaned back onto the couch as she spoke, her hand moving instinctively to hold the wound on her belly.

Lok cursed under his breath. "Raask, do you know anything about your family's magic? Where it comes from?"

Raask nodded, of course he knew. "The Morlok bloodline is naturally predisposed to greater magic, and we have some kind of kink in our genetics that make us react far stronger to white lithe than any other. Theoretically, we also receive magic from the land itself. But—"

"But no Skierkan ruler has truly completed the trials since Bjor Morlok, the first ruler of Skierka." Fen finished Raask's thoughts. He continued, "That's where Lok and I have just come from. Dorid and Dorida have confirmed that the Gaulic forest will back you. The magic won't settle into you until you are officially king, but that shouldn't matter as you will have the support of our creatures and the wood itself."

Raask looked at Fen, his heart sinking into his chest with the weight of his gratitude. "Thank you."

Fen merely shrugged. Raask knew better than to think it was a favor to him, but still, he was grateful. The creatures of the wood were nothing short of nightmares. For them to fight on the side of the rebels, if things were to go south, if Raask was unsuccessful in killing his father, it could be the difference between a failed rebellion and a revolution.

Lok shook his head, still obviously frustrated, still grieving too. "Raask that isn't right, it may be what you were taught but it's not right." He exhaled messily again. "Your magic isn't a *kink* in your *genetics*, it's from a deal that Bjor made. If you don't believe me, the church kept hidden documents with the truth of what happened."

Raask's eyes shot to Lok, "What are you talking about?" That couldn't be right. He would have known. Somebody would have told him. The Irridesci or the King or any of his tutors. He'd trained from the best tutors in the entire realm in history in sciences and religion and his own lineage, he would have known.

Lok ran his hands down his face once more. "Your magic isn't a kink in your damn genetics, Raask. If that was true, then there would be more people with the abnormality. And it would have reached your cousins and extended family too."

Raask twisted his face. "I don't have cousins."

Lok peered at him over his hands, "Yes, you do."

But he didn't. At least not on his father's side. And his mother's side, he had never known. He knew they existed, but they had never come to the palace, and when he asked his mother, she told him to never ask of them again. They didn't even show up to her funeral.

"Respectfully, Lok, what are you talking about?" Raask was tired and beaten down. Even after the hit of white lithe, the heavy toll of guilt and grief of the day had been too much.

Lok took a seat, still nervously fidgeting, constantly in movement. "We are cousins, Raask. My parents married young and had my sister soon after their wedding. And when she was born, at the time with the Morlok last name, the Irridesci took her. Then my father, Taug Ollen, took my mother's last name to prevent it from happening to their future children. And then your father scoured the records of him. My father said he did it to protect him and his family, but from what I've seen of the King, I don't know if he's capable of such things, even before the magic tainted his soul."

This could not be true. It just couldn't. His father, who had never shown kindness, would not go to any lengths to protect his family. Because if this was true, his father was capable of kindness, protectiveness, love, and had just chosen to not give any of it to him. Old wounds from being raised with cruelty rose in his chest. Idly, Raask stroked Aria's calves and ignored her heavy, worried gaze. He felt her gaze move from him, and when he turned towards her, he saw her look back and forth between him and Lok. He wished they were in private so he could ask her what she thought of this. If she knew somehow, as she always seemed to know, or at least sense, everything. Could she smell the familiar bloodline in them both? Damn, he had blood magic, shouldn't he be able to tell such things? Skullin's scythe, if this was true, why didn't his father ever show an ounce of care or protective feelings for him?

He could feel the pain that settled in his bones long ago begin to stir. Careful to keep his face straight, embarrassed by his feelings and needing to focus, he kept the muscles of his face relaxed, just as he'd practiced for years in the mirror. To keep a straight face, devoid of emotion, in the face of pain and even worse, confusion, was perhaps the greatest lesson he could have learned from his father. Maybe that would have to be enough.

He watched Lok. His black hair and the twist of grief and pain on his face. His nose, strong and hooked, just like his father's. Maybe like Taug's too, for he'd only heard of the formidable blacksmith, never seen him. Perhaps that was by design of those around him.

"And you don't have magic?" Raask asked.

Lok shook his head. "My father lost it, once he changed his name. He said he used to feel the magic of Harik in his veins. Not anymore." Harik, God of Forging, the same god the Rakkei prayed to, and built temples in the name of. It made sense for such a famed blacksmith.

"Is that who Bjor made the deal with?"

Lok shook his head. Aria groaned in frustration. "Are you kidding me? Lok, just tell us the whole Gods-damned story and tell us now." Raask was not envious of the look she shot at Lok, who had the right mind to look at Aria in fear.

"Well you know that before Bjor Morlok led the human revolution—before the war, humans were at the bottom of the food chain. Not exactly slaves, but we had no magic and therefore nothing to offer a world that revolved around magic. Because of that, there weren't many humans back then. So the humans grew angry and resentful. We started killing the other creatures. And in turn, they started killing us. Humans were on the brink of extinction. So Bjor became desperate."

"Determined to save his race, he climbed the Red Peaks. And the Gods, curious of the human who successfully summited Mount Disparadi, answered his call. Bjor then told them of the troubles the humans had faced. Asking how the Gods could have given every other creature magic but them, and how they were supposed to live and survive without any powers of their own. Tsu felt pity on him and the humans, for humans were built in his image and he saw this as his own failure. He ordered the Gods to spread their blood across the Arkts. Each drop that landed transformed into lithe. A different type from each God, and the stronger ones had different types that formed from their blood. Bjor thanked the Gods and they went on their way. All except for one."

It was Aria who spoke first. She knew, somehow, as she always seemed to. "Voskulle." The name of the God of War, the partner to the Irridesci, settled over the room like a dusting of snow. Lok gave one solemn nod.

"Voskulle could smell the blood on Bjor. Where the others saw a man desperate for a chance in the realm, Voskulle could see him for who he was; a vile and cruel man, who enjoyed spilling blood, not for retribution but for the love of killing. And Voskulle made him a deal, he told him that he would help the humans with their way. And give the rest of his bloodline, the kings at least, magic that overpowered even the strongest of magical creatures in the realm. All Bjor would have to do was continue to spill blood. It's why the Irridesci take and torture. They believe it takes them closer to the Gods, or at least just one God. They become Saints of Voskulle, and Voskulle continues to bless the Morloks with greater power, as long as they keep spilling blood."

Raask didn't know what to say. Everything he had known was a lie, but he couldn't understand why no one had told him. It made sense that the public wouldn't know, but why not him?

"What else?" Aria asked. Her eyes scanned Lok's face, causing Raask to look him over again. Of course, there was more.

"Voskulle didn't tell Bjor everything. And the Irridesci, they know things that the Morloks don't. They've learned things from their *prayer ceremonies.*" Lok looked into the fire as he spoke. The prayer ceremonies of the Irridesci were torture, maiming, and disfiguring. And Lok, whose sister was taken by them, had suffered a great deal at the hands of his family. Or *their* family now.

Lok continued, his voice dry and cracked. "The extra magic that Voskulle placed into your bloodline, it's—it's too much for a human. Humans aren't meant to hold the magic of the Gods. And Voskulle's magic, it's tainted, poisonous, and rotten. And the more it is used, the more blood that is fed into it, the more it'll turn the one using it."

"Turn?" Aria and Fen asked at the same time. And the white snake climbed down the legs of the table, slithered towards the couch, and up towards Aria's hand, where it wrapped itself around her hand like a hug.

"The more magic that's used by a Morlok, the more that it's fed, it takes over their soul. You'll lose yourself, Raask, and in your place will be someone power-hungry, bloodthirsty, and soulless."

"Someone like my father." Raask barely recognized his own voice.

"Yes, it'll turn you into someone like your father."

Raask's heart stopped in his chest. And the only noise that entered the room came from the crackling fire and the snake as he seemingly whispered something to Aria. He looked at her, expecting to see the mirror to his own heartbreak, instead she was scanning him. Her brows furrowed and jaw tense, she was thinking, and thinking hard, but certainly not heartbroken. Satisfied by wherever her train of thought led her, she met his eyes and gave a small nod. She believed everything would be fine, or she had a plan—whatever —he trusted that nod as if it were the word of a God.

Lok, who was too overcome in his grief, didn't notice the look between the two.

"It sounds like I'm the right one to kill him then. And whatever comes after, we'll deal with it as it comes." Aria gave a moan of disapproval, obviously at the notion that Raask would be the one to kill his father and not her. He didn't argue with her. All he wanted was to rest, gather his strength, and then go kill the King with the creature that he loved at his side.

Whatever came after, they would handle it. Because they could handle anything together.

CHAPTER 27
VIGGO

Viggo was overcome with fear and anxiety and for the first time in a long time, hope. There was hope in his heart.

He was worried sick about Mayta. He felt her soul disappear from this realm, at the end of the bridge in the back of his mind, was still her brightness and love, but it was fuzzy. She was speaking to either the Sistros or the Gods, and he could feel nothing but brightness and warmth from wherever she was. So he was worried, of course, he'd always worry about her, but he could sense that she was alright.

She was alright. And so was Raask. Raask was alive. He was back and he was probably pissed at Viggo, but he had to see him. He'd hear from Mayta once she came back to this side of the realm, but in the meantime, he'd had enough delaying things. The army was as trained as they could be. As big as they would become, a few Luruvians even opted to stay and help fight. This was it. This was their moment.

He would announce that night, after dinner was over, that they would set sail in the morning for Skierka. He had already spoken to the leaders that morning. King Agar, Taura the Terrible, Silia, and the twins, they had all agreed. They'd all trained. They've rested. And tonight they would feast.

Plates of raw fish and shelled creatures were passed around as the army dined along the shore. Tonight, they would eat under the stars. Sweet drinks of Surtrian sugar liquor sloshed in glasses and bellies. Laughter came from each table and each table was a mix of different creatures and humans from different countries. Together, they had banded.

After the fish had been eaten, bones and all—thanks to the wraiths and the syrens, Viggo watched as King Agar's servants began to pass around the sweets. As Viggo and the other leaders sat at the table closest to the shore, in front of two massive bonfires, he watched the faces of his men and women who had fought with him for years, who had known what it meant that he had the King's servants make Amia's wheels. A soft chewy almond cookie, dipped in chocolate. Modeled after the pottery wheel that Amia, Goddess of the Arts, created the world within.

King Agar's servants wore the skins of the giant snakes of the Boai jungle around their necks, allowing their tails and heads to flow loose into the wind. The King himself had placed the body of one of the giant snakes around his neck in a similar fashion. To the Surtrians, this was their tradition on the eve of battle. They believed in channeling the power of the snake.

And Viggo, he didn't have a grand or spiritual reason for serving the cookie on the nights before battles. It started because he'd eat them nervously when he first joined the war. The cookie was the one sweet his mother would eat, and they reminded him of her. As he grew in the ranks, more soldiers joined his tradition.

Viggo explained the tradition to the other leaders, now sitting at the head table with him. Skender to his left, Emir on his right and Silia to Emir's left. Silia, who had been loud and brash since Viggo met her on the battlefield all those years ago, had not been the same since the Skierkan attack on the wraithkin's home. Emir was constantly at her side. His large hands held her small fists under the table as he whispered what sounded like soothing words into her ears. Skender's eyes, like Viggo's, roamed over the tables. Constantly assessing. Observing.

On Viggo's right was the king, at the seat of honor of course, as they were sitting on his island. On King Agar's right was Diya Latifi, co-ruler of Luru, who constantly stared doe-eyed at the King—who had been making constant jokes the entire meal, or really ever since Diya arrived.

Next to Diya was Mei, the other co-ruler of Luru. She seemed quiet for most of the meal. Her smooth black hair shone beneath the light of the silver moon and each time she nodded her head politely at Alia, the child leader of the Surtrian syrens, who adored sharing bloody tales and was too young to notice Mei's aversion to violence with her looks of disgust. Taura sat at the end of the table. It was her stories that Alia was telling. Taura stared coldly at her plate. As the general of the Abisian syrens, she was acting as the leader of their kind. It would be her syrens who would lead them across the Dahs. And her syrens who would help their army march the shores and onto the land. The first feet to hit the Skierkan shoreline.

Her eyes met his, she gave him a small smile and a nod. He was a General too, and he alone could understand how she must be feeling. Generals are told what to do. They lead their army, but it is not at their word that their army dies. It had been hard for him too, when the revolution first began. Without Aria or Mayta, it was Taura that had to agree to lead her people into whatever sat ahead of them.

There weren't many of her people left. And the ones who were left, would all be going into battle. None of the leaders mentioned it when Viggo announced his plan earlier that day, but they all understood. If they lost whatever was waiting for them on the other end of the Dahs, there would not be enough soldiers left to fight any longer. Not from the Abisian Syrens, not from the Skierkan revolutionaries, not from any other nation that had been willing to fight.

He took a deep breath in, and a long one out. The laughter had ended, and the whispers had begun. Heavy, daunting, and scared whispers overtook the camp. All eyes fell on their table. And Viggo, who had made the call, made the decision to end their training and take them back to Skierka, prepared to stand. Only King Agar's hand sank onto his shoulder. The King shot him a look as he rose. Viggo obeyed the silent order and remained in his seat.

"I would like to thank each and every one of you for what you are about to do tomorrow." His voice boomed across the war camp. Silence overcame the shore the moment he stood. The waves seemed to cease crashing, and the jungle birds stopped singing. It was like the entire realm awaited his words.

"Some of us have been here for quite some time." He looked down at Viggo and squeezed his shoulder with kindness and pride for the work that they had done together. Even if it all went to Helk, they had fought the good fight together, and that was something that the Fire Monger King could never take from them. "Some of us have no choice. To fight or to lose everything they love, everything they cherish. And some of us, made the decision to risk their every-things for a greater realm. No matter where you fall, I want to thank you." He raised his glass of straight Surtrian sugar liquor, a brown as dark as tree bark, and drank the entire glass in one shot. The sound of the gulp was audible to Viggo and the others at the top table. "Now drink and be merry. Tomorrow we set sail for Etra."

As one, the entire camp lifted their glasses into the air and drank.

On strict orders from Taura, and Alia who ordered her syrens to do whatever Taura said, the syrens were not allowed to sing nor create any violence. So they danced under the light of the silver moon. The Surtrians were the first to join them, followed by the Luruvians and then by the drunkest of the Skierkans. The wraithkins were the only ones who didn't dance at all. They drooped their heads low at their tables. The wraithkin had been hunted down, just like the syrens, only they were never enslaved. Instead they were hunted for the slaughter. Too dangerous. Too unruly. Their kind never submitted to Morlok rule. Instead they lived along the edge of Skierka, high up in the Red Peaks, high enough to be unreachable by the Skierkans, moving along the mountain passes, always on the move as it was what kept them safe... until now.

The leaders remained at the high table, not joining in the revelry. Many of them looked at the wraithkin, praying to the Gods that this would not be their people in the future, grieving over their losses. Even their lunar wraiths seemed heartbroken. They did not play in the moonlight. Like their human counterparts, they kept their heads low, laying on the sands, groaning and lounging instead of hunting or playing.

Viggo retired to bed early that night. He laid in his bed in the Jungle Palace, listening to the sounds of the revelries all the way from the shore.

The next morning, Viggo packed his bags, and walked to the tucked-away cove on Boai, where they hid the warships. Soft buttery light crept in from the horizon and over the long green vines and large flat leaves that brushed against Viggo's skin as he walked. The sunlight had only just begun to edge onto this side of the realm, and already it was unbearably hot.

Viggo expected to sit alone among the boats and wait as his army trickled in.

Only the shore was littered with the sleeping bodies of the syrens who had slept on the beach, along with their weaponry. They slept in layered circles, centered around Taura and Alia, who fell asleep hugging each other. From far away, at the edge of the jungle, Viggo could see that Taura was awake. Holding on tightly to the young warrior ruler of the Surtrian syrens.

Giving them their space, Viggo initially remained tucked along the edge of the jungle. One by one and group by group—the army arrived and the syrens awoke. A heavy breakfast of sweet fruits, heavy breads, and boiled jungle-bird eggs was handed to each person along with a packed bag filled with blankets, daggers, bandages, dried meats, breads, and nuts. The Luruvians who would not be traveling with them, and the Surtrians who would remain on the islands, stayed up the entire night packing the bags.

By mid-morning, they had left. Viggo had spent a great deal of his life on these islands, and he tried not to consider that this might be his last time in Surtr. He didn't care for training in the heat, but he had lost his boyishness on these islands. He'd become a leader, a traitor, and then a leader again on Boai. Somewhere along the line, the Jungle Palace had become a second home to him. He swallowed back the sorrow, needing all of his focus on what was to come as they departed for Etra.

The syrens, along with the smaller of the sea wraiths, tugged the warships out of the cove. Spikes in various shapes and sizes swam along the edges of the boats as the wraiths used the currents to push them. The Dahs was large and unrelenting. The trip to Skierka could take anywhere from a week to several months, and Gods-knew how long it would be for the Skierkans or the Surtrians who remained in place.

It was mid-afternoon when one of Viggo's soldiers called him to the edge of the boat. Sitting on top of the head of a sea wraith was Taura. The wraith's head was the size of a horse. And while it swam along the side of the boat, its long serpentine neck twisted so the wraith looked directly over the top of the boat. While this warship was filled with mostly Skierkans who had grown up terrified of wraiths, and had now gotten more and more used to them in recent months, they were still terrified. There was an eerie silence across the boat as the wraith looked along the top of the ship. Its massive eyes bulged out of its head and its mouth curved up in the most terrifying smile that Viggo had ever seen.

Viggo laughed at the sight. He knew Taura would not bring her wraith this close if there was any risk to his army or the boat. And it was just a ridiculous sight. "Taura, is there a reason you're terrifying my army?" Viggo called over the winds and the waves. Taura herself laughed at this as Viggo strode to the edge. He gripped the wooden posts for support, with the help of the wraiths and the syrens this boat was going faster than he had ever traveled before. And while if he fell, the syrens would fetch him, he still didn't want to fall.

"Yeah well Dragna gets a kick out of scaring humans, and I couldn't resist." Viggo laughed again at seeing her sitting on top of the creature's head, gripping the two spiked horns for support as she sat cross-legged in her humanic form.

"Well, while I love getting to finally meet Dragna, is there a reason you summoned me?" Taura's wide smile faltered as her eyes shot back down to the sea below. Immediately, Viggo knew that he would not get his wish to remain out of the Dahs.

He leaned over the edge of the posts, sensing an air of secrecy.. "Viggo, what I am about to say to you, you can't react to. Understand?" He nodded tightly, keeping his smile plastered to his face in case anyone was watching. "Rahn has requested to speak to you."

Viggo, whose father was one of the original Gods, who could sense the woman he loved still at that higher plane, speaking to the Sistros, was stunned. Was the Gods Agreement just an empty conversation? It seemed like each God was secretly ignoring their pact. "Rahn? The God of the Seas? He wants to speak to me? And he told you?"

Taura giggled. She actually giggled. Viggo threw up his hands in disbelief. He had hardly seen her even laugh and now she was giggling. "Yes, he lives down here with us. He said he met you last year."

He had no clue what Taura was talking about but sighed. Rahn was his father's brother, making him his uncle. One of the three originals. He would not deny him an audience. He looked down at the raging black seas below and grimaced. "You will not survive that drop, godling. Just—here," she extended her hand and with strength he didn't realize she had, she literally pulled him onto Dragna's head. "Hold onto this horn, I'll hold this one. And don't let go." Before Viggo had time to process, Dragna took off.

She leapt into the air in a giant arc, the wind slapped Viggo's face with the blunt force of a hammer before Dragna twisted into the air and dove down into the Dahs. The thick, heavy, black layer at the top lasted only a second with the speed and weight of Dragna. Her horn was slick in his hands, and he struggled to keep his grip as she continued tunneling further and further down into the Dahs. The blackness ceased and vibrant blue waters appeared. But the water was rushing into his eyes, and they were travelling so damn fast Viggo was essentially a clueless extra weight to Dragna.

Until she stopped.

Dragna extended her wings—or flippers, or Viggo wasn't entirely sure—and immediately she slammed to a halt. At this point, Viggo had held his breath for a long time and endured a lot of force. Spots crept into his vision. He was about to pass out.

"You didn't bring your lithe?" A gentle voice echoed into his mind. One that Viggo immediately recognized. The large cow-like creature that had saved him last year floated in front of him. Rahn, Viggo realized, this creature was the God of the Seas. "I will return him to his boat when I am finished, you may leave now." Taura removed Viggo's hand from Dragna's horn with a slap. Faster than any creature had any business being, they disappeared into the currents as Viggo began to sink.

Suddenly a bubble of air appeared, exhaling all the water out of the space with a whoosh. Viggo panted, immensely grateful to be able to finally breathe again. He sank to the bottom of the air bubble, standing on the edge as if the water beneath was hard ground. "I have watched you for quite some time." The creature—the God—remained outside of the air bubble, only a few inches away from Viggo.

Unsure of how to respond, Viggo just nodded, still panting slightly from the pressure of the water and the loss of air. "Thank you for saving me... again."

"Neither myself nor my brothers have had any children for many, many, many years. You are the first godling, at least that I am aware of, in quite some time. So those of us who know, have developed quite fond feelings for you. I have helped to protect you all these years. Since you were a young boy sent to war, I have watched over you and protected you from down here."

Viggo swallowed. He thought of Raask, his mother, and Kel as his family. That was it. It never occurred to him that there were others who saw him for who he was, others that loved him from afar. "We cannot have children of our own, two Gods that is, yes we can make species together, but not our own children with one another. So, we sometimes *foster* the ones that keep our attention and protect them as much as we can. I have protected you as you are my nephew, but Loor and I, we have grown quite fond of Aria and Mayta." Viggo realized then that this was not a friendly family chat, but a talk from someone who had loved Mayta from afar as well, who knew how he felt for her.

"I see," Viggo smiled at the creature. "She is speaking to the Gods now, right?"

Rahn nodded. "She has been there for a while."

"I can feel her, she's alright." It was true, he felt her in the presence of warmth and holiness.

"Yes, but like my home among these black seas, time does travel differently there. Yet still, this is too long. I cannot travel to Mount Disparadi. And Loor can't see her through the mountain. And we have grown worried for our little one."

"I won't hurt her, you have my word." Rahn rolled his massive eyes at Viggo. "Yes, that I know you won't do. Believe me, if you did, my Loor would have your throat. But we are worried about our Mayta and our Aria. We need you to rush to the palace. As quickly as you can, or more correct, as quickly as I can take you."

Viggo twisted his head. "What do you mean?"

"I will be pushing you to Etra, with my help, you will arrive in the night. And I will do my best to ensure that as little time as possible has passed."

Viggo looked at Rahn carefully. His heart refused to settle and instead raced with concern. "What do you know? Why are you doing this favor? Is Mayta alright?" He could feel her there, shrouded in warmth and light, she felt happy. But he could not afford to be wrong, not about Mayta. Again he knocked on the bridge to her mind, again she refused to let him in. Something was going on. Now he was sure of it.

"We have heard the whispers of the prophecy." Rahn's voice boomed into his mind and with it, the calming sensation of warm water settling against his skin like a hug. Just as his father did with his shadows. Rahn continued, "What you are racing towards, on the other end of my sea, is a bloodbath. One so great, and so terrible, that it has been foretold it'll turn the Dahs red. And while you have a unique ability to walk among the land of the dead as well as the living, and would do well in death. Our girls would not. I want your word that you'll do what you can to save them."

His mouth and throat went dry. Enough blood to make the Dahs red, that sounded like a massacre. Again he tried to enter Mayta's mind, it felt so warm and light wherever she was, the feelings seeped out from the bridge to her mind like the light surrounding a closed door. Maybe he could tell her to stay there, stay out of harm. But she wouldn't let him in. His heart ached with desperation. He had to get to her.

"You have my word."

"Very well then." Kindness rang through Rahn's voice, and before Viggo had time to ask him any questions, his bubble began to float through the Dahs. It started slowly before building speed. Dragna had taken him very deep. And through the safety of his bubble, he had a moment to appreciate the beauty of the Dahs. A deep blue water filled with colorful creatures, each with large sharp teeth. He watched as a massive shark ambushed a whale, rushing swiftly from the deep and arcing to bring it down with it to the bottom of the Dahs. Blood gushed from the whale along with little pieces of its entrails. The smaller creatures swarmed the bits that fell off in the ambush. And then he was too far away to see the rest, but he looked down at where the shark came from—seeing nothing but blackness beneath. There was a strange magic in the Dahs, something that had made the inner section, but neither the top nor the bottom, vibrant and otherworldly.

His questions surrounding the dark sea vanished the second the bubble lifted him out of the top of the Dahs, straight through the black toxic waters along the surface and shooting him like a cannon out of the water and onto his ship. He landed with a roll, slamming his shoulder hard against the wood, and then his belly, his other shoulder, his ass, until he rolled to a stop directly in front of Skender. All Viggo heard was the loud crunch of Skender chewing on something, only to look up to see that he was gnawing on the legs of a dried jungle spider. Viggo looked up at Skender as Skender looked down at him, there was silence on the deck of the warship despite the hundreds of soldiers aboard.

After a moment of them looking at each other, Skender seeing that Viggo was alright, and Viggo realizing that he *was* in fact alrigh, laughter erupted aboard the warship. Because sometimes, when there was so much darkness ahead and just as much darkness behind, ridiculous moments couldn't go without a laugh. The entire ship continued their fit of laughter and Viggo could swear he could hear the syrens snickering beneath the waves.

He stood, now feeling the bruises that were forming across his body, and gave his army a bow. "Thank you, thank you." Once everyone settled back to their business, he threw Skender a look over his shoulder, to which Skender gave a slight nod and immediately followed.

They called Emir over as they walked back towards the edge of the ship where Taura was once again awaiting on top of Dragna. Once he filled them in on what Rahn had said, Taura commanded the syrens to board the ships and warn their wraiths. Her and Dragna then rushed ahead. Viggo grimaced, watching the speed at which Dragna could swim. Her long serpentine body moving through the water like a shimmering wave of death.

When they were almost out of eyesight, Dragna lifted her long neck high above the water and let out an ear-shattering screech filled with clicks and gurgles. Silia's lunar wraith swooped down from high above the clouds and hovered by Dragna's head. It was an odd sight—watching the two wraiths communicate.

They often hunted one another.

Like the humanoid creatures, the wraiths also had to learn to let go of their prejudices and work together. Luckily, Taura and Silia handled those relations. And even luckier, it appeared that Dragna and Silia's lunar wraith, Ago, seemed to have a *fondness* for one another. The massive dark gray beast hovered right by Dragna's head. His long, scaled wings beat steadily with imperceptibly small movements, appearing as if Ago was truly just floating in the air.

To Viggo's understanding, not all lunar wraiths could do this. But Ago was one of the strongest and most aggressive of his kind. It was a wonder to watch the deadly beasts as Taura relayed the information to Silia. That those travelling in the water will be pushed with the aid of Rahn. The lunar wraiths would have to swim as close to the sea as possible, trailing their claws in the water to be aided with the magic of Rahn and not be left behind.

As the two leaders converged, their wraiths nuzzled their cheeks against one another. As they parted ways for Silia and Ago to share the news with the other wraithkins, Dragna remained where she was. Even from this great distance, Viggo could see her large eyes searching the clouds for Ago. As the other wraiths swooped below the clouds, skimming their long talons against the water, Ago and Dragna led the pack side-by-side.

Once each syren had boarded the ships, the currents began to settle. And for one small moment, it seemed like the Arkts itself stilled. Then they took off. Wind rushed through their ears Waves crashed relentlessly against the boat. A few people screamed and most ducked closer to the deck to remain on the boat and not fall into the black waters below.

Rahn had told him that they would be there sometime within the night. Viggo didn't know what to believe before, but now, he knew it would be true. At this point, all Viggo could do was wait. The day passed quickly and slowly all at once. Viggo did his best to speak to as many soldiers as he could. Taking a note from King Agar, who resided on the ship to the left of Viggo's, he thanked as many people as he could and reminded them what was at stake. To live in a free realm. To live a life of safety and comfort without fear of a greedy power-hungry ruler. To go to sleep knowing that their families would be safe. He reminded them that these were their goals. He put their nerves at ease, played games of Four-Footed Monk and passed out food and water. All the while, his mind kept falling into the haunting image of a Dahs turned red with blood.

CHAPTER 28
ARIA

It was anything but hard to convince Raask that he needed to sleep. All of the white lithe in the world wouldn't be enough for what they were going to do.

But Aria was not human, so rest wasn't as necessary for her. She didn't need it to recharge her magic or herself too much. But most importantly, if she did sleep, she would not be the one to kill the King. And this was perhaps the most important thing she could do in her entire life. The one thing she had worked towards. Aria *would* be the one to kill the King. And that was that.

It wasn't that she didn't believe Raask could kill him, it was that she *did*. And Aria, she may be a monster for a lot of reasons, but she didn't mind adding one more reason to the list by taking this meaningful kill from him. This was one thing she just couldn't let go of. She had to be the one to kill him, feel his last breath on her teeth and his blood on her fingers.

She waited until he had fallen asleep. She *would* have drugged him with some cobalt lithe, but she didn't want to risk him waking groggily in case things didn't go as planned. Or even if they did, she'd want him alert while they celebrated. He fell asleep quickly. And she stayed for far longer than she planned to. Listening to the sounds of his breathing like the currents that coursed through her cave back home. He looked so different now. But he was still hers.

She ran her long fingers through his hair. White now, no longer golden like the sun. Fen, who would always offer his bed to her, and therefore Raask, was out sleeping on the chair by the fire while Lok slept on the couch. Night had fallen a couple of hours ago and Aria relied on her syrenic eyesight to see Raask in the dark. His chest rose and fell with each labored breath. And ever so carefully, Aria traced the outline of Raask's tattoos. The swirls, Morlok crest, the symbols she did not know—not yet at least. She couldn't wait to ask him about each and every tattoo and scar that marked his body. But that could wait. Aria had a king to kill.

And Raask... He would be a great king. Dueling with his father, showing his greatness, would be *something*. But it wasn't what the Skierkans needed. The Skierkans needed a ruler who could rule without a bloodthirsty reign, show the strength in peace.

But in order for there to be peace, there must first be a reckoning. And that was exactly what Aria was built for. She would need to play the villain that ruthlessly slaughtered the King and his followers, to clear the path for peace.

With a gentle kiss on Raask's forehead, Aria got up out of bed, and crept out of the bedroom. The second she cracked open the door she heard Lok's loud snoring. Her eyes moved to the entryway, where Fen sat, wide awake in the wooden chair by the door, staring out the window with Jor coiled snugly on the armrest. Aria's weapons were already laying against the door. And Fen's were strapped to his body. More than she could count.

Silently, she skulked over to him and strapped the daggers to her thighs, arm, and ribs. They slid against her black leather bodysuit with the ease of an act done a thousand times. On the kitchen counter sat the box with the arm that Caden Callady had created for her. Her scrutinizing gaze lingered on the box, thinking of the clever man who created it.

He too, believed in a better realm. She didn't feel ready to use the arm in battle, she'd only practiced with it a handful of times. But she couldn't leave it behind. Caden Callady deserved a part in this. He gave his life for the revolution, and she would have it noted in the history books that the revolution was won with his help. She wouldn't let him be forgotten.

Fen watched her eyes and without words, knew exactly what she wanted. Somehow, in the little time they had spent together, they had grown to know each other to the point of anticipating each other's actions. Their thoughts. Their needs. It was no surprise to Aria when she opened the door to see Fen armed and waiting for her.

Silently, he opened the box to the prosthetic limb and helped her strap it to the little piece left of her arm.

The metaled-lithe powder, a sparkling black and white, the matching colors to the new limb itself, sat in a little velvet bag. She scooped some into her nail and snorted it. It smelled of metal and a salty ocean, not unlike her home in the caverns. An image of a young Caden Callady sloshing through the caverns on the edge of the Zojz flashed through her mind. Maybe it wasn't such a terrible thing to care for humans, some of them didn't seem so bad.

Perhaps she was growing. Maybe this was what the realm needed now. After years of prejudice and slaughter, maybe they needed to learn to care and really see one another. She didn't think she would ever be capable of such things, of loving, and caring, for a human or even humanity as a whole, but maybe she could. Maybe she could be more than simply destruction incarnate.

When she was strapped up and down with weaponry, she took one long look at Fen's apartment—for the second time that day—and quietly opened the door. Her black hair hung in one long braid that landed between her shoulder blades and slapped into her back with each heavy footstep. Fen was as human as she was, and could also see supremely well in the dark. Where Aria was a creature of the deepest pits of the most treacherous black seas, Fen had heralded from the shadows of the forest. A different kind of darkness, but darkness the same.

They ran side by side the whole way.

Their boots, shined black leather, were Skierkan-made and therefore incredibly efficient at running on ice. Their toes gripped onto the frozen streets as they ran, while the cold air stung their lungs. Skierkan winters were some of the worst in the realm and the running warmed them.

Too quickly and not fast enough, they arrived by the edge of the Gaulic. The dense forest buzzed with the magical creatures inside, radiating an eerie power. Unlike the white lithe that resided in the walls of the palace, the Gaulic felt like the power of life. The Bleached Palace buzzed with a dark power, like the air moments before lightning, a feeling of dread and vulnerability.

Fen wrapped his arms around Aria. He smelled of spiced clove and warmth, and no longer reminded her of a wet dog. He too, wasn't as bad as she assumed at first. She tucked her head into his chest before pulling away. "I'll see you on the other side," Fen said with a wink. He only whispered it, but his deep voice seemed to echo against the stillness of the night.

A part of her heart ached to leave her partner then and there. Somehow, he had become someone she trusted. Quickly, her dampened mood elevated once again as she realized what he was about to do. Fen was going to grant Aria her wish. He ripped his shirt off and took off in a run towards the forest.

The snout came first. Along with the teeth. Then his spine seemed to grow and arch until it deflated in on itself, before growing once again, only this time with thick brown fur. Legs sprouted from where his arms had been and claws ripped out from his nail bed.

He galloped into the shadows of the Gaulic in his hylbra form. As large as a horse, with teeth and claws nearly as sharp as hers. She heard him long after she stopped seeing him, smiling at the sound of seeing and hearing her friend in his natural form for the first time.

"See you on the other side," she whispered, smiling to herself as she broke off into a sprint towards the Bleached Palace.

The buzz of the storm grew stronger with each harrowed step. She had lived in this palace for months, and knew it better than she knew the clunky metal arm that pumped at her side with each run. She hid behind trees, careful to avoid the stables, and the Irridesci tower that seemed to grow more alive in the dark night. Only when the light of the silver moon faded and gave way to the indigo moon's deep light did Aria sprint between the hedges of the gardens and to the one place she knew would not be guarded.

She climbed the stone walls of Raask's tower just as she climbed the Callady Estate's. Her claws punctured the stone, leaving behind a trail of holes as she threw herself up the wall, over and over and over again. She grimaced each time her body slammed against the wall. Her feet would hit first and she'd arch her back away to make as little noise as possible. But eventually she began to give, when she got high enough to not be heard, her body would slap the stone and vibrate through her bones. But she kept going. Forward, always forward.

When the stone changed from the old, worn-out white lithe-bleached stone, to the new and shiny one that arrived after the wraith attack, she knew she was close. Only two more jumps and she was hanging above his window. Swinging back and forth a few times, she broke the lithe-enforced glass with the tip of her boots. She prayed that nobody heard the glass break or saw it falling through the air. She swung one more time, and landed in his room, directly on her ass.

Most of the glass fell off her thick leather bodysuit when she stood, but other parts required a moment of pulling and tinkering as she worked with the prosthetic arm Caden had given her. Purple blood sizzled on the ground below. Bubbling and warping the wooden floors while she focused on manipulating the metaled fingers to delicately pinch and remove the glass shards. A far from simple task that took way too long. As she worked, she debated changing her blood to a humanic red or leaving it violet and acidic.

As king, Raask wouldn't sleep in these chambers anymore anyways. Her purple blood sizzled and smelled of burning wood as she began to leave Raask's old bedroom. Her eyes lingered for a moment before shutting that door.

Clothes and books were strewn everywhere. Food had rotted and molded over. The bed was unmade and his ostentatious jewels and shiny rings sat on his desk with a thick layer of dust. Aria grabbed a short blade that leaned against his bedframe. The blade he had commissioned for her when she had lost her arm, Arachni. She slid it into the thigh strap she'd left empty. Enjoying the weight of it against her hip.

Aria—long ago—decided that the Fire Monger King lacked a heart altogether. But if there ever was an argument for him having one, the untouched bedroom of his beloved dead son was it. The thought rocked her to her core. Sharing a feeling with that disgusting man.

She gagged and let the door shut loudly behind her as she raced down the spiral staircase to the rest of the palace in pursuit of blood.

Her steps were light and silent, just as she'd practised all those nights.

The cold harsh air and the raw buzz of power from the white lithe twisted together as they swam up her nose and down her throat. She ran through the palace, slicing through the air like a flung blade. There was one thing holding her back from slaughtering each and every guard that remained loyal to the Fire Monger King, one rebel that she needed to move to safety before she unleashed herself upon the castle.

The one guard who would be stationed at the bottom of Raask's tower, where he said he would be nightly in case Aria needed him. He was sitting, which of course was against guard protocol, and reading a book with a half-naked centaur on the cover. "Did you get to the part in the cave with the sprites?" She asked.

A smile tugged at the corner of his lips. He peered up at her, his eyes hesitated on the weaponry, leaving his smile faltering. "Where can I take them?" His family.

"Take them to the Gaulic, Fen has instructed the creatures to keep an eye out for you and take you to safety." Zaries rose, placing his book into the inside pocket of his cloak. The once-round guard smiled at her. A thousand memories raced through her mind, and in each of them, they had all started with her and Zaries. He was the first human she had ever considered more than meat. More than a vessel for cruelty. He was one of the only friends she had ever made that didn't start and end with a respect for her as a bloodthirsty queen. They had laughed together. To anyone else that may mean nothing, nothing at all, but to Aria, it was the first step in a long journey out of the depths of pain and sacrifice.

"What will you do, with the other guards? They have families, many of them remained out of fear and not loyalty." His eyes bore into hers. "Just as you have done things to protect yours, they are protecting theirs, Aria."

She understood what he was telling her. It was something she had learned this past year. That there was more to the monsters. She had tried to do things with less blood, appointing Mayta to the throne with Raask, but that hadn't worked. This war wouldn't end until there was only one side left. And maybe it wasn't fair to the ones who stayed out of fear, but she didn't care. Raask would be king, a more just and peaceful king. She would be the fire that razed the kingdom down so he could build one anew.

Aria always knew that she was not the one who was meant to rule. Mayta had the disposition for that. Raask was an ideal king in every way. And Aria? She was meant to bleed the way for the better rulers. Once this war was over, she could step aside and allow the others to take over. Then, and only then, could Aria finally rest.

She was so close she could almost taste it. One more bloodbath. One more slaughter. She'd allow herself to revel in it, too, and then she could rest. The weight of the realm wouldn't be on her shoulders anymore.

"Thank you," her voice was far quieter than she anticipated. He was doing what he should do in his place, looking out for his kind, but now it was time for her to do what she had to do.

"Goodbye, Aria." She watched as he left down the long hallway she'd have to travel to reach the rest of the palace. She gave him a few minutes. A few minutes that she spent leaning against the white lithe-bleached walls, imagining what lay ahead.

A horn, blaring loud, echoed across Etra. Zaries had betrayed her. She removed Arachni from her belt and prepared. Slowly, she walked down the hall. Swinging her blade from front to back and to the front again. Over and over again. She swung the blade, hearing it whistle through the air like her own call to war.

She reached deeper into the hallway where it opened up and windows sat on each side of the walls. Guards were running alright, but not towards her—towards the Dahs. Zaries had not betrayed her. Etra was being attacked, presumably by her allies. Anger filled her stomach, pumping her veins with more power than she knew what to do with.

Her allies had finally come to the shores of Etra. Her army had presumably finished their training. They were supposed to warn her. Make plans. Not just show up and start killing. Her breaths grew ragged. The first thing the Skierkans would do was increase the King's guards and store him somewhere safe, somewhere they could easily defend. She could no longer slip in unannounced among the shadows and darkness of night, instead she'd be facing prepared guards stoked with the adrenaline of battle.

The only advantage she'd have now, was striking hard and fast while the majority of their forces rushed to the shores.

Her feet carried her through the palace. She knew it well, she knew the guards well. She remembered many of them, hearing the songs she played for them on the harp, hearing their voices turning to screams as she slit their throats. Three down. Many more to go.

Raask's tower was close to his father's corridors, but she doubted theKing would remain there now. If she had to guess, he'd be in the war room.

It was no time to guess, but guesses were all she had.

She ran down another hallway as six more Vermilli turned the corner. They took one look at her and drew their blades. She threw a dagger at the one leading the charge, it landed in his throat and he fell to the ground clutching at his neck. The next one threw a dagger at her that bounced right off of her metaled left arm. The next sunk into the sensitive flesh above the prosthetic limb. Aria grimaced before removing it and flinging it back to its owner, where it sunk into her right brow, piercing her brain. When she finally met them in the middle of the hall, she wasted no time in impaling the woman in the center, swinging her body to the left and punching the throat of the man on the left side of the hall. Not dead but momentarily collapsed, she focused on the woman on the right end of the hall. She rammed her shoulder into her, pinning her against the wall and grabbing her own dagger that sat against her leg, slitting her throat then turning around and throwing it into the last one's heart.

Quickly, she grabbed Arachni from the chest, and continued her run. Blood poured down the blade and covered her hand. Sloppy, and she knew better. A wet blade, a wet handle, a disastrous combination. Heavy footsteps fell down the hall as more guards came. Each one she slaughtered, turning killing into an art form. She knew where to puncture, how to throw the blade, how to kill. Her mouth watered at the smell of the blood and meat.

She impaled the one in the front, taking the one behind him out too as she pushed the blade hard enough and far enough to gut the guard behind him. Taking advantage of the hard metal of her metaled lithe left hand, she smashed the face in of one guard with one quick punch. His skull crunched and impaled his own eye. Bodies fell like rain. Blood, as endless as the Dahs, puddled on the floor of the palace. She kept her blood syrenic, violet and acidic, as deadly as her. She used her metaled arm as a shield whenever possible, but a gnarly dagger had cut across the side of her neck.

Bruises blossomed across her face like a bouquet of wounds from battle.

The deeper she got into the palace, the more skilled the guards became. Guards turned into soldiers, who turned into higher and higher ranking members of the Skierkan military. Each kill came naturally to her.

Her mind emptied as she killed. No thoughts, no planning, no course of action, only the beat of her heart and the scent of gore.

Before she knew it, Aria had killed her way to the battle room, and through it. The King was not there, but other Skierkan loyalists were. At that moment she didn't care for their families, or their lives. All she cared for was the movement, the dance of battle and the songs of their screaming.

But where was the King? Where was he? She racked her brain. Tracing the different rooms of the palace in her mind. Did he even know that she had come for him? She had to see his face. She couldn't live another second without feeling his blood in her hands. She needed this. It was her purpose. Her only salvation. The heavy weight of her ancestors rested on her at every second, she felt their shame and disappointment. Finally, finally that would end.

Then she heard it. War had come to the Bleached Palace. The impenetrable fortress. Screaming. Weaponry. The whistle of arrows. The blast of cannons. War was here. Another blast of cannon and with it the realization that the Fire Monger King was cruel, but he was no coward. He would not be hiding in the palace. He would be fighting.

Just as she would, when the killers came to the palace, she wouldn't let her guard hide her, she'd stand outside and fight. Her breaths were heavy, the wounds had started to accumulate on her and she was feeling the pain. One moment, she sat and listened to the beat of her heart, the throbbing of her head, and the sounds of the war. What if Raask was not her mirror, the other side of the coin, but the Fire Monger King was? They both hungered for blood. Reveled in their cruelty. Only he had won, and her ancestors had lost. When she killed him, would she rest and allow the others to rule? Or would she continue to crave the glory of battle?

The one moment she gave herself had passed. Again, she sprinted through the palace. Anyone who had stayed behind, she had already killed. No longer masking her steps, she stomped through the palace until she was racing down the stairs of the grand entrance.

Here. Here was the heart of the massacre. Another moment, she needed another moment, as she took in the scene. Red cloaks of all shades fought the rebels: Skierkans, syrens, wraithkins, Surtrians, they all battled together. With more precision and power than any magic wielder should have, the Fire Monger King sat on his throne and appeared bored as he carefully lit the heads of her people on fire, miraculously avoiding his own army as hers burned into ashes.

The horror of the stench of burnt flesh and the blood of her people was pushed aside as Aria understood what needed to be done. She ducked onto the stairs, hiding behind the railing. If the King saw her, she'd be burned to ash in seconds. She had to be precise, smart, and lethal. This was it, her entire life had led to this moment.

A plan fell into her head like an anvil. She could sprint back up these steps, take a running leap into the air, swinging onto the Skierkan flag and onto the King before he saw her, before anyone noticed her. She was fast. She'd been training. And nobody knew she was there. She could do it. She'd have the King's blood on her hands, and she'd finally feel her retribution.

She'd be free.

Free.

Staying hunched over, she raced back up the steps, sticking to the shadows as best as she could. Then running. Her feet slammed in front of each other, one after the other. She ran. Forward, always forward. Leaping into the sky and onto the red and black flag decorated over the grand entry, ignoring the ashes of her people as they swarmed the entire room into a fog of decay.

She was a killer. She was fearless. Ruthless. Bloodthirsty. Cruel. The Queen of the Abisian Syrens. The most feared creature of the realm. Her hand brushed against the soft fabric of the flag. Desperately, she clung to it, getting ready to pump her body, twisting it to fall on top of the King where she would behead him with her claws.

Her claws.

They slid out of her hands at the thought, ripping apart not just her nailbeds, but the Skierkan flag. She did not grasp onto the flag, instead, her claws ripped all the way down the fabric and to the floor of the grand entry far, far below. She felt it only for a second before the darkness came for her.

CHAPTER 29
MAYTA

As life as she knew it began to literally crumble all around Mayta, all she could think about was the man on the other side of the dark bridge in the corner of her mind.

She could feel him as he tried to get in. A gentle knock that evolved to a more hurried and desperate thunder, before altogether disappearing. The bodies of her victims were gone, and the shadowed, musty cave had fallen apart until a lavish golden room stood in its place. Still Mayta did not want to let Viggo in. She was scared, so unbelievably scared of screwing up and disappointing everyone, that she couldn't bear it if Viggo witnessed her failures firsthand. So she kept that door locked shut as she took in the details of the room.

Gold was everywhere. The dark stone of the cave floor had fallen to Gods-knew where and Mayta stood in a liquid gold puddle that spanned the entire room. The thick liquid was warm, but not hot. And when she lifted her legs the gold did not stick to her, it merely glided right off and back to the floor. The walls were adorned with floor to ceiling windows with a gradient of the same deep gold at the bottom, lightening to a buttery yellow at the top. The ceiling was the only black thing in the entire room, the only darkness and break from the unrelenting brightness. A throne sat in the center of the room. Made of the same gold puddled on the floor, only it was hardened and shaped with long rays shooting out of it.

At first, Mayta was alone. She was sure of it. And all she could smell was heat and metal. A primal part of her recognized where she was before she was able to put the words to it. Once the God appeared on the throne, the word rose into her mind like a new dawn: Baldrei.

Mayta was in the presence of the God of the Sun, Baldrei. He sat straight against the back of the throne. Oddly, he appeared to her as a human. He was large and muscular with the same deep brown skin of the Surtrian syrens. Atop his head was a bed of light blonde curls that appeared halo-like. Along with the magnifying presence, there was a subtle pull towards him that was innate when in the presence of a God, or at least she had heard so from the old fairytales, the only other clue to his Godliness was the liquid gold in his eyes. His gaze burned into her, hurting her eyes, as she remembered herself, she sank into a single-legged kneel. It would have been proper to lower her head, but she couldn't help herself, she couldn't look away.

Baldrei smiled at her. A warm and beautiful thing. Mayta didn't know much about the sciences of the world, but she did know that all life began with the sun. Now that she was in his presence, she understood this on a deeper level than ever before. Baldrei, God of the Sun, was in a way responsible for all of the life in the realm. The plants. The sea creatures. The humans. All of it, bowed to him for what he had done for them. Freyite may be the Goddess of Love and Fertility but Baldrei... In a way, he was the original giver of life.

"It is an honor to meet you Mayta, Princess of the Abisian syrens." His voice was soft and smooth like a sugared drink. "You may rise," He added when she remained kneeling.

She rose to her feet, feeling the warmth of the gold floor fall off of her knees. "Thank you," Her voice was quieter than she had meant it to be, and while the God seemed to be kind, he was still a God. And Mayta was not foolish enough to believe for a second that this God cared at all about her. The Gods had made a pact to stay out of the business of the mortals like her. And while they lounged in their holy realm, her kind had been hunted and enslaved. Endless slaughter for centuries had gone ignored and unchecked. An anger that Mayta didn't know was there began to rise into her throat.

Baldrei drew in a long breath through his nose, seemingly sniffing the air and releasing it with a sigh of pleasure. "You are angry at me, aren't you, little one?"

Mayta shook her head. "No, sir."

"Well, maybe you should be." He winked, slow and languid.

"I have come to hear the prophecy from the Sistros." Mayta kept her voice even, stealing some of the power she felt from her anger with the Gods, and shrinking away from the consistent worry of failure that had sat heavily on her chest ever since she'd left the palace. Helk, since she was born, she had been afraid. Afraid of being captured by the Skierkans. Afraid for Aria. Afraid for her people. Always afraid, while these Gods refused to step in and create a more righteous realm.

Mayta did not want to be afraid anymore. And while she wasn't feeling particularly brave, she decided to act like she was anyways. Just because she preferred her knives in the kitchen than in a sheath strapped to her thigh didn't mean she wasn't mighty. She could be formidable if she wanted to. She could be strong. She *would* be brave. The realm was counting on her. Viggo. Aria. Taura. The syrens. Those silly women of the courts that she loved. The goblins who worked in the gardens. Everyone. She would hear the prophecy and if it foretold that there was nothing left but misery and pain then she would not leave until they told her the path to freedom.

She was a kind person by nature, but today, she would be fearless too.

"I have come to hear the path to peace in the realm." Mayta

corrected. It wasn't just the prophecy, not really. What she needed was the answers to how to defeat the Morloks and leave behind a better realm.

As Baldrei nodded, the liquid gold in his eyes shifted, causing a twinkle to reflect sharply across the room like a sunbeam. He smiled smugly, making it obvious that he believed this to be the right answer. Mayta let out a small sigh of relief, allowing her shoulders to fall from their tension. "Luckily for you, if it's the prophecy you want, I can put you back into that cave with the Sistros—who were planning on eating you by the way. *Or* I could tell you what it is you really want and send you where you need to be."

Without invitation, Mayta walked closer to the God's throne. She narrowed her eyes on his, assessing if there was any truth to his words. He laughed quietly at the face of her scrutiny. "You know, you are different up close." Instinctively, she took half a step back.

"What do you mean?" Her brows furrowed as she considered his words.

"Do you think you were the only one watching him all these years?"

She knew who he spoke of. The charming prince. The kind man in a sea of cruelty. The prince of the sun, and the man she had killed. "Do you know he walks the Arkts again?" Baldrei's words sliced through her like a sword to the gut.

Baldrei laughed again, louder this time, more brazen and full of ridicule. "Tsu alone has kept the God's pact, little one. And it seems that Kel sent the prince back. It has been done before, only once, but it has been done. The one you call Skullin was once human. It was many years ago, but I remember." Fear cracked onto her face. She couldn't help it, she couldn't hide it. A powerful man with a vendetta against her had come back from the dead, evidently with the favor of the God of Death. "Don't worry, he doesn't seek revenge, not against you anyway."

Mayta swallowed a lump of air. She felt it as it slipped all the way down to her spinning gut. For some reason, she didn't quite believe him. "Do you know that he is the key to your salvation?" While she was certain Baldrei was speaking of Raask, her mind flashed to an image of Viggo. "Yes, him too," Baldrei added, somehow aware of her thought.

"Please, just tell me what to do, how do I save them?"

She felt his gaze on her, feeling the entire weight of the sun's power with it. He said he had the answers, so when would he stop toying with her? But... Something had changed in his eyes. The light and playfulness that was just there had disappeared, leaving in its place the worst thing she could imagine from him. Pity.

Mayta tried to summon the anger that she had felt before, but she just couldn't. It wasn't anything but a mask for her fear anyways, a more comfortable emotion, but not an honest one. How bad was their future to draw a look of pity from the God of the Sun?

"If I tell you what is about to happen and what will need to be done for you to reach your realm of peace, it will not happen. So listen to me, listen to the words that I can tell you. Listen, little one, for the fate of your loved ones relies on how well you listen to this."

Mayta nodded, walking closer to ensure she didn't miss a single word, a single change in tone, anything.

"Your realm relies on balance. For power comes sacrifice. And for the Fire Monger King's reign to end, your revolutionaries will need to lose your most powerful. But the leader who will rule over Skierka will not be the same. Grief will tear their heart in two and another reign of blood will follow in its place."

Their most powerful? One face fell into her mind. A face that she couldn't bear to lose. Heartbreak nearly ripped her chest in half. Eyes wild, gasping for breath, she did her best to remain focused.

And then the God held out his hand, his golden robes slinking down to his elbow. He withdrew a small dagger from somewhere beneath his robes and cut a harsh line down his palm. Then, quickly, he raised his palm, full of golden blood that looked a little too similar to whatever thick golden liquid rested on the floor for Mayta's comfort, and held it to his eye. He then delicately stabbed at the corner of his eye, where the skin of the lid met the corner of the nose. On the tip of the dagger, was what Mayta could only assume was a tear. He mixed it with the blood on his palm. Swirling the knife around the cut as Mayta would mix a gravy.

As the knife moved, the blood and tears mixed, becoming thicker and thicker. The God kept his eyes closed and whispered something to himself in a language Mayta could not understand. Then the liquid started to glow and shrink until it hardened into what could only be some form of lithe she had never seen before. Perhaps, a form that had never existed before.

He held out his hand with the sparkling gold lithe in it. Mayta hurried forward, opening her palm. Baldrei dropped the golden lithe into her hand, it fell like any other rock, only it was far heavier than she imagined of such a small rock. It was barely larger than her thumbnail and smelled like an odd combination of sweet florals and metallic blood.

"When you return to your realm, you will bring this to the next ruler of Skierka, and you will make sure they bring this on their quest."

"That's it?" Mayta asked, feeling like the task was too small for what was about to happen.

"Yes, my sweet child. And when what is done is done, I am going to cut off the sunlight to your realm. You may not believe me now, but I am going to do it to protect your realm from the eyes of the Gods who would like more excuses for blood. But I will bring it back when the time comes."

He couldn't be serious. "How will we survive without the light?"

"You will survive, just as you always have. The realm will need you then more than ever. Remember that you have a light of your own to give, Mayta the Precious." She blushed hearing the name her people had coined for her.

She did her best to remain brave, but everything he was saying was truly the last thing she wanted to hear. "But why, why are you doing this? Why are you helping us?" She asked, smashing her lips together as she tried to keep herself composed.

Baldrei's lips curled in a smile. Either subconsciously or out of showmanship, beams of light shot out from him in a halo. "Do you know anything of the Hawthorn lineage?" Mayta shook her head, she had never even heard the name. "Well, long ago, I fell in love with a human with the name of Hawthorn. And Raask, he is the last of that line. A beautiful and sweet baby boy who has held the weight of the realm on his shoulders since birth. I believe—no—I know that he is capable of great things. And I will do what I can to protect him and the humans."

"And taking your light from us? That'll protect us?" Mayta didn't understand any of it. What was it about this rock? What was the quest someone would take? And how could there be a peaceful realm without their most powerful?

"It won't be forever. I promise. Only until it is safe for the other wandering eyes of the Gods to see our plan."

She still didn't understand, but she really had no choice but to trust him. "Are you sure? Aren't you mad at me for what I did to Raask?" Guilt lingered in her voice.

But Baldrei shook his head. "No, you do not see it now, but by killing his humanity, you saved him. You'll understand soon. Now you must hurry off. Go, and remember to be strong."

She felt like collapsing into the puddle on the ground. Like pulling out her hair and letting out a scream. "Mayta, you have the kind of strength that comes once in a millennia, and it is exactly what the realm will need. Do not give up. Do not force yourself into another's ideals of strength. Stay true to your heart. Give the golden lithe right away. And trust that even if things aren't as you may want, they will be as they are needed to be."

With that, the golden room began to fade into the cold sunlight filtered through the pine needles of what could only be the Gaulic forest. The radiant smile of Baldrei was the last thing she saw before her soul settled back into her mortal body, back against the icy ground.

Cold, wet, snow seeped into her skin while the clashing blades and the smells of gore registered into her senses. All she wanted to do was curl into a ball and cry herself to sleep, but instead, she rose to her feet, and walked towards the shadow of the palace.

CHAPTER 30
VIGGO

They came in the night. By ship. By wraith, both lunar and sea. By the grace of Rahn, they came.

For the first time in over an entire sun cycle, Viggo stepped foot onto Skierkan soil. He wore his armor, the heavy black helmet with the Morlok crest imbued with white lithe. Spikes jutted out from the shoulders and along the crown of his helmet resembling his dark Skierkan crown. He debated removing the white lithe of the Morlok crest, a raven with its wings extended over a moon. Symbols had power, but the white lithe itself was power, and he needed all the help he could get in controlling his magic. Too much was at stake.

So he covered the crest. With the fur of a bear that wrapped around his neck and flailed behind him like a cape. He would not be associated with the Morlok legacy today, today, he would need people to see him as himself. The Skierkan Bruin. The title he earned long ago, fighting for the very people he would be fighting with and against today.

The boots of his armor trudged through the shores of the Dahs. The war ships were too big to dock any closer to Etra. So with the help of the syrens, they were escorted and kept safe from any curious Dahsian creatures. The syrens kept up their end of the bargain, distracting and removing the sharks and eels—the creatures that would bump into their legs under the dark, thick waters of the Dahs. In turn, the humans would lead the siege on the land. The syrens had gotten better at land combat, but they were not as fluid as they were in the waters or as those born with legs. It was their time.

The black sand of the Dahs felt so different to the light fluffy sands of the Surtrian islands. He forgot how unforgivable Skierka was, how it felt like the land itself wanted to dissuade any life on the island. It was colder than he remembered too. The coldness assaulted his skin and bones, wafting in from the waters that seeped in between his armor at his legs and settling onto the hair of his chest.

As the General, Viggo remained in the front. Taura the Terrible at his side and King Jag Agar on his other side. Skender, Emir, and Alia were behind them, spread out equally along the shore. Silia and the other wraithkins remained high up above, careful to not cast shadows across the silver nor the indigo moon. They would remain hidden until Viggo gave his signal.

He expected the Vermilli to have already sounded the alarm. Expecting to see the band of red cloaks across the shore as they were every night he had been in charge of protecting this land. He strained his eyes looking for a single Vermilli. This shore was where Etra was the most susceptible to attacks. Not a single red cloak was stationed along the shore. And the usually sprawling Salt District seemed quiet. The nocturnal part of town filled with drunkards and gamblers was never quiet at this hour. How much had changed in his homeland due to the war he'd started?

He shook off the question, scanning the Salt District one more time to confirm that there were no hidden armies that somehow knew they were coming. Then he looked to his side, at Taura the Terrible, walking with long strides, she gave Viggo a nod. He turned to King Agar, who strode evenly with his chest puffed out and chin up high. The skin of a snake hung off his back like a scarf, rippling through the harsh Skierkan winds. A curt nod from the king and Viggo magically amplified his voice, "People of Skierka, I am your General, Viggo Morlok. As your General, my greatest concern has been the safety of you, your family, and our land. And as your General, I am giving you the opportunity to reach safety. My war is not with you, it is with your King. We ask you, for your safety, to remain indoors. We will not be breaking into any houses or businesses. We are only coming for the palace." His eyes fell upon the Bleached Palace, towering high above the city. A massive white structure with towers and bridges and a band of red-cloaked Vermilli stationed like a sea of blood, protecting the nobles and the King when they should be placed protecting their people along the Dahs.

He should have felt angry, to know that when given the choice, the King chose to protect himself over his people. But it was not anger that settled against his bones and into his gut. Like the first dusting of snow ahead of the long Skierkan winters, Viggo felt settled and sure of what was to come. The band of red lining the grounds of the Bleached Palace meant one thing and one thing only —that Viggo had been right.

For years he had felt tortured and tormented, wondering if he was doing the right thing by betraying his people. Raask was here somewhere. Somewhere, in one of these buildings, in one of these houses, was his brother whom he loved more than anything or anyone. Viggo had done wrong by him, so devastatingly and disgustingly wrong. But now, he was doing the right thing. There was no longer any question. That red band of trained soldiers, lining the most powerful palace in the entire Arkts, was the answer and reassurance he had been searching for. His power rose inside of him. For once it was not an unsettled ocean of rocking waves and alarming lulls. His power rose as a sure and settled thing.

The alarms began. The wave of red cloaks raced down the hills towards him.

Viggo lifted his sword high above his head. Moonlight glinted off of the sword as he flicked his wrist from side to side, signaling to Silia for the lunar wraiths to descend. Taura the Terrible, at the sight of his raised sword, let out a bloodcurdling shriek. With it, the syrenic drummers rose from the depths and beat their drums. Donning their human bodies, the syrens slunk through the shore, holding their drums in their hands like babies. They beat the drums over and over again, to the heartbeat of their Queen. A quick rhythm, but steady as Viggo's magic that thrummed in his veins.

The alarms shrieked, continuing on and on, a loud and shrill noise. The drums beat as the syrens threw themselves into each pulse. And then the syrens began their song. A low hum, a deep and aching melody of grief and retribution. They'd come for revenge.

The song filled the cove with a heavy layer of syrenic magic. Viggo felt it right away, the increased strength, more power and speed with each movement. None of it compared to the focus the syrenic magic instilled in him. Battle clarity. With the help of the syrenic magic, Viggo looked upon his homeland with the eyes of some of the oldest and most evolved predators.

The Surtrians were the first to join the syren's song. Skender and Emir thumped their chest along with the beat of the syrenic drums. Their orange slashes swayed in the wind. Their famed swords remained along their sides—the Rakkei did not lift their weaponry in showmanship. They believed in the holiness of weaponry and found it distasteful to raise a weapon as anything less than a promise to kill. They would not draw their swords until the first Skierkan came to attack. And then they would be unstoppable.

The wave of red came crashing down. The first wave of Skierkans was nearly upon them. A solid mass. Wearing warm leathers, boots made for the icy, snowy terrain, and armed with some of the best weaponry in the entire realm.

Underneath his heavy black helmet, behind the pockets of shadows and darkness that he kept on the ready, sat a dark smile. For the greatest armor and weaponry in the world would not save them from what was to come. And he had given them every chance to do the right thing, and now... Now he would not have to feel bad for what they were about to do.

This confidence, self-assuredness, it felt damn good.

And the sight of Silia and her sister leading the lunar wraiths? Even better.

They came faster than any arrow. The lunar wraiths kept their long wings tucked close into their body as they shot through the air. Long shiny claws grabbed onto the Vermilli soldiers and ripped them apart. The lunar wraiths, in one fell swoop, obliterated the massive wave of Vermilli soldiers racing to the shore. Discarding their bodies in the Dahs behind their forces, they bled out into the black waters, turning the cove into an ocean of blood.

Viggo could hear Silia's wooping, and her wraith's roar of triumph clear above the ever-ringing alarms and the drumming and the humming of the syrens. Silia, his friend, was triumphant. Viggo looked back at Emir who tracked Silia and her sister through the skies with his eyes. His lips tightened in focus. No smile, not until the day was done.

Viggo continued forward into the heart of his homeland. Trudging through the leftover entrails and blood that stained the snow. This time, he would not stop until he had saved his homeland and left a path towards a righteous ruling to the only one who deserved it. Or at the very least, he'd die trying.

CHAPTER 31
RAASK

Raask stretched his hand out towards Aria, looking to pull her closer into him, only to be met with cold sheets. The smell of her lingered on the bed. She must have stayed for quite some time before running off. He should have known. If he had given it half a second of thought, he *would* have known better than to fall asleep trusting that she would be there when he awoke. Aria may love him, but she loved her duty and her people more than anything. And she had one Helk of a self-sacrificial streak that he was working against.

He breathed in the scent of her on the pillow. Salted caramel. He let the smell settle over his nerves as he dressed. Quickly throwing on leathers he found strewn across the room. Fen's bagged leather pants had a good stretch to them, and Fen was a massive man, so Raask had to use a rope to belt the pants. All the combat leather tops he found were coated in disgusting combinations of sweat and blood. He considered going fully shirtless, or throwing on a heavy fur. But it was still winter. So he found a sleeved leather top that left his chest bare. He had decided to stop running, so maybe it was best

that his people saw who he really was. And in the heat of whatever
waited for him, he was sure that he wouldn't get too cold.

Lok was sleeping on the couch. Fen had obviously already left
with Aria, taking most of the weaponry in the apartment, but Raask
collected a handful of swords and daggers before planning to wake
Lok up. The palace's alarm sounded. A disgusting shrill noise. Lok
woke with a startle, jolting upright with wide eyes.

What had Aria done?

Lok and Raask looked at one another. A thousand memories and
thoughts silently transcended through them, all concluding with the
fact that they had to go to the palace, that the rest of their lives were
waiting on the other side of today. Raask tossed Lok a heavy sword,
he let it land on his lap, studying it briefly before getting up and
dressed. Before they left Fen's apartment, Lok patted him on the
back, "Let's go get your girl."

Raask wanted to say something about going to get revenge,
going to kill the King, anything really, but he figured that Aria had
already killed the King, hence the alarms. The cold night air
assaulted their faces as they rushed through the streets. The sound
of stampeding Vermilli echoed from up ahead, Lok and Raask hid in
the shadows of a gem storefront as the Vermilli rushed past towards
the Dahs. What *did* Aria do?

They were nearly at the palace by the time Raask felt a surge in
his blood magic. He felt the constant hunger easing, bubbling and
reacting to what could only be bloodshed. He turned back, now at
the top of the hills that housed the palace, and caught the sounds of
the wraithkin ripping apart the Vermilli and their excited cries afterwards. He watched as a couple of lunar wraiths dropped off hordes
of bodies far off the coast, and then settled his gaze on the army that
stood on the black shore. A familiar helmet led the charge, thrusting
a familiar sword high up into the air. He could see drums beating,
but could not hear them from this distance. The tension in his chest
settled slightly, as long as those drums continued, Aria was still alive
and safe. He knew she could take care of herself, but the sight of

those drummers, so in tune with her heart, eased the pit in his stomach that quickly came back at the sight of his brother again.

Viggo who had been his protector his entire life only to turn into his would-be killer. Raask understood the toll of magic, how it hungered for violence. He could run away from that, for just a little bit longer. He'd had a year to process what had happened to him, and how he felt about his brother after it. And it hadn't been enough. He was hurt and heartbroken, but he loved Viggo. He loved him. At the end of the day, that was really all there was to it. So he'd forgive him, he'd still hurt, but it was time to move on.

Luckily, for now he could kick that can a little bit further down the line.

Raask turned back around, facing the Bleached Palace. He was about to enter, declare who he was and either take the throne or find Aria and help her do it, when he heard a canine yipping from the Gaulic. Golden glowing eyes stared at him from the black forest. The golden eyes stared intently at him before fading into the blackness. Raask could take a hint, even if he didn't want to. Lok and he shared a look before heading into the cover of the forest, following the tracks of the beast. Large canine tracks that abruptly turned human led them the way to Fen.

His voice was dry and husky, "You can't go in there, not just yet."

Raask shook his head. But it was Lok who spoke, "He is the future King of Skierka, he can do whatever he wants." Fen leaned against a tree, allowing Raask to take in the fact that he was completely naked besides a thick strip of fabric he tied around his waist like a skirt. Raask, who did understand the grandeur of the situation before them, did his best not to laugh. He couldn't wait to tell Aria about this, she'd die laughing.

"Thank you, for everything, but I am going to go in there and help her."

Fen shook his head, sighing with annoyance. "You think she can do what she has to do with you there? She won't be able to focus. Believe me, you want her to be focused."

"Didn't you listen to me? If anyone can kill the King, it's him. She needs him there." Lok was fidgeting, his eyes kept drifting to the shadow of the Irridesci tower just ahead of them.

Fen ran a hand through his hair, and huffed. "I did listen to you, that's why I think Raask should focus on taking down that tower and cutting off his father's connection to Voskulle."

Lok laughed, a dark and twisted sound. "It doesn't work like that. We could burn it down now but all of the sacrifices, all of the bloodshed, that's what fueled his power."

"It does. It works exactly like that. Voskulle was growing angry with the King. Before you officially joined our movement, Mayta and I had been scoping out the Irridesci. And Voskulle, he's pissed at the King. If we destroy that tower, chances are Voskulle may pull the magic in the Morlok bloodline. But even if it doesn't work like that, if the King lives after today, it'll cripple him in the future. And more importantly, now is a better time than any to put an end to the twisted sacrifices." Fen turned his eyes from the tower and looked at Lok, immediately his jaw relaxed, and the tension left his eyes. "You're not the only one who has lost family to them."

Raask who had been aware of their religious practices his entire life, and had never done a single thing to stop it, became all too aware that Lok's sister was his cousin. For many, many years, his cousin had been tortured in a building he'd visited and been trained in, and he had never done a thing to stop it. How many families had children taken for the power of his family?

The sounds of war had grown closer as they remained hidden in the woods. The clash of swords and screams of anguish and triumph. All that blood. It made its way into the pool of his magic in his core. He had to use it while he still could. Aria, she never needed him. She could handle herself. She could do this. But the people in that tower, they have needed him and have been waiting for someone to step in.

"Okay. Let's go." Raask barely recognized his own voice, the directness and stillness felt foreign to him. But good. He had decided to step up and stop running, this is what that looked like. "You bringing your friends or is it just us three?" Raask asked Fen.

Fen's lips curled upwards in a slight smile. In answer, dozens of glowing golden eyes appeared behind him. Slowly, the hylbra stalked forward. Like wolves, only the size of horses and with claws the size of fingers. Their spines sloped high and dropped off steeply giving them the appearance of a constant stalk. Their snouts were long and ended with rows upon rows of sharp teeth. Their fur— some a twilight black and others a muddy brown. But their eyes, each one glowed a golden amber. Suddenly Fen's face began to elongate. Sharp teeth cracked through the blunt human ones. His skull twisted and contorted into a snout and his ears flattened into his skull while long ones began to form on top of his head.

It was a gruesome and truthfully disgusting thing to watch, made only worse when the whole process paused in some kind of disfiguration in between human and hylbra as Fen paused his transformation. His eyes, one the amber of a hylbra, one brown and human, stared into the edge of the woods just past Raask and Lok.

Snow crunched as someone ran towards them. The hylbra bowed their heads low and Fen retracted his wolfish form and returned to a human state as a blur of red hair barreled towards him and tackled him in a hug.

Fear pumped into Raask's chest as he recognized Mayta. For the first time, he realized she had been out of the picture for quite some time now, giving him peace of mind and a break from the constant mental images of dirt covering his dead face, coating his throat and lungs.

"How did it go?" Fen asked Mayta as they both straightened. She nodded, radiating with happiness to see her old friend. Her mouth opened and snapped shut when she saw Lok, and then him.

Her eyes shot to his chest and the Morlok crest tattooed in white lithe, she stumbled a step backwards. "So it's true, you're here."

He clenched his jaw, doing his best to settle the fear that bubbled in him at the sight of her. And then she moved. Quick. Too quick. She raced over the snow, Raask braced himself for whatever she had in store for him now, to finish the job, finally kill him for good, right when he decided to finally make a difference.

Her hands wrapped around him, and she pulled him closer to her and... And she hugged him. She was hugging him. Maybe out of instinct or maybe out of fear, he found himself hugging her back. Her big head and hair buried into his chest. "You killed me," Raask couldn't tell if he was asking or confessing. She patted his back and Raask began to feel warm and comforted. Undoubtedly, she was using her magic to soothe him, but he couldn't be mad at her when feeling so calmed.

"I'm sorry. I thought you were going to be like your father. I was wrong." Mayta pulled away and stared him down with those big watery green eyes. How could she kill him and *he* ends up feeling bad for her? Oh Gods, Viggo was going to be in a world of trouble with this girl.

Raask cleared his throat, feeling overwhelmed with serenity from her magic, guilt for hating her for so long, and the residual fear from being hugged by the creature that had killed him. "And now you *know* that I'm not like my father?" Last time he saw her as himself she was whispering in his ear about killing him. That kind of thing didn't just disappear, and unlike his brother, Raask didn't have a lifetime of love and good memories to convince him that she was safe.

Mayta nodded, somehow looking so sure of herself. "By my count, you have a couple of Gods in your corner, as well as Aria, Fen, Viggo, and as Hauth, you've gotten the support of the people. I can see that I was wrong. And I think—for what's about to come—you'll need to trust me in order to save her."

Raask's muscles tensed. "What do you know?" Nausea and worry took over, along with a surge of his blood magic. He turned to look back towards the palace, at all that spilled blood. Without waiting for an answer, he took off.

Faster than he had ever run, he ran to her. He dodged swords and arrows. Fists and kicks. He ran. The wind whistled in his ears and his boots skidded across the snow, but his feet kept pounding against the ground. On and on he ran. Mayta said something about the Gods being on his side, so he prayed and he prayed for her. Red cloaks blurred past him, Surtrian soldiers blurred past. He ran.

Power swirled inside of him, with each pump of his thundering heart, he felt more power accruing. The power he had been saving to use to kill his father, he'd use it for her. Everything he had, he'd give it to her. Gods, she had to still be there. Wouldn't he feel it if she died? Wouldn't he know? He'd have to know.

He whipped through the battle and straight through the front entrance of the Bleached Palace. Vermilli guards blended into the puddles of their own blood on the floor, only a few remained standing in an overwhelming sea of rebel soldiers. But nobody moved. It was like the entire battle halted in the halls of this palace as Viggo and his father battled.

His brother's dark magic crackled like whips of black fire as he dodged the endless bursts of bright orange flame from their father. The fire burst through the air with a whoosh. For each fireball, Viggo countered with a whip of his death magic that swallowed the flame whole. Their father was fast and aggressive, leaving Viggo mostly in the defensive.

His father looked tired. The toll of his fire magic showed on his face, a mangle of burns and scar tissue. He'd always kept it hidden in the shadows of his own flames, carefully held above his head so it was impossible to get a good look at his face, too blinding and shadowing the mess that he had made of himself. But today all of his efforts were put towards killing his son, Raask's brother. The flame bursts were aimed at Viggo's head. At his own son.

Raask began to pool his blood magic. He pulled all of it, all of that blood that spilled on the snow and the floor and within the Dahs, he pulled it to him. It started slow, before beginning to build.

A scream echoed from behind him. Raask turned back, still summoning the blood into his power, when he saw it was Mayta who let out the Gods-awful sound. She had collapsed to the ground in hysterics. Everything stopped as Raask followed her line of sight.

It was her.

He knew it by the sound of Mayta's anguish. But nothing could prepare him for this.

Her skull was... was dented. Pressed in on itself like a crumpled towel. The blood centered back into the room, no longer pulling towards him as he let it all go and reached to her with his magic.

There was nothing there. No heartbeat.

All he could feel was the burnt walls of her arteries. He recognized the technique. He'd seen it done and had even felt it at brief moments. His father had boiled her blood. And she was gone.

Gone.

There was a stillness to his grief, a brief moment where everything in the realm seemed to stop and listen to the sound of his heart cracking in half. Then the blood began to pull to him. Faster than lightning, all that blood that had shed, staining the Dahs and the snow of Etra red, he pulled all of it into his grasp and flooded it down his father's throat. He took several steps forward as he watched. His hand was outstretched towards his father, shaking with the pressure and immensity of the magic he was controlling.

He poured it down his father's throat. Up his nose. Pushing into his eyeballs before they burst. Raask lifted his arm up high and slashed it down as he used the blood like a whip, ripping into the skin of his father, releasing even more blood into his power. Again and again. He felt the moment his father's heart stopped. It happened quickly, but he ignored it and kept going.

The heavy hands of his brother wrapped around him, pulling him back. It was only when he blocked his sight from their father that Raask stopped. He sank against his brother, exhausted and broken. He couldn't do this, he couldn't go on. "It's done, Raask, you can let go."

Raask would never let go. Not of her. "It's done," his brother's soothing voice whispered into his ear. Viggo pulled away, only enough to address the room. "The reign of the Fire Monger King is done. If those who remain on the side of fire refuse to conform to the new regime, you will be brought into our dungeons as a political prisoner or face the wrath of my brother, the new king. Fall to your knees if you accept the new regime."

He heard the sounds of bodies hitting the floor, but all Raask could focus on was her body, laying there. It must have hurt, dying like that. He should have been with her. He hadn't been there for her.

Viggo, under his breath whispered to Raask, "Hold it together for now. I'll bring you somewhere private after. They'll hold onto this memory." Raask knew Viggo was right, but he had a hard time caring about anything else right now.

Viggo's voice sounded so very far away. He had to strain to listen, and even then Raask felt like he was listening to his brother's speech from six feet under. "This war is over. The Surtrian Islands are no longer the territory of Skierka. The syrens are now recognized as a humanoid class and may not be owned or hunted. And the Irridesci practice will now be outlawed. I'm offering temporary forgiveness for the soldiers who fought on the side of the previous king. We will build a greater Skierka, but in the meantime, we have to heal."

Each soul listened carefully to his brother, for, at some point, he had led each and every person in this palace. And when he finished speaking, he looked solemnly into Raask's eyes and gave him a nod. Raask turned his gaze from Aria's body, and instead watched as Viggo picked up Mayta—who had been laying on the ground eerily still and silent. Raask followed close behind as they silently went up the stairs and away from the eyes of the Skierkan people.

They stepped over countless bodies as they made their way through the palace and into Raask's old tower. It was dusty and seemingly untouched—other than purple blood on the ground and broken glass. Moving on instinct, Raask swept his hand over the bed, shaking off the fine layer of dust before Viggo placed Mayta onto the bed. Raask himself sat at her side.

He had yet to trust Mayta, but at this moment, they were both broken shells of themselves, forever lost to the same grief and a love for the same creature. He would not trust her, but for now, there was nobody else he'd rather sit next to as he confronted the idea of living in a world without *her*.

He had gone so long without knowing of her. He buried his head into his hands, unable to understand how to go back to a world without her. Going back to being alone. His mind wandered back to the cold sheets he awoke to this morning.

"Raask, you need to know something," Viggo paced back and forth, carefully avoiding the pool of purple blood.

"Not now, Viggo. Just, just let me sit." He spoke into his hand, but he was sure Viggo would get the point. Instead he halted in front of him and crouched so they would be at eye level.

"It has to be now."

He picked his head up, feeling disconnected from his own body and this realm. "What?"

"I might be able to save her. But first I have to tell you some things, things I've been avoiding." Raask stilled, unsure of what Viggo was talking about. There was no saving her. She was dead. Gone to this side of the realm. To this side... of the realm...

But hadn't he been killed too?

Raask turned to Mayta whose eyes were watching Viggo. "Ask him, ask him to bring her back." Mayta had mentioned multiple Gods were on his side, that's what she'd said earlier when she apologized for murdering him. And there was his brother, who had been gifted with the magic of death, and he who had been brought back from death itself.

A dark understanding overtook Raask. He now understood. A missing piece of the puzzle of all of the tiny little mysteries of his life had fallen into place.

"Will he do it? Will he bring her back?"

"I don't know. But we can ask him."

Raask stood. Pooling whatever strength he could for his quest to the underrealm. Mayta's small, cold hand reached out and grabbed his wrist. He turned to her, swallowing back the mirrored grief in her eyes. She opened his palm, gently, before reaching into her pocket and dropping a surprisingly heavy golden rock into it. "You'll need this."

He didn't understand, but he pocketed it anyways.

His brother summoned a pool of swirling blackness that oozed like oil. It covered the window of his room and leached onto the stone walls like a living, breathing thing. Viggo turned back to Mayta and swallowed. "Do not let anyone in here. Some will be happy about what happened today, many won't want to see Raask on the throne. Nor will they respect you as the queen of the syrens. We have enemies here still. I will be back as soon as I can, but please, try to stay safe." Raask watched as Mayta stared, hollow, at his brother.

The death of the Fire Monger King would not end the years of hatred and prejudice that had been the core of Skierka for far too long. The Skierkans needed him. They needed someone to lead the way. But his first duty would always be to her. This was all supposed to be for her anyways.

So Raask, neither sure of himself nor the land he was about to enter, stepped foot into the darkness and succumbed to the swirling sensation of falling as he prepared to beg for the life of the creature he loved.

EPILOGUE

ARIA

It hurt badly enough that she had welcomed her death. She accepted its warm embrace and said goodbye to the realm of the living. A world, a part of the realm, that she did not belong to anymore. She did not remember her journey to the underrealm, only the smoothness of a leathered glove, the comfort of a thick, heavy, black cloak.

Now there was nothing but blackness and emptiness. She rested against what felt like a cold, damp stone, out in the open. She rested there, with her eyes closed, for what may have been days or possibly seconds. Did time even exist down in the realm of the dead?

She did not weep. She did not think of those she left behind.

Instead she allowed herself to empty. It felt good to be empty. She wouldn't mind if she spent eternity in emptiness. She sank into it like an icicle above a fire. Perhaps she would fade back into the ether and find peace.

But Aria, she should have known better.

For there was no peace for the wicked. And certainly, no peace for the cruel like her.

The sound of her mother's shrew and crisp laugh fell across the emptiness like a crack of thunder. "You think you deserve peace, girl?" Her mother's voice echoed across the silence as Aria prepared to pay penance.

She curled in on herself, stiffening against the rock, hoping that she would blend into the harsh stone and stay hidden from her mother. For a moment all was silent. Until she felt herself being dragged by her ankles with the familiar claws of her mother.

Dive deeper into the world of The Songs of Beasts.

Scan to join Samantha Gonda's Substack for series news, bonus content, and more, including *an exclusive bonus chapter.*

ACKNOWLEDGMENTS

It has been an absolute pleasure writing and publishing this book!

To my family & friends — Thank you for your continued support and love. None of this would be possible without you.

To Merle Bennett and Fergus Edmondson of BeRead — I owe so much of my journey to you and your wonderful team!

To Wilhelmina Asaam — This book, and series, are far better because of you and your hard work.

And to you, the reader — This past year has felt nothing short of a dream. Thank you to everyone who has continued this journey. Who have reached out on socials. Have left reviews and recommended the book to friends. THANK YOU!

ABOUT THE AUTHOR

Samantha Gonda is an award winning fashion and beauty publicist. After completing her degree in Communications and minors in Italian Studies and Economics at the University of Massachusetts Amherst, Samantha briefly worked as a certified personal trainer.

Originally a New Englander, Samantha now lives in New York City where she spends her free time meticulously planning her next trip, watching horror movies, and making a mess in the kitchen.

instagram.com/authorsamanthagonda
tiktok.com/@authorsamanthagonda